THE ASSASSIN'S STORM

THE ASSASSIN'S LEGACY SERIES
BOOK 3

LIBBY WEBBER

To request permission contact Libby Webber of Dead or Alive Press at DeadorAlivePress@gmail.com

ISBN 978-1-7377811-8-9 (hardcover)
ISBN 978-1-7377811-7-2 (paperback)
ISBN 978-1-7377811-6-5 (ebook)

Book design by Libby Webber

Dead or Alive Press
Jacksonville, NC

www.libbywebber.com
www.libbywebber.com/deadoralivepress

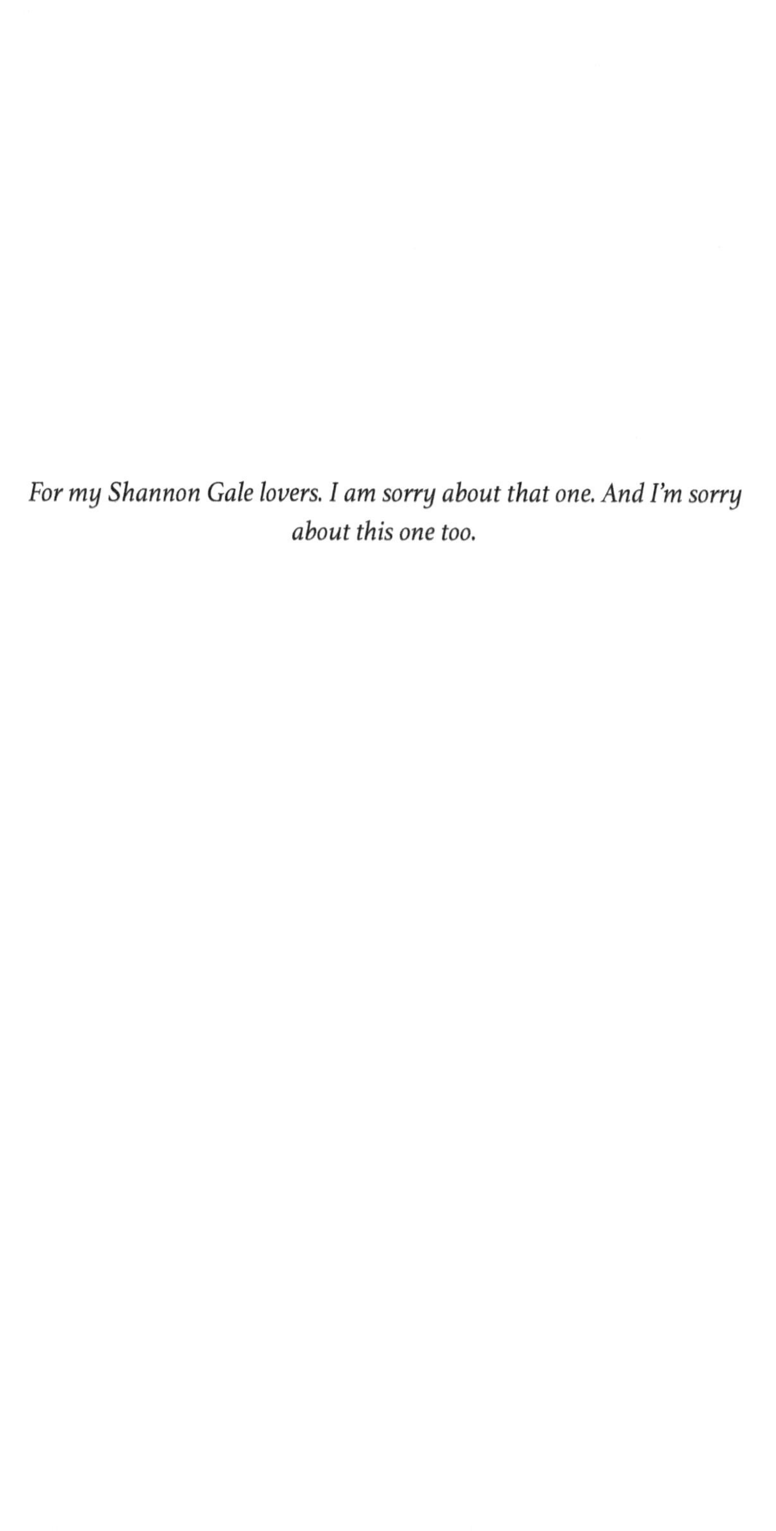

For my Shannon Gale lovers. I am sorry about that one. And I'm sorry about this one too.

PLEASE BE AWARE

This book contains sensitive topics including violence, foul language, and violence against children (not in detail). This book is recommended for mature audiences.

SEVEN YEARS AGO

1

KARA LOURDE

"**Ms.** Lourde?"

Kara Lourde pulled her eyes away from the urgent message she'd just received from the Onyx Division. This was the third fuckup they'd had this year on a black ops operation, and they had less than twenty-four hours to fix it, or it would be her problem. Laura leaned in the doorway to Kara's office at Langley, the fluorescent lights accenting the bags beneath her blue eyes, her face frazzled. Laura had been Kara's secretary for six years and was what Kara would consider a friend—if she had any. "What's up?"

"The Director of Operations is here," Laura said softly.

A cold dread snuck down Kara's spine. 'Like here, here?' she mouthed.

Laura gave a slight nod, eyes widening. Fuck. "Thanks, Laura. Let him in."

Laura stepped back, the Director filling the doorframe. His pristine blue suit made Kara self-conscious of the two-day-old outfit she wore. The black slacks were dusted with white powder from wiping her hands on them after eating the only thing she'd found in her desk—powdered donuts—and coffee stained her white button-down, which was stale with sweat as they monitored the Onyx op.

"Kara, I'm glad I caught you in the office."

"Of course, Sir. Where else would I be?" She stood and rounded the desk, extending her hand, and he accepted. She closed the door behind him and returned to her desk, opening the large bottom drawer on the right and pulling out a fresh shirt. "Do you mind if I. . ." She held up the shirt.

"Not at all. And stop calling me sir when no one is around—I basically raised you." He dropped into the chair in front of her desk and looked away.

She stripped off the dirty garment, the cool air caressing her bare skin. "Calling you Uncle George in the office is never going to happen. Stop asking."

He laughed.

She pulled on the fresh shirt and buttoned it up. "You're here about Onyx," she said.

He turned back to her. "This is top priority. What am I going to tell the Deputy Director when he asks why we have subpar assets on this task?"

Kara released a heavy sigh and sank in her chair. She untied her bun and raked her hand through her tangled hair. There wasn't an acceptable answer. Hale Security had been unavailable for this operation, and the Director needed it done. It was the Onyx Division or asking the S.E.A.L.S. to step in, which would have required a butt-load of falsified information she'd had neither the time nor manpower to create.

"I'll handle it," she assured. "Even if I have to do it myself, he'll be dead by the end of the week."

George shook his head. "What's the allotted window?"

"They still have 22 hours." Yet she couldn't see Onyx pulling this off. She should have insisted on waiting until Hale Security was available. If they didn't have multiple concurrent operations with Onyx, Kara would have pulled the plug on their contract months ago. If they failed again, she would need to call in freelancers—Underworlders she'd rather not be in business with. "I'll call Tom, in and we'll make some calls."

George nodded and pushed himself out of the chair. "If you need an extra hand—"

"I will not, but thanks."

"Make sure you eat something besides donuts." His eyes fell on the wrapper in her trash bin. "Your mom has been hounding me about how overworked you look for a secretary." They shared a knowing look. Her mother meant well, but George and Kara were all she had left, and the idea of them both working in intelligence frayed her nerves even if she believed Kara only pushed papers for her uncle. "Ask Laura to go get you some real food. It's why you have her."

Kara nodded and gave him a smile. "See you at Wednesday Night dinner." She waited until he left before checking the encrypted window that flashed in the corner of her computer screen. Great. They'd failed to breach the property, sending the target into hiding. She rolled her eyes and dropped her head to her desk. The best part of her job was coordinating the black ops units that Langley denied existed—the thrill of knowing she handled the cases no one else could. The worst part was running it with a skeleton crew. She closed her eyes. She may not sleep for the next two days, but she could get a nap in.

A knock sounded on her door. George probably insisted Laura grab them some lunch. "I'm not hungry," she called out.

"There is an Agent Brinks here to see you," Laura said.

Kara sat straight up, her heart ramming into her ribs. It'd been years since she'd heard that name. Christopher Brinks had been her partner at the FBI before the CIA recruited her. They'd been diligent in their cover for her; people couldn't even get to this portion of the building without multi-biometric scans.

"Well, send 'em in."

Laura nodded and stepped away. Kara straightened in her chair, pulse thrumming. It had been a lifetime ago, but she and Chris had been close—they'd been family. She'd risked her career to help keep his son, Shaun, out of jail, and he had stood by her side as she packed her things and to move in with him after leaving her abusive ex. After leaving the FBI, work became her life, and those from her past slowly fell off the radar.

Someone moved into view, engaged in conversation with Laura. This was not the Agent Brinks she knew, and her heart sank. The woman donned black slacks and a soft purple shirt, effectively highlighting the nonconforming touch of purple in her neatly tied bun, which fell outside the prescribed regulations. "I'm not sure what department you work for," Kara said, annoyance spilling through her tone, "but on this side of Langley we require appointments."

The Agent turned, and Kara gasped, the unforgettable mismatched eyes bringing her to her feet. The last time she'd seen this woman she'd been just a girl sitting inside an FBI interrogation room, still in her holiday pajamas, with tears in her eyes. They'd scooped her up during a raid, with rumors that her computer skills rivaled the best the FBI had in the business. After five hours of intense interrogation, she made a deal with Chris. All traces of the paperwork they had completed disappeared, and the sixteen-year-old waved as she walked out of the building.

"Well, I'll be damned," Kara said, genuine shock in her words. "I never expected to see you working for the CIA."

"Oh, I'm not," Storm said and shut the door. "But the CIA fits you better."

Kara's guard went up, her hand poised to hit the emergency button beneath her desk. "How the hell did you get back here?"

"I'll get to that."

Kara shook her head. This was far from the timid girl she met all those years ago. "You know, it takes some balls to walk in here impersonating an intelligence officer, although I admit, impressive. A single press of this button and you spend the rest of your life at a black site."

"Impressive?" Storm chuckled. "I think we can agree it's downright impossible." She took a seat in front of the desk, folding her feet beneath her. "And we both know I wouldn't be in there long."

Kara didn't doubt that. She could recall at least three other occasions where Storm was caught—and then out of custody, all traces of her erased, within hours. The first time, Kara had helped Chris clear Storm's name, but now she either had a lot of favors stacked away or was in with some powerful people. Kara kept her hand over the button.

Storm nodded at her, a glint of victory in her eyes. "Please, go ahead and press it—it won't work."

Kara's fingers hesitated for only a moment, then she pushed the button. It was a silent alarm, however, the phone should ring in confirmation of its receipt. Kara kept her eyes on Storm, the silence wrapping her in fear. She glanced at the phone, but it remained silent.

"Brinks sent me," Storm said, unfazed by Kara's attempt to have her detained. She pulled out a folded piece of paper and opened it, turning it around. Kara's name was scrawled in Brink's handwriting across the page. "I come in peace," she assured and tucked the paper away. "And you can frisk me; I'm not packing."

Kara nodded, and the fear dissipated. "How is Brinks? We lost touch a few years ago."

Storm's face darkened. "He's dead. It's one reason why I'm here."

Fuck. A pang of sadness echoed in her chest, and she lowered herself into her seat, removing her hand from the button. She should have tried harder to stay in contact with him. "When? I haven't heard anything."

"You wouldn't have. It happened a few days ago."

"Damn. How's Shaun handling it?"

"Not good," Storm admitted.

"Any idea what happened?" Kara could name a laundry list of people who would want her old partner dead. He dabbled in the Underworld enough to get the bad guys off the streets and the really bad guys in his pocket. Storm remained quiet, and Kara made a mental note to pull up the information on his death later and stared at the woman sitting in front of her. "Laura said you scanned in as Agent Brinks. Does this mean you and Shaun. . ."

"No." Storm's face contorted with mild disgust like when someone asks if two siblings are married.

Kara chuckled. Her computer pinged, and she glanced at it. Onyx sent another update. She would check it in a minute. "So, what's the real reason you're here? You could have emailed, called, shit—sent a carrier pigeon to let me know about Brinks and not risk being caught."

"I have a proposition I believe can be mutually beneficial, and what better way to showcase it than to show up here," Storm said. "Most importantly, though, it will solve your current. . ." she waved her hand in front of her as if trying to find the word, "issue. . .with the Onyx Division."

Kara tilted her head. "Excuse me?" There were six people in the building with the security clearance to even know about her division, The Graveyard. It was a clandestine division of the CIA that didn't exist on paper and handled the most unsavory players in the political moves against America.

"You should check that message. However, I can tell you Onyx has lost tracking on your target."

Dread rolled in Kara's stomach. She couldn't afford another fuck up. "How could you possibly know that?"

"What if I told you I wrote the program that made this," she gestured between herself and Kara, "possible? And this is just the beginning of what my program can do."

"I would ask if you are here to sell it or to blackmail us."

Storm gave her a half smile. "How about a partnership?"

"I'm listening."

Storm straightened in the chair. "Onyx has just royally fucked up what should have been an easy execution, and your neck is on the line. You also have the finest of cracks in your cyber security that I took advantage of. Now, we can let I.T. know so they can fix it, or we can keep it between us, and I can give you access to one of the most powerful cyber weapons created."

"What are you playing at?" Kara swallowed hard.

"I have a team in place to take care of Onyx. In fact, I have a team in place to take care of Hale, too. You haven't told Uncle George, but they've been selling classified information for the past six months."

Kara cocked her head. That was a piece of information she hadn't shared with anyone, but nothing Storm said so far was false. Plus, the act of bypassing the CIA security system and cyber walls garnered a shred of respect. "I'll admit, I'm intrigued. Tell me more." She'd just promised her uncle that she would handle this, and then, as if sent from God—or Chris—a solution.

Storm straightened, her face lighting up with excitement. "There is so much. But what you would be most interested in at the moment is biometric data and facial recognition manipulation. Pull up the logs for this section of the building."

Kara held the woman's gaze. It could be a trap. Storm had already admitted to being in their system, and Kara didn't want to be the one to open up floodgates for a full infection.

"You don't trust me."

Kara shook her head. "I know nothing about you except that I risked my career helping Brinks set you free."

"Did you ever learn why?"

Kara shook her head. That was the thing about Brinks—she trusted him, and he never gave her a reason not to.

"Because I got Shaun out of trouble with the Legacy."

"The Legacy?" Kara asked. This meeting just kept getting more interesting.

"Have you heard of them?"

Kara nodded. "Of course. A shadow organization dedicated to the American people. Protects them from threats both domestically and abroad, especially from the government. They've been a thorn in my side, rightfully so. But they are deeply rooted throughout the government agencies and impossible to extract. They are not someone I'd willingly cross. How did Shaun end up on their radar?"

"A story for another day." Storm checked her watch. "We are running out of time. If you check the logs, you'll realize that Storm Brinks never stepped into this building. In fact, you are speaking to a ghost. When you pull up security footage, I am already erased. My program will change the way your black ops run. You will be more effective, have less time in the office, and maybe even get laid."

Kara's fingers itched to check the logs, but as she moved the mouse, another alert from Onyx appeared. She ignored it again. More time at home sounded good right about now.

"You said partnership," Kara recalled. "With whom?"

"At this moment, does it matter?" Storm leaned forward. "You've had four failed missions in the last eight months. Onyx and Hale have become more unreliable, so you've pulled back from using them as much and passed off the mission to the military, which only works because we are at war and Congress is turning a blind eye. Once the war passes, you'll be back to scrambling."

Kara stared wide-eyed. "How the fuck could you know any of this?"

"This is what my program and the company I work with are capable of." Storm checked her watch again. "And more. Should I send my guys in?"

Kara scoffed. "You aren't vetted. There's no track record. I know Onyx and Hale. They're trouble, but it's reliable trouble. I don't even know who you work for."

Storm held her gaze. Danger and cockiness sat behind those eyes. "Legacy Inc."

Kara's mouth fell open, and she sat back, a chill racing through her body. Legacy Inc had been on the CIA radar for the last five years. The play on the Legacy name was brilliant. The Legacy was a shadow, a nightmare of vigilantes protecting civilians, and known to only the vilest of people. But Legacy Inc was a respected and feared corporation. On the surface, they ran security. But underneath, they were ruthless, effective, and untouchable. "Jesus, Storm, how did you get involved with them?"

"A boy," she said with a sad smile, her voice softening. "Isn't it always a boy?"

"I wouldn't know," Kara answered. "I can't send unvetted people into the middle of a mission with my name on it or I'll be the one dragged to a black site before the night is through." Then a thought struck her. "Did you set this up?"

"Their lack of ability? No. I saw an opportunity and took advantage of it. Legacy Inc is looking to secure exclusivity with The Graveyard and create a name for itself. And I need a partner."

"Why bring it to me? The Director is a few halls down."

Storm leaned forward. "Kara, listen to me. I'm here because I owe you. You need to be rid of your current assets, and I'm providing the means to do so. And I can assure you, Legacy Inc is only interested in two things: money and prestige. Being paid to be the only ones to handle the CIA's filthiest laundry checks both boxes."

"The Graveyard has a long history with Onyx and Hale.

Severing ties does not look good in the intelligence world or the Underworld."

"The intelligence world is in a constant state of shifting," Storm countered. "And Legacy Inc is at the top of the Underworld. You go with us, and we will handle the backlash from the other organizations and guarantee your missions are complete. We will even finish their current assignments free of charge."

There it was, in between the words, the veiled threat—Legacy Inc would eliminate the competition, regardless. "How much will this cost us?"

"Far less than what you're paying now."

Kara sat back and folded her hands on her stomach. There was something she was missing. Storm was a criminal—a cyber genius—but her track record didn't indicate any type of violent crime connections. She'd been more of a Robinhood criminal than a terrorist. Another alert popped up on her screen. "You say 'mine'," Kara noted, "not 'ours' when discussing the program."

"Because it doesn't belong to Legacy Inc, although they don't know that. It belongs to me, and if you agree, you."

"Again, why me?"

"You have something to lose. You've been passed over for promotion twice now. What happens after three? Your uncle will have to let you go, and you'll probably find a boring job in personal security." Kara raised her eyebrows at Storm's words. She was only aware of one time she'd been passed over. Storm's features softened. "And Brinks spoke highly of you until the end. I sought you out on his recommendation."

Brinks had sent her. That alone was worth giving Storm a chance. "What are the terms?"

"Legacy Inc is requesting exclusivity of all the Graveyard's operations."

"Are you also exclusive to the Graveyard?"

Storm shook her head. "But we will take the pay decrease in exchange for your exclusivity."

That wasn't a bad deal. "Communications?"

"Completely secure and happens through my program, Storm-Link. It's already loaded onto your system. We can call this a test run. Let me give the go-ahead, and we will eliminate your target for you in the next two hours. If you're impressed, we can set up an official meet."

"Exclusivity cannot be your only term." Kara drummed her fingers on the desk. "If Brinks sent you, there is another reason."

"This program will give you access to things you'll want to share with your intelligence friends, but it will shut down the second it's being used for anything but what I've designed it for."

"Understandable," Kara agreed. "But there is something else."

"Are you going to check the messages?" Storm asked, eyeing the computer screen and not answering her question.

Kara swallowed—a pit heavy in her stomach. This much communication during an operation meant things had gone south. If what Storm was offering was true, those messages wouldn't matter. This could be the end of her career or the very beginning. "No," Kara said. "Send in your team."

"Do you mind?" Storm gestured to the computer. "I left mine in the car." Kara hesitated. Again, the idea of giving Storm access to her computer left her feeling vulnerable. It only took one mistake for their system to be compromised, but it clearly already was as Storm sat in front of her, unchecked by security.

Storm smirked. "No problem. You'll learn to trust me soon enough. Can I use your phone?"

Kara nodded and pushed the secured landline across the desk. Storm picked it up and dialed. "Send 'em out," Storm said and then looked up at her. "Do you care if there are Onyx casualties, or would you like them all alive?"

"What?" Kara said, surprised.

"Onyx. What would you like done with them?"

"Alive and detained," she replied. This was an audition, after all, and bringing in live targets was far more difficult than dead ones.

Storm nodded in appreciation. "Did you get that?" Storm asked into the receiver. "Good. Be safe, Mase." She hung up the phone.

"Why give me the option?" Kara asked. "Eliminating them would have saved you trouble later."

"I'm not a fan of death," Storm admitted.

"I knew you weren't a stone-cold killer," Kara said.

"No." Storm smiled. "Just in love with one. You will have confirmation within the next hour."

If Legacy Inc pulled this off, she would have no problem with exclusivity. She studied Storm as the woman settled back into her seat, picking at her cuticles. There was something still left unsaid. "There's more. What is it?"

Storm gave a small laugh. "Once they have proven their worth, I have a personal favor to ask should something happen to me."

"What do you mean?"

Storm cocked an eyebrow. "I'm delegating a shadow deal between the CIA and Legacy Inc. I'm sure you can let your imagination run wild and still not accurately depict the type of danger I'm in."

Fair enough. It'd been years since Kara worked in the field. She made arrangements and deals and paid money. It was easy to forget how dangerous her game of chess was for the players. "What is it you need?"

"There's a woman named Maureen Seward. Her dossier is already on your computer. Should something happen to me, swear to me, she never gets her hands on this program."

Kara cocked her head. "You've created a mastermind cyber

weapon and are brokering a multi-billion-dollar deal on behalf of Legacy Inc. Why are you worried about this woman?"

"It's complicated."

Kara didn't buy it. "Who is she?"

"I can't explain right now, but one day, she is going to be the person you need to worry about. I understand this is a big ask."

Storm hid it well, but Kara spied the fear in her posture. It was the first time she'd shown even an ounce of it since walking into this office. Whatever threat Maureen Seward posed terrified her. "I'm assuming you've already written into the program for it to shut down should she get her hands on it, so what you're asking is if something happens to you I should—"

An unfamiliar soft whoosh sounded from her computer, and a purple screen she didn't recognize flashed across it. Storm checked her watch and then grinned. "Right on time. That would be StormLink," she said. "You ready to see what it's capable of?"

PRESENT DAY

2

———

AERON

*A*eron, please.

Aeron stared at Luke's body on the office floor, her entire being trembling. Luke's last words echoed in her mind. *Aeron, please.* His slack face taunted her. He looked at peace—even with his now disfigured features, the worry lines were un-creased, his brow not furrowed. She hadn't seen that look on his face since before she eliminated Shaun. She'd only ever wanted to save him, get him out of danger. But getting him out and saving his life were two completely different things. Her father had said as much—warned her she'd have to get messy. She hadn't realized 'killing your boyfriend and plotting your not-so-dead-mother's murder' messy was what he'd meant.

"You should sit down." Aeron pulled her eyes away from Luke to Mason standing beside her, aware Katherine and Griffin were talking near the desk. How could they be so calm? So, cavalier? He slid his hand on the small of her back, eyes widening. "Aeron, you're shaking. Are you feeling okay?"

"I was yanked from death only to deliver Luke to the grave. I'm really fucking far from okay," she said, but didn't step away from him. The trembling increased, and she swayed. Nothing in the world made sense anymore. Her entire team—her family—they were all gone while her mother was alive. Yet she was the furthest thing from what Aeron remembered, from the high regard that people had when they spoke about her. They used to rave about her kindness, her willingness to do whatever it took to save innocent people. The woman she had met was heinous, there wasn't a single kind thing about her.

Mason nodded. "Come here." Aeron let him guide her to the wall. She leaned against it and slid to the ground, failing to keep her eyes from finding Luke's blank face again.

"I'm sorry," she said, not sure who to direct it at; Luke, Mason, or herself. She'd failed all of them. How the hell had this gotten so out of her control? A single lie. That was all it had taken, and then another and another. Lies were nasty like that. Once said out loud, they took on a life of their own, twisting and hiding in the truth, just enough to make it impossible to take them back. She had lied to keep everyone safe—to save the Legacy and Luke. She shook her head. The weight of all those dead children left black marks on her soul. If she had told Luke the truth about his granddad from day one, could she have stopped him from becoming a monster? Would he still be alive? Would any of them?

"What are you thinking?" Mason asked, squatting beside her.

She turned to gaze at his bruised and blood-smeared face. His bloodshot eyes stared back, but he remained calm—a steady ship in a treacherous sea—and she latched on to the comfort he provided. "I wish I never lied to him." Her chin shook, and tears burned in her eyes again as she let them blur Mason's face from her vision, a longing so deep aching in her chest. "I want to go home," she said between sobs. It made no sense—she didn't have a home—not literally or metaphorically. She'd destroyed them both. "I don't even know what that means anymore. I have no one. Nowhere to go. But I want to go home."

Mason wrapped his arms around her, and she leaned against

him, her body shaking from the tears, the pain, and the loneliness. "I'm sorry I failed you, Aeron." He stroked her hair, letting her cry against his chest. "You've lost so much, and that hurts. It feels like your soul has been ripped from your body, shredded, then rolled into a ball and shoved back into your heart. I know. And I'm sorry." He sniffed, his breath hitching, before he continued. "But you are not alone. I will always be here." His words were like a warm blanket. He had always been there, and she believed he always would. "And you have Ivan and Kat."

And her mother.

But she swallowed the urge to say a word about her mother. Instead, she nodded against his chest, her breath shaking, the tears subsiding for the moment. She pulled back to see his eyes brimming with concern. "I don't want to anymore," she said, tears fighting to come back.

"You don't have to," he said, not needing to ask what she meant. He cupped the sides of her face and placed a kiss on the top of her head. "Once we get out of here, you never have to again if you don't want to."

She nodded, the fight against her despair a losing battle. She never wanted to fight again. To lose someone again—she wouldn't survive it. How Katherine and Luke could choose vengeance she would never understand. This pain was too raw to think of anything else. To plan, to lie—that's what started this whole massacre. A lie to save the man and the life she loved.

"Did we do it?" Aeron asked. "Shut down the hit list?"

Mason drew his eyebrows together. "I'm not sure." He pulled out his cell phone and scrolled, and a comfortable silence fell between them. He frowned.

"What is it?" she asked.

"I'm having a hard time pulling it up. How's the shoulder?" he asked.

Aeron gave a small shrug, discomfort deep within her joint.

The miracle drugs Mason had supplied were wearing off. "Uncomfortable."

"How about everything else?"

When Aeron rose from the dead, Mason explained the extent of her injuries. In the brief span of six months, she had died, broken too many bones, been shot, stabbed, shot again, and experienced enough emotional damage to cripple even the healthiest person's immune system. After tonight, he had promised a long rest, with Luke by her side to help her heal.

"Sluggish," she answered. "Exhausted. I feel like I should be dead." She gave a small smirk, the irony of that statement not lost on either of them.

He returned her smile. "Do you want to sleep?"

It was a reminder of how well he knew her. Sleep was her cure-all. Stressed? Sleep. Angry? Sleep. Broken-hearted? Sleep. For those few moments, she could pretend like it was possible to wake up from this nightmare and try it again. She looked over at Katherine and Griffin, his smile lighting up every time he looked at her. She would never catch that kind of smile on Luke's face again. A sob choked her, and she dropped her gaze to her knees. "I want to forget," she said.

3

IZZ

Izz Montgomery followed Maureen out of the Senior Assassin's office, not daring to look back at Mason, or Luke's dead body. But Mason's gaze burned into her back. That wasn't how it was supposed to go down. No one else was supposed to die. Aeron's broken sobs echoed down the hall, and Izz quickened her pace, falling into step beside her boss.

"What now?" Izz asked, gauging Maureen's stride and posture. That was the third unplanned death this week, and when things go unplanned, Izz's day goes bad. She had been Maureen's right hand for the last ten years—one of the few in the Alliance who knew the whole truth, and one of only three in the Syndicate who knew about the Alliance. But more than that, she'd been Maureen's friend. Izz had seen the darkness inside of Maureen and what it hid from the world—a mother and a lover broken and pieced back together with jagged shards of glass.

Maureen's jaw tightened, and she picked up her pace. She hid it well, but believing Aeron was dead rocked Maureen to the core. Finding Aeron alive and ready to kill her—well, that would shake anybody—the ice-cold queen included. How the hell had Mason brought her back?

"We need to swing by the lab to grab hard drives and vials for Dr. Jones before they burn this place to the ground," Maureen said.

"How do you know they won't follow?" Izz asked, looking back over her shoulder.

"Because they have bodies to bury and a vault to categorize." Maureen stopped outside a sliding glass door. "And Mason knows better." She brought her hand to the scanner.

"Will that work?" Izz asked, eyeing the sensor. It's not like they needed to worry if the alarms went off, but it seemed too simple.

"It should. I paid Rosemary a lot of money to return my biometrics to the system." She placed her scarred hand on the reader. It lit up beneath her palm and the door slid open. She smiled at Izz, the twisted map of scars on her face shifting. "See?"

"What are we looking for?" Izz looked around the cold room and shuddered. Dr. Jones gave her the heebie-jeebies. He dabbled in some futuristic shit—most of it was hypothetical, and Legacy Inc had been his professional playground. But the Syndicate—aka the Alliance to anyone inside the inner circle—had been his experimental laboratory. She'd seen some of the fucked up shit his drugs did to his test subjects. She shuddered again just thinking about them.

Maureen handed her a list. "Grab these. I'll grab the hard drives and files."

Izz nodded. She spied the blue coolers used for transport under one of the silver metal tables. She snatched it up and moved to the walk-in freezers that ran along the back wall. The hand scanner blinked at her. "Maureen?"

"What is it?" she called from the office.

"Hand scanner."

"Use yours. I had Rosemary upload it as well."

Izz could hear the smirk in her voice and smiled, too. She slammed her hand onto the sensor and the door popped open. A chill ran through her as she propped the door and stepped inside, the temperature dropping to nearly freezing. Three walls of shelves surrounded her, sitting above locked freezer drawers. Her breath rose in a puff in front of her. She fucking hated the cold.

It took a moment for her to realize he kept them numerically, and she found the first three drugs easily enough. Vials 850 and higher were locked away. She pressed her thumbprint to the black pad, and the drawer unlocked and slid forward. Glass vials clinked together as she pulled it open. There was a technicolor of fluorescent liquids in the vials. She scanned the numbers and grabbed two trays. She checked the next two drawers. Finally, her eyes fell on Vial 879. She picked up the tray, three vials missing from it, and lifted them from the cooler.

"I bet that's what Mason used." Izz whipped around, nearly dropping the whole thing. Maureen stood in the doorway—eyeing the vials in her hand before her gaze shifted to the next set on the shelf, all of which were accounted for. A smug smile crossed her face. "I doubt Aeron's enjoying much of her trip topside at the moment."

"What is it?"

"Vial 879 is a prototype to delay death," Maureen said. "Although it also had limited success in resuscitating the dead. However, all of Dr. Jones' attempts with just Vial 879 proved unsuccessful in the long term."

Izz lifted a bottle higher, inspecting the completely clear liquid. Maureen moved closer, and Izz handed it over. A faint green color was visible in the tiny bubbles as Maureen gave it a small shake. Izz had never heard of any drug that could bring back the dead.

"Are you sure she was dead?"

Maureen's eyes glossed over. "I've only heard him cry like that one other time—when I put him under Sin and he re-lived Faith's death over and over for days. Aeron was dead enough for him to think, at that moment, that he had failed to save her."

Maureen passed the vial back, and Izz secured it in the tray, transferring it to the blue soft-sided cooler. "Don't forget 880."

Izz grabbed the last samples. "Are we going to talk about your children?" she ventured.

"What's there to talk about? My son—" Maureen paused, her breath hitching. "Decius is dead. And Aeron might as well be too. I'm resigned to dealing with Katherine the same way I dealt with Rosemary—let her hang herself."

"That's your daughter," Izz said, shouldering the bag.

"She was never mine," Maureen whispered. "Katherine belonged to Rosemary from the day she was born."

Izz shook her head. "Obviously not."

Maureen glared, and Izz smirked. "But your daughters aren't dead. So, what is the plan? Because the Syndicate is going to need answers and direction soon on this rogue mission. And now that the truth about Katherine is out and Elijah is dead. . . Are we moving back to the Alliance with you rising from the dead or. . ."

"You let me worry about the Syndicate and the rest. Tell Dash we're ready." Maureen held out the bag of hard drives, and Izz took it, shaking her head. They'd lived a triple life for as long as Izz had been her right-hand lady. They changed Maureen's name to Amara, opened the Syndicate, and rose through the Underworld to keep her hidden from Elijah and keep her kids safe. But now? What were they going to do when Katherine started calling her Maureen and making waves that the Alliance was alive and well? Maureen's head was still worth a pretty penny across the world— even with her dead.

Maureen gestured to the door. "Wait in the hall. I'm lighting it up."

Izz released an aggravated sigh. Keeping up with what Maureen wanted took more energy than fucking the entire Tampa crew. "If you wanted them dead, I would have handled it in the office and saved ourselves a whole bunch of trouble."

"I don't want them dead," Maureen patronized. "But without Luke, I've lost my leverage. Now, if they want me as an enemy, they'll get the full treatment."

Izz nodded, a pang of sympathy shooting through her heart. Those girls had no idea what they were in for. She sent a text message to Dash and he shot a thumbs-up back.

"He'll be out front," Izz called before stepping into the hall. Her ears strained for any movement or noise from the office, but all was silent except her heartbeat hard in her chest. When Mason had said Aeron could be unpredictable, Izz doubted that even he ever thought she would pull the trigger on Luke. And declaring war on Maureen? There wouldn't be much Izz could do for him now.

Maureen appeared a few moments later. "We've got about five minutes before they're alerted," she said and strode off down the hall. Izz followed, not glancing back at the flames dancing in Dr. Jones' office.

They exited out the front door of Legacy Inc Headquarters and into the streets of DC. Dash's white Audi idled behind the ambulance they'd arrived in, and Izz paused. Why the fuck would he bring the Audi?

"Dash isn't going to let me in his car like this," she said, looking down at the fresh blood.

"He will if he likes breathing," Maureen countered, and there wasn't a hint of the humor in her voice Izz was used to hearing after a successful mission. But technically, this hadn't been a successful mission.

Izz didn't argue. She pulled the passenger door open, and Maureen slid into the front seat. Dash leaned forward across Maureen's lap. "You're fucking walking," he said, disdain painted across his face. Maureen pressed her gun beneath his chin before

Izz blinked. He swallowed hard enough for his Adam's apple to bob up and down. "Or at the very least, pick the chunky parts off."

Izz looked down at the chunks of Luke stuck to her shirt. Fair enough. She closed Maureen's door and pulled the shirt over her head, folded it in on itself, and slid into the backseat. She dropped the shirt to the floor and fought off a shiver as the winter air bit at her. The sooner they got back to Tampa, the better—fuck this cold.

Maureen lowered her gun and put her seat belt on as Dash pulled from the curb. "Where to?" he asked.

"The safe house. We're not going home just yet."

4

KAT

*K*at looked away from Aeron and Mason, blocking out Aeron's cries, her eyes falling on Luke. Her chest ached. This was not the ending she pictured. Luke and Perry helping her run this empire had been the vision. Suits and ball gowns, not tears and caskets. She pulled the grimy piece of paper with Kara Lourde's name on it from her back pocket, turning it over a few times. The ache in her chest increased. Maureen had damn near destroyed them all for this. There would be nothing on this earth that could stop the hellfire that Kat planned to rain down on that bitch.

But first, she needed to focus on StormLink. She and Perry had halted several operations while trying to shut down the list —reporting to a faceless screen name made it feel less important, but now she had a name to a very real and powerful person, and the consequences of what they'd decided on felt insurmountable. How would she even start that conversation? 'Hi there Director Lourde, funny story—I pulled back a majority of my people from your critical missions, most of whom I slaughtered in the last few days, while combating this pesky hit list. If you could give us a few more days to pull ourselves together, that would be great.' She shook her head and gave a dry laugh. They were fucked.

Griffin's hand grabbed her elbow and turned her to him, eyes searching from his seat on the desk. Kat glanced at the dagger protruding from his leg and blood-soaked pants, staining the desk beneath him. She pulled out her pocketknife and flicked it open. She needed to see how much damage Izz had done.

"Are you going to stab me, too?" Griffin joked, eyes crinkling with mirth.

Kat shook her head. "No, but I want to get these pants off you and see how much damage there is before I just yank it out." A smirk slid across his face, sending warmth to her center, pushing the matters of StormLink from her mind for a brief moment. Everything else might be a shit show, but Griffin was back where he belonged, by her side. "Why are you smirking like that?"

"I made you a promise about this desk," he said, patting the wood beneath him. "I plan to keep it."

She bit her lip to hide her smile and refocused on the blade in his leg. "Shut it," she said before he could make another comment, but warmth still spread through her face. The last seven years had been heavy and angry. Perry filled some of the void Griffin had dug into her heart. The warmth dropped from her face like an anvil into her stomach. Perry—he was really gone.

"What's wrong?" Griffin switched gears, all the lust in his voice gone as his hand slid beneath her chin and lifted it to meet her gaze.

"I want to give Perry a true burial," she said softly. "Luke and Decius too." The ache that settled in her heart felt like it would never leave. So many dead for a fucking piece of paper.

"We will." He ran his thumb along her cheek, and she leaned into it. For a moment, they were teens again, comforting each other through trials and pain. Kat swallowed and pulled his hand from her face. "You might want to hold on to something."

She cut down the front of his jeans beneath the blade, exposing his leg. She winced when he sucked in a breath, Griffin's knuckles turning white on the edge of the desk when he picked up his leg so she could cut the hanging fabric free. The entry wound didn't look nearly as bad as it could have. In fact, Izz's aim hadn't been deadly, or even life-threatening. She'd embedded the blade partially into his leg—deep enough to slow him down, but not enough to take him out of the game.

"That actually doesn't look too bad," Mason said from behind her. Kat looked back at him.

"Yeah," Kat agreed. "I'm surprised."

"I'm not," Mason said.

"What does that mean?" Griffin asked. "She seemed pretty intent on killing me after I—"

"We'll get to that," Mason responded and looked intently at Kat. "We have a bigger problem."

"Lay it on me," Kat said, the list of issues growing by the minute.

"The hit list is still live." Mason held out his phone. She glanced at the live site, her lip curling in disgust.

"I really hate that man," she said, a sour feeling overcoming her stomach. Having Luke open the vault was supposed to reset the system; clear the hit list; give her a fresh start. "If he wasn't already chopped into pieces and scattered around, I would pull his body out and filet his skin just for my own satisfaction. What about StormLink? Is there something we need to do there?"

"We should ask Mike Barnes," Griffin supplied. "Senior had several meetings with him the weeks before he died."

"Who the fuck is Mike Barnes?" Kat asked. She'd never heard the name, although she was learning there was a lot she'd never heard.

"StormLink's only authorized personnel," Mason said and

raised an eyebrow. "I thought he was due for elimination a month ago."

Griffin frowned. "He was. And then out of the blue, Senior said to let him be."

"That's strange," Mason said, and Griffin nodded in agreement.

"Why is that strange?" Kat asked.

"StormLink personnel have a very short shelf life," Griffin said, his hand drifting to his thigh, a small groan leaving him. "Someone take this thing out, or I will."

"I've got it," Mason said, moving closer to Griffin. "That way you can start cataloging the vault."

Kat appreciated his word choice—you can. He wasn't ordering her around; he was delegating for her because, at this moment, she was the head of Legacy Inc. The entire empire her granddad built was now at her fingertips, and she had no idea what to do next— what secrets she needed to know, what files were the most impor- tant. She was the Head Mother Fucker in Charge, but Mason was the one with all the secrets, all the power, all the connections.

Kat nodded and stepped back, eyes skating behind Mason to Luke's still form, and Aeron—her sister—sitting propped up against the wall, eyes closed. She felt Mason's gaze on her. "I gave her a painkiller," he said, "to take the edge off while we figure this out."

Kat's gaze lingered on Aeron for a few seconds longer before she pulled her eyes back to Mason. She hated that she needed him so much right now. "What should I be most concerned with?"

"Everything Maureen touched," Mason said, pulling gauze from his cargo pants pocket. "And anything with the names Syndi- cate, Hale, Onyx, or Storm."

"What are those?" she asked, a few of the names sounding only vaguely familiar.

"Competing Security Agencies," Griffin interjected. "Well, at least the first three. I'm assuming Storm is in connection with the program we use?" He looked at Mason, who nodded.

"What do you mean 'competing'?" Kat asked.

"Did you think we are the only black ops security firm out there?" Mason asked, shock coating each word.

Kat bit back her reply and glared at him. Of course, she didn't. It just never occurred to her that there was any legitimate competition. They were fucking Legacy Inc.

He held her glare for only a moment, then shifted his focus to Griffin's wound. He grasped the handle of the dagger and looked at Griffin. "Ready?" Mason asked. Griffin nodded, and he yanked the weapon up, a slew of swears leaving Griffin's mouth. Mason staunched the bleeding with the gauze before he looked back at Kat.

"Onyx and Hale were the CIA's go-tos before Legacy Inc. Before Storm—" he broke off for a second, and Kat didn't miss the emotion sneaking into his voice. He took a deep breath and exhaled. "Before Legacy Inc introduced StormLink to the CIA, proving why we were the best for the job. They were hardly an issue after we culled them down to bare bones. The Alliance helped keep them at bay, too, although Elijah had no idea. The Syndicate is the cover name for the Alliance. But word that we—you—are vulnerable will continue to spread quickly in the Underworld, especially with Rufus out causing mayhem."

Ice crept up her spine. More things she didn't know. "How far in the dark was I kept?" Kat asked, words barely a whisper, gaze bouncing between the two men. She was supposed to take over Legacy Inc, to serve beside Luke. Supposed to. . .not be anything, because she wasn't a Wayward. She'd been a sacrificial pawn and now reached the other side of the board to be crowned queen without any idea of what that actually meant.

Mason's voice was soft when he answered. "As far as possible."

"And whose decision was that?" Kat asked.

"Not mine," Mason assured.

A lump of emotion lodged itself in her throat. She nodded and turned toward the vault, not wanting either of them to see how much that admission stung. Fuck the Waywards. She was a—well, she didn't know what she was—certainly not a Seward. Had Aeron's dad known about her? Did Mason know who her father was? *No.* She stuffed the thought deep down. Whoever her father was, he had no influence on who she became. She didn't need them, just like she hadn't needed a mother; either of them.

She stepped into the vault, the temperature around her dropping a few degrees. This wasn't the cold vault she had heard about; a quick glance around confirmed there were no hard drives in sight. Shelves lined the walls on either side of her, the traces of her Granddad's meticulous organizing sprinkled in the dumpster fire Maureen had left behind. She righted a few overturned boxes on her left and toes aside a few dumped on the floor spying the lockboxes still arranged in perfect order on the shelf, save the few Maureen had opened. Where would he keep them if not in this vault?

She scanned the small room again. The back wall was bare, a waste of valuable storage area in such a high-tech room. She moved toward it, looking to both sides for a scanner. Given the large number of hidden passageways in the building, she assumed he would have one here. She shifted the boxes, moving them out of her way when a label on one of the dumped containers caught her attention: Mason St. James.

Kat glanced back through the entrance. A conversation between Mason and Griffin was just out of earshot, while Mason was still working on Griffin's leg. She shifted the papers that remained in the box, a handful of official mission reports written by her granddad. The word 'Storm' jumped off the page, and she picked it up, dread creeping into her spine. She knew nothing about this man, not really. Just that he had his hand in everything.

Everything. How was that even possible? She picked it up, eyes scanning the coded document.

"Find anything good?" Mason asked, his voice much louder than just seconds ago. Kat jumped. She placed the document face-down on the shelf beside the box and looked up at him. Mason surveyed the mess on the floor while using the bottom of his t-shirt to wipe the blood from his hands, not paying her any mind. "Fuck me. She really went to town in here."

"How's his leg?" she asked, calming her racing heart.

"He'll be fine," Mason started. His face contorted as he sniffed the air a few times. "Do you smell that?"

Kat inhaled a few short times, the faint trace of something burning reached her nose. She met his eyes across the vault, fear stabbing its way into her heart. They were going to lose every-thing, the documents, the servers. She looked into the office, eyes falling on Luke. She was going to lose Luke and Perry.

Kat pushed her way past him, back into the office. Griffin was already gone. "Start taking pictures of everything in there," Kat said. "I'm going to see what's happening." She sprinted down the hall toward the smell. Tendrils of smoke trickled around the bend from Dr. Jones' lab, and Kat ran faster. She broke the corner and ran smack into Griffin's chest, bouncing off and landing on her ass. He reached down to help her, but she leaned to see around him. Flames licked the windows of the laboratory and small explosions of his vile concoctions erupted as the fire tore through the room. Kat's gaze jumped to the passage door across the hall, just feet away from Perry. She could make it.

"Are you good?" he asked.

She pushed herself up, not answering, and stepped around him, eyes locked on the door. Griffin's fingers brushed her wrist, but she yanked away. "We have to get Perry," she said, her voice barely a whisper as her feet moved her forward.

"No," he said. "There's probably minutes before the fire barrier of that lab gives. We have to get Aeron and—"

An explosion rocked the hallway. Kat covered her face and dropped to the ground as debris shot toward them. They needed to get Aeron and find another way out of the building. But her heart pumped a single thought through her as she got to her feet, like an invisible string pulling her forward—Perry.

Griffin got to his hands and knees beside her, his concerned gaze on her. "Are you okay?" he asked.

She nodded, though she barely heard him over the ringing in her ears. She opened and closed her jaw a few times and pressed her fingers into her ears to clear them. "Perry—"

"We have to leave him," Griffin said.

Kat shook her head, panic and fear encapsulating her chest. She just wanted to see him one more time. Before she could think about it, Kat bounded to her feet, taking off toward the steel door. "No!" Griffin roared. She'd made it only a few paces when his arms encircled her waist, yanking her off her feet. He dragged her backward, the pull of the string attached to Perry going taut and then snapping.

A sob broke loose from her chest. "Let go," she screamed, wriggling against Griffin's impossible grip. He carried her around the bend, away from the heat of the flames. He placed her down against the wall, caging her in with his body, arms holding him up on either side of her as his breath came in short bursts.

Tears streamed down her face, the sudden hole inside her raw and gaping. Perry had been her right hand. Her rock, her best friend, her brother. And now she wouldn't be able to bury him or say goodbye to him. It was as if the small hope of giving him a proper burial had been holding her together, and now. . . "Get off me!" Kat shoved against Griffin's unmovable chest.

He only shook his head. "Katherine, he's gone."

The delicate way he said it broke her composure. Moisture sat in his eyes, and it pulled another sob out of her. His hand moved to her face, thumb stroking her cheek. "He's gone." He pressed his forehead to hers, their noses touching, his breath slowing, and she matched it while she rolled her thoughts and emotions into a ball and shoved them deep inside her. They needed to get back to Aeron and secure the vault. And she hadn't killed Maureen yet. She took in a calmer breath, smoke attacking her lungs, and she nearly choked. She wiped the tears from her face. "Okay."

Griffin's hand slid to hers, and she followed him back to the office, pausing briefly to grab the UBS drive from the scanner and slip it into her pocket. They stepped over Luke, his body now covered with broken-down cardboard from the vault, and Griffin closed the door behind them. Mason looked up from the vault floor. In the stark light of the metal room, she could see just how haggard he looked. He was a completely different person than he had been 48 hours ago. Sharing secrets was supposed to lighten the burden, but the secrets that Mason had spilled seemed to do the opposite. He and a drowsy-looking Aeron were furiously sliding files beneath their phones and tossing them aside. Aeron didn't look up. "Fire?" he asked, and Kat nodded. "I should have seen that coming. How much time do we have?"

"Minutes," Griffin said. "It just breached the hallway. None of the emergency systems activated."

"She must have had it written somewhere in the coding when Rosemary added her palm scan back into the system." Then it was like a lightbulb went off in his head and he looked up. "I wonder if she flipped Barnes."

"That would be a problem," Kat said.

"A big fucking problem," Griffin agreed.

"Tell me there's another way out of here," Kat said. The passage door nearest them was inaccessible, and their next exit just exploded.

"The vault." Griffin nodded his head forward, and Kat raised an eyebrow at him.

"You think Senior wouldn't have built himself a backdoor? It's a passageway to the StormLink vault and exits through the cold rooms. It's been need-to-know only. I don't think even Rosemary knew about this one." Griffin looked over at Mason.

"She didn't. Kat, your palm anywhere on that back wall should open it," Mason added and pocketed his phone.

Kat didn't see a scanner to plug Ivan's USB in to override the previous programming. "We haven't fully updated the system yet," Kat countered.

"That wall is blood-only access—or well, family access, I should say, although no one was to know about it." He reached a hand down and helped Aeron to her feet.

"And how do you know about it?" Kat asked.

"How do I know anything?" he countered with raised eyebrows. "Trust me. You'll be able to get us out of here at least. Now when we get to the command center downstairs. . ." he tipped his head side to side. "Let's hope Ivan's code takes over quickly so you can open our exit."

"I have the small thumb drive." Kat patted her pocket.

Mason shook his head. "That won't work for the StormLink doors."

"Awesome," Kat said, letting the sarcasm drip into every sylla-ble. She scanned the mess of documents around the room. "What about all this?"

"We grabbed a lot of information, but the vault should survive the fire as long as it's sealed."

Kat took a deep breath and moved to the back of the small space. A soft musical tone played when her palm connected to the smooth surface, and the wall's middle portion rose into the ceiling, blasting ice-cold air at her ankles. A thrill shot through her. The door revealed a soft-lit staircase leading into a dark abyss, the first four stairs illuminated.

"Have you been down this way? Either of you?"

"It's been years, but yes," Mason said.

She looked expectantly at Griffin.

"A handful of times this past year. He's been doing a lot of work on StormLink."

Kat didn't like the sound of that. She looked down the cement stairwell, pulse thrumming in her neck, and placed her foot on the first step. The light traveled down another stair. She took a few more tentative steps; the light matching her footfalls. She looked back at Mason. "Alright, you guys file down. I'll seal the vault behind us."

Mason stepped past her, Aeron followed, moving more slowly, and then Griffin in the rear. She grabbed his arm as he passed, whispering in his ear. "I need you to keep an eye on her. If anything happens—she's priority number one. Promise me."

His jaw flexed a few times before he nodded. Kat returned to the entrance, taking a last look at her office. Smoke crept beneath the door near Luke, and she swallowed back the sadness. He'd deserved so much better. "I'll keep my promise," she said to him. "I'll keep Aeron alive. And wouldn't you know—I have just as much to lose this time..."

Kat pulled the heavy door toward her, the lock sliding into place as it shut. Moving toward the exit, she paused by the stack of files she'd found on Mason, still face down. She gathered a handful of loose papers off the shelf, folded them, and stuffed them into her pocket before stepping back into the stairwell. As she placed her hand on the nearby scanner the steel door lowered, sealing the vault and dropping her into darkness.

5

KAT

*K*at traced a hand against the cold wall and started down the spiral steps, the feeling of being in a black void crushing in on her senses. It only took a few moments to catch up to the others, the soft blue glow at their feet the only source of light. They moved aside and let her take the lead. With each step, the temperature dropped. This far down, they had to be in the basement, if not deeper. She rounded the final bend and stopped short, Mason bumping into her. The soft blue light that guided them shot along the landing and then beneath a glass door in front of her. The cement room beyond came to life, and it was underwhelming. She took a tentative step forward, and the glass door slid aside.

"So, this is it," Kat said as she stepped into the freezing and nearly empty room. Two locked cages sat against the right wall, the whirring of servers inside them filling the area. A row of blank monitors hung along the left wall, and a console dominated the center of the room, the Legacy Inc rook bouncing around the three screens above it.

The four of them filed into the tiny space. Aeron swayed when they stopped, and Kat reached out to steady her. "Hey."

Aeron didn't answer. Her eyes rolled to the back of her head, and she slumped forward into Kat's arms. Kat shot a look of concern to Mason as Griffin came up beside her.

"Here." Griffin slid his arms beneath Aeron and picked her up like a doll, cradling her against his chest.

"How long do we have in here?" Kat asked.

"This runs on a completely different power grid. As soon as there is a change in temperature or anything, it will self-seal. We'll maybe get a 20-second warning. Maureen knocking out the emergency alerts for headquarters probably bought us a few extra minutes, but not much." Mason took a seat in the blue high-back office chair at the command center and held out his hand. "Ivan's program?"

Kat reached into her bra to pull out the larger USB drive and handed it over. Mason plugged it into the console, and they waited with bated breath as the computer loaded the program. The StormLink logo took center-stage on the middle screen: the word 'StormLink' with the black jagged S akin to a lightning bolt, and a blue, purple, and white streak of lightning woven through the letters. But as the program loaded, the streak of lightning flickered, and the entire logo rose out of a pink cloud. Kat had to admire the work. She was sure her granddad's lip curled every time he had to log into this program.

"Are we sure this is going to work?" she asked as sweat dripped down her back, unsure how long they had before this room became their tomb.

"Nope. But we can at least get it started and, hopefully, it will get the hit list down."

Kat didn't know what any of the scrolling code meant, but every time it took longer than a second to load a screen, her pulse raced for no other reason than she was completely ignorant of what was happening. She walked away from the computer and toward the vault door, the lights dimming as she moved.

"That'll be our first warning, I bet," Mason said as he typed furiously away at the keyboard. "Get that door open."

The hand scanner blinked at her, and she ran her fingertips along her thumb as she approached. In theory, she should be able to open this door. She placed her palm on the cool surface and waited. The quick prick of her finger was a reassuring sign. The vault lock disengaged, and she let out a whoop of excitement when the door slid into the wall, opening up to the cold room.

Kat wasn't sure what they would find behind the door. Carnage? Irreparable damage? Would the room be destroyed and littered with the bodies of Underworlders and rogue assets who'd overrun the building? But it sat untouched, with rows and rows of hard drives locked inside towers within similar cement walls, the blue lights giving the ambiance of an alien ship.

"Mason, StormLink runs everything, right? The buildings, the missions, the blackmail?"

"Yeah." He leaned his forearms onto the console, eyes fixed on the screens again.

"And these servers here, they house all the information?"

He nodded, not looking up. They couldn't afford to lose any of it. The lights in both rooms dimmed to red, the emergency lights shrouding the room in a dark haze. "We have to go," Kat insisted. She motioned Griffin to go ahead of her, and he moved slowly with Aeron, the limp in his leg more pronounced. "Get her out of here. Mason and I are on your heels." She turned back to Mason, but he was now at the cages along the wall, punching in codes, trying to unlock them. "What are you doing?"

"If I can get the cages open, we can at least take parts of Storm-Link with us. Give Ivan a fighting chance."

"To what?" she asked.

"Re-write the program."

The thought hadn't crossed her mind. It would be great if he could—but it wouldn't do them any good if they were both sealed in this tomb and left to die. A mechanical sound churned near the glass doors, and a steel wall slowly lowered to the ground as if hearing her thoughts. These rooms were built to be recovered.

"Leave it," Kat said. "We can come back to the vaults in a few days. C'mon." She headed toward the door. But as she crossed the threshold, she realized Mason wasn't behind her.

Griffin had already made it to the hall outside the cold room, an identical steel door lowering in front of him. "Katherine!" he called.

She looked back at Mason. He frantically typed numbers on the keypad again and again. The other steel door behind him was halfway down.

She hesitated for a moment, then ran to his side and grabbed his bicep. "Leave it," Kat said, exasperated. "StormLink is important, but now we know StormTracer is Kara Lourde. We can start over."

He ripped his arm away and glared up. "I'm not fucking leaving this behind!" he snapped, the glint in his eyes sending a warning note down her spine.

What the fuck. Kat's mouth dropped open. It was the second time she'd seen him lose control, and it intrigued her—what triggered this kind of emotion from the steel vault himself? Was it the prospect of losing all this information? Of losing their link to Kara? Their advantage? But now was not the time to start a therapy session. "It's not a goddamn suggestion, Mason. It's an order. We're leaving."

Her words seemed to sink in, and he clenched his jaw, nodding. Kat pulled him to his feet, and they raced through the vault door. They made it only a few steps into the cold room when the door to StormLink slid home, fast and deadly. She and Mason exchanged a glance and bolted toward the now almost closed exit.

The steel descended from the ceiling as Griffin strained to force the glass doors back open, the mechanical wheels not moving. Mason grabbed onto one, and the two men pried them open enough for Kat to dive under the steel death trap. She turned on her knees and took over for Mason, her muscles straining to keep the gap open as he rolled to safety with only inches to spare.

Kat and Griffin released the glass doors and dropped to the floor beside Mason, the collective sighs of relief filling the air as the last few feet of the cold room disappeared from view.

"Well, that was fucking close," Griffin said. "What took so long?"

"Nothing," Kat said, glancing at Mason. He'd already gotten to his feet and was checking on Aeron. There was something about him she was missing—a piece that made him tick. A piece that was just threatened. "Let's get the fuck out of here."

6

AERON

*A*eron stirred as Mason lifted her off the ground, the red flashing lights burning her eyes. "We're almost out," he said to her gently. She nodded against his chest, the world spinning around her. She shut her eyes again. Her mother was alive. She was alive and wanted them dead. The thought chased itself around her foggy brain, the jarring sensation from Mason's movements not doing much to help her thought process.

"Thank you, Ivan," Kat said from beside her, and Aeron opened her eyes to see they were now in the stairwell. They raced up the stairs, each jolt of her body a reminder she was alive—it wasn't a pleasant reminder. A sudden burst of cold fresh air assaulted her senses, and Aeron opened her eyes as Mason carried her out of the building. They made it only a few steps when he stumbled, Aeron falling from his grasp to the ground on her injured shoulder. A scream shot from her, and she rolled to her stomach, trying to see what caused him to drop her. Mason pulled his gun, and he fired toward the street.

"Get her out of here!" Katherine called. Aeron looked toward her, their eyes meeting for the briefest second. Katherine furrowed her brow and shook her head.

Someone grabbed Aeron by the arm, and her world tilted. Pain radiated through her, but Griffin's tight grip didn't relent until she got to her knees, and he could scoop her up beneath her armpits. Bullets danced around them, the ground exploding with each miss as he half dragged her to cover behind a stone wall. Her mouth fell open as she took in the early morning scene—the soundtrack of bullets and sirens surrounding them as Legacy Inc headquarters burned, the flames licking the sides of the building.

"Let's move," Griffin said and grabbed her arm. Aeron yanked it free.

"I'm not leaving without them." He glared. He could glare all he wanted. "I'm not leaving without them," she reiterated. "Give me my gun. We can help them, or you'll have to knock me out and drag me away." Mason had told her Griffin was as loyal to Katherine as Aeron was to Luke. The thought did not bode well at the moment. But she could see the war waging inside him—follow Katherine's orders or follow his heart.

It turned out he was more soldier than lover. He lunged and tossed her up over his shoulder like a rag doll, her world tilting upside down. She tried to brace against his lower back, but her injured arm gave way and another scream left her. He didn't wait for her protests. He ran toward the side of Headquarters. Aeron gripped his shirt, trying to reduce the bounce of his steps, but his compromised gait made every other step feel like a stab to her shoulder.

"Stop!" Aeron yelled. "Griffin, Stop!"

He didn't slow until they were around the corner and out of the line of fire. He finally lowered her to the ground. Her legs shook, and she turned away, dropping to her knees and emptying the bile from her system. Her entire body trembled, a chill seeping deep into her bones. She felt like she was dying—again.

Griffin pulled her to her feet, slipping his arm underneath her armpits and she swayed against him. "You good?" he asked.

Aeron closed her eyes, trying to find her center again, pushing him away as her equilibrium pulled left and right. She dropped to her knee, concentrating on the ground beneath her and the sounds around her as the smoke-filled air seized her lungs. She held up her hand, a single finger raised, instructing him to wait. It only took a few seconds for her world to stop moving. She opened her eyes and flipped her hand over. Griffin grabbed onto it and pulled her to her feet. She followed him around the building, concentrating less on where they were going, and more that she kept her feet moving one after another. Aeron's heart raced faster than she could ever remember it doing, and her breath refused to keep pace with her. Griffin reached Kat's car and pulled the door open. He didn't say a word, his hand tapping against his leg the being only indicator of his impatience.

An explosion rocked her forward, and she stumbled, Griffin catching her. They looked back as fire erupted from the upper floors. His jaw flexed. She climbed into the car, her trembling body sinking against the cold leather. "Here." He pulled her gun from his waistband and held it out. She took it, the warm metal heavy in her hand. Luke's head snapping back flashed in her mind, and she cringed against it, her heart racing.

"You okay?" He raised an eyebrow, eyes searching her like he could see what she was seeing.

She nodded her lie and readjusted her grip. She would never be okay again. Another explosion of glass shook the car, and Griffin took several steps back toward the building. "Go," Aeron said. "I can man the getaway car."

He shook his head. "Katherine would castrate me." He got in the driver's seat instead, starting the car and pulling from the curb. "She needs me here."

Aeron huffed. "And if she dies trying to get to us?"

"She won't," Griffin said, his voice full of conviction. "Mason will make sure of it." He kept his eyes fixed on the side of the building, though, and Aeron looked too. It seemed an eternity before they saw movement. Finally, she spied Katherine's red hair as she sprinted toward them, a familiar petite blond that made Aeron's blood boil following, covering Katherine and firing shots back the way they came as their leader sprinted toward them.

Aeron scooted over as Kat reached the car and slid into the backseat.

"What the fuck happened?" Griffin demanded.

"Hit list," Katherine said, taking deep, gulping breaths. "Cover her. Mason is on his way."

Griffin didn't hesitate and jumped out of the car, his aim protecting Alexis as she fired. Aeron waited with bated breath—where was Mason? Katherine's breathing slowed beside her as she opened and closed her left hand, which was covered in blood.

"Were you hit?" Aeron asked.

"No. I ripped open my tricep again." Katherine said, annoyance in her tone. Aeron could relate. Slick moisture slipped down her chest from her shoulder, and she was pretty sure it wasn't sweat.

"What is she doing here?" she asked, nodding at Alexis.

"She's a bottom feeder. She came looking for Luke—looking for sanctuary, to feel important, to be in the mix when decisions are made."

"Why?"

"Because it makes her feel useful," Katherine said, annoyance slipping into her tone. "Money to someone like her only goes so far. When she found out Luke was dead, she pledged loyalty to me."

Aeron wanted to tell her she didn't trust Alexis, but she knew nothing about her—except the image of her and Luke in the hotel room was forever seared into her brain.

"Here they come, push over." Aeron scooted to the door as Alexis and Mason sprinted toward them. Alexis slid into the back seat, slamming the door closed. Mason half-slid, half-vaulted over the front of the car, whipping the passenger door open and slamming it closed behind himself just as quick.

"Let's go!" he said, but Griffin had already pulled from the corner.

"We need to secure the area," Katherine said, leaning forward.

"On it," Mason replied. "There's a fire chief who owes me his life." Calling the Chief was the tactical move, but more importantly, the hazardous material that sat within headquarters needed to be contained. The last thing any of them wanted was a kid riding by on his bike, being accidentally poisoned.

Aeron dared a glance at Alexis, but the woman kept her eyes on the burning building. She thought back to the file Ivan had given her. She'd only skimmed it. It seemed less important after her dad died—after Shannon.

Katherine cleared her throat and turned to Alexis. "I'll be reassembling a team within the next 48 hours. If you can bring me information on Mike Barnes and anything on what my granddad and mother were up to, you will guarantee yourself a seat at the table."

Alexis' eyes glowed with anticipation. "Absolutely. You can reach me here." She passed a small piece of paper to Katherine. "I'm good to get out at this corner." Griffin pulled over a few blocks from the building, and they watched Alexis disappear into the crowd.

Katherine tapped the back of Griffin's seat twice, and he pulled away. She folded herself in half, laying her face against her knees. "Are you okay?" Aeron asked. Aeron knew that feeling of sadness, leaving your home and watching it burn—witnessing your legacy disappear into the night. "I know that was your home."

Katherine gave a small laugh, the sound muffled by her legs. "I don't have a home," she said, and Aeron fought the urge to hug her.

"I don't like her," Aeron said.

"I don't care," Katherine rebutted. She heaved a sigh and sat back up, looking at her sister. "We wouldn't be in this fucking predicament if you were a little less trigger-happy."

"Katherine." Mason's voice held a note of warning, but she wasn't wrong. Aeron's face burned, her eyes pricking with moisture. She opened and closed her mouth a few times, but pressed her lips together instead. There was no defending what she'd done, and she was too tired to, anyway. Aeron turned away, staring out the window, her arms folded, supporting her injured shoulder the best she could. At some point she'd lost her sling, the pain a constant that she tuned out—or maybe her body just couldn't feel the pain anymore. It was hard to tell what anything felt like—except the guilt that ate her up.

7

———

IZZ

*I*zz braced her hands against the bathroom counter, Dash's erection pushing against her as his fingers traced familiar paths over her towel. She tipped her head to the side and he moved her wet hair off her neck to make room for his lips. He ground against her again and she arched back. The feel of his body against her pushed all thoughts from her mind. She reached up and wiped the fog from the mirror, wanting to see the hungry look in his eyes. Instead, she met the intense gaze of Eileen Gale standing in the doorway. She hadn't seen her since the Playhouse. She looked rough, her face bruised and cut, but her eyes were as clear as the day she'd walked Izz into this life. Izz didn't stop moving, though, her hand winding through Dash's hair, encouraging him to suck harder on her neck as she asked, "Where the fuck have you been?"

"Making the runs to Tampa," Dash said, his lips moving to her shoulder.

Izz caught Eileen's smirk in the mirror and gave a small laugh when Eileen answered. "She wasn't talking to you, Dash."

Dash's fingers froze beneath Izz's breasts, and he looked up, too, body going rigid against her as he saw Eileen's reflection.

"Five minutes," Izz negotiated, eyes on Eileen as she continued to move her hips against Dash. He didn't respond, and Izz noticed his gaze was still locked on Eileen.

The older woman shook her head. "Kick rocks, Dash."

He removed his mouth from Izz's neck and took a step back, the hint of fear in his face. His gaze bounced between Izz and Eileen before he nodded and skirted past the older woman, eyes downcast and not a word to either of them. Izz turned and leaned against the counter, arms crossed. "You are the biggest cock block."

"If you're fucking the help, something went wrong in the last few days."

She wasn't off the mark. "Have you talked to her?" Izz asked. Eileen shook her head. Izz took a deep breath. For as long as she'd been in the Alliance, they'd had one high-priority mission that trumped everything: to protect their children. Losing Luke wasn't just a loss of leverage for Maureen, it was a complete failure of Izz's job, and the words burned on her tongue as they passed her lips. "You should know we lost Decius at the Playhouse."

Eileen's face fell. "How?"

"I'm not sure. We also lost Luke last night."

"What the... *how*?"

"Aeron shot him."

Eileen's jaw dropped open. "Motherfucker. How is Maureen handling it?"

"She threatened to blow Dash's brains out when we got in the car and then retreated to the office."

"So not well," Eileen surmised and heaved a sigh.

"I'm sorry about Luke and Decius," Izz said. "I know..."

"You know nothing, Izz." Eileen stepped into the hall. "The office. Ten minutes."

Izz let out an aggravated sigh. "I could have fucked him for five of those!" she called out as Eileen disappeared from view. But she dried off quickly and pulled on jeans and a t-shirt, the fabric sticking to her skin. Eileen was Izz's oldest confidant and friend, and the reason Izz sat comfortably as Maureen's right hand. When Eileen brought her in, Izz's only job was to make Maureen's life easier. Tie her shoes, get her food. But it was also to keep her safe, reporting back to Eileen if Maureen seemed too melancholy or stopped taking her meds. Then in walked Maureen's right-hand man—Mason St. James. Dangerous, fucking hot, yet somehow also kind and funny. He taught her how to live, how to feel, how to be valuable. He changed her life.

Izz took the stairs two at a time toward the office. The safe house they occupied as headquarters was a five-bedroom home in Arlington, VA. It was a tight fit with twelve of them—although it was only supposed to be a temporary stay.

Eileen's voice carried through the cracked door, anger lacing through the soft words. "How could you?"

"Decius is dead!" Maureen snapped, the emotion catching on the last word.

"And whose fault is that?"

"Luke's," Maureen said matter-of-factly.

"And who kept him under Sin until he could no longer tell the difference between reality and hallucination?" Eileen pushed. "We can play the blame game all day, Maureen, but you haven't been the same since Andrew died."

Izz froze at Eileen's words. She could enter the room, and the women wouldn't even bat an eye, their argument continuing like it was a normal Tuesday. But in the last year, the tension between the two had risen, Eileen calling Maureen on her bullshit, and Maureen staying on that bullshit. Being anywhere near Maureen when Andrew's name came up usually meant someone was losing their head. Izz liked her head.

"Yeah. Well, Luke killed him too," Maureen said.

"He died to save Luke," Eileen said. "Aeron—"

"The girls aren't coming home," Maureen said, her voice rising. "Katherine made that painfully clear."

"And what home do they have to come to? You tortured Luke. *Tortured*," Eileen said, her voice rising.

"You were just as eager to find out what he knew about Shannon," Maureen countered.

Izz turned to the sound of movement on the stairs behind her. Keara Gale, Eileen's oldest daughter, emerged into the hall carrying a tray of to-go cups. "Coffee?" she asked, her eyes dancing.

The words brought a smile to Izz. "You are my favorite. How did we ever survive without you?" she said, reaching out to take a cup.

"I ask myself that every day. You coming into the meeting?"

Izz took a sip of the drink, the warmth filling her chest. She could sneak away still and Keara would cover for her, but if anyone was taking the brunt of Maureen's anger about losing Luke, it should be Izz. "Well, I'm not sending you in there alone."

They pushed the door to the office open, the conversation halting as they entered. Maureen sat at the head of the table, legs folded underneath her, and Eileen sat to her left, leaning back in her chair, her anger melting as her sight landed on her daughter.

"I have caffeine," Keara said, walking the drinks over. "Black with two sugars," she said, handing Maureen a cup. "And cream and sugar." She handed the other cup to her mother and took a seat beside her. Izz rounded the other side of the table, dropping into the position next to Maureen.

"Thank you, Keara," Maureen said, all venom gone from her voice. "Do you have the Playhouse casualty list?"

Keara took a sip of her own drink before answering. "We lost twenty at the Playhouse. I updated the TTT (Top Tier Teams) roster, but we need to fill their spots. We have several critical missions on deck."

Izz let out a low whistle. When Maureen ordered them to the Playhouse, she had wanted to bring Luke in alive. Izz doubted she anticipated the carnage Katherine and Rosemary brought to the table.

"And what about the assessment of the garage afterward?" Maureen asked.

"Afterward?" Eileen asked.

"We had intel on where Mason and the kids were," Maureen said. "We went to retrieve them, but Rufus crashed the party."

"With some of ours?" Eileen asked.

"No," Keara said. "A group of Underworlders. From what I pulled from the spotty security footage on site compared to the bodies we recovered there, he entered with twenty, left with none."

"The question is, where is he now?" Maureen asked.

Keara shrugged. "I lost sight of him after the garage."

"He'll show up," Eileen interjected. She took the lid off her cup, the steaming rising into the room. "He always does."

"What else do you have for us?" Izz asked.

"The Tampa crew is requesting an extended time off after covering for when we moved them to New York. They had minimal losses—two."

"That's less than I expected," Izz said. "Considering they went in blind halfway through. Mission success otherwise?"

Keara nodded.

"Did you guide them?" Izz asked. Keara had been asking for more responsibility since being brought into the inner circle. Her leadership skills were phenomenal and one of the greatest assets of being a Guide was that no one knew how old you were to complain.

Keara nodded again, a smile dancing on her lips. "Right on," Izz said.

"Grant them extended leave," Maureen said, all business. "We will bump them to tier one when they return."

"Are they ready for that?" Eileen asked.

"Doesn't matter," Izz said. "Out of the five tier-one teams, Blue Bloods came home with 2 of 5; Falcons with 1 of 5; Serpents with 2 of 5; And the Playhouse completely wiped out Badgers and Obsidian. We will have to rebuild all of those teams from the tier twos."

Eileen's eyebrows shot up, but she nodded.

"What else?" Maureen asked, her focus on Keara.

"There's movement reported on Hale this afternoon with word of Legacy Inc's demise plastered all over the news. Mel wants to know if she should move into phase two," Keara said.

Maureen sipped her coffee and turned to Izz. "How deep did you get in with Derek Hale?"

"As deep as his dick could get," Izz said and smirked when she caught the pink tinge on Keara's cheeks.

Maureen nodded. "Good. Be on standby. Keara, tell Mel to pull back from their current assignment, but await new orders." Izz's mouth dropped open. Pulling Mel's operation would take the protection detail off Aeron and Katherine. She glanced at Eileen, her jaw ticking with unsaid words.

"Will do," Keara said.

"And then set up a video call with headquarters for tomorrow. I'll start promoting the lucky fools who didn't die. That will be all." Maureen dismissed the younger girl, and the room sat in quiet tension until her footsteps retreated.

Eileen rounded on Maureen. "Are you fucking insane? Pulling Mel sets back everything the Alliance has accomplished."

"Mel's operation was to keep competing firms out of Legacy Inc's way. With Elijah, dead there is no Legacy Inc."

"I think Katherine would argue with you on that," Eileen countered.

"Then she should have thought of that before telling me to fuck off."

Eileen released a cry of frustration and stood up. "What even is your end goal anymore? First, it was to keep them safe. Then it was to transition them over as soon as Elijah was no longer a threat. And now?"

"And now I need to do damage control," Maureen said, leaning back in her chair. "The Alliance has failed—it's dead. We should let it die. I have assets who need me, and we retrieved Elijah's contact in the CIA. The focus now is to secure that position before Hale has the opportunity."

Maureen's words paused Eileen's next thought, and she looked to Izz for confirmation. "We got the contact?"

"We got it."

"Who?" Eileen asked.

"Kara Lourde," Maureen supplied.

Eileen's eyes widened. "Not who I was expecting. What are your plans for the girls?"

"I've waited this long—I can wait a little longer for them to see the errors of their ways. I want them here—Mason will make sure they arrive. Until then, I have a business to run."

"And where is Mason?" Eileen ventured.

Maureen and Izz exchange a glance. Since Shaun's death, Mason's standing with Maureen had been on a rocky footing. He'd begged Maureen to pull the kids back from the Institute, but she and Andrew had a long game they weren't willing to share or deviate from.

"Where do you think?" Maureen said, and Eileen nodded. It was no secret Mason would do anything to protect his charges, Izz just never thought she would see the day he and Maureen were at odds. "But. . . I may have something to change his mind."

"Rufus won't be enough," Eileen said.

Maureen shook her head, and Izz leaned in closer, wondering what she could have that Mason would give up his lifelong oath for. "No. But learning what happened to Storm might do the trick."

8

AERON

They pulled onto a gravel driveway, the rough movement jarring Aeron awake. Outside, tall trees lined the road. Katherine leaned forward between the two, listening intently to Mason's phone call while pointing directions to Griffin. Mason was speaking quickly in. . .was that Gaelic? She tried to listen more closely. No, he was speaking Irish, but her brain felt too foggy to decipher the words beyond that.

Katherine looked back, eyes widening from seeing her awake. She remained silent, but motioned for her to get out of the car and follow. Mason remained in the passenger seat, phone glued to his ear. He offered her a tense smile and waved his hand for her to join the others inside.

Aeron trailed behind Kat and Griffin, their footsteps muffled by the dew-covered grass. They rounded the back of the house, and the morning sun broke over the treetops like a harbinger of hope. Her eyes hovered over the picture-perfect moment—a new day and a surreal reminder she should be dead. She wanted to be dead.

"Shoes off," Kat said, leading them through the back door and putting hers on a shoe rack. Aeron and Griffin followed suit, closing the door behind her. She glimpsed Kat's clothes from the Playhouse in the trash bin, stiff with dried blood. A knot lodged in her throat as she saw a flash of Decius screaming in pain on the Playhouse floor. "Do you want a drink?" Kat asked, not looking back as she entered the next room. "I need a drink."

Aeron shook her head, unable to get words out, and followed her through the door frame, scanning the area. To the right was a set of comfortable-looking couches and a wall of monitors filtering through security footage, but Kat made a beeline for a bar to the left, where a laptop sat open.

Kat forewent a glass. She snatched a bottle of clear rum from the shelf and took a long gulp. A sigh left her when she lowered it and then pulled down a bottle of Macallan. A pang of sadness hit Aeron. She had seen the New York Edition bottle in her father's collection. It was expensive, rare, and saved for special occasions.

Griffin reached for it. "You still stock it?" Surprise coated his words.

Kat poured him a glass and held it out to him. "I hated you. Not your taste in alcohol."

"Did you really hate me, though?" His eyes crinkled when he smiled, reaching for the glass.

Kat held it just out of reach, a smile dancing on her lips as well. "I bought this bottle from your rare whiskey dealer several years back, because I heard you were looking for it."

His mouth fell open. "So petty," he said and laughed as Kat handed the glass over.

Aeron's heart cracked—she would never have that again. The easy banter after a mission. The relief of seeing your team through the chaos. She averted her eyes away from them and back to the laptop where a can of energy drink sat next to it—Ivan's favorite energy drink. "Katherine," Aeron said around the knot in her throat. "Whose laptop is this?"

"Um, either Dom's or Ivan's. I'm not sure. Did you want a drink?"

Aeron's heart stuttered in her chest. "Ivan's here?" The immediate longing for his familiar gaze, his bone-crushing embrace cutting into her and pulling her to the stairs.

"Yeah," she said.

That was all Aeron needed to know. She bolted up the stairs, ignoring Katherine's calls for her. She took the narrow steps two at a time, bumping into the metal door at the top. Her heart pounded in her chest, and her head swam. She shouldn't be running upstairs—she should be dead. Two hands grabbed her before she could tumble back down.

"Easy there," Griffin said, his voice soft in her ear. "I've gotcha." He reached around her and opened the standard soundproof metal door.

The world went from silent to flooding with noise: laughter, screaming, the clinking of plates, and Aeron paused. There were more people in the house than she thought. What if Ivan didn't want to see her? She couldn't take another person looking at her the way Katherine had when. . . No. Ivan wasn't Katherine. He would understand. She stepped into the room, squinting against the bright white kitchen.

The kitchen was massive. Across from her was a grand walk-in pantry and a hallway to the right. She peered left and found Ivan's tall lanky form hunched over the kitchen sink as he scrubbed a metal mixing bowl. Her entire nervous system was going haywire, the noise of the room buzzing in her ears and traveling down her entire body. She nearly tripped over her feet as she closed the distance to him. He still hadn't noticed her.

"You missed a spot, Darth," she said, voice shaking.

He spun around; the bowl clattered into the sink. She smiled. Just being near him brought a comfort she yearned for. But her smile faltered. His face paled, mouth dropping open, as he took two steps back—as if he'd seen a ghost.

"Aeron," he whispered. Tears filled his eyes as they roved over her from head to toe, his hands held out as if trying to see if she was real. Not the response she was expecting.

"Oh, shit," she said, her stomach flipping. "Mason didn't tell you."

Ivan shook his head, his entire body trembling. "Oh, my god. You're alive."

Tears burned her eyes, and she threw herself at his chest. His arms wrapped around her. Her shoulder and body protested the tight hug, but her soul cried out in relief. It was like being home. This was what she needed. She never wanted to leave his side.

He pressed his wet cheek into her hair. "You were dead. I held you." He stepped back again and raised his hand, fingertips hovering by her cheek. "How is this possible?"

"I don't know," she said. "We'll have to ask Mason."

His eyes roved over her again, his brow creasing with displeasure. "He brought you to headquarters?"

She nodded, not wanting to speak about the last 24 hours at all.

"Did you guys even—"

"Aeron!" a small voice yelled out from the other end of the room. The blood froze in her veins, and she slid her gaze past Ivan to the long table on the other side of the kitchen. Eight children, still in pjs, sat eating pancakes with their eyes on her. It seemed all the blood in her body drained to her feet, making it impossible for her to move.

Eliza stood on the chair, flour down the front of her nightdress and in her hair. She waved a whisk in the air. "Look! It's Aeron! Where's Luke?"

A harsh ringing started in her ears, and the world tilted around her. Where's Luke? Luke was. . .she shook her head and stumbled back, bumping into Griffin, who steadied her. She pressed her eyes shut and bowed her head, the image of his head snapping back replaying in her mind.

No.

She hadn't slept and had been snatched from the brink of death just hours ago. Those kids weren't really there. It had to be a side effect of nearly dying because Mason had said they were dead. Luke had said they were dead.

She swallowed hard and opened her eyes again, stepping away from Griffin. The eight faces stared back at her. Owen, Eliza, Penelope, Caroline, Robin, Jack, Ryan, and baby Scarlet. Each very much not-dead. Unlike Luke. Her breath wouldn't come, her chest tightening, the pain reminiscent of being shot. She looked down to be sure she hadn't been.

"Aeron?" Ivan said. He reached forward, and she pushed him away. Maybe he wasn't real, either. No. She must be hallucinating. There was no way all those kids were alive. Because that meant she killed Luke for. . .for what?

"Let her be." Griffin stepped between her and Ivan.

Ivan protested, and Aeron used the moment to retreat toward the doorway.

The kids were coming closer now. She needed to go. Anywhere. She bumped into a solid body and turned, panic rising in her chest. Mason looked down with concern written on his wrinkled brow, Katherine right behind him. The room spun, moving in on her. There were too many people. Too much noise. She couldn't breathe. In, out. In, out.

Mason reached for her, and she stepped back out of his reach. "Don't you touch me."

"Aeron," he said. "Please." The words gripped her around the throat, and she shoved him hard.

"Get away from me!" she cried. She shoved him back another step, clenching her hand in a fist and pounding on his chest. "How could you! How?" The words broke from her, a sob catching in her throat.

"Aeron, I didn't—"

She wouldn't listen to his lies a moment longer. She retracted her right arm and punched him across the face. He stumbled back and grabbed his jaw, opening and closing it a few times, but didn't come closer. Good. She was tired of the men in her life using her like a pawn. "You lied to me," she ground out. "You're as bad as my father. No—you're worse because I believed you with everything I had."

Aeron pushed past him and Katherine. She needed to get away from those kids. Away from all of them. Soft footsteps followed her back down to the basement. Aeron ignored them and headed for her shoes. She needed air.

"Where are you going?" Katherine asked from behind her.

"I don't know, but I can't stay here," Aeron said. Her hands shook, the laces falling from her fingers. Kat sighed and pushed her hands out of the way, sitting on the floor in front of her.

"Where are you going to go, Aeron?"

It was as if a bucket of ice had drenched her. She had nowhere to go. No one to go to. Everyone was dead, and it was her fault. She killed Shaun. She killed her father. She killed Luke. Hell, she killed Ernie, Decius, and Shannon too—if she'd just told the truth, none of this would have happened. But she couldn't stay here with those ghosts. She couldn't trust her own perception, because if she was being honest, she'd felt off since she woke up in the back of a moving car in Tommy's lap, yanked from death. Her system moved sluggishly and her heart beat painfully with each strike against her rib cage—but she couldn't tell if it was a side effect of escaping death or a reminder that she'd killed so many of the people she loved.

"I don't know, but I can't stay here with those. . .are they real? The kids?"

Realization dawned on Katherine's face. "You didn't know."

Aeron's vision blurred, and she choked on a sob. "I thought he killed them. Mason told me he killed them. So I killed him," Aeron said. "I shot my best friend—the man I loved—because I thought he'd turned into a monster. I—" Breathing was now impossible. Each pull of air used too much energy. "I—I—"

Katherine stiffly wrapped her arms around Aeron and she leaned into her, painful cries rocking her body.

"You did the hard thing. It had to be done," Katherine said over Aeron's sobs.

But Aeron shook her head. "No, it didn't! He could have—I should have—"

"Aeron?" Ivan called from behind her.

She turned, wanting to be near him again, and felt a prick in her neck. Her hand flew up to the spot, and she looked wide-eyed at Katherine, who held a syringe in her hand. "Sorry," she said before Aeron's world went dark.

9

KAT

*K*at looked up at Ivan, Aeron's unconscious form now heavy in her lap, as she tried to stop her sister from falling to the floor. Her sister. God, would she ever get used to that? Ivan's wide eyes just stared at her. She hadn't told him Aeron was alive. There hadn't been time, and what if they hadn't made it out of headquarters? Kat needed to see for herself that Aeron was alive and well. Well, at least she was alive. "Don't just stand there, help me." He didn't move, eyes locked on Aeron.

"Did she say she killed Luke?" His words felt like a slap. A reminder of how fucked up this entire situation had become. She'd just wanted justice for Shay; to stop a madman from killing people.

"Yes," Kat answered, her left arm trembling from holding on to Aeron, the pain medication nearly worn off. "Come help me."

Ivan's lanky frame moved closer, his face a mask of disbelief as he continued staring. "What did you do to her? Is she okay?"

"No, she's not," Mason said, emerging from the darkened stairwell, his busted lip giving Kat a sick rush of joy. "And it's just a sedative." Ivan stepped out of his way, and Mason slid his arms beneath Aeron's armpits, helping Kat carry her to the couch, moving slowly to not jar her arm.

Kat breathed a sigh of relief as the pain subsided, running her hand over her biceps to encourage blood flow. She glanced back at Ivan, his eyes glued to Aeron like she would vanish if he looked away. She understood the shock he was feeling, and the new wave of concern that weighed on his shoulders—she'd felt it when Aeron stepped through the door in the office, even though Mason had said she was alive. They'd said goodbye, they'd taken Aeron's death as a catapult for going after Maureen, and they'd grieved, even if for a short moment, and Kat could bet he was thinking the same thing she was—could they really go through losing Aeron again?

Kat sat back on the coffee table, watching Aeron's still form. Her chest moved steadily up and down, and for right now, that would need to be enough. They had too much to do to worry about her, but how could she not? She eyed Mason wearily, the fresh blood from Aeron's hit beneath his lip. She had half a mind to punch him again.

"Why didn't you tell her about the kids?" she asked.

"There wasn't a chance."

"But you've known for months," Kat countered.

"I didn't have proof," Mason said.

Kat tilted her. "That's a lie. You told Luke you had proof he was saving the children weeks ago."

"And you told us at Ernie's you had confirmed he killed them," Ivan said, his voice rising several octaves. "You said—"

"That I had confirmed a few, but for all appearances, they were all killed," Mason finished for him. "I know what I said. I didn't say he killed them all." But Kat saw the shame cross his face.

"I had confirmed for you," Kat reminded him. "We talked at length about them."

He gave a small smile. "We did. But I didn't put my eyes on

them myself until a few minutes ago. I wasn't telling her anything until I was sure."

"So you let her believe Luke killed them all?"

"I didn't think she would kill him over it." His voice was barely a whisper.

Kat's heart constricted. He'd lost just as much as they had, maybe more. Her hand slid to her back pocket, resting on the files she'd grabbed before sealing the vault. Would any of them ease her mind about the man she was, metaphorically, getting into bed with?

"I think she killed him for more than just that," Kat reassured. "The Sin really did a number on him. Where's Griffin?"

"I asked him to wrangle the kids so I could help with Aeron," Mason answered, and Kat had the sudden urge to run up the stairs to see what that would look like. They had once been playful, immature even. But that was before, before Shay, before her granddad had strategically stripped them of any innocence and left them on a path of vengeance. "Do you have a guest room I can use for her?" he asked.

Kat nodded. "She can have my room. I won't be sleeping anytime soon." Or ever again, she thought. She was sure as soon as she closed her eyes she would see them all: Perry, Luke, and Aeron, all dead. "How did you do it?" Kat whispered. "Bring her back?"

Mason took a seat on the side of the couch, gaze on Aeron. "I didn't bring her back. Not really. I just delayed her death in hopes of getting her out. I slipped her a dose from Dr. Jones' stash."

Kat blanched and fought off a shiver. She would forever be grateful for Dr. Jones' experimental drugs that allowed them to continue through pain, but his personal stash of experiments she stayed far away from. "You thought she was going to die."

He nodded. "I honestly thought it hadn't worked, and I had the awful feeling that maybe I'd sealed her fate by trying to save her." His voice broke, and he wiped a tear from his cheek.

Kat looked back to Aeron, tampering down the ugly feeling fighting to reach her chest—jealousy. She couldn't think of a single elder who cared for her the way Mason cared for Aeron. Everyone who should have loved her had deceived her; used and abused her; and then abandoned her. Even Griffin, in his quest to protect her, had abandoned her. But not Aeron. The jealousy subsided, morphing into fear. Aeron had run to her rescue, twice. Aeron had risked everything for her, and Kat couldn't bear the thought of losing her before she even got to know her. "Whatever we decide to do, she stays out of it. I want a medic and full-time protection for her."

Mason nodded in agreement. "Absolutely. Dr. Jones is out of the question. He moonlights for the Alliance."

She huffed, pinching the bridge of her nose. Did everyone work for the Alliance? "I can call Dr. Shea," Kat suggested.

"I have someone even better, but you won't like it," Mason said. Kat shifted her gaze to him and raised an eyebrow. "Eileen Gale."

"Absolutely fucking not."

"Hear me out—"

"No. She's buddy-buddy with Maureen."

"And so was I. Eileen is the only reason we knew where to find Luke."

Kat gave a dry laugh. "And look how well that turned out."

"I trust her," Ivan interjected. Kat spun to look at him. He'd been so quiet she nearly forgot about him. "I was working with her and Andrew this past year."

"And also moonlighting for the Alliance," Kat said.

"I didn't know that," Ivan said, his tone defensive. "I was Andrew's apprentice, and that's it. But I got to know Eileen. She's one of the good guys."

"None of us are the good guys." Kat shook her head and turned back to Mason. "I don't trust her."

"Then don't. But she loves Aeron like a daughter."

Kat laughed, a loud, disbelieving laugh. "Said to the woman abused and abandoned by not just one, but two mothers." Mason flinched in response. "My answer is no. Now, we can't bring anyone here, especially with the kids. We'll set up for Aeron to be checked out by Dr. Shea." She looked at Mason, waiting for his confirmation. She could tell he wasn't pleased, but he nodded in agreement.

"And what about the kids?" Ivan asked. "What are we going to do with them? We can't run a full-scale operation while hiding equipment and weapons from a gang of nosy children."

Kat rolled her neck a few times. "The plan, if I didn't make it, was to send them to the compound in the West Indies with Dom and Gunnar. I have a network of families ready to take them in. But I need one of them here to help you re-write StormLink."

Ivan gave her a blank look. "What are you talking about?"

"We may have lost StormLink," Mason said. "Maureen lit the building up as we were installing your program. The room is on lockdown, but we won't know until the debris is cleared if anything survived."

Ivan stared at them. "Is it air-gapped?"

"For now. We need to locate Barnes for more information," Mason said. "But in case we can't, I think you can re-write the program."

"That's impossible. People tried for years. No one can re-do her work."

"Not according to Storm," Mason said, and Kat noticed the fall in his voice. "There has never been an issue with StormLink, so I've never had to ask you, but before she died, Storm said she coded you into the original program. Somewhere in here," Mason tapped his head, "you have the keys to unlock it."

"But I don't have access to the original program."

"The Alliance does," Mason said.

Kat whipped herself to face him. "What?"

"It's a downgraded version," Mason said quickly. "And I don't even know for sure if what she put in there will help you at all, Ivan, but I can try to get my hands on it."

Kat wanted to know exactly how he intended to get his hands on anything the Alliance had after he'd just threatened Maureen's life. But she was learning it was best not to ask questions and let him come through.

Kat looked back at Ivan, her faith faltering with each second that ticked by until he answered, "Oh, okay. Does that mean you shut down the hit list?"

Kat and Mason exchanged an uneasy glance. "It hadn't been when we entered the vault, but maybe when Protocol 2 went into effect, the hit list went offline?" she said, hoping that it had.

Ivan moved to the bar, turning on the laptop, hands flying over the keyboard.

"Well?" Kat asked, a knot in her stomach pinning her down to the table.

Ivan turned back toward them and shook his head. "It's still active. However, no one has claimed Decius, Perry, or Luke."

"Fuck," she said beneath her breath. She braced herself on her knees and stood, pain ricocheting through her tricep. She swallowed back the groan begging to escape, a sudden sadness trying to creep in instead. They'd lost Luke, Perry, and so many more in the last few days. She killed her mother—god, had it only been two days since she killed her? It felt like a lifetime. She needed rest, she needed bodies, and she needed answers, like how the hit list was still running with StormLink down.

"Can you figure out what the hell is going on with that?" she asked Ivan.

He nodded. "But I'll need access to better equipment than we have here."

Mason tilted his head, a thoughtful expression crossing it.

"What?" Kat asked.

"The Institute," he said. "Ivan's computers are in Luke's apartment there. And there's a cold room."

She dared to let a smile cross her face. "Get started on what you can here. I'll send Gunnar and Dom down to help."

She gave one last glance to Aeron, who somehow looked older. Maybe it was just the weight Kat knew she carried now. She hadn't had the courage to pull the trigger on Shay—neither when Granddad demanded it, nor after his torture. Who would she be now if she had? Who would Aeron be when she gets to the other side of this? She gave a slight shake of her head and turned to Mason. "Get her upstairs. I'm going to clean up. Once she's settled, meet me in the kitchen."

Kat leaned against the counter, her cup of coffee warming her hands while she waited for Mason. She turned toward the footsteps coming down the hall, questions about Aeron on the tip of her tongue, but Griffin stepped into the kitchen. His cheeks were red, his eyes glinting with mischief as his long curls danced around his shoulders. "You have more of that?" he asked, gesturing toward the cup.

He glowed in a way she hadn't seen in years, and it pulled a smile to her face. He'd changed into jeans and a t-shirt after Betty re-treated his wound, but the jeans were already torn and stained with mud and grass. "Sure." She turned and grabbed a mug from the cabinet, not surprised as his arms wrapped around her. He pressed his chest against her back, his cold nose nuzzling into her neck. She gasped in surprise, and he laughed, but the sound died in his throat as his hand moved to her torn tricep, fingers gently skimming over the fresh dressing Betty had applied.

"How is it?" he asked, taking the cup from her as she spun around.

Fine had been the immediate answer to pop into her mind. The short-snipped response she would have given him just days ago. But this was her Griffin—childlike, spontaneous, full of mischief. It was hard to shed the armor she'd worn for so long around him. "Betty says I need to have someone more skilled look at it. But Dr. Jones' Lidopen patches are doing the job for now. How's your leg?"

"It'll heal." He took the coffee, and she eyed his limp with concern as he moved to the table. He took a seat, and she followed, sitting in the chair across from him.

"But you're still limping. Did you have Betty put on a patch?"

He shook his head. "We only have a few left. Your arm and Aeron's injuries need them more than I do."

"That is idiotic," she said. "I need you to function at one hundred percent. Go get fixed up by Betty."

Griffin's brown eyes stared at her, eyebrows drawn together, and she could see the argument forming. But he changed the subject instead. "What's the plan?"

She took a deep breath and then sipped her coffee. There were eight people in her inner circle at the moment. Griffin, the Reaper, whose name still carried a ton of weight in the Underworld. He was the deadliest human she knew, and if he were to be believed, more loyal to her than anyone else in the world. And Kat wanted to believe that he was. But she'd seen the way her granddad could manipulate and morph a person into something unrecognizable. A night of confessions and great sex did not clear the slate. His actions in the office, however, earned him some brownie points.

Then there was Mason, the wild card, who had connections everywhere and ties to nowhere. He was her most valuable asset at the moment, but she was also unsure if she could trust him. But he had not lied to her. And he had delivered on every promise he had made so far. And Perry trusted the fuck out of him.

She had Star and April, two formidable reapers whose skill set would prove useful. There was Ivan, her only hope for restoring StormLink. His fighting abilities were unknown, but his loyalty to Aeron made him an unwavering ally. Dom and Gunnar had been with her since before Shay's torture. Her two tech geniuses with zero combat skills, and who she never wanted to drag into a fuck up like this. They should have gone back to the West Indies the second she confirmed Granddad was dead. And finally, there was Aunt Betty, a potential wealth of knowledge about Maureen, and a mid-level medic who was a liability by being on the hit list. But if Betty stuck around, Kat wouldn't say no.

Half of them were battered and bruised, hanging out with a foot in the grave, while the other half were so disconnected from the dangers of the Underworld, she wasn't sure they would survive a fistfight, let alone a battle with the Alliance. But the clock ticked against them, literally. StormLink had been shut down; the hit list was still very much alive; and these were the only people she trusted to not try to kill her or Aeron.

The plan? There was no plan. Whenever problems arose, the rule was to only focus on what she could control—the immediate issue that she could shift to her advantage. But in this moment, everything felt out of her control. "I don't have a plan yet. I need more information. We need a status report on what's left of head-quarters. We need Mike fucking Barnes. I need to start tracking Kara. And I need the hit list squashed. I need to—" She sucked in a shaky breath. She needed a moment to process the carnage she had led over the past week. Time to pack away the pain sitting heavy in her heart.

Griffin scooped her feet off the chair beside him and moved them to his lap. He rubbed along the side of her legs, the gentle touch sending serotonin through her. She put the mug down, and her eyes drifted closed. "When was the last time you slept?" he asked, voice low.

She kept her eyes closed when she answered, but could feel the heat of his gaze on her. "In bed with you the other night."

"Would you like to repeat the experience?"

She smirked, and his hand traced up her leg to her thighs, heat filling her, distracting her.

"You're no good to us on an empty tank," he said.

She cracked an eye open, biting her lip. "And you would like to fill me up?"

He ran his tongue across his lips. "Do you even have to ask?" His hands continued their soft circles on her thighs, pulling her guard down with each rotation, her body reflexively relaxing. "Come lay down," he said. "The world can wait to be saved."

That was one problem she could handle right now, forgetting the pain. She gave a soft smile, and nodded pulling her legs from his grasp and standing up. She left her cup on the table and grabbed his hand, pulling him to his feet. "C'mon. I know just the spot."

Gunshots echoed in the distance, and Kat raced toward them. Her face was slick with sweat as her bare feet pounded against the sidewalk in Central Park, each step jarring her body. It was dark and empty, except for the screams. "Kat!" Shay's voice yelled out. She ran faster, the shots getting louder, Shay's screams getting closer. "Kat!" She rounded a bend and came up short. Shay kneeled in the middle of the walkway, his beautiful face beaten, his eyes bloodshot as he pleaded for death. Tears streamed down his face, carving tracks through the blood and mud on his cheeks. "Please. Just do it."

Kat glanced at her empty hand, her granddad's gun materializing in it. She looked back at Shay and shook her head, heart pounding in her throat. "I can't—don't ask me."

"Please," he begged.

"You couldn't protect him." Kat jumped at the voice by her right ear and turned as her mother appeared beside her. "And you can't protect her." Her mother nodded back toward Shay, but he was gone. Luke knelt in his place, staring up at Aeron, the gun now gone from Kat's hands and held firmly in Aeron's.

"Please," he begged Aeron, just like in the office. Kat wanted to run to her, stop her from killing him—but her feet wouldn't move, her voice didn't work.

"How long do you think before she turns that gun on you?" Kat whipped around to see Maureen standing to her other side, that twisted smile on her mangled face. "Haven't you realized yet? No one wants you, Katherine. No one needs you. You were born to be forgotten."

No. That wasn't true. But her voice wouldn't work. Her eyes pulled to the scene of Luke and Aeron, but this differed from the office. Aeron's hand was steady, her features hard.

Aeron looked over at them. "Why didn't you protect him?"

"She's talking to you, darling," Maureen said.

"I—I didn't—" Kat couldn't catch her breath. "Aeron, I tried!" Aeron shook her head in disappointment.

"You were my biggest mistake," Maureen said matter-of-factly. "But Aeron knows how to make the hard choices."

"Please!" Luke was gone, Shay in his place once again, begging at Aeron's feet.

"Don't!" Kat tried to lurch forward, but Rosemary and Maureen grabbed onto her, holding her back.

"She has what it takes," Maureen whispered in Kat's ear. "She belongs with me."

"Aeron, please," Kat begged, her gut clenching when she realized those were Luke's last words.

Aeron pulled the trigger, and Kat screamed out. Shay's body went rigid, his head moving backward in slow motion before dropping to the ground. His body turned back into Luke's. Kat yanked her eyes away from him and back toward Aeron, who now held the barrel beneath her chin.

"No! No! No!" Kat screamed, her voice going hoarse. She tried to twist free of the women holding her, but their grips tightened into her upper arms. Pure panic beat through her body with each heartbeat. She couldn't lose another person. "Don't!"

Aeron's expression remained serene as she turned the gun instead on Kat.

"Goodbye, Katherine." Kat looked toward Maureen in time to see her smile in pleasure as Aeron pulled the trigger.

Kat jolted awake, her heart pounding into her ribcage. Her hands flew to her chest, feeling for the bullet hole. It took a moment to realize she was in the master bedroom at the safe house, in an empty bed, and someone was pounding on the door.

"Red! This is important!" Gunnar shouted through the door.

"Give me a minute," she called, closing her eyes as the image of Aeron executing Shay seared into her brain. She took several deep breaths, pushing the nightmare away. But the images and Maureen's words clung to her like seaweed. Pushing the covers aside, Kat made her way to the bathroom. She splashed cold water on her face, bracing her hands on the counter as the water dripped off of her.

Her deep breaths quickened, and she choked on the sobs, the raw pain of witnessing Shay's torture as fresh as the day it happened. Nightmares starring him had been few and far between the last several years. Rehashing his torture with her mother must have undone the wall she'd built around those memories. And sleeping with Griffin probably bulldozed the rest of it. A few more splashes of cold water calmed the sobs. She dried her face on a towel and tossed it on the bed, spying Griffin's prized bottle of Macallan on the nightstand, still nearly full. She unlocked the door, which Griffin must have locked before leaving. "Yes?"

Gunnar looked down at her with wide eyes. "If that madman asks, I did not wake you up." Kat raised an eyebrow. "He said if any of us woke you, we'd be dismembered and used as firewood."

That sounded like Griffin, and she didn't bother hiding the smile his words invoked. "How long was I sleeping for?" Kat asked, stepping back and letting him in. She moved to the armchairs where she'd told Betty about Perry and sat down, swiping a bottle of water from the table and taking a sip.

"Eighteen hours? Give or take. I don't know how much of that was sleeping and how much was. . .well, not sleeping," Gunnar said, averting his gaze and trailing off. "Griffin left about twelve hours ago with Mason. They headed back to headquarters to see if anything was salvageable."

Kat nodded. She wanted to be mad at Griffin for leaving, and Mason for going without asking her. But she and Griffin had talked over tentative plans before she fell asleep, and she had to trust that they could gather information without being microman-aged. "What's so important you woke me up?" She rubbed her neck, her body sore from too many battles so close together, but she felt rested for the first time in a while.

Gunnar opened and closed his mouth a few times. "Well, you see. . ."

"Spit it out."

"Shay's missing."

The blood ran cold in her veins. No. *No.* "What do you mean missing?" She had spent millions making sure he was hidden, protected, cared for. How could he possibly just vanish?

"The compound was raided two hours ago—"

"And you didn't wake me immediately!" she snapped, her

blood pressure rising. An image of Aeron pulling the trigger on Shay popped into her head and then morphed into Maureen shooting Shay, that twisted smile on her ugly face.

"We just. . . Kat as soon as I knew I. . ."

She nodded, unable to speak, her body trembling with rage. "Who else knows?"

"Just me. Dom and Ivan are working on StormLink data."

"Good. Let's keep it that way."

Gunnar remained silent as the possibilities spun through her mind. Who would have been able to track him down? Who even knew about him? Granddad—dead. Her mother—dead. Perry—dead. Griffin—Mason? Mason had known about Shay. How long had Gunnar said he'd been gone? Twelve hours. More than enough time to—no. She shook her head. She couldn't go down that path. But if Mason knew. . .

"Keep digging into it and get Mason and Griffin back here," she said, the intensity of her anger subsiding and leaving behind the sweet taste of vengeance on her tongue. "I think I know who has him."

10

IZZ

The bar bustled with people and noise. Groups huddled around tall tables covered in beers and baskets of nacho chips, oblivious to the threat walking right past them. Izz scrunched her nose in disgust and pushed through the crowd toward the bar as music blared from the karaoke stage where a blonde woman sang off-key with her sorority sisters cheering her on.

Izz spied a tall brunette leaning forward on the bar top, her attention completely on the man beside her. As she spoke, however, the man's eyes remained focused on his drink. Izz didn't know how; the woman's thick ass peeked from beneath her cut-off jean shorts and if Izz wasn't here out of concern for the man, she would bring the gorgeous woman home herself.

But she was here for Mason—her friend—she reminded herself when she reached the bar. Izz dragged her eyes from the perfectly round ass to the woman's face. The roar of the music had lessened, and Izz cringed for the woman as the conversation reached her ears.

"It's all in your perception," the brunette said. "If the sky is blue, but you're wearing rose-colored glasses, it's now purple."

"I wouldn't get your hopes up," Izz interjected, close enough now to step between the brunette and Mason, forcing her back a few steps.

"Excuse me?" The brunette put her empty glass down and raised an eyebrow at the interruption.

"Don't," Mason said, putting a hand on Izz's shoulder.

"She would be a fucking downgrade, Mase. I'm offended."

"What did you say?" the woman demanded, liquid courage blinding her to the reality of the situation.

"You may have a real nice ass—but you couldn't calculate the velocity needed to drop a target 1000 yards out on a windy day in the middle of a fucking rainstorm," Izz said.

Mason stood up behind her. "Knock it off," he said, pushing Izz aside and looking at the brunette, whose brow furrowed in confusion and anger. "Ignore my friend," he said. "I apologize for not being more attentive tonight. Perhaps some other time." Mason picked up the woman's hand and kissed the back of it. Her face flushed, and she nodded, backing away and giving a final wary glance at Izz, who sent her a smirk and flipped a middle finger in response.

"Nice, Izz. I wasn't here picking up some ass. I'm fucking working. What are you doing here?" Mason dropped onto the bar stool. He picked up his glass, stared at the empty remains, and put it back down.

"My bad." Izz looked over at the woman. She stumbled to a gaggle of other inebriated ladies, all appearing to be in their late twenties, maybe early thirties, enjoying a girl's night out. The group turned a cohesive accusatory glare on her. Izz smiled and gave a small wave back. They turned away, and Izz chuckled and signaled to the bartender. She held up two fingers and then pointed to the empty drink. The bartender nodded, and Izz returned her attention to Mason. He looked like shit, eyes blood-shot, a busted lip she didn't remember seeing in the office, and a weight she hadn't seen him wear before. That woman must have been really drunk—probably what Mason had been counting on.

They waited in silence for the drinks, Izz turning the information about Storm over in her head. Her original plan was to tell him that Maureen knew something—but seeing him torn up like this? She didn't have enough information to punch another hole in his gut just yet. The bartender finally returned and placed two more drinks in front of them. Izz slid a $100 across the bar and enjoyed the view of his ass as he walked away. Mason pulled the new glass closer to him, swirling it a few times before taking a swig. Izz did the same, her nose flaring as the Green Label Jack Daniels hit her senses and tipped the amber liquid into her mouth.

"What happened to your face?" Izz reached out and ran her thumb along his busted lip, but he pulled away. Okay. Not ready to talk about that. She changed tactics. "Maureen's not leaving town," she said, leaning against the bar beside him.

He looked up from his glass, then dropped his gaze to where her Alliance markings sat, and back to her face. "Is this a courtesy warning or an official one?"

"This is me getting some air." Izz knew when to make herself invaluable and when to make herself scarce. The way heads were rolling back at the temporary headquarters, she didn't want to catch any of that heat. "How's the Reaper?"

"He'll live." Mason took a sip of his drink. "You have to be careful there. He won't just kill for her—he'll die for her."

"That's what I was trying to prevent." She'd seen the way the Reaper looked at Katherine, and no one else was supposed to die in that room.

"Yeah, but did you have to stab him?"

Izz groaned. "Trust me, I already got an earful from Maureen."

"Speaking of," Mason adjusted himself on the barstool. "What does she have planned?"

Izz slowly shook her head, eyes on the glass in her hand. "I don't know. She's in rare form. I've never seen her like this."

"I have," Mason said, but didn't elaborate. A pang of jealousy raced through her, the harsh reminder that Mason had Maureen's right hand before she came along. "She lost her husband and kids in the space of a few weeks," Mason said. "That will fuck you up."

"She didn't lose the girls."

"Yes, she did," Mason countered. "The moment she took Luke, she lost them."

Izz couldn't disagree and took a sip of her drink. Maureen had made that play without her—pushing her aside to work with Rosemary and Rufus.

"What's your play then?" Mason asked.

"Same as it's always been. Answer when she calls."

He gave a half-hearted laugh. "You're living the same life I am, Izz; too many secrets will drown you."

"It hasn't drowned you," she countered. It amazed her how he balanced the life he chose. Between the kids, the Legacies, and the Alliance—she would have snapped a decade ago.

"I'm burying three of my kids—if you think I'm not drowning—"

"I'm sorry," Izz said. "That was insensitive. I should have pulled Luke from the room sooner. I didn't know she would kill him. How is she?"

She noted the slight tick in his jaw, and he took a deep breath, eyes still on his tumbler. "The first thing I said to her when she woke up—you can't kill your mother." Izz settled onto the stool beside him. In the twelve years they'd worked together, throughout the atrocities they'd done in the name of the Alliance, she had never seen him like this. "I made it explicitly clear: Maureen could not be touched. I said it over and over and over. Then I warned Kat. But I never once said 'don't kill Luke'."

"We couldn't have known she was going to kill him."

"I should have," Mason said. He shook his head, tears slipping down his cheeks. He brushed them away. "I was so worried about Luke that I missed every sign from Aeron."

"That's not fair." Izz took another sip.

"She killed her father, Izz. I should have pivoted right there." He slammed his finger on the bar top with the last two words and then dropped his voice to a whisper. "I lost all of them. Luke killed Decius. Aeron killed Luke, Kat killed Perry. And I nearly. . ." he swallowed hard. "I nearly lost her."

Izz's ears perked. "How did you save her?"

He shook his head. "I thought she was dead in that garage, Izz. I swore I'd failed." He dropped his head on the back of his hand, resting on top of the glass. "When she woke in the back of the car, I nearly crashed the fucking thing."

"But you saved her," Izz said. "Like you always have."

"Did I save her? Or did I just deliver her to her own personal hell?" He looked up, his eyes red with moisture.

For fuck's sake. She cupped the side of his face and he pressed against it. The warmth spread up her arm, and she stroked his cheek with her thumb. "We can't stay here," she said, leaning into him. "Your place or mine?"

He picked up his glass and finished the dregs, then took her unfinished drink and downed it. "Yours. I haven't cleaned up all the blood at mine yet."

She nodded and laced her arm around his waist. "Let's go."

They'd done this dance a thousand times, lips on skin and fingertips dancing beneath clothes, moving as one down the hallway to Izz's apartment. She would take anyone willing to bed, but it was Mason who filled in her missing pieces. He pretended not to see the gaps in her bravado covering the pain of her loneliness, her failure, her fear. But tonight, that was her job. Make him feel anything and everything except the self-disgust and pain that haunted them all.

They reached her door, Mason pushing her back against it, hands sliding over her ass, lips moving from her mouth to her ear, nipping at her lobe. His hand left her ass and grabbed the door handle. She unwound her hand from his hair, reaching for the key to unlock it. "Hold on. You'll need this." But the door swung open, and she stumbled back, all thoughts of fucking him senseless, gone.

"Since when do you leave your door unlocked?" Mason asked, his focus sadly off her body and his eyes, clearer than when she found him in the bar, scanning the room.

"I don't." Izz closed the door behind her and flicked the light switch—it remained dark. She removed the knife from her belt and heard Mason pull his gun from his waistband. Creeping forward into the pitch darkness, she navigated the studio apartment with ease until her shin slammed into the out-of-place coffee table. She sucked her teeth and swallowed the vulgarities wanting to spill out.

The light in the corner flicked on. Izz threw her knife, and it flew past the man, embedding itself into the wall. His eyes widened, and he raised his hands in surprise. Then slowly, he reached down and pulled up his shirt the Syndicate tattoo nearly jumping off his pale skin. Anger flashed through Izz's entire being. No one knew of this address except Mason and Maureen. She studied his face again, the soft brown eyes, the messy, dirty blonde hair. She had seen him before. . .in the command room. He was just a mid-level intelligence agent.

"I was just sent to—"

"Check in on me?" Izz asked in disbelief. She stepped her foot onto the coffee table and rubbed her shin, Mason coming up beside her. The man dropped his shirt and nodded. "Did you think you hit it big? When she asked you to come here?" Izz let the sarcasm seep into every syllable. The man swallowed hard but didn't answer, eyes flicking to Mason and back to Izz. "No. You must have royally fucked up to be sent to check in on me."

"Mason, I won't say anything," the man said, looking past Izz.

A weighted sigh left Mason. "I know you won't, Scott." Izz looked over her shoulder at him. He couldn't be serious.

"You know him?" she asked.

Mason nodded and moved to the kitchen area. He opened the fridge and took out a pitcher of water. Izz flicked her gaze to Scott, who was frozen, eyes glued on Mason. When she looked back at Mason, he'd picked out a yellow mug and was filling it with water. "Did you want any?" He held up the pitcher, the other hand sliding to the drawer in front of him where Izz kept a Sig and a suppressor.

"I'm good," she said. "You?" She turned to Scott. He pulled his eyes from Mason and looked at her.

"No. I'm—"

They didn't get to find out what he was as Mason's near-silent bullet found a home in the side of Scott's skull. She released a long breath. "Fuck me."

"That was the plan," Mason said, a smirk crossing his face. "But we should probably clean this up."

Izz looked at the growing pool of blood, frustration vibrating through her. This had been the closest place to a home she had ever made on her own—her sanctuary. "How fucking dare she? Loyalty check me?" She turned to face Mason. "She fucking sent a mid-level pawn to loyalty check me?!"

Mason sipped the water, putting her Sig back in the drawer. "I mean, you are fucking the enemy right now—unless you're fucking me on her orders."

"You know better than that," Izz said softly. She stepped over Scott's body and yanked her blade from the wall, re-sheathing it before taking a seat on the couch. "And we don't have to clean this." She nodded toward the body. "I'll call the crew." A laugh left Mason, a full, boisterous laugh she hadn't heard in a while. His eyes crinkled, and he leaned forward on the counter, pulling a smile to her face. "What?"

"Is this—" he laughed again. "Is this you telling me we can still fuck because a cleaning crew can come in?"

A laugh rose out of Izz, too. Yeah, it was. She needed the release, and he needed to forget. She stood and tossed a blue blanket over Scott. They could fuck on the bed, they could fuck in the kitchen, hell, they could fuck on the floor next to Scott. She just needed Mason's hands on her body, his lips pulling the cries from her lips. "Yeah. Get your ass over here."

Izz spun the flip phone in her hand, the small display indicating she had two missed calls from Maureen. One missed call: nothing dire. Two missed calls: Maureen was getting anxious. Three missed calls and Mason would be picking out her coffin. Mason had left hours ago, their de-stress session doing nothing to lift the weight he carried. The phone vibrated again. *Maureen.*

Izz flipped the phone open, biting back the urge to snap *what*. "Yes?"

"Where the fuck have you been?" Past Maureen's anger, Izz caught the under-toned panic she'd only heard one other time— when Mason was nearly executed by Elijah under the Legacy treason by-laws.

"Where do you think I am? I need a clean-up crew. Your boy Scott didn't make it." Maureen didn't answer. "Maureen?"

"Where are you?" she asked, voice lower, but the panic was still there.

There had never been a time when Maureen had asked her

that question and meant it. At any moment, Maureen could pull up the tracking system and know where she was unless. . . "I'm home. What's wrong?"

"There's a problem with the tracking system."

Izz's blood ran cold. In the nine years of using the program, there has never been a glitch, and now? "StormLink?"

"I think so. The bitch must have connected them when she sold it for Elijah." Izz didn't miss the venom in Maureen's voice. She'd never found out what happened between her and Storm, and she was too chicken-shit to broach the topic with Mason. However, after the girl went missing, they'd expended an ungodly amount of resources to find her and came up dry. It wasn't until the night Mason was almost executed that they stopped their searches.

"I'll be there in thirty. The clean-up crew?"

"I'll send them over."

Izz hung up the phone and looked around the apartment. She and Mason had spent more nights here than anywhere else. It was her sanctuary, a place Maureen hadn't even known about until recently. Now there was a dead Syndicate member and cleaning crew on the way to invade her space. She tossed the phone on the bed and moved to the closet. She pushed the hanging clothes to the right and pulled her knife back out. Painted wood paneling surrounded the bottom third of the closet. She pressed the blade into the corner where the front drywall met the faux paneling on the left and slid the knife up and down, slicing away at the paint. It took a few minutes, but the paneling gave way, popping off with a small cloud of dust. She moved it aside and reached into the hiding spot, pulling out a go bag and slinging it over her shoulder.

She moved around the small apartment, collecting weapons she'd stashed and the few personal items she didn't feel like replacing: her favorite lingerie and sex toys. She dropped the items on the kitchen counter and unzipped the bag filled with cash, passports, and a single photo she'd forgotten she'd stored there. A knot of emotion lodged in her throat as she reached for the picture. Two teens sat on the beach in North Carolina, pure joy spilling across their faces as they laughed at some joke their friend had told them. It had been the first day of the best summer of her life—her and her brother and all the freedom in the world. She hardly recognized the girl in the photo anymore—that kind of joy didn't exist in her world. It died the day he did. When she joined the Alliance in exchange for the name of his murderer, she left everything behind—except this. Maureen had tried to convince her to let it go, but Izz insisted, and Maureen relented.

She put the picture back inside the bag along with the rest of her items and shouldered it. She glanced toward Scott and sent a half-hearted apology his way before stepping out into the hall.

11

KAT

Kat leaned back in the armchair beside Aeron's bed, turning over the folded files she'd swiped from the vault. She hadn't opened them yet. Aeron slept soundly, only waking for a few minutes when she had entered. After her nightmare, Kat just needed to see her, to know that she was safe. Make sure Maureen wasn't lurking in the shadows. And she needed a place to think. Shay was missing. *Shay was missing.* Since she'd heard the news, a hole had shredded its way through her heart, and Kat was positive it would never heal. The video footage Gunnar supplied gave nothing away. The operation was clean and effective, leaving only her guards dead. They hadn't touched any family members asleep in their beds, but they had wrecked the place leaving, a very clear message for her: *Come get him.* And she would—but until they sent her something else, there was nothing she could do.

She and Perry had spent years building a network to protect him. The compound itself was nearly a fortress, and whoever had taken him sorely underestimated who they were stealing from. She would find them and pour every ounce of stolen vengeance on them. Someone tapped lightly on the door. Kat took one last look at her sister and tucked the unread files in her pocket before leaving the room, her promise to Luke ever present in her mind. Griffin's brown eyes scanned her when she stepped into the hall and closed the door. "I got Gunnar's message. What's going on?"

She wanted to tell him—but this was a conversation that needed both him and Mason present. "Let's wait for Mason."

He raised an eyebrow but didn't argue. "How is she?" he asked instead.

"Resting. We talked for a few minutes, but she just needs time to heal." She signaled for him to follow. "Did you find Mike Barnes?"

He shook his head. "Mason's taken the lead there. Star and I tracked down all the remaining reapers, though."

"You mean the ones who wanted to kill me for the price still on my head?"

"No." He shook his head and laughed. "I may have been wrong about Star being unable to protect you. She's fiercely loyal. Those reapers are no longer among the breathing. The remaining ones were reminded of the oath they took, and who lines their pockets."

That brought a smile to Kat's face. "I'm glad she's okay. I was worried when she took that bullet the other day."

"Well, we had raided Dr. Jones' stash before Maureen and Izz showed up. She's on the mend, but a break for all of us would be beneficial. I posted the reapers at the Institute. Ivan and I went in, and he set up some firewalls and such, but he wanted to come back and collect a few things before moving there."

"Any word from Mason?" she asked. She didn't want him to know she hadn't heard from him, that every possible thought of betrayal had raced through her mind, that she was pretty sure she was a kid playing grown-up right now. They entered the kitchen. Ivan sat at the table eating a bowl of cereal, eyes glued to a tablet.

"No. He hasn't checked in?" She shook her head. "He'll be here. Coffee?"

"Thanks." She sat beside Ivan. "What do you have for me?"

His eyes didn't stray from the screen as he answered. "The hit list is deeply integrated into a CIA server so I can't touch it. I moved on to tracking Kara, who had been taking full advantage of the facial recognition spoofer, and I had hardly a trace of her until two days ago. I think she got too comfortable having her face hidden from the world, but I have her entire daily itinerary for the last week." He swiped through a few pages on the screen and then turned the tablet toward her. "She's a sucker for sweets. Hasn't missed a morning donut since I started tracking her."

Ivan finally looked at her, his bloodshot eyes set into bags on his face. They were all starting to look like walking dead. "This is phenomenal, Ivan," she said. "Truly."

"I'm not done," he said, turning the tablet back around. "There is a shadow program of StormLink on the Institute servers. Someone made a backdoor, and recently. They've been uploading and downloading sensitive materials, but I'm not sure exactly what yet. But all programs went down when the main server went offline. We got lucky—Luke had my main computer at his place. I started a firewall protocol and am running diagnostics that will take hours on a server that large. Mason might be right—I think I found Storm's writings in the code, but it's encrypted and password-protected. I'm working on it," he assured, "but I can have you a functional version of StormLink in a matter of weeks." He huffed a breath, his word-vomit coming to an end.

Weeks. That was both amazing and way too fucking long. "Great work," she said. "How many of those energy drinks have you had and when did you last sleep?"

He shrugged, but she could guess he hadn't slept since they brought Aeron home. "Have you seen her?" she asked.

"Yeah. But—"

Griffin slid a cup of coffee in front of Kat, and she wrapped her fingers around the steaming mug, the heat racing through her hands. She smiled up at him and turned back to Ivan. "But what?"

It took him a few moments to find his words. "Is she going to be okay? Not physically. But like. . ." he dropped his voice low. "We spent the last six months doing whatever was possible to save him. She—she killed her dad to save him—"

"And he killed children to save her," Kat said, breaching the horrors of what Luke had done out loud for the first time, but it was all she thought about while she sat with Aeron, watching her sleep. The things people did in the name of love, especially when that love was threatened by something they did—it was terrifying. When she'd lost Shay, her world fell apart. It was easy to look at her and see the vengeance she'd chosen. That wasn't her first choice. She'd walked into her granddad's office with the expectation she would never walk back out. She'd never told a soul that, not even Griffin. But when he'd tried to stop her from running in there, the day she'd learned about Shay, it triggered something inside her—a will to live, because not all was lost. It was dumb luck her granddad would rather mentally torture her than put a bullet in her head. It gave her a fighting chance.

"What Luke did was unforgivable," Kat continued. "He knew he lost her the night he killed Gabe, but he had to keep going. Not only to keep Aeron alive, but to save as many children as he could. Add that to the fact Maureen pumped him with enough Sin to kill two men. . . Aeron didn't kill Luke, or the monster he'd become. She put to rest the man she loved—because he was already dead." She let out a long breath. "To answer your question—I don't know. And I don't know her well enough to gauge that. But she's going to need you to help her." The image of Aeron pressing the barrel beneath her chin flashed through her mind.

Ivan's mouth had fallen open while she talked, and he closed it, swallowing hard before asking, "And if I can't? If I'm not enough?" Kat didn't want to think about that possibility, although at this rate, Ivan looked like he would wither away before Aeron.

"One day at a time," Griffin said. He held his hand out for the tablet, and Ivan passed it over. "We have a track on Kara. That's good work."

Ivan nodded, looking anywhere except at Griffin. Kat bit her lip to keep from laughing. "Thanks, Ivan. Can we hold on to this?" She pointed at the tablet in Griffin's hand.

"Yeah. It's just a mirror of what's going on downstairs. You just can't change anything on it."

"Perfect," she said. "You should get some sleep after you eat."

He took another bite of cereal and shook his head. "Gunnar and Dom are—"

"Ivan," Kat said sharply, cutting off his spiral. "You're no good to her dead—that includes brain dead from lack of sleep. We are in a holding space while the headquarter's rubble is cleared. Take advantage of it. I don't know how long it will last."

His gaze bounced between her and Griffin before he answered. "O-Okay." He finished his cereal in silence. Kat turned over the information about Storm in her mind. It seemed this dead girl had a lot of sway with two integral members of her team. She needed more info. Ivan rinsed his bowl out and headed for the basement.

"Hey," Griffin called out. Ivan paused, and Griffin pointed upstairs. "I don't think sleep was a suggestion."

Kat sipped the coffee while she waited for Ivan's footfalls now heading up to recede. "You're being nice to him." It was a change of pace from the other night in headquarters.

"Well, I scared the shit out of him when we went to collect the reapers," he said with a satisfied smile, and then it faded. "Plus, I've been in his shoes." Griffin leaned back and draped his arm across the back of her chair. "Loving a girl who loved someone else, and having to watch them slowly self-destruct as they try to save said boy from damnation."

The hole in her heart pulsed, and she looked over at him. Their story wasn't a love story—it was a tragedy. They may have finally found their way back together, but at what cost? She swiped through the programs running on the tablet, stopping at the security cameras where the kids were playing in the backyard. It had snowed while she slept, and apparently, kids liked to have snowball fights and build snowmen. Who knew? All she ever learned to do in the snow was survive hypothermia and how to navigate treacherous terrain.

She watched them play. Betty lobbed snowballs as she raced from tree to tree. Caroline rounded Betty's hiding space, her tiny snowballs hitting their target. Betty fell to the ground, pretending to die, and Caroline jumped up and down in celebration before sprinting off. If Kat had any experiences like that as a child, she couldn't remember them. She knew that Luke and Perry had, and that Aeron and Decius probably did, too. How different would her life have been if Maureen had kept her? Would she have had memories of playing in the snow? Building sandcastles on the beach? A happy childhood? A pulse of longing hit her, and she scowled.

"What are you thinking?" Griffin asked. He reached his hand across, lacing his fingers through hers.

"That I cannot wait to kill Maureen," she said, a fresh wave of determination and injustice racing through her system, calming her.

A security alert flashed in the corner of the tablet: movement at the front of the house. The screens switched automatically, showing Mason parking in the driveway. "About damn time." She took one more sip of her coffee and stood. "Let's meet him downstairs."

They reached the basement just as he entered, and it took

everything Kat had to not pounce across the room and start demanding answers. He stopped short when he met her gaze, but she noticed his black hoodie covered in dust and grime, and his jeans more ripped than usual.

"Where the hell have you been?" Kat asked.

He slid off his shoes, set them beside the rest, and joined her at the bar. He pulled out his cell phone and placed it in front of her. The device was twisted and cracked. "I did get Gunnar's message. I just couldn't respond."

"What happened?" Griffin asked.

"I fell through a weak spot in the rubble," he said. "We should start traveling with a backup as long as StormLink is down. I didn't want to risk being picked up on any unnecessary cameras, but the vault has been located. April will have it transported to the safe house of your choosing. However, it will be a few more days until we may even reach the cold room—if anything is left."

"What about Mike Barnes?" Kat pulled out a bottle of water from the mini fridge and took a long gulp. She'd been running through all the scenarios where someone could have learned about Shay. Most who knew about him were dead, except for Mason and a few trusted souls. But Perry had used the StormLink servers to create an alias for Shay and hide him amongst the assets. If Shay's identity had gotten out—what other sensitive information was out there? She was getting really tired of chasing techies down. "Tell me you have something."

He held out his hand, signaling for water. She passed one to him. He opened it and downed the drink before releasing a long sigh. "Nothing yet. What's so urgent?"

It was Kat's turn to sigh. "My compound in the West Indies was compromised. Shay's missing." She looked between the two men. Both knew something about her operation there, Griffin from his intimate knowledge of her, and Mason—well, she was about to find out. Griffin's eyes widened, his jaw going slack, and Mason stilled. "Please, don't both speak at once," she said.

"How long?" Mason asked.

"Five hours," she said. She felt Griffin's gaze on her and ignored it. She hadn't expressed her fears about Mason to him, but at every turn, she expected Mason to pull the rug from underneath her feet. To laugh as she fell. To turn his back on her like everyone else.

Mason's gaze stayed locked on her. There was no visible change in his demeanor, but she knew he was doing the math: how long it would take to grab Shay and make it back here. "Ask me," he said, the words smooth, non-accusatory. "We don't have time for the mind games your granddad played. So, ask me."

Instead of goading her, the words diffused her fear. If he wanted power, he could have taken it at any moment—even before her granddad died, she'd bet. She shook her head. "That answered my question. What do you guys know about my operation down there?"

Griffin spoke first. "I don't. After I became his Reaper, I made it a point to not look into it. Senior tasked me with looking for Shay, and I consistently lied. Said there was nothing to find."

"He looked for him?" Kat said, surprised.

"Every year," Mason added and held her stare. "When he realized Griffin wouldn't give him a single bit of information, he called me." Kat could feel the color drain from her face. "You have a compound in Montserrat, set into the mountains that costs roughly two million dollars a year to maintain. Your strip club in New York, Rockstars, funds it, and then some. Shay is there with round-the-clock care, along with a small arsenal of guards and his family. I'm assuming that was your base of communication for your hostile takeover."

Kat opened and closed her mouth a few times.

"I didn't find him until this year," Mason assured. "And Elijah never knew."

"How did you find him?" she whispered. She made sure to never visit and the money from Rockstars was routed through multiple dummy accounts.

"When Perry chose the West Indies instead of coming home. He hated the tropics. Too hot. If I didn't know him so well, I would have never thought to look."

"Well, fuck. Does Maureen know about Shay?"

He sat back on the bar stool. "Not to my knowledge. I don't know anyone that does."

"Well, clearly somebody did," she snapped. She pinched the bridge of her nose. "I even had Perry put him into StormLink with an alias for another layer of protection. But with the facial recognition scrambler down—I'm hoping we can find him. I have Gunnar looking into any international database he can get access to while Ivan is doing what he can on the program. If he comes across any footage, we should know in a matter of minutes." The familiar pluck on her battered heartstring hit her chest hard, and she covered it with her hand. Would there ever come a time when Perry's name didn't cause such a physical reaction? She cleared her throat, trying to shake the feeling.

"Maybe that's how they found him," Griffin said. "Because StormLink is down."

Mason shook his head. "It's offline. The protection programs are down, but sensitive information shouldn't have been leaked."

"Unless it was backed up to a secondary location," Griffin said. "Ivan and I were at the Institute. He figured someone has been in that program, moving information around."

"I don't understand," Kat said. "Who would even know to look for Shay? He was untraceable."

"Your mother," Mason said. "Rosemary," he clarified.

"And she was working with Maureen," Kat said, connecting the dots. Fuck. She leaned her forearms on the bar and dropped her head to them. Even if they could link Shay's disappearance to Maureen—they would have the entire Syndicate to contend with. Nearly three hundred assets. Maureen was untouchable. "Okay. There is nothing I can do about Shay right now." She looked back up, gaze moving between the two men. "Perhaps it's time Kara learned she's not as invisible as she thinks she is."

12

KAT

Kat leaned against the wall outside the pastry shop, the oversized sunglasses restricting her vision. The specialized glasses helped trick the facial recognition programs, but they gave her a headache. A sickly sweet aroma wafted out each time the door opened, accompanied by the soft ring of a bell alerting the employees they had more customers. She kept her eyes down, staring at the security footage on her phone Dom had live-streamed for her, careful not to drop the white paper bag in her hand. Kara Lourde's favorite morning indulgence: powdered donuts. If Kat was going to bombard her in the streets, the least she could do was have a peace offering available.

After twenty minutes of waiting in the cold, Kara stepped into the security footage. She rounded the corner nearest Kat, eyes down on her own device. Kat pocketed the phone and stepped directly into her path.

"Pardon me," Kara said, attempting to step around her, not looking up.

Kat stepped in front of her again, doing the do-si-do dance people do when trying to get out of each other's way. An exasperated sigh escaped Kara, and she brought her eyes to Kat's face. Kat lifted her glasses for a moment, and shock flashed in Kara's expression before she schooled her features, eyes scouring Kat as if looking for the threat of a weapon. "I'm here to talk," Kat assured. She held out the white paper bag. "Your usual."

Kara Lourde scanned the area, her eyes clocking Griffin on the roof, and Star just down the road. Kat didn't see any extra detail for the woman. She nodded and accepted the bag. "To what do I owe the pleasure, Ms. Wayward?"

Kat didn't know whether to be offended or flattered that Kara knew who she was. "Let's walk," Kat suggested, turning away and walking forward into a crowd of people exiting the subway station and filing onto the sidewalk. Kara fell in step beside her.

"I have to be honest," the older woman said. "I'm surprised to see you alive, let alone walking the streets of DC."

Kat nodded. "That's actually why I am here. I wanted to know if you could shut down the list and return the contracts to us."

Kara shot her a sideways glance. "That's not possible." She opened the bag and removed the white powdered donut. She took a bite, eyes drifting closed as she savored the pastry.

Heat flushed Kat's face. "Ms. Lourde—"

"Director Lourde," she corrected. "I had an agreement in place with your grandfather. As soon as protocol six was activated, I opened the bidding."

"Protocol six?"

Kara stopped walking, eyes scanning the area, and Kat followed suit. "Protocol six was his doomsday plan: clear the board, and erase the storm," she said, head tipping slightly. Kat nodded in understanding. His plan was to destroy Legacy Inc and StormLink.

"His plan obviously failed," Kat responded.

"Did it? The list is live, and the program went offline. There is no way to shut it down now." She took another bite of the doughnut, white powder raining down on her black jacket.

Kat bit her lip. This was not what she was expecting. "According to my source, you can. It can only be done now from your end."

"Well, then your source is mistaken."

Kat didn't buy that for a second, that she would allow the use of a program she couldn't control. "What did he have over you?"

"Excuse me?"

"Leverage. It was his currency. So what was it? I'm here to clear the table and start fresh. I want to show you we can work together."

Kara finished the pastry and wiped her hand on her pants, leaving a white smudge. She crumpled the bag and shoved it in her pocket.

"You misunderstand," Kara said. "What we had was a mutually beneficial arrangement. I could have cut ties at any time."

Kat stared blankly. That was impossible. Her granddad didn't do business without having leverage.

"You don't believe me." Kara resumed walking, and Kat fell in step beside her. They were only a few blocks from Langley now, her opportunity to convince Kara to shut down the list shrinking by the second.

"Director Lourde, I promise you, I am more valuable to you alive than dead—my whole team is. We just want the opportunity to prove it."

Kara gave her a pensive look. The truth, was she didn't need them. Protocol six probably put a huge strain on her operations— she and Perry had tabled any non-critical missions, Kat blindly guessing what to do.

"Unfortunately, it's all already in motion, Ms. Wayward."

"Kat," Kat interrupted. "I'm not a Wayward."

Kara raised an eyebrow, but continued. "The contracts are in negotiations elsewhere. And unless you have a way to reactivate StormLink, you honestly are no use to me."

"Please," Kat said, "Maureen has probably already reached out and said the Syndicate can handle this, and they could. What I'm asking—"

"You mean Amara," Kara interrupted, raising her eyebrow again.

Kat hesitated, realizing her misstep. Fuck it. If Maureen was playing hardball, so would Kat. "No. I mean Maureen Seward."

It was Kara's turn to pause, the shift in her facial features alerting Kat that she knew the name—and it was not a friendly knowing. "She's dead." The confidence in her statement gave Kat pause—like Kara had double and triple-checked the fact that she was dead.

"Don't I wish it," Kat half mumbled, and then, "I can guarantee she is very much alive and gunning for this. From one brilliant woman to another, don't give it to her."

"And how—how would she know who I am?" Kara asked, and her entire demeanor shifted, from a woman who knew just how much power she wielded to someone who learned for the first time Santa might not actually exist.

"The same way I did." Kat pulled out the folded piece of paper with Kara's name on it and passed it over. Kara licked her lips before opening it. Moisture gathered in her eyes, and she nodded like she knew what she would see when she did.

Kara stopped in front of a black sedan, the rear door opening of its own accord. Her entire body language shifted. She was guarded, and Kat realized that this would be the last face-to-face meeting she would get. "Thank you for this." She held up the paper. "I feel for you, Kat. But you have a target on your back now, and I have powerful people who need results and don't care how I get them. I won't risk it."

"What if I can get StormLink back up?"

Kara gave her a frown, studying her like a misled schoolchild. Kat hated the feeling but didn't move a muscle. "If you get Storm-

Link up and running, we will have a different conversation all together."

"And what about Maureen?"

"If what you say is true—"

"It's true."

"Then in no uncertain terms—she is off limits until I say otherwise."

Kat's mouth dropped open. She was not expecting that after Kara's reaction. "What?"

"I'll need her alive," Kara said. "Reach out to me when you get it back up. Until then, good luck. I look forward to working with you."

13

AERON

"That's war," Aeron said, looking at the pair of twos on the bed as excitement jutted through her body. She was down to four cards and needed a win. She could play poker blindfolded but, apparently, war required no skill and all luck— which she seemed to be out of lately.

"Ready?" Griffin asked. She nodded. "One, two, three, war." Aeron flipped her last card—another two. Griffin flipped over a queen. "I win!" He sat at the end of her bed, legs crossed and long hair pulled up, a dart stuck through it. He looked comfortable in his gray sweatpants and black t-shirt. Aeron grimaced. He had beaten her at almost every single card game they played.

"That cannot be. How many twos are in this deck?"

Griffin chuckled and collected his bounty, shuffling the deck again. "Another round?"

She nodded. She'd gotten used to waking up to people in the room. There always seemed to be someone around to make sure she didn't slip into a coma or trying to force her to eat. Spoiler alert: she wasn't hungry. She normally woke up to Dom or Gunnar in the room. They were quiet, usually working on a tablet, and left her alone. When Katherine had stopped in, her visit had been short on Aeron's end. They'd talked about what to do, who to trust, what plays would be most beneficial with their limited knowledge until Aeron broke the news to her—she was done fighting. Katherine hadn't argued, but had a single request: they put their brother to rest before anything else happened.

When she woke to Griffin at her bedside, it didn't take a genius to figure out some shit had hit the fan. He wouldn't tell her what, but if Katherine had assigned her personal Reaper to Aeron— things couldn't be good. He'd only confirm she and Mason went to retrieve Decius' body, and that they were having a meeting right after. Aeron swallowed hard at the thought of Decius and adjusted her aching body on the bed. The pull of the I.V. in her arm reminded her that she was not getting any better—Aeron would wager she was getting worse. Her brain worked slower, like she was walking through mud to find answers. And her body was tired —so tired.

"But just one more," she said and closed her eyes, leaning back against the headboard, trying to keep her mind busy. "I never thanked you for pulling me out of the building," Aeron said. He paused in his shuffling, and she opened her eyes to find him staring hard at her.

"And I never apologized for trying to kill you in the Playhouse."

She laughed. With all the chaos and death, she'd forgotten he tried to execute her in the bullpen. "We can call it even then. Deal the cards." The cards flew across the bedspread.

"You know he cheats, right?"

Aeron looked up at Ivan in the doorway, and her heart stuttered. She hadn't seen him since her arrival. He held a tray of food in his hands and a guarded look on his face, eyes on Griffin. She glanced at the Reaper and raised an eyebrow. He *had* won almost every hand they played. He quirked his eyebrows. "You can't cheat at war."

"If I find out you've been cheating. . ." She laughed at his wide eyes. She liked him. He was kind, and protective, and quiet. And he didn't ask questions, which she appreciated most of all. How many times can you say you're fine until people believe it? He'd shown up with a deck of cards and a glass of scotch—for him—and a cup of tea for her, and didn't seem upset to be babysitting her instead of protecting Katherine. She glanced at her untouched tea, much like everything else in the room.

"Hungry?" Ivan asked.

"Starving," Griffin answered.

Ivan's eyes narrowed as if deciding how far to push his luck with the deadliest man on the East Coast. "Too bad. This is for Aeron. Yours is in the kitchen."

"Let me guess, in the cupboards, uncooked," Griffin said with a grin.

Ivan grinned back, and it caught Aeron off guard. "There is food on the stove. Owen is watching it."

Aeron's pulse quickened at Owen's name, but Griffin's eyes lit up. "Do you mind if we continue this game later?" he asked.

"Not at all," Aeron said, confused by his enthusiasm. He scooped up the cards and his now-empty glass and headed out of the room.

Ivan took his seat and placed the tray in front of her. "You should eat." He took the cover off and revealed cut cucumbers and watermelon. His eyes stayed averted from her, and her chest tightened. "Even just a few bites, please."

"Did you make this for me?"

He shook his head. "Owen and Eliza are the chefs."

Everything in the room stopped. The kids. She'd spoken to no one about them since she woke up in this room. She'd been too afraid to ask Katherine about them. What if she was hallucinating? What if she wasn't? "Are they really alive?" she whispered.

She saw the moisture gather in his eyes and he nodded. "Luke saved eight of the twelve kids."

"Baby Scarlett?"

"Alive and well downstairs," Ivan said.

A wave of relief washed over her, and then the cold reality hit—she killed Luke. He'd become a monster, and she killed him. But had she killed him because of what he'd done? Or because of what her mother was going to do to him? Her heart skipped several beats and her vision tunneled, her lungs not cooperating with her brain.

"Aeron?" Hands shook her shoulders. Her lungs sucked in a long gasp of air, and Ivan's face came into focus inches from her face.

She took a few gasping breaths. "I'm okay." The lie is automatic at this point. "I'm okay." But his concerned gaze didn't waver.

"Please, eat something," he said again. "You're not even able to stand."

He was right. Of course, he was right. "Okay." He sat back and held out the plate for her again. And even with all the turmoil inside, her mouth watered at the sight of the watermelon. She picked up a piece. It was off season, and the fruit did not have any of its sweet juiciness of the summer, but her stomach rumbled, and she took several more bites. "Happy?"

He nodded. "Feel better?"

She did. "Yes. What time will Katherine be back?"

"A few hours."

The room fell silent as she ate, and not the same comfortable silence she and Griffin had shared. Ivan watched her take each bite, his lips pressed together, his hands folded in his lap. She could see the words swirling behind his eyes, and the active decision in his frown to shut them down.

Aeron couldn't take it a second longer. He'd been like this since she showed up, like he wasn't sure he was happy she was alive or not. The thought hurt more than the physical damage she'd endured. Feelings usually did, though. "I'm sorry about Shaun," she said. She'd had a lot of time to think the last few days about her choices, and all the things she wished she could undo. But thinking about them would never, ever, change the damage she'd caused. So she would start where she could.

"You haven't spoken to me in days, and that's what you're leading with?"

His words were not what she was expecting, and anger fizzled in her. "I haven't spoken to you in days? You've been avoiding this room like the plague. You won't even make eye contact with me," she whispered, forcing her eyes to stare at him until he looked up. It only took a moment for him to raise his head, and she continued. "I'm sorry for the pain I caused. I should have said that to you as soon as I learned you were close. If I could go back, I would have told Luke no."

He didn't answer right away, and her heart skipped several beats. It was the only thing she could think of that was different between them now—the knowledge she killed Shaun. She wanted him to look at her the way he had before she'd died—like she mattered. "Thank you," he finally said, looking away again. "That means a lot."

A weight lifted off her chest, but it wasn't enough. There was still a barrier between them, something tangible she couldn't grasp onto. She swallowed hard, the pressure in her chest threatening to choke her until they cleared the air. "Ivan, did I do something?"

He snapped his head up. "Wha-what? No." He shook his head.

"What's going on then? Because I feel so disconnected," she admitted. "And alone." The words brought a lump to her throat, and she looked down at the empty plate. She was alone because she'd killed the most important people to her, and was betrayed by the rest—except for Ivan.

"Aeron." He heaved a sigh and moved the plate to the nightstand, sitting in the chair beside the bed. "I don't know how to help you."

"Help me what?" she asked.

"Just—help you."

She nodded, emotion threatening to silence her. She had spent the last several days in a funk. Angry. Broken. Depressed. But she couldn't stay there—she wasn't built to stay there. She needed to say goodbye to the ones she'd lost, and then she needed to go far, far away. Away from this life, away from Ivan, before he ended up dead, too. Because that was what she brought to those around her —a death sentence.

"I'll be okay," she said. "I want to shower and maybe eat a little more before the funeral."

"Are you ready for this?" he asked.

Aeron grabbed her glass of water and took a long sip. She wasn't ready. Was anyone ever ready to bury their brother? But they needed to put him to rest—she needed to say goodbye.

"I could prepare for a thousand years, and never be ready for this," she answered.

"I don't think that is what Kara had in mind," Mason said, his voice low and seething. Aeron paused in the hallway outside her room, hair dripping down her back.

"She practically begged me to keep her alive," Katherine said back, just as low. "What do you want me to do?"

"Not invite her here. Aeron will be—"

"I'll be what?" Aeron asked, stepping into the room. It had been cleaned, the bed was made, and some clothes were laid out for her. Katherine was rummaging through the closet, Mason sitting in the armchair by the bed, leaning forward, elbows braced on his knees. They both looked up when she entered.

"You don't look like death's bride anymore," Katherine said. "How do you feel?"

"Like I left him at the altar and he sent his hellhounds after me," she said back. Katherine nodded with a small chuckle. Aeron closed the door behind her. "I'll be what?" she asked again, looking at Mason, anger coiling in her gut. He had lied to her. It was the only thought that existed in her mind when she looked at him.

Mason didn't look at her, though. He kept his eyes on the ground when he answered. "That you'll be pissed to learn Katherine wants to invite Maureen to the funeral."

Aeron snapped her gaze to Katherine. "No. Absolutely not."

"Tactically speaking—"

The coil snapped, and Aeron rounded on Katherine.

"Fuck the tactics. That is my brother."

"Listen to me," Katherine said. "I spoke with Kara. When she learned that Maureen was alive, she requested I keep her that way. I need a way to gain her trust. What better way than an olive branch?"

"Any other way," Aeron said.

"Aeron—"

"Get out, Mason," Aeron said, cutting him off. "I don't want to see you. I don't want to hear you. I don't want to know you." The words hurt as they came out, but they landed the blow she'd hoped. His brow furrowed, and he nodded, leaving the room.

"I get you're pissed," Katherine said once he was gone.

"You don't get anything," Aeron said, her anger fading as quickly as it came, exhaustion wrapping its tendrils around her legs, pulling her to sit down on the bed. Maybe she should have been eating more. "I destroyed everything I ever loved for a lie. I'm not ready."

Katherine sighed. She pulled down a black hoodie from the top of the closet and pulled it on. Then she tugged off her sweatpants and replaced them with a pair of jeans before looking back at Aeron.

"Please don't bring her here," Aeron begged.

Katherine held her gaze for several seconds, then pressed her lips together and nodded. "It's probably better we don't, with Betty on the property and the kids. It was just a thought."

"It was a dumb one," Aeron said.

Katherine cracked a smile. "I don't have those often. Keep it to yourself. Do you need help getting ready?"

Aeron looked at the clothes, realizing they were exactly what Katherine was wearing. "I think I'll be alright. Come here."

Katherine approached with caution, and Aeron reached out and grabbed one end of the string hanging from the hood and pulled it free.

"You know," Aeron said, tossing the string aside. "Just in case."

The air was frigid, and the ground frozen solid. Aeron's breath rose in front of her, the heavy winter jacket bundled around her. It was too cold to bury him, plus where would they anyway? The entire Seward Legacy was buried back in Connecticut, on a property that no longer belonged to her. No. Mason had suggested they do a warrior burning.

And after telling him to fuck off in as many languages as she could think of, she agreed. But burning a body wasn't as easy as it looked on screen. They needed high temperatures and a lot of time, as it takes hours to burn human remains. He'd enlisted Star to help prepare and watch over the operation.

The pyre sat in the middle of the expansive backyard, Decius' body wrapped in a white sheet laid on top. The image stopped her in her tracks. He was gone. Her chest ached, and she couldn't take another step. Her everything was laid out beneath that sheet. Did he look the same? Was it even him? She took a few tentative steps forward, pausing again. Did she want to see him?

A light touch on her elbow startled her. She spun, a cry of pain leaving her as she tried to move her injured arm. Mason wrapped his arm around her, and she leaned into him.

"I'm sorry," he said, concern furrowing his brow. "Is it okay?"

She took a few breaths and nodded. "Yeah." She looked back at the pyre. "Can I see him?"

"Aeron—"

"I need to know it's him. I need to. . ." She needed to see his peaceful face, the one like Luke's. The last vision of her brother, bloody on the operating table, was not what she wanted to remember. "Did they fix him?"

Mason nodded. "Come on."

They approached the table, each step closer, Aeron second guessing if this was what she wanted to do. They were suddenly right by his side, Star clearing away to give them some privacy. Mason reached for the sheet, and Aeron grabbed onto his wrist before he could raise it, the cold nipping at her fingers. "Wait."

Moisture pricked at her eyes, and she didn't even try to stop the tears. That had been a losing battle the last few days, and she let them flow down her face. She took the fabric from him and lifted it. Decius' face stared back at her, scars and all. She swallowed the sob of disappointment. A small part of her had hoped Mason had been lying to her mother. That he had saved him because how could Decius have left her alone? How could he have left her? She lowered the sheet back down and met Mason's tear-filled gaze. "I tried to save him," he said.

Aeron just nodded, not trusting herself to speak. Footsteps on snow announced the arrival of more people. Aeron looked back up to see Katherine, Griffin, Ivan, and Betty approaching.

Everyone was there. It was time. "Did you want to say anything?" Mason asked her. What could she possibly say? None of these people knew him. None of these people loved him the way she had. No one here would appreciate her grief for him—except for Mason. As mad as she was at him for lying, they were in this moment together, and Decius would want her to give him some grace.

"I don't know what to say," she admitted.

"You say whatever you feel needs to be heard."

"By who?"

"By anybody."

Aeron nodded, and the others joined them around the pyre. She took a few deep breaths, her eyes focused on the white sheet. There was so much to say, and nothing all at once. How was that even possible? But if she didn't say anything, no one would know how amazing he was; how dedicated, impossibly hard-headed, and funny. He was funny.

"When we were little," she said to Decius, "you and I would talk about the future as if it was infinite. We would imagine the people we would save, the trips we would take, the way we would change the world. What we would do if we didn't live this life. I wanted to be an astronaut. You wanted to work for the FBI but said you would work part time as an astronaut, so I didn't have to go to space alone. You never wanted me to be alone." The tears burned her eyes, and it took a few deep breaths before she could continue. "We knew it was a fool's dream. We knew we would die younger than most—we would go out violent and swinging." She took a shaky breath. "But it didn't matter because you were with me. I thought we would go out together."

She blinked the tears free and looked up at Katherine. "Decius was a protector. Once you had his loyalty, he would go to the ends of the universe to protect you. It didn't matter how you fucked up. He loved with every ounce of goodness he could hold on to in this life. And he was fun. He played as hard as he worked, and almost as hard as he loved." Her eyes scanned over the others, and she turned to Mason. "He wouldn't have been those things without you," Aeron said. "None of us would have been what we were without you. You taught us to keep our humanity and hearts front and center. And right now, I hate you for it." She half sobbed and half laughed. "But without you, we would have been terrible humans."

Aeron wiped her face. This was impossible. Her boxes might never close inside her again.

"I, uh. I have something for you." Ivan said. Aeron looked up at him, the unease in his eyes. "I thought you might want this, all of you."

Ivan pulled an envelope out of his jacket pocket and held it out to her. Her fingers shook in the freezing cold, and she couldn't open it. She held it out to Mason for help.

"What is it?" he asked.

"Pictures," Ivan whispered.

Aeron's throat was too tight to speak as he pulled out a photograph. A picture of Lesley, taken from her file. She took it from him, her hand shaking, and not from the cold. She had been so bright and young—she had so much life to give. Her only crime was being on their team—collateral damage. "I'm sorry," she said to the photo and laid it on Decius' chest.

"There should be another one," Ivan whispered.

Mason reached into the envelope again and pulled out the other photograph. She swallowed hard when she caught the tremble of his chin as his eyes scanned the image. He held it out, and a cry broke free from her. It was a group shot they'd taken at Club Sapphire last year. Each of them with a smile that broke Aeron's heart to look at. Justin, Keara, and Perry sat on the back of the couch, drinks in hand. Keara wore an obnoxious, sparkly dress, and Perry and Justin wore tuxes. She, Shannon, Decius, and

Luke sat at their feet in similar outfits. None of them actually looked at the camera, and the laughter was almost audible in her ears. They had been celebrating Shannon's birthday. Her fingers shook as she took it from him. It was one of the few pictures they'd ever taken as a group.

"I found it in Luke's apartment," Ivan said. "I know you don't have bodies, but I, uh. . ."

"Ivan this is. . . Thank you," Aeron said and passed the picture to Betty. "Perry was family," Aeron said. "And we don't have a body, but he deserves to be sent off with all the honor of any Legacy heir."

Betty covered her mouth. "He looks so happy."

She passed the picture to Katherine, and Aeron met her eyes as they snapped to her.

"You forgot Luke," Katherine said. It felt like a knife in Aeron's heart. Forget Luke? She could never. But she didn't deserve to speak of him—to think of him. "He may have lost his way," Katherine continued, "but Luke deserves to be sent off as a warrior, too."

"To Luke," Mason said. He picked up a long stick that had been soaking in oil, stuck it inside the small fire pit, and it caught instantly.

Katherine stepped forward and grabbed a stick, copying Mason. "To Perry."

Ivan followed suit. "To Ernie."

Aeron choked on a sob. Ernie—the first man to show her what family should really mean. To show her compassion, unconditional love. As if at the thought, she could smell the garage, a wave of emotion threatening to drown her. She hadn't deserved his sacrifice.

Betty picked up a stick. "Decius."

Griffin held out the final stick to her, a sadness in his eyes she could relate to—as if he'd lost the world and come out on the other side. The wood was rough in her cold hand, the fire a warm welcome as she lit it. "To Lesley, to Justin. To all of us," she said. They were all dead men walking, anyway. She looked at Katherine, her eyes still on the photo, tears rolling down her face. Katherine swallowed hard and looked at Aeron. She nodded but didn't put the picture down.

Aeron couldn't wait another second. She laid the flaming stick on the wood lined along the base of the pyre, everyone following suit. It didn't take long; the accelerant feeding the flame along the table. Mason grabbed her by the waist and pulled her back a few steps.

The fire danced in her vision, and she couldn't pull her eyes away if she wanted. She'd tried so hard to protect them, but in the end, it didn't matter. Now, she watched her future, her past, her entire reason for living go up in flames.

14

KAT

$\mathcal{K}$at stared at the picture in her hand, her gaze finding Perry. He looked younger. His tux jacket was open as if they'd been dancing, and she could see the sweat on his brow. And while he laughed, his eyes were on Shannon, in all her beautiful glory. Her hair was wild and curly around her head. She and Aeron were leaning on each other for support as they laughed. She hadn't understood before why he was so drawn to the bottle after she died—this picture captured every ounce of his love, and her heart beat painfully.

They never talked about his Legacy life. He wanted to keep that team as disconnected from Legacy Inc as possible. She could see why—he truly lived two completely different lives. She looked to Luke, his arm around Decius, and the two of them leaned into each other, Decius grabbing his side in laughter. This is what she'd stolen from him—what she failed to grasp—what he killed to protect. His life was full. It was perfect. Happy.

She finally focused on Decius. His smile was the same as the night in the Playhouse. The moisture that stung in her eyes escaped her control and rolled down her cheeks. She swiped at them angrily before placing the picture on top of her brother; the flames licked at her wrist as she placed her torch in. He had been stolen from her—her life swapped without her consent. Fire burned in her veins with the only thing that ever truly made her feel alive—vengeance. Aeron was right not to let her invite their mother. She may have never made it off the property alive.

They watched the fire consume for nearly twenty minutes as the smoke rose high into the air. Slowly, the group dispersed. Griffin placed a kiss against her head.

"I'm going to check on the kids. Will you be alright?"

She gave him a half smile. "You really like those kids."

"And you really don't." There was no venom in his words, just curiosity.

"I don't *not* like them," she said with a small laugh. But she hadn't given them a chance. She had saved them, and she would make sure they were set up for life. But that was all she could afford to give to them. "I love seeing you so playful with them. Go." She gave him a push. "We'll meet in about an hour in the kitchen." She watched him jog off, his gait looking better than it had a few days ago.

Betty came up beside her. "When are you going to tell him you're sending the kids away?"

Kat looked up at her aunt. She didn't think anyone gave the woman the credit she deserved. She was stronger than any of them, living in this hell for as long as she did. "I will," she said. "But he deserves a bit of happiness right now."

"I think you are all the happiness that man needs. Would you like me to stay here while you have your meeting?"

Kat turned to face her, spotting Aeron and Ivan heading inside. "No. I need you there. And then I need you to pack. You're going with the kids when they leave tomorrow."

"Excuse me?" Betty raised an eyebrow.

"I need you to escort them to the islands. And I'd like you somewhere safe."

Betty scoffed.

"Please, Aunt Betty. I can't—" She couldn't lose another person. "I'm about to take Maureen head-on. If she finds you, I think the hit list payment would just be a happy bonus. And I promised Perry I would protect you."

"I don't need protection," Betty said.

"Oh, you don't need to tell me that. I saw you chop up his body. But this isn't your fight anymore. This is mine. And I need to know the kids are protected, and I can't afford to send a reaper. If you want back in, after I kill my mother—again—you will have a place at my table."

Betty was quiet for a moment and then nodded. "For those kids, I will sit in the fires of hell." She turned and headed back toward the pyre. Kat watched her and Mason exchange words, and then Mason and Star headed her way.

"An hour?" Star asked as they approached. Kat could see the chattering of her teeth.

"Yes. We'll meet in the kitchen," Kat said. "There is hot cocoa in there now. You'll have to fight with Griffin and the kids for it, though."

The idea seemed to excite her, and she hurried ahead of them. She and Mason fell into step, retreating to the warmth of the house.

"Can I ask you a question?" Kat asked.

"Shoot," Mason said.

"Who was the other woman in that photo?"

"That is Keara Gale," Mason said, confirming Kat's suspicions.

"That would be Shannon's older sister and Eileen's oldest daughter."

Mason nodded.

"You said 'is'," Kat said. "She's alive?"

"Yes."

"Do you know where she is?"

He nodded again, his jaw clenching in a way that Kat now knew meant he would not say anything else.

"Is she a threat?"

"No more of a threat than Eileen."

They reached the house, but Kat wasn't ready to go inside yet —there were too many people. She headed for the basement entrance instead. "You say that as if I don't see her as a threat."

"You shouldn't." He pulled the door and held it open. She stepped past him, sliding her shoes off just inside the house, her toes tingling from the change of temperature.

Kat dropped the topic and took a seat on the couch, pulling out the file on Mason she still hadn't read. She tapped it on her knuckle, her stomach flipping in anticipation. She hadn't read it because she wanted to hear from him first. Wanted to give him an opportunity to confirm or deny anything she found in the file without her hackles being raised. Luke had blindly believed the information in the documents their granddad handed over, and look where that landed them. Who's to say he didn't fabricate everything in that vault? The thought filled her with dread.

"Coffee?"

She looked up. Mason had rounded the bar and pulled out the coffee maker.

"Yeah. I'll take a cup." She adjusted herself on the couch, leaning over the back, chin resting on her arm. "Who was Storm?"

The bottle Mason had been using to fill the coffee maker dropped to the bar top, water flooding the surface. "Shit," he said under his breath. He grabbed a bar towel, righted the bottle, and cleaned up his mess.

Kat waited as he finished filling the coffee machine and turned it on. He pulled down two mugs and placed his hands on the bar beside them, eyes downcast. She pushed herself off the couch and rounded it to the bar. She tossed the folded file onto the surface between them, the mission code MM16-GHOST-613 stamped in the corner. He looked up. "Have you read it?" She shook her head. "Why not?"

"After seeing what he did to Luke, I don't know how much I trust anything that man wrote down. I wanted to hear it from you before I dove in."

Mason released a huff of laughter and nodded. He poured them both a cup of coffee and slid one toward her. "Creamer?"

"In the mini-fridge."

He passed it to her and let out a long breath as she sugared up her drink. "She was the genius behind StormLink."

"I know that. Who was she to you?" Kat clarified, her patience waning.

Mason interlocked his fingers around his mug, quiet for a few moments, his brow crinkling. Finally, he looked up. "Storm was. . .she was everything. A rebel, wicked smart, sassy, loud, a risk taker." He ran his tongue across his lips. "A lover and a royal pain in my ass." A sad smile slipped across his face before he could school it, and Kat's chest constricted.

"Although I could guess," Kat said, "what happened to her?"

"I don't know." Mason dropped his guard, pain and confusion sitting in his eyes. Kat swallowed hard as he continued. "One day she was just gone."

"Like dead. . .or. . ."

"I don't know," he repeated, and Kat caught the emotion she'd heard in the office. "I never found a body. And no one took credit for killing her—and let me tell you, I smashed heads looking for answers."

"Who would have wanted her dead?"

"Everyone. She was a pioneer in her time. What she created, everyone wanted a piece. Her list of enemies was longer than your grandfather's."

"But she built the program for Legacy Inc. I would imagine that afforded her protection."

"Well, technically, she built the program for the Alliance. But Storm and Maureen did not see eye to eye. I don't know what the tipping point was, but she sold the program to the CIA with the endorsement of Legacy Inc instead of the Alliance."

"She stole Maureen's chance to take down my granddad," Kat realized. Mason nodded. "If she went behind Maureen's back, then she went behind yours, too."

"Like I said: royal pain in the ass."

"But you loved her," Kat said.

"With everything I had," Mason admitted. "There had come a time I risked everything to find her, my allegiance to the Alliance, and my oath to the Sewards and Waywards that I would protect their children. I was hours from elimination, chasing a ghost." He pointed at the folded piece of paper. "That was the mission where I had to finally let her go. If she was dead, no one was taking credit, and if they did, what then? If she had left on her own, she didn't want to be found."

"And if she was held against her will?" Kat asked.

He was silent for a moment. "I had to choose between failing her and failing you kids. If I had found her alive and anything happened to any of you, she would have skinned me alive."

"You chose us over Storm?"

"I chased her ghost for as long as I could. When it came down to it, yes. I chose what I knew I could save. What she would have wanted me to save."

Kat stared in surprise. How could this man have chosen to protect her? He didn't even know her. How long had he been protecting her?

"Is that why you agreed to help me?"

"There are a lot of reasons I agreed to help you. The first being you are a brilliant, driven woman with a fierce heart."

The sudden swell of an emotion she couldn't identify caught

her off guard and it took a moment for her to realize what it was: gratitude. "Thank you."

He gave a small nod. "I don't know what's in that report and I don't remember much from that time. I was high on grief for most of the year. But if that is what I think it is, I had reached out to a member of the Syndicate, who was doubling in Onyx at the time, to see if they had any information on Storm. The kids' first Guardian, Sarah, followed and reported me to Senior for selling information.

"It got—messy. I'd been working alongside her for years to keep an eye on the kids. She'd suspected I was not completely loyal to the Legacy and managed to gather some evidence. She wasn't wrong—she just wasn't right, either. With the help of the Alliance, I framed her for the treason and made sure she didn't make it out to save my own ass. It's not my proudest moment, but had I not done that, I would have never been able to step in as their Guardian."

"You what?"

Kat snapped her head to the stairwell. Aeron stood at the bottom of the stairs, her mouth agape. Damn it, that girl moved like a shadow.

"Aeron—" Mason said, straightening up.

"Fuck you, Mason." Aeron turned on her heel and left.

Mason dropped his head into his hands. "I should have never taught her to be so fucking stealthy."

Kat looked back toward the stairs. She should go check on her, but honestly, there were too many other things that needed her attention. "What just happened?"

"She just learned I'm the reason her first Guardian was killed," he murmured.

"That sucks," Kat said, remembering witnessing the death of Jackson, hers and Perry's Guardian in DC. But it hadn't slowed her down—it fueled her. "She needs to grow up," Kat said. "This is the life. Lies, compromises, guilt."

Mason picked his head back up. "She's just a kid, Kat. A kid who lost everything. Give her a break."

"She's an assassin. We don't get to be kids."

"Isn't that what you're trying to change?"

His words halted her thoughts. It was exactly what she was trying to change. "Fuck. Should I go check on her?"

"No. Give her some space. She needs to grieve in her own time. Grab that box over there, near the wall."

Kat turned around to find a file box tucked between the wall and the armchair by the couch. She brought it over to the bar. "What is it?"

"Some of the photos Aeron and I took, and any notes I thought would be useful." He pulled out the files, already organized. She recognized Griffin's scrawl on the sticky notes, along with Ivan's chicken scratch.

"I didn't know you were working on this," she said, but there was no accusation in her words. It was on her list of things to get done, but not high enough to be a plan. The fact he had done it brought on that feeling again. . .but it was more than gratitude, it was trust, loyalty.

"Well, you can't be the next Senior Assassin until we can get Legacy Inc back online. I figured this was the closest thing until we get the vault here in a few days."

"I don't want to be the next Senior Assassin," Kat said suddenly. She wanted to bury Maureen and make her regret throwing her to the wolves. Wanted to steal every piece of her empire and destroy it. She wanted to prove that everyone who bet against her was wrong. "I want to be the first Kat—" Kat what? She wasn't a Wayward, and she wasn't a Seward. She looked up at Mason. If she asked, Kat believed in this moment he would tell her who her father was. But it didn't matter. She was just Kat. She shook the thought from her mind. "Legacy Inc is dead. And it should stay dead. I want to build something better. Be someone better."

Mason opened his mouth to say something, thought better of it, and closed his mouth.

"What?" she asked.

"Nothing. Pass the coffee."

They fell into silence as they categorized the most important tasks to be tackled, what assets remained available, and their growing list of enemies, more rolling in as the hours ticked by. They created three piles: Assets, Problems, and Compromises. She stared at the problem pile, bigger than all the rest. She couldn't do what she'd always done—worry about what she could handle immediately—because everything was urgent.

"Alright," Mason said, sliding over a spreadsheet he'd filled out by hand. "First column was the total number of assets within Legacy Inc, including overseas divisions: 157."

"I didn't know we had that many overseas."

"Well, technically speaking, the two teams in South America are Syndicate assets. So that drops it to 129."

Kat flicked her eyes at him. "You flipped an entire division?"

Mason nodded. "Recruited would be a better choice of words. But it cost me more than it was worth." He didn't elaborate, just continued with the spreadsheet. "Spain had 28—no idea how many Carl took for his failed op—but I cannot reach anyone there so we will need eyes on the ground. Ireland and Japan each sit at 14. Both are awaiting payments, to continue their work."

Kat scanned the document. There were 6 reapers left after Star and Griffin had culled them down, and Mason had even included Dom, Gunnar, and Ivan.

"How much money are we talking right now to get them back in the game?"

"Ireland is owed two million and Japan three million."

"What about Division Three and the reapers?"

"Total? You're looking at about ten million." Mason said. "But that is because he was killed right before payday. It was bad luck."

She let out a whistle. There were too many moving pieces at the moment, and as enticing as it would be to call Ireland and Japan home, knowing she had ready backup was comforting. "Do they know of the change in command?" Kat asked.

"They know something is up because StormLink is down, and they haven't gotten paid."

"Okay." There wasn't much she could do about the international divisions at the moment. Pay them or kill them. "Are they the same scum that the divisions here were made of?"

"Does it matter?"

"Yes," she said. "Perry and I. . .we were going to find a balance between Legacy and Legacy Inc. Find that sweet spot of business and duty." Mason gave a small laugh. "What?"

"Maureen wanted the same thing. But somewhere along the line, she lost sight of that goal."

Her spine prickled at being compared to Maureen. "What happened?" Kat asked.

"I wish I knew."

"What was she like?" Kat asked before she realized the words had slipped out of her mouth. "Before. You don't seem like the type to follow someone like the Maureen we met."

"I'll need a stronger drink for that conversation," he said.

Kat rounded the bar and pulled down the first bottle of Jack that her fingers touched and handed it to him. "The meeting can wait for us."

15

AERON

Fuck Mason. Fuck Kat. Fuck all of them.

Aeron slammed her door closed, anger swirling in her chest. She wanted to scream and hit something. Wanted to demand Mason explain himself. She wanted someone to come and fix this fucking mess she created. She wanted her brother and Shannon and Luke.

A small sob broke free, and she shook her head. Did she really just hear what she thought she did? A knock on the door interrupted her spiral, and she ignored it. Had Mason sacrificed their first guardian? Had her mother and father helped him? Why? Sarah had been there for Aeron, a woman in this man-infested world who showed her how to hold her own when she had no one else because her mother—her mother had abandoned her. She wanted answers. Needed them. But how could she trust Mason to give them to her?

Another knock. "Go away!" she said hoarsely. She needed to get out of this house, away from all of these people.

The door opened instead, and Ivan's head peeked in. "What happened?"

"Nothing." She sat down on the bed. Leaving would be impossible. Ivan's security setup was one of the most secure she'd ever seen. Unless she knew the cameras—could change the cameras. "I need a distraction."

"I can do that." He closed the door behind him and dropped into the chair near the bed. "We've got cards. And I can probably dig up some board games."

"How about drinks and you bore me with tech talk until I pass out?" She quirked an eyebrow at him.

"We have the meeting in an hour."

"Have you met anyone on this team? Alcohol is the coping mechanism that gets shit done." He opened and closed his mouth a few times, the scars on his face dancing. "I just buried my brother," she said. The painful thump of her heart wasn't as strong. She'd buried her team and the box in her heart along with it.

"Okay. Okay," he put his hands up. "I'll go grab us a bottle."

It only took him a few minutes to return, his cheeks red, and he pulled out a bottle from under his shirt. A smile spread across her face. Griffin was going to kill them, but it would be worth it.

"Where did you get that?" she asked.

"I didn't want to chance being seen, so I snuck into the master bedroom and swiped it from the nightstand. Is this any good?"

"Oh, I would bet a few hundred it is divine." She opened the bottle, savoring the sweet aroma. Griffin had excellent taste. She raised the bottle to him. "To freedom," she said and took a sip. It tasted exquisite, exactly what she would expect a $25,000 bottle of whiskey to taste like. It went down like honey, and she closed her eyes, savoring the taste, the pull to take another shot tugging at her mind. She held the bottle out to him instead.

He took it tentatively. "I don't know about this."

"Don't be a saggy sack of balls," she said, doing her best to channel Shannon, a small sliver of guilt wedging into her heart.

She could trust Ivan—but if Kat found out he'd helped her skip off the property, she'd be furious. If Aeron tricked him, she took the gamble Kat would be way more forgiving. "Drink."

He put the bottle to his lips and tipped it back. His eyes scrunched closed, and he coughed. He passed the bottle back and pressed his fist against his mouth. "Swallow," Aeron said.

His eyes watered as he did, and he opened his mouth, tongue hanging out. "That was. . ."

"Your first taste of real alcohol?" She laughed. Genuine joy coasted through her, and she rode the wave. "You'll get used to it." She took another sip, the burn going down smoothly. "What geek stuff have you been up to?" She moved over, making space for him. They sat shoulder to shoulder, and he pulled the tablet out. What she wanted to see was the security system, but he protected that information like a vault.

"A lot. I'm working through rebuilding StormLink." He pulled open a window filled with lines of code she didn't understand.

"Can you work on it now?"

"No. This just has the running mirror of the main computer. I keep it with me for security alerts and any updates."

"So, who is manning the computer?" She took a stage sip this time. To get off the property, she needed to have a clear head, and to get where she was going, she needed to be sober to drive.

"Gunnar. He's watching the cameras and working on tracking down Shay. I can't do much with StormLink at the moment, so all focus has shifted to tracking him down."

"Who's Shay?"

Ivan looked uncomfortable.

"Who is Shay?" she repeated.

"All I know is he's an asset that is super important to Kat, and he's been taken. He's priority number two, next to shutting down the list."

The list. She had almost forgotten about it. "How is that going?"

"Not much traction." He pulled up the hit list.

"May I?" He handed her the tablet. She took another stage shot from the bottle and passed it over. "Don't let me drink alone," she said.

He took another sip, his reaction not as bad. She raised an eyebrow, and he took another. Perfect. She scrolled down the list of names. The alcohol gave her a padding between her emotions and logic, and she looked at the information with a more critical eye. Her finger hovered over her name, a large 'unconfirmed' beside it. Was she really going to find anything in here to help her?

"You know, by the third shot, it's not so bad," Ivan said. Aeron glanced over at him, and he took another swig. "I'm really glad you're not dead."

Her pulse thumped hard in her neck. "Me too. Where are the security cameras?"

He looked up, eyes becoming red. "Swipe up. The eye icon. There." He motioned with his hand, and she followed his directions. The carousel of security footage popped up. She spotted the kids in the kitchen; Griffin in the living room with Owen; the pyre burning in the backyard, Betty standing watch. Beside her, Ivan took another, longer sip, and Aeron took the bottle from him. She still needed answers.

"What's the coverage?" she asked, the footage moving at its own pace. She tried to move it, but it was simply a projection of whatever Gunnar watched downstairs. "How do I get this to respond to me?"

"When I thought you were dead," he said, leaning into her. "My entire world collapsed."

Her finger froze over the screen. She hadn't thought about how other people would feel about her death—she had just accepted the fact she wasn't dead herself. "I'm sorry," she said. "How do I get this screen to respond to me?"

"You can't," he slurred.

"Awesome," she whispered to herself. "How far does the signal reach on this?"

He sat up and looked at her. "Why?" His eyes were glassy now, and she took half a real sip and passed the bottle back to him. "Like if we were to take a walk, how far would the tablet respond?"

"I don't think I can take a walk," he slurred. "I have a meeting. And this room is spinning."

Good. She watched the cameras flip through a few more cycles, only recognizing a handful of the rooms. If she was going to get off the property, it was going to take some luck. But if everyone was at the meeting, then she had a shot to get to the cars. "When do the alerts go off?"

Ivan leaned back against the headboard. "Movement in the front. Or on the perimeter."

She could work with that. "Thanks, Ivan."

He sat up straighter, his body wobbling side to side. Aeron climbed over him off the bed and headed for the closet. She needed footwear if she planned to make a run for it, and her sneakers were by the basement door.

"Wha— are you lookin— for?" he slurred.

"Shoes."

"I can't do the walking thing."

"That's okay, I can walk alone." She looked over, and Ivan was laid out on the bed now. He was going to be sick and have a massive hangover. The sliver of guilt grew. He had been nothing but kind to her. She found a pair of slightly too-big sneakers in the closet and pulled them on before returning to the bed. His eyes stared at the ceiling, blinking slowly.

"It's spinning. Like a tilt-a-whirl. Is the ceiling suppose' to be spinning?"

She gave a small laugh, and he looked at her instead. "You're beautiful." His words twisted something inside Aeron, and her mouth suddenly went dry. "I never got to tell you when you were alive before."

"That I'm beautiful?" she asked. The words warmed her in a way she hadn't expected.

"That I love you."

The world went silent around her, a soft ringing in her ears starting. "What—what did you say?"

He pushed himself up, hands reaching out to grab onto her waist and she let him, stepping closer. "I love you."

No. Tears stung her eyes, and she held them back. How could he love her? How could he even know her? She killed Shaun. She killed Luke. No one in their right mind could love her. Should love her. She was damaged beyond repair. "Why?" The word fell out before she could stop it.

"You're smart and funny. You scare the living daylights out of me." He brought a hand up to cup her face. "You gave me something to look forward to every day."

The tears spilled down her cheeks, and she brought her hand up to cover his, turning her face and kissing his palm.

"Come with me," she said, sniffling back in her emotions.

"I'll go wherever you want," he said, "as soon as I can stand."

She gave a half smile. He couldn't go with her. He had to shut down the hit list, needed to bring StormLink back online. Kat needed him more than she needed Aeron. She grabbed the bottle, took one last stage sip, and handed it back to him. "One more for the road," she said.

He shook his head and laid back, eyes falling closed. She watched him for a few minutes until his chest rose and fell steadily. Aeron placed the bottle on the nightstand, sending a silent apology to Griffin, and turned back to Ivan. He slept peacefully—for now. With a finger, she traced the scars along his face.

She needed to leave him because anyone who loved her wound up dead. She placed a kiss on his forehead. "See you later, Darth." She covered him with a blanket to make sure he was harder to find, slid the tablet into her hoodie pocket, and headed toward the front of the house.

16

KAT

*K*at scanned the group of people sitting around the kitchen table. This was it. The people she trusted to help her build an empire—the people she counted on to help her kill Maureen—all except Ivan and Aeron. Mason, Griffin, Dom, Gunnar, Star, and Betty sat in silence as she checked the clock hanging on the wall for the third time. She didn't expect Aeron to show, but Ivan had yet to let her down.

"Has anyone seen him?" she asked.

"Last time I saw him, he was leaving the memorial with Aeron," Star said.

Kat shook her head. "We saw her after that, and she was alone." She exchanged a worried glance with Mason. Maybe she should have gone after her.

"Maybe they're fucking?" Griffin suggested. Kat sent him a dubious look. "What? That boy needs to get laid."

Mason scrunched his face up in disgust. "Please stop. They are like my children."

Kat fought the smirk itching to cross her face. Ivan getting laid wouldn't be the worst thing to happen to that boy.

"Maybe he just lost track of time," Gunnar suggested.

"Or maybe he finally fell asleep," Griffin offered.

Kat nodded. That wouldn't be a bad thing either. "Let's keep moving. I'll update him after. Star, once the pyre is out, I need a status report of what is happening at our overseas locations. Mason has already reached out, but StormLink was our primary source of contact. Until Ivan has his program up and running, everything must be done the old-fashioned way—face-to-face. If they aren't loyal, dispose of them. And this isn't an ultimatum, 'be loyal or die'. This is 'you are loyal or you're dead'. Got it?"

Star smirked. "Yes ma'am. Do we still have access to the jets?"

"Yes. And Ivan—once I find him—will keep you updated with locations and communications as he gets them. Aunt Betty—"

"Betty is fine, dear."

"Betty," Kat corrected, "I need you to patch up who you can, and then prep the kids."

"Where are they going?" Griffin asked, and Kat caught the slight disappointment in his voice. She hadn't had the opportunity—or maybe it was the courage—to tell him ahead of time.

"Home, with Gunnar."

"What!" Dom said, standing up. "No."

Gunnar grabbed his cousin's arm and pulled him back down. "We've already talked about it. I can run point from the compound back home, same as I've always done. You're needed here to help Ivan."

Dom looked between his cousin and Kat, as if weighing his words before answering. "How can you be sure they'll be safe there? With Shay missing—"

"I'm sending Betty," Kat said, "and moving the Caribbean division to run point at the compound. Whoever took Shay already got what they wanted and left the family alone—sleeping in bed. I don't expect they will be back." Dom nodded, but Kat's gut gave a nasty twist—what if there was something she was missing? She swallowed and pushed the feeling aside.

"That's it. Gunnar and Dom, take a break and help Betty with the kids. Mason, Griffin, let's go find our sleeping beauty."

The house, although big, didn't have a ton of rooms to search. There was the Master Bedroom, the two kids' rooms, Kat's room—where Aeron was currently held up, and then the other guest room they'd stuck a few twin mattresses in to make sure everyone had somewhere to sleep. She headed for Aeron's room. The door was closed, and she hesitated before barging in. What if Aeron and Ivan were. . .no. Aeron was too torn up, emotionally and physically, to be doing anything. She pushed the door wide, Mason and Griffin on her heels.

At first, the room looked empty, and then she saw Ivan's hair poking up from beneath the covers. She ripped the blanket off, the smell of alcohol overwhelming. "You've got to be. . ." She scanned the room again. No Aeron. She searched the immediate area for Ivan's tablet. Gone.

"Mase, call the boys and get them to the security cameras now. See if they can locate Ivan's tablet. I don't see it." She roused Ivan as Mason stepped into the hall. "Hey, Ivan."

"I can't walk, Aeron. My legs are jello-y, and I think my head is glued to the bed."

"Where is she, Ivan?" Kat asked.

"Who?" He couldn't even open his eyes.

"Well, he got fucked. Just not the way I was thinking," Griffin said. He held out his prized bottle of Macallan—half empty. "I'll fucking kill her."

"There's plenty left," Kat said, standing up and looking around the room. The closet door was open.

"Do you see any cups? They drank straight from the bottle," he whined. "I can't drink now. It's got backwash in it."

"I'll buy you another," she said.

"You don't have any money," Mason reminded, returning to the room. She shot him a glare. "They're looking," he said, holding up the phone for her.

She did a quick inventory of the closet. A pair of sneakers were missing. Damn it. "She's making a run for it."

"To where?" Griffin asked.

"She has nowhere to go," Kat said.

"Mason," Gunnar's voice sounded from the speaker. "His tablet is in the driveway. I see her. Shit—she's wiring one of the cars."

Mason met her concerned look. "She's probably already disabled the tracking on it, and if not, she'll drop the car as soon as she can."

Dread encircled Kat's heart. "She doesn't know that the facial recognition is down." Mason swallowed hard. "I need to go after her," Kat said. "Griffin, you're with me. Mason, make sure he doesn't die of alcohol poisoning." She took a step toward the door, adrenaline pumping through her, but Mason put his hand up.

"You can't go anywhere," he said.

"Fuck you. I can do whatever I like."

"The bounty on your head," he reminded her softly.

The adrenaline plummeted and with it her heart. She couldn't do anything or go just anywhere. She was stuck in the house until Ivan and Dom shut down the list.

"I can still go," Griffin said.

"We won't be able to catch her," Mason said.

Kat glared at Ivan. He should have been working on the program and not cuddling up to Aeron. She gave him a hard shove. "Get up!" He didn't budge. She looked up at Griffin. "Go after her."

"Of course."

"What about the other reapers?" Mason asked.

"They'll follow me because I will pay them to," Kat said.

"You don't have—"

"We claim them: Rosemary's, Decius', Luke's, and Perry's

bodies. I know you well enough by now that you took the evidence needed, just in case."

Mason was silent for a moment, and then nodded. "I don't have Perry's, though."

"That's still 18.5 million."

"StormLink is down," Mason reminded.

"Then we better sober him up and get him to the Institute. The list isn't down, so I say it's worth a shot. Maybe Mike Barnes has a backdoor we can trace." She looked down at her techie, drool forming on the bed beneath his cheek. "Griff, get going. I'll have Dom send you any updates."

He placed a kiss on her forehead, hand running over her ass. "I'll bring her home," he said and left.

"And us?" Mason asked.

"I'm going to haul his ass into the shower and get him sobered up. You're going to stop me from killing him."

They dropped Ivan into the master bathroom shower. She checked his pockets, pulled out a cell phone, and passed it to Mason. "Try to call her." Ivan only stirred a bit. That bottle had been almost full when she saw it last. She turned the water on cold, grabbed the shower head, and brought it right to his face.

He inhaled a nose full of water and woke up, arms flailing, feet kicking. He drew a hand down his face and pushed Kat's arm away, panic in his eyes as he gasped for breath. She redirected the nozzle. "Where is Aeron?"

"I—I don't—"

She put the water back in his face, and he struggled to get out from underneath it, anger pulsing through her body. Aeron was in more danger than she realized right now. "Where did she go?"

Mason grabbed her wrist and pulled the water from his face. She looked up at him. "You can't waterboard him."

"I'm not," she said, and he let go of her. She pointed the shower head down, still spraying him with water. He took several deep breaths. "What happened?" she asked.

"I heard the door slam and went to check on her. She was upset about her brother. Wanted a drink and to be distracted."

"Distracted how?" Mason asked.

"With boring tech talk. What was I drinking?" He grabbed his head, swaying slightly. "I swear I only took a few sips."

"You just chugged a $25,000 bottle of whiskey. A single shot is really all you needed."

His mouth fell open. "What?"

"What did you talk about? What did she say?"

He shook his head, eyes going wide in panic. "I—I—" She brought the water back to his face, and he sputtered. "Stop it!" She aimed back down again, Ivan now shivering. "I don't remember. She talked about taking a walk. Something about the security cameras." He dropped his head back, the water dripping down his face from his hair, eyes looking at the ceiling. "I told her I loved her, and she fucking left me."

Kat let out a long sigh and turned the shower off. She tossed a towel at him. "She left all of us. Get dressed. There's still a bounty on her head and no surveillance protection." She turned to Mason as Ivan clambered out of the tub. Mason grabbed her left arm and yanked her forward. A hiss of pain left her at the contact and the sound of yacking sounded behind her as Mason pulled her from the splatter zone. Pure alcohol spewed out of Ivan once, twice, three times. Griffin would be fucking pissed.

"Feel better?" Mason asked.

Ivan wiped his mouth with the towel and then looked up at them. "I'm sorry."

"Don't be sorry," Kat said. "Just get this cleaned up and meet us downstairs. We need to get to New York." Kat walked back into the master bedroom and took a seat on the bed. She wanted to be mad at Mason for chasing Aeron away. To be mad at Aeron for being too fragile to stay. She just wanted to be mad, and Maureen was about to see just how mad Kat could be.

"Where would she go?" Kat asked him.

Mason closed the bathroom door and leaned against the frame, arms folded and ankles crossed. "She wouldn't be dumb enough to go back to Ernie's."

"I didn't ask where she wouldn't go," Kat snapped. She cupped the back of her neck and rolled her head a few times. She couldn't afford to have Griffin chasing after Aeron, but she also couldn't afford not to. Her list of enemies tripled after speaking with Kara—her only saving grace was that no one knew Amara was Maureen. "How bad would it be if Maureen's identity got out?"

"Bad," Mason said. "And I'm not just talking about in the community. I'm talking internationally. She led the team through some of the most harrowing executions and heists during the early years of Legacy Inc. We pissed off some seriously powerful people. If they found out who led those operations and that she was alive? I was alive? We would be fighting literal armies. It's one of the reasons she built the Syndicate as big as she did."

"Well, shit."

17

———

AERON

*A*eron pulled into the packed parking lot of Rita's Diner. Sweat dripped down her back, her good arm shaking as she navigated to the employee parking around back, not seeing Tommy's or Rita's cars. She owed them the biggest apology. She parked beside the cook's pickup truck and turned off the car. The world swirled around her. Unbuckling her seat belt, she leaned against the cold glass of the driver-side door.

Her eyes fell shut, her breathing shallow. This was just a pit stop. One last goodbye. One last apology. Her body shivered from the cool contact, but before she could lift her head, the door opened. Aeron jerked back, reaching for a weapon that wasn't on her hip. Pain shot through her body at the reflexive motion, and her eyes fell on Tommy.

"Hey, Princess."

She let out a small sigh of relief. "I didn't see the Impala," she said, shoulders relaxing, her face grimacing in pain.

"We left it behind when. . ." When they fled and the property burned, Aeron finished in her head. He reached out a hand, and she accepted his help climbing out of the car. "What are you doing here?"

The cold nipped at her feverish body, and she scanned the area for any threat. But the only danger was slipping on the ice-covered walkway to the kitchen entrance. "Is Rita here? I wanted to talk to both of you."

Tommy held open the security door for her, hands bracing her hip as her feet slid on the restaurant tiles. They passed the kitchen, the smell of food turning her stomach. She caught sight of the full dining room, servers moving non-stop from table to table. He guided her to the manager's office. The room was small, with a vault built into the wall, a desk sitting in front of it, with piles of papers and old menus strewn across it. To the left was a card table, staff shirts with Rita's Diner logo on it, a retro black and red jukebox with Rita's Diner in bright yellow in the middle, the slogan Burgers, Fries, Shakes, Pies across the top, and of course, a nondescript classic convertible. The restaurant theme was 1950s. Big red booths, milkshakes, fries, and the best breakfast Aeron had ever had. She loved this place almost as much as she loved Ernie's. She looked back at Tommy.

"She'll be here later," he said. "It's been a rough few days."

"I'm sorry." Aeron took a seat in the blue plastic chair in front of the desk. "I wanted to tell you both—I never wanted this."

"Aeron." His voice fell, and took the seat beside her, leaning forward on his elbows, eyes pinning her in place. "Your father gave us the option. We knew how it could end. Rita knew." Emotion lodged itself in her throat, and she just nodded, unable to talk around it. His eyes scanned her, and she shivered. "Does Mason know you're here?"

"No. Mason isn't who he says he is, okay? And right now, I don't trust him." Her body shivered hard. She couldn't stay here long. There may not be CCTV, but being near her was dangerous. "Do you have some ibuprofen?"

Tommy rubbed the back of his neck. "Yeah. Want something to

eat? Mike is running the kitchen today—he makes that French toast you love."

She shook her head. "Just the meds."

"Why else are you here?" he asked, opening the top drawer of the desk. Items clanged around until she heard the unmistakable sound of pills in a bottle. He tossed them to her. Her arm didn't move at her command, and she missed. The bottle bounced off the floor and rolled to the door. He let out an exasperated sigh. "Fucking hell, Aeron. You should be in a hospital."

"I should be dead." If she said it enough, maybe it would become true. But that wasn't her luck.

"You were. But apparently, you're too much of a pain in the ass even for Death."

"Excuse me?" she said with a laugh.

"That's what he said when you showed up," Tommy said, rounding the desk and picking up the bottle, a smile tugging at his face when he turned to her. Something in her chest stirred. When she lived at Ernie's, they would fight, and bicker, and make life miserable just short of pissing off Ernie. She forgot how much she enjoyed that, and suddenly, she didn't want to leave, but she needed to.

"Here." He opened it and handed her two. She looked from the pills in her hand to him and raised an eyebrow. He dropped two more into her palm. She nodded her head once, eyes moving from the bottle to her palm. He dropped four more. She nodded and popped them in her mouth, forcing herself to get them down without water. He handed the bottle to her, and she pocketed it. "I was hoping to grab one of the go-bags and a medic contact."

He nodded. "I figured you weren't sticking around."

He moved to the vault, and Aeron closed her eyes, letting her head drop forward, the back of her neck stretching. "Listen, don't tell Mason I was here."

"You're not in any condition to be giving demands," he said. She heard the vault open.

"It's a request," she countered. He stopped moving, and she looked up at him, but his gaze was on the door. She looked over too, eyes falling first on an expensive pair of loafers, and then traveling up the dark blue tailored suit, finally resting on a man's face. He was fair-skinned and looked to be in his early forties, with black hair cropped close to his head. He offered them a smile that almost reached eyes so dark, they looked nearly black behind his glasses.

"Sorry to interrupt," he said.

This man did not fit into the casual diner demographics she loved about Rita's. He oozed power and violence. She could spot the almost invisible scars on his knuckles and face. "Sorry, is there something we could help you with?"

He quirked an eyebrow. "I'm actually looking for you, Aeron."

The sound of her name leaving his lips sent a chill down her spine and she noted not once did the man look at Tommy. But the aura around him screamed danger, and she had a feeling the longer he was in Rita's the more likely bloodshed would soon follow. "I'm sorry, but who are you?"

"Oh, don't you worry. We will have plenty of time to get acquainted. If you don't mind, I would like to take this somewhere more private."

"I do mind," Aeron said. "I don't fancy being killed in a back alley by a stranger."

He laughed. "Your head is worth too much money to handle in a back alley. Let's go."

Fuck. She looked at Tommy, his face white as a sheet, a gun from the go-bag trembling in his hand. He shook his head at her, eyes wide. "Aeron, no," he whispered.

Either this man was going to kill them here in the restaurant, or he was going to wait for Aeron to leave and grab her then. "Put it away, Tommy." She pushed herself up, her body screaming in response to the movement.

"Aeron, no."

"I don't think I have a choice," she said. "I'm not letting you die, too." She looked back at the man. He hadn't moved a muscle, watching the interaction with nothing short of amusement. "I'll go with you." The words barely made it through her lips, her body trembling. "But no harm comes to him."

"Okay," he said and stepped aside, arm wide, to let her pass through the doorway.

"Princess," Tommy pleaded, the nickname like a knife to the heart. The look of betrayal on his face mirrored the night she left with her father.

She wanted to tell him to pick up that gun and shoot her. To not let her leave. But there was no use fighting. She swallowed hard. She should have stayed at the safe house. There were words she should be saying, last goodbyes, messages to pass on. But she couldn't find them in the clusterfuck that had become her mind. She scrunched her eyes together, but as soon as the words formed, they disappeared, and she let out a sigh. "Let me go," was all she could manage.

He lowered the gun, head bobbing up and down.

"Just to be on the safe side," the man said. He pulled a black rectangular box from his back pocket and opened it, revealing a syringe. "Be a good boy and have a seat."

"You are a hard kid to track down, you know that?" the man asked from the driver's seat of the SUV. Aeron bristled at being called 'kid' and refused to answer. They drove in silence for an hour. Aeron's right arm was zip-tied to the passenger door handle, her knee bouncing with nervous energy. She stared out the window, the scenery moving from the tree lines of Connecticut to the highways in New York. She had no idea who this man was, or what he wanted. A simple bullet to the forehead in the parking lot would have landed the cash attached to her life.

His phone rang, breaking the silence, and Aeron looked over at him. "Barnes." His eyes skirted toward her as the person on the other end of the phone spoke rapidly. "I've got her." His eyes raked over Aeron again and she shivered. "It should be an easy swap. Will do."

So, he wasn't taking her for himself. She was being traded—for who? "Who are you?" Aeron asked.

"Mike Barnes," he said, like she should know who the hell that is.

"You should know I'm worth more dead than alive."

"Don't sell yourself short," he said with a laugh. "I've been looking for you for a long time—even before the list came out. I was looking for Decius, too, but I saw he was claimed. Sorry about that."

Aeron swallowed hard, the sincerity in Barnes' voice like salt in a wound, and she turned to look back out the window. The reality that Katherine had claimed his body like they had planned washed over her, and tears pricked at her eyes. "Yeah, well, it's the cards we're dealt in this life."

"In the Legacy life," Barnes said the last two words with renowned respect. "Quite the bloodline you have there."

"I don't know what you're talking about," Aeron said, repeating the words ingrained in her since birth. The hit list hadn't said anything about her being Legacy—no one should know that.

Barnes gave a small frown and nodded his head. "It's okay. You'll talk soon enough."

The ice-cold hand of fear gripped Aeron's heart. Agreeing to go to her death—that was an easy choice. She hadn't really thought about who this man was, who they were connected to. He wanted a paycheck, and Aeron was happy to oblige at this point. She didn't want to fight, to run, to be responsible for any more unnecessary deaths.

But there were definitely things worse than death. Sin, for one. The image of Luke, bloody tears streaking down his face, ghosts haunting him unseen by the world. Men like Rufus, looking to get their fill of prey before killing them—or just never killing them.

"Who do you work for?" Aeron whispered, afraid to hear the answer.

"Oliver Hale," he said, a smirk dancing across his face.

Dread sank deep into Aeron's bones. The name didn't ring a bell at all, and the thought scared her more than if it was Rufus or her mother. At least she would know what to expect, know that Katherine and Mason would have a fighting chance at finding her —if they decided to come looking. But a complete stranger? She was screwed.

They rode in silence, Aeron fighting to keep her eyes open. They finally turned off the highway and into an industrial park. With each warehouse they drove by, Aeron's heart leaped into her throat, flashbacks to the Playhouse carnage all too fresh in her mind, and Aeron did the one thing she never thought she would. She prayed. Prayed to whatever was out there that she would die of her injuries before they reached their destination—that he would just kill her for the bounty. That somehow, Mason would find her before this man trafficked her—because he always found her. She thought back to Sammie, the first girl she ever killed for. The fear in her eyes when Aeron had been dragged through the door had fueled Aeron then—but now it terrified her.

They drove up to a four-story tall office building, the parking lot full of cars and people. Barnes pulled around the back to a warehouse entrance, and the garage door closed behind them.

Barnes winked at her. "This will only take a moment." He hopped out of the car, and Aeron squinted against the brightness as she tried to sit taller to see where he went. They'd pulled into an empty space—no storage, no other cars in sight. Just a blank room, full of possibilities.

The trunk of the SUV opened, and Aeron looked back, spotting Barnes beside the last person she expected to see—Rufus. His eyes glinted with mayhem as the sound of a briefcase opening and a keyboard being used hit her ears.

Panic surged through Aeron's body, snapping her focus into place. She tried to shrink herself smaller in the seat, biting back the cry of pain that clawed its way up her throat. She failed, and it came out as a whimper.

"Who's that?" Rufus asked. Sweat formed on her brow, the pain in her wrist and shoulder begging to be acknowledged.

"Where are they?" Barnes asked, not answering the question.

"The kid is here," Rufus said.

"And the woman?" Barnes said, irritation in his voice.

"Insurance. You'll get her once I have Red."

Aeron kept herself small, not daring to even look in a mirror.

"That wasn't the agreement," Barnes said.

"And I've been around long enough to know where my value ends. You get the hacker when I get Red. Where's Shay?"

Barnes let out an aggravated sigh. "Derek's bringing him. You don't want to fuck with Hale on this. The boy without his mother is useless. Here, send her these videos. It will put her in a spiral, and she'll come running."

"But you did bring somebody."

The rear door slammed shut and a knock sounded on her window. She instinctively looked up, meeting Rufus' hungry gaze. The passenger door yanked open, pulling her with it, and she tumbled out of the car, her feet trying to find purchase on the cement floor as her arm stayed attached to the handle. A scream left her when she bounced against the door. She landed on the ground, jostling the shoulder which, should be in a sling, her weight twisting her other arm. Blackness tunneled her vision, and she fought against it.

"Hello again, Aeron." His dirty combat boots with specks of mud and something akin to blood on them stepped into her view. Her eyes traveled up dark blue jeans hugging massive thighs and over the black button-down shirt rolled up at scarred and scabbed-up forearms. Finally, her gaze stopped on the all too familiar face of Rufus, his nose broken and bruising beneath his eyes.

The sight reminded her of Katherine, and despite the panic, she smiled. "The broken nose really made an improvement," she said, gritting her teeth and finding her voice. "Still an ugly fucker, though."

He smirked. "I thought I killed you in that garage."

"And I thought you would have jumped off a bridge by now, looking in the mirror every day. I guess we're both disappointed."

Barnes laughed, but stepped between her and Rufus like a shield. "Without the hacker, she's not up for grabs."

"C'mon," Rufus said, leaning around Barnes, eyes raking over her body. "Let me borrow her for a few hours."

Aeron's insides turned, the thoughts of what Rufus could do to her in a few hours flashing through her mind.

Barnes shook his head. "Derek's on his way with your trade. I can get Oliver to pay you triple what she's worth. Plus, you'll have the payout from Katherine."

"Money can't touch what she's worth to me," Rufus said, pulling his eyes from Aeron. "What she's worth to her mother."

Barnes' jaw dropped, and it took a few moments for him to respond. "Her mother is dead."

"Don't I fucking wish it," Rufus said, the venom in his voice tangible in the air. It was probably the only thing she and Rufus would ever agree on.

Barnes looked from her to Rufus again. "Maureen Seward died in a car crash, February 2008."

"And rose from the dead as Amara McVey—leader of the Syndicate."

Hearing her mother's name did not comfort Aeron in the slightest, and the look in Barnes' eye as he re-evaluated her sent chills through her body—or maybe that was the fever. She was so hot, and cold, and dizzy. She closed her eyes, the darkness whispering to her to just fall asleep.

"Is this true?" Barnes asked. Aeron felt a foot nudge her ribs and peeled her eyes open. "Is your mother alive?"

"Can you call someone who abandons you a mother?" Aeron asked, disgust swelling in her. "Who tortures the man you love? Who threatens to kill you? Does that sound like mother-worthy qualities?"

"Is she fucking alive?" Barnes demanded, squatting low and getting inches from her face.

The intensity switch from calm to angry startled her and cracked the little composure Aeron had left. Tears burned as they left her eyes, and she nodded, pulling away from him as far as her trapped arm would allow. Her mother would never come for her. But Katherine would. And if Katherine was coming here, so were Mason and Griffin. She held onto the shred of hope, as small as it seemed, that she would be saved—or at least see them one more time before she died.

Barnes stood back up, brushing invisible dust off his pants. "Change of plans, Rufus. Aeron's off the table, but I'll help you secure Katherine before we leave."

18

IZZ

"Have you talked to Mason?" Eileen asked.

Izz looked up from the word search she'd picked out. Eileen leaned against the kitchen counter near the sink, an apple in hand. Izz returned to her puzzle. "No." She hadn't spoken to him in days—and didn't intend to. He'd made his decision. He could have convinced the girls to give Maureen a chance —could have made them see the benefit of joining them.

"Has your pussy talked to him?" Eileen asked, pulling out a chair at the table and taking a seat.

"Sadly, she has not," Izz said, circling the word *Winchester* on the page. "You think I'd fuck the help if I had other options? I saw him the night after Luke was killed. He wasn't doing well."

"Does he know the biometrics are down?"

Izz put her pencil down and sat back, meeting Eileen's curious gaze. "No. I know who feeds me. Why the questions?"

"Because he's my friend, too," she murmured. "And I'm worried about him."

"As long as he's keeping the girls alive, she won't touch him," Izz assured. She'd been telling herself that since they left Legacy

Inc headquarters, because the alternative was a decade of wasted work.

"Do you think she's telling the truth about Storm?" Eileen asked.

Izz ran her tongue across her teeth. "She's your bestie."

"And I've been out of the loop."

Izz sighed. "I think if she wanted to break Mason, this would be how she does it—true or not."

"If she knows anything. . ." She took a bite of her apple.

Izz shook her head. "We won't know until she wants us to." She held her hand out. Eileen rolled her eyes and handed over the apple. Izz took a bite, the crisp sweetness hitting her tongue. She finished it in a few bites.

"Satisfied?" Eileen asked, an amused look on her face.

"Never," Izz joked.

"Well, grab another on the way. Let's check in."

Izz grabbed a fresh apple from the counter and pocketed it before she followed Eileen to the office. Her ears strained for the sound of yelling or general disdain from ahead. But the air was filled with the whir of electronics and typing. Keara and Rebekah looked up from the table, now covered in laptops and screens. "Hey," Rebekah said.

"Hey," Izz said, a smile sliding onto her face. Rebekah was Izz's favorite techie in the Syndicate, with blonde hair that fell to her waist, eyes like golden honey, and an ass that looked like it was out of a fitness magazine. "Where's the boss?"

"Hasn't been in yet," Rebekah said, shooting a smile back at Izz. They hadn't slept together—yet. But Izz was sure the time would come.

"Anything we should know about?" Eileen asked, walking into the room and putting a hand on her daughter's shoulders.

Keara shook her head. "Biometrics are still down, but all other communications are working fine. All assets are accounted for, and missions are going smoothly."

"Good work," Eileen said.

"You should know—they claimed Rosemary, Decius, and Luke's bodies," Keara said, her voice catching. "Mom—are they all dead?"

Eileen sighed, and Izz looked over. Keara's eyes were rimmed red, and she looked like she hadn't slept. "Darling." Eileen leaned against the table, looking down at Keara. "I'm afraid so. Only Aeron is left, and we are working like hell to find her. Have the programs tossed out anything that could be a match?"

"Not yet," Rebekah answered. "But we have it searching for all four of them."

"Call me as soon as something pops," Izz said. She shot a look at Keara, catching her eye. "I'm really sorry, kid." Keara nodded, and Eileen pressed a kiss to her daughter's head before heading toward the hall. Izz closed the door behind them. "Where the fuck is she?"

"Let's check her room."

Eileen didn't bother knocking on Maureen's door. She pushed it open. Maureen paced the room, phone glued to her ear. She looked up when they entered but said nothing; the anger swirled around her like a cape. "Thank you, Mel." She hung up and tossed the phone on the bed, which was already covered in papers and tablets.

"What's going on?" Eileen asked. She took a seat on the bed, pushing the piles aside. Izz dropped into the chair by the window, folding her feet beneath her.

"I need two teams to go clear the Legacy Inc vaults. There will be an opportunity to take them in the next twenty-four hours."

"Aren't we worried about Katherine," Izz said.

Maureen's lip curled in disgust. "Katherine is too busy scrambling, picking up the pieces she scattered on her quest for vengeance. She doesn't have the manpower to stop us."

"What about Mason?" Eileen asked.

"He's drowning," Maureen said, her words mimicking Mason's at the bar were unsettling. "He won't be thinking clearly, at least until the bodies are buried, and he can calm Katherine enough to get her to listen and heal Aeron enough to teach her to stay alive."

"I think she knows how to stay alive," Izz said.

Maureen shook her head. "Aeron grew up in an invisible world, but their faces are no longer hidden from scouring eyes. He'll have his hands busy keeping her hidden. If there is one thing I know about my daughter, she runs. And she has a lot to run from right now," Maureen said.

"Okay. So, you want two teams to the vaults?" Izz asked, pulling out her phone.

"Yes, but tier-three. I need all the top teams we have left to go after Hale."

"Wait, what?" Izz said. "Hale Security? As in the current holder of the Graveyard contracts?" There was no way she could prep the teams for such an invasion. "I haven't even finished a full assessment of the teams left."

"I don't care," Maureen snapped. "Hale's a threat that needs to be dealt with. I can rebuild later."

"Since when is Hale a threat?" Eileen said with a laugh, standing up again.

"Since always," Maureen said, raising her voice and turning to look at her best friend. Izz sat back, melting into the chair as the tension rose in the room. "Why can't people just fucking do what I say?" She looked at Izz. "Send the teams to the vaults and Hale. Then you," she looked back to Eileen, "track down Rufus. He has a long overdue appointment with the newest vials of Sin."

"Excuse me?" Eileen asked, closing the distance between them. "As much as I would absolutely love to do that, I'm not your gofer."

"Then what the fuck are you doing here?" Maureen asked.

Izz's mouth dropped open, but Eileen responded so quietly, Izz almost didn't hear her. "You're hurting, and I get it. I miss them too. But jumping blindly at anything that feels like a threat isn't the answer."

"This is my company," Maureen yelled. "I can do whatever the fuck I like."

Eileen shoved Maureen. Izz unfolded her feet, ready to intervene, if needed. Maureen glared, but didn't retaliate. "You would be nowhere without me," Eileen said. "You would be dead in a fucking ditch thirteen years ago if it wasn't for me. Your daughter would be dead if it wasn't for me. Do not speak to me like I have not been here for you this entire time." Maureen didn't answer, and Izz removed the apple from her pocket and took a bite. This could be a while.

To her surprise, Maureen didn't push back. She just glared and repeated, "Hale is a threat."

Eileen's mouth fell open, and then she gave a small laugh. "Since you've been thinking so clearly lately, give me one good reason why."

"Because I fucking said so."

"Great fucking reasoning. What about Mason and Katherine?" Eileen asked. "You going to kill them, too?"

"I'm going to do whatever it takes to protect the best interest of the Syndicate," Maureen said. "Mason knows that."

Izz took another bite, the juice dripping down her chin. She wiped at it.

An exasperated sigh left Eileen. "Just be honest for five fucking seconds! What is going on with you?"

"Hale is a threat," Maureen said, sticking to her guns. "He has always been a threat to me."

Izz's apple paused halfway to her mouth, and she furrowed her brow. She knew every threat to Maureen's life. That was her job—

her entire purpose. She knew every enemy, every secret, even ones that would make Eileen want to put a bullet in her best friend. "What do you mean?" Izz asked.

Maureen gave an almost apologetic look. "I'm responsible for the death of his wife and kids."

Izz laughed, lowering the apple. "So? You're responsible for the death of a lot of wives and kids and husbands. What makes Hale so special?"

"This one is more personal. If he finds out I'm alive—that Maureen Seward is alive—we will become the number one target. And now that he has the funds from the Graveyard? We'll be in trouble. I need to strike first."

Thick silence filled the room. Maureen wasn't angry. She was scared, and that filled Izz with dread. She had witnessed Maureen in despair, excitement, chaos, but never before had fear crossed her friend's face.

Eileen turned to Maureen. "Are you serious about Hale being that big of a threat?"

"When have you known me to be anything but?" Maureen asked.

A knock interrupted them. Maureen cleared her throat. "Come in."

Keara opened the door, holding a tablet in her hand. "We had an unusual message come in. Given the circumstances, I thought you'd want to know right away."

Izz took another bite of the apple and got to her feet, reaching for the tablet, the email already open.

Subject: Remember When?
You always made one hell of a comeback, Maureen.

Attached was a picture of a young boy around twelve and a girl a few years younger. The boy's brown hair was slicked back, his tux perfectly fitted. Pride radiated on his face as he smiled and clapped from the front row of a theater for the girl on stage. The girl beamed down at him, her pink tutu swaying behind her.

"What the fuck," Izz said.

She tossed the apple in the garbage and handed the tablet to Eileen. "I don't recognize them," Eileen said. "Could you trace the sender?" Keara shook her head.

Maureen took the tablet, her face darkening. "Did we receive anything else?" Keara shook her head again.

"What is it, Moe?" Eileen asked.

Maureen remained quiet, staring at the picture as if transported to another time. The map of scars on her face softened, her mouth downturned.

"Keara, find out where this came from," Eileen said. "Message us as soon as you have something." Keara nodded and headed out of the room. Eileen turned back to Maureen. "Who's in this picture?"

Maureen licked her lips, a small laugh leaving her. She took a seat on the edge of the bed, eyes still on the photo. Izz and Eileen moved closer. "Me." She zoomed in on the little girl. Her face was bright and flush, the stage lights hitting the glitter on her costume. "You know, before, I loved to dance. I came to New York when I was ten. I wanted to be a ballerina or on Broadway."

"And who's the boy?" Izz asked, her brow furrowed. She knew Maureen had come to New York as a child to live with an aunt after her parents died. Then she joined the Legacy, and like Izz, she had no one to go back to.

Maureen moved the screen, bringing the boy into focus, and Izz saw moisture gather in her eyes. "That's my Ollie. Our parents didn't care what I did, but Ollie—he was always so proud of me. Came to every show he could until I stopped dancing. Until I met Andrew."

"Your brother?" Eileen asked.

"Your parents?" Izz asked, her gut sinking.

Maureen nodded. "Maureen Seward didn't have a brother. She didn't have parents. Just an aunt who raised her and died a timely death." She zoomed back out, taking in the whole picture again. "Olivia Hale had a brother, though." She passed the tablet over, meeting Izz's gaze. All emotion vanished from her face, replaced by the familiar stoicism. "And I broke his heart, wrecked his family, and then disappeared off the face of the earth."

"Hale?" Izz asked, her threat assessment going into overdrive. In their current state, if Hale attacked, they wouldn't last the week. Who gave a fuck what their backup plan was if they were dead? And then it hit her—Maureen was a Hale. Everything Izz ever knew about her was a lie. Every instance that Izz had spent protecting her was compromised because she had never been given all the information. It stung, but Izz swallowed back the feeling of betrayal, a more pressing question in her mind: What else had Maureen lied to her about? "Oliver Hale? Are you fucking kidding me?"

"You know me better than that, Izz," Maureen said and looked at Eileen, whose face represented everything that swirled inside Izz right now: shock, betrayal, and worry. But Maureen continued as if she didn't notice or care. "If we're done questioning my decision-making skills, I need our teams prepped to take on Hale."

19

KAT

Kat looked over at Mason. He sat across from her at the coffee table in his residence at the Institute. It was very much a bachelor pad. Neat, nothing out of place. No personal items—like he'd barely lived there at all, except for the bottles of liquor on the counter. It looked like her place.

Betty, Gunnar, and the kids had successfully headed off to the Caribbean. Katherine and Mason decided to escort Dom and Ivan back to the Institute. It offered more than she could imagine. Not only access to the cold room and StormLink, but housing, a medical ward, training rooms, a full arsenal her granddad hadn't emptied yet, and a place she'd never thought to look: his main office. She'd been there a handful of times, but she had been so focused on the Legacy Inc headquarters, that she'd forgotten he had a whole other life here in the City. But she hadn't had the energy to go up there yet.

"Isn't there an easier way to do this?" Kat asked.

"No," Mason said, placing a paper on the growing pile in front of him. "Not if we want to keep the information out of anyone else's hands." They were hours into categorizing another box of pictures from the vault, looking for anything that would lead them to Mike Barnes or whoever had Shay.

"Ugh. Where is the pile on Maureen?" She'd found a handwritten file they'd snapped a picture of referencing a Maureen McCall—maybe her mother's maiden name. But it wasn't in her granddad's handwriting, and Maureen was at the bottom of the shortlist right now. He pointed to a pile he'd moved to the floor, and she dropped it on top.

The pile was growing bigger by the second, and a deep part of her wanted to dive into it—learn more about the woman who rejected her before she even had a fighting chance. Find the weakness that would break her. Her phone buzzed on the table, pulling her away from the daydream. She picked it up and answered as she reached for another file, this one mentioning Storm. "What's up?"

"After four years, I will never take you answering the phone for granted again," Griffin said.

His soft voice eased the storm raging in her heart, and she smiled. "Did you find her?" Kat asked, hope rising in her chest.

"Sort of. Is Mason there?"

"Yeah, hold on." She waved to get Mason's attention and put the phone on speaker. "Go ahead."

"I followed up on the Rita's Diner tip," Griffin said. "She was here, but not for long."

"Where did she go?"

"I'm going to say nowhere good. When I arrived, the manager, Tommy, was unconscious in the office. Said Aeron turned up in terrible shape looking for a go-bag. Before he could convince her to stay, a man came in looking for her."

"Who?" Kat asked.

"No idea, but according to Tommy, he was dressed in a nice suit with really expensive-looking black shoes. He had a kill-you look about him, reminded him of Aeron's dad."

She looked at Mason, watching the wheels turning in his head. His eyes fell slowly closed. "Did we get a better description?"

Griffin laughed. "Better? No."

"Is Tommy okay?" Mason asked.

"The kid seems fine. Shaken, but fine," Griffin supplied, and Mason's shoulder relaxed. "I've got nothing else here. The trail is hours cold and they don't have any cameras. Where to, boss?"

"We're at the Institute. See you soon." She hung up and leaned back against the couch. She turned her gaze to Mason. "What are you thinking?"

He let out a long breath. "Who the hell would grab Aeron and not just kill her? There are no alerts from the hit list yet."

Her phone buzzed again, a text from Ivan.

Ivan: COME HERE

That boy needed to learn some etiquette. "Looks like Ivan has something. Let's go."

She followed Mason through the Institute down to the cold room, trying to keep track of where everything was. The building was a maze. She'd only been inside the Institute to go to her granddad's office. They made their way to the basement, and through glass doors like the ones at Legacy Inc. Computer monitors lined the wall straight ahead. Ivan sat at the command center in the middle of the room with Dom hovering over his shoulder. "You summoned me?" Kat asked. Ivan looked over his shoulder, a smile on his face that promised good news.

"So whatever Mike Barnes was doing in the system—he jacked it up. And he was definitely in both systems. I was able to track some of the logins," Ivan said.

"If you look at the third screen," Dom said. "You can see the pathway of changes, but it's encrypted. We're still trying to decode it."

"So, you brought me here to tell me you found nothing?" Kat asked.

"I would never," Ivan said, and Kat was glad to hear some excitement back in his voice. "Check this out." He pointed to the right side of the screens. A map popped up, green dots moving around.

Kat's mouth dropped open, and she moved closer to the screen. It was the tracking portion of StormLink.

"You got it back online?" Mason asked, coming up behind her to look. It was clearly a map and trackers, but there were no distinct identifiers, and not nearly enough to account for all of Legacy Inc—well, maybe. She had killed a lot of them.

"Not really," he said. "The entire system is glitchy. Like I cannot access the communications, or mission files, or archives, but I have access to track whoever these people are, and they will randomly pop up and then disappear."

"Is there information attached to them?" Kat asked, reaching out for the screen.

"Yeah. Pick one," Dom said.

Kat pointed to the closest blinking green light. After a few seconds, a message box opened up, displaying the StormLink biometrics report she'd seen hundreds of times.

-- ASSET BIOMETRICS REPORT --

NAME: PUMPKIN

GEO: 41°23'28.4 N, 73°32'08.8 W

HR: 82 bpm

TEMP: 98.6°F

RESP: 18 bpm

BP: 120/80 mmHg

O2 SAT: 98%

MOVE: 5,000 steps / 3.5 km / Moderate activity

ENV: 23°C / 40% Humidity / Air Quality: Good

BIOMETRIC SIG: Confirmed
STRESS: Low
COMM STATUS: N/A
FALL DETECT: No incidents
BIOMETRIC ALERTS: None
MISSION STATUS: Green
-- END OF REPORT --

She didn't recognize the name, though, and Mason chuckled beside her. "What?"

"Click another one," Mason said. Ivan did, another report popping up, the name SPIKE at the top. "These are Legacy Inc and Syndicate members. Spike, aka Izz. Pumpkin? That would be Griffin. But it doesn't make sense. They shouldn't be on the same system."

"I know," Ivan said. "It's like Mike Barnes was trying to mash versions of what he swiped together, which is where he failed. See, Storm encrypted them, making them detrimental to combine. Try without the passcodes and it ruins all the programs."

"And what if you have the passcodes?" Mason asked.

"Then you have an upgraded version of StormLink," Ivan said.

"Keep working and print me a list of the names as they show up," Kat said, turning to Mason. "We are a step ahead of her for once."

"And yet have no use for the information," he said, heading to the door.

"For now. Good work, guys," Kat said, patting Ivan on the back as she passed. "You said there's a training area here?" she asked Mason.

"Yeah."

Good. She needed an outlet. "Lead the way."

The Institute's training room was massive. Mason slid his shoes off and stepped onto the matted area, Kat doing the same, rolling her neck a few times and bouncing from foot to foot.

"What do you want to work on?" he asked.

"I just need to. . ." Perry always knew what she needed. She never had to explain it. God, she missed him. "Flow," she said. "I need to flow."

He nodded and bowed. She returned the gesture, and he attacked. Her feet were off the ground, her back hitting the padded floor before she could react. She spun, putting her legs between them. She covered her head as his fist came down, the dull ache in her tricep registering as he made contact. Her free hand grabbed his ankle and her opposite foot wound around the back of his knee. With a quick pull, he stumbled back, and she jumped to her feet. He tossed a punch, and she parried, stepped behind him, and wrapped her arms around his waist. With a tug, he dropped to the ground, his feet entangled with hers. He smirked as she found herself trapped beneath him. His fist came down, light touches to every spot that would be a devastating blow. She sat up through the blows and wrapped her arms around him. With a push of her legs, she slammed them both backward. Mason's hand stopped hitting her and based above her head. She rolled them over.

His eyes narrowed as she threw an elbow toward his face, pulling the force and barely grazing his nose. She smirked and popped up to her feet. He did the same, and they started again. It was mental freedom, a form of mediation nothing could touch. Her mind and body became one, responding to the moment, the second, the here and now. There could be no worrying about Aeron or Maureen. No thoughts of all she lost, of what she feared, because when they slipped in, Mason would strike, and she would be dead. Then they would reset, and he'd up the pressure, add the weapons, and pull her from her mind one move at a time until she laughed, her cheeks hurting from the sheer respect that as good as she was—he was better.

"Can I join?"

Mason's dull blade paused at her neck, his knee on her face pinning her to the ground. It was the third time he'd gotten her there, and Kat really wanted to learn how he did it. She looked toward the entrance. Griffin leaned casually in the doorway, arms crossed and curiosity on his face. "Two on one?" Mason asked.

"Boys versus girl?" Griffin added.

The pressure on her face released, and Mason helped her to her feet. "Sure," she said. Without waiting, she secured Mason's wrist and spun, dropping to her knee. He spun with the momentum and released the knife into her grasp. She sliced at him, the blade brushing his cheek first on one side and then the other. He stumbled back, and Griffin lunged. Kat met him halfway, their bodies slamming into each other, and she let the knife fall to the ground. She ducked beneath his arm and rounded to his back. He spun toward her, and she kicked at his knee. He went with it, dropping low and spinning. His other leg whipped at her, and she dove over it. He lunged from his knees, and she kicked back, knocking him in the chest.

She smiled when he landed on his ass. Griffin smirked back. He bounded to his feet, dodging her jabs, and ducking under her hook. Kat grunted as he landed a blow to her ribs. He swung again. She blocked and then thrust her knee toward him. He countered, and scooped her legs from underneath her, picking her up like a child and tossing her to the ground.

A laugh left her as she rolled to her stomach and pushed herself up, her left arm shaking slightly under her weight. The meds did their job. She couldn't feel the pain, but the damage still needed to heal. "I can't believe you just did that."

"I can't believe you just let me." He advanced, and she shot forward, meeting him halfway again. She threw an elbow, and he leaned back, winding his arm around her waist, spinning with her momentum, and slammed her into the wall. Strong fingers snaked around her throat.

They stopped moving, chests heaving, faces inches from each other. He stared hungrily at her and licked his lips as his hand drifted from her neck to her hip. He leaned in and placed a kiss on her lips. Kat's body arched into him, eyes falling closed as his other hand cupped the back of her neck, drinking in the taste of him, the comfort of his body pressing into her.

"Hey, I hate to interrupt," Mason called out, and she mentally cursed him. "Hey!"

Griffin pulled away, his dark eyes dancing with mischief. "Sorry, boss," he whispered.

"I didn't tell you to stop," she replied, the smile on her face impossible to hide. She stepped past him and looked at Mason. "What's up?"

He held up her phone and then tossed it. It landed in her outstretched hand, a notification labeled URGENT on the screen. She used her thumbprint to unlock it, and a message from one of Aeron's burner phones popped up. Electricity shot through her. "It's from Aeron."

She opened the video message, and the relief evaporated. Her heart froze, then beat so painfully she thought her chest would break open any second. Her eyes wouldn't look away, her cheeks burning with rage. She kept the sound off, but she didn't need the sound to hear the screams that accompanied the video.

"Kat?" She looked up from the footage of Shay, heart jumping to her throat as if she'd gotten caught doing something she shouldn't. She met Mason's concerned look. "What did she say?" Kat swallowed hard and shook her head. She turned the phone around, unable to say anything. His face paled, and he snatched it from her.

Griffin moved past her to watch over Mason's shoulder, and

his eyes snapped closed, face scrunched against the images he too knew were there. Mason's eyes, though, didn't move from the screen as he took in the torture Shay had endured all those years ago. He was dying in the video right now for the second time. He would be resurrected and killed at least six more times. Where the hell did Aeron get this? Why would she send it? The answer was easy: she wouldn't. But that meant someone else had. Kat closed her eyes, the failure setting into her bones. Someone had Aeron—and they weren't planning on just killing her.

"Where did you get this?" Mason asked.

"It was sent from her phone," she said.

Kat willed the images of Shay away, but all that happened was Aeron replaced him in each memory seared into her psyche. Fuck the hit list—she was done hiding. All she wanted was to go straight to Syndicate headquarters, knock down doors, and bust open skulls until she found Shay and Aeron. She wondered how loud Maureen could scream—if there was enough damage from the car accident that she could literally melt the skin off Maureen's body without her feeling it so she could watch and anticipate the pain as Kat moved to her unmarred skin.

"How long did they torture him?" Mason asked. She opened her eyes and took back the phone, Mason's pained look not helping her at all.

"Days. I watched hours of curated footage—that footage. I could tell you every breath he took, every twitch of his body, every tear that fell from his eyes." She let out a long breath. "This has to be Maureen. No one else knows about Shay." She took a shaky breath, and Griffin moved beside her, but the sudden closeness was suffocating, and she shook her head, taking a step back.

Mason shook his head. "I'm not sure it's Maureen."

"Who else would grab Aeron and not just take the bounty?" Griffin asked. "Senior would have kept that in the vault. Maureen knew exactly where to find Kara's name. She had plenty of time to snag other information."

"Or Elijah had it loaded onto StormLink, which still points to Barnes and whoever he is working for," Mason countered.

"Or both, because Mike Barnes works for her," Kat said and released a long sigh. If anything happened to Aeron or Shay—how could she live with that? "How many are too many?" she asked.

"What?" Mason furrowed his brow.

"How many sacrifices are too many when trying to revive two fallen empires and get vengeance?" Kat asked. The image of Shay flashed into her mind, only this time it was Aeron strapped down. Griffin's arms wound around her and she took a deep breath, his scent calming to her nervous system. "When do I look in the mirror and say it's enough?"

"For people like us, it is never enough. From the first day we take a life we start running, and we can never stop, because the day you stop running is the day you realize it was, and always will be, too many."

"You're fucking terrible at pep talks," Kat said.

He laughed. "What is it you want?"

"I want it all. The power, the money, the safety, the name—the vengeance. I want to save the good people and kill the bad ones."

"Then do it," he said, as if it was the most obvious answer in the world.

"How?" In moments like this, when she had no idea what to do next, and she was sure her choices damned those closest to her, the imposter syndrome ran deep. How could she run anything—be anything—when she had to rely on others? When she even had to ask the questions? Her granddad had never relied on anyone, but how had that served him?

"I don't think there is anything on this earth you couldn't get if you really wanted it. I just witnessed you wipe out Legacy Inc in a single night. There are only two things that can truly stop you, Kat:

a bullet in your head," he put his finger on her forehead, "and your own self-doubt." He moved his finger to her heart.

She smirked and swatted his hand away. "That's a better pep talk." She looked back at the phone, her lips turned down, unease simmering in her gut.

"So, who has Aeron?" Griffin asked. "And do they also have Shay or just the video?"

If Maureen wanted her dead, Kat knew in her heart she would be dead. So who would grab the two most important people in her life right now? Who even knew about them? She opened the phone back up, fingers hovering over the keyboard. What if she. . . Kat typed a reply to the video. *Where?* She turned it for Mason to see and raised an eyebrow.

"Couldn't hurt to ask," Mason agreed.

Her thumb hesitated over the button for a few seconds before she hit send. The worst that could happen was no answer. The response bubbles popped up immediately, and her heart jumped into her throat. Maybe there was something worse.

A picture came through this time, and her chest tightened. Rufus held the phone, Aeron in a chair beside him, and the accompanying text:

> Unknown: Come and get her, Red.

The world around her darkened as the reality sunk in: Rufus took Aeron. That monster had her sister. Screams from the Playhouse echoed in her mind. Hers, Perry's, unknown souls who she'd gladly let take the punishment Rufus wished to do to her.

"Kat?" She could hear Griffin's voice, but the rush in her ears muffled him. Rufus had her family. She gasped for air, but her lungs spit it out as quickly as she took it in. Griffin moved her to the ground, pushing her back against the wall, taking her hands in his.

"Close your eyes." His voice sounded as if it moved through water to reach her, but she listened, concentrating on his voice. She let him talk her through the familiar grounding techniques until her vision cleared and she could hear again. Her breath regulated, and she accepted the water he offered, dropping her head back on the cement wall.

"Sorry," she said, heat flooding her cheeks. She took another sip of water. She hadn't had one of those in years.

"Never apologize for remaining human," Mason said. He grabbed the phone from the ground, his gaze immediately returning to her with hatred so deep Kat nearly flinched as he ground out, "Rufus."

Her lip curled, and she nodded. Mason passed the phone to Griffin, and he stiffened beside her. Rufus always had an unhealthy obsession with her, one fueled by the fact she was off-limits to him. Was this Rosemary's doing from the grave? She would have known Mike Barnes, and she was grossly intimate, it seemed, with Rufus. Could this be payback for killing her mom?

The phone pinged, and Griffin checked the message, a disbelieving laugh leaving him. "He sent the fucking location and a 24-hour warning."

"Good. Let's go." Kat clambered to her feet, the world swimming around her for a second, and she stretched out her arms for balance. Mason grabbed on to steady her.

"We're going to need help, Kat," Mason said. "This is Rufus. You took two armies into the Playhouse, and he still survived."

She shook her head, a shiver running down her spine. "Rufus always hated the fact I was untouchable."

"Are untouchable," Mason assured. "He's not putting a finger on you. Let me see it." Griffin passed the phone over, and Mason opened the image again. "He only shows Aeron. We can probably assume he doesn't have Shay."

"Then who the fuck does?" Kat spat, panic threatening to claw up her chest again. How much more was he going to suffer for loving her?

"I don't know." Mason turned the phone around and pointed at the corner of the screen, where a few pairs of feet could be seen. "But Rufus doesn't have the resources to pull off the raid on the West Indie's property. So, the bigger question—who is he working for?"

"How sure are you that it's not Maureen?" Griffin asked.

"Ninety-six percent. Dealings with Rufus are tumultuous at best. No one willingly works with him if we can help it."

Ninety-six percent was going to have to be good enough. Every second that Aeron was with Rufus was a moment of trauma Kat couldn't take back. She turned to Griffin. "I need you to gather the reapers and Division Three. We have the payout from the hit list to cover the debt, so let them know they will be paid."

"Are you sure?" Mason asked. "We can reach out to Hale, see if they can spare some assets, and we can pull the overseas assets back."

She shook her head and took another sip of water. "Star hasn't given a full report yet, plus there's not enough time. I don't know anything about Hale—which needs to be rectified as soon as possible. And do you really want to give Rufus another second with Aeron?"

Mason's face darkened with a predatory look that both frightened and excited her.

"Exactly," she said. "Let's get to work."

20

IZZ

"So, what now?" Izz asked, looking up at Maureen and Eileen, burying her anger as deep as she could.

"We cripple Hale's ability to complete Kara's orders. Full elimination of his numbers," Maureen offered, "which we should have done all those years ago."

Izz laughed at the ludicrousness. "We are functioning at half, and without trackers."

"I don't care," Maureen said. "I've survived too long to let my brother take me out now. We hit the vaults tonight at nine. There are decades of blackmail stored in there, and we roll on Hale at midnight." Her eyes glowed with excitement.

Izz checked her phone. That gave her twelve hours to prep, transport, and organize a full-scale raid on an unknown target. She let out an aggravated, "No."

Maureen glared, and Izz glared right back. "What?"

"I said no," Izz repeated, her heart thumping in her throat when Maureen stepped toward her, but Izz didn't move. "It is not humanly possible to pull that off. And I'm not putting our teams at risk. Plus, we already lost the element of surprise."

Maureen's face didn't give a thing away, and Izz waited for her to say something or strike.

"Does Oliver know about your kids?" Eileen asked, pulling Maureen's anger away, and Izz took a small step back, releasing a shaking breath. Eileen picked up the tablet, looking at the picture again.

Maureen waved a dismissive hand. "Aeron and Decius, yes. Katherine, no." That would put Aeron right in the crosshairs—and if Maureen was right, which she usually was—Aeron would be easy pickings.

"Does Mason know?" Eileen asked.

"No. And I know what you're thinking—we can't tell him."

"Aeron's life is at risk," Izz argued. He had the right to know there was more than just the hit list target on her back. There was a revenge target as well.

"As long as he does his job—"

"How the fuck can anyone properly protect someone without all the information?" Izz snapped.

Maureen's face morphed into a sneer. "I would never put you at risk. Any of you."

"Could have fooled me," Izz said, anger now sitting just below her skin. Maureen stepped toward her again, and Izz matched her pace.

Eileen slid in between them, hands raised. "Enough. Get some air, Izz," Eileen suggested.

Maureen's glare burned into Izz, a chill racing through her. "Yeah. Okay." She left the room, hands curled into fists. Izz would never have let the Playhouse mission fly so freely had she known about Hale. Protecting Maureen's identity was the top of her priority list, and Izz had thought it a calculated risk. She knew how to handle Rufus and Rosemary—she knew she wasn't making it out alive. And there weren't too many people who would care if Maureen Seward rose from the grave once Elijah was dead. But had she known about Hale? Making sure Rufus didn't make it out alive would have been her main task. Fuck.

She pushed past the people in the hall and headed straight for her room. She slammed the door closed, trying to funnel the energy that was building in her chest. Where the fuck was Dash when she needed him—where was Mason? She scanned the room, clothes tossed around, some hers, some not. The dresser was littered with gun parts and oiling supplies, empty glass tumblers, and a bottle of vodka Jude had left in her room before they'd departed for the Playhouse. Izz snatched the bottle up and poured herself a glass.

She took a seat at the edge of her bed, elbows resting on her knees, leaning over the shaking glass in her hands. She took a sip, face scrunched with the burn. Maureen had lied to her. Maureen had *lied* to her, the person she swore to keep nothing from. She took another sip, moving between anger and hurt, but right now, anger was winning. Every single mission she'd done, every security detail—was worthless.

Her bedroom door cracked open. Izz looked up, hoping to see Dash, or someone she could bury herself in. But Eileen's face met her instead. "What?"

"You good?" Eileen asked.

"No. And unless you're here for me to fuck my feelings out, leave."

Eileen rolled her eyes and entered the room, the door clicking closed behind her. "Hale hasn't been seen at work in two days," Eileen said. "Mel just—"

"Good for fucking Mel," Izz spat and took another sip, her body giving a small shiver. She hated vodka. She hated everything right now. "Maureen—or Olivia—or whatever the fuck she wants to be called now, can cozy up to her next, and lie to her." Eileen sat beside her, the bed sinking beneath the weight.

"Everyone who comes into the Legacy has a past they don't talk about, Izz."

"She swore she would never lie to me," Izz said. "How can I do my job if I don't have all the information? How can I protect her? Protect the kids?" She downed the rest of the glass and held it out for Eileen to refill.

Eileen sighed but complied with the request. "Everyone lies. We're no different—how many times have we lied to protect her from herself?" She grabbed the bottle off the dresser and filled the glass back up, taking a sip herself before passing it back, disgust crossing her face. "Why are you drinking this?"

Izz frowned. "It was the first thing I found. What if Hale had found out about Maureen just a few days earlier? Imagine the havoc of the Playhouse then?" Jude's dead eyes flashed in her mind. She'd been one of their best.

"Relax, Izz. Has she ever led us astray? She had it covered."

"Why do you always defend her?" Izz snapped and stood, glaring at Eileen. The world wobbled around her, and she took a sip to steady it. "She's a liar—she's—"

"Watch your tongue," Eileen said, voice lowered. "That's family you're speaking of."

"She doesn't give a damn about family. She doesn't give a damn about any of us." Eileen reached for the glass of liquor, and Izz pulled it back. "No. She put everyone at risk lying to me."

"You are not the only person she counts on to keep everyone safe, Izz. That's too much for one person. It's why she has me and had Mason."

"Did you know? Did Mason?"

"She had her reasons."

Indignation burned in Izz's chest—or maybe that was the vodka. She burped, tasting the vomit already, and swallowed it back. Eileen reached for the glass again, and Izz handed it over. "Do you think he'll go after the girls?"

Eileen placed the full drink on the dresser. "If he's anything like Maureen? Yes."

Izz's head pounded. She removed the hair tie and shook out her mohawk; the pressure released from her scalp. What did she know about Hale? Not nearly enough. "He's a businessman," Izz said. "I do have a contact, Hale's cousin, Derek. I will have to meet in person—he's more of a fuckboy than source material. But I'll get what we need from him."

"I have Keara and Rebekah switching gears as well, and Mel is on her way in."

"I'll get with Dash about the vaults," Izz said. And then let out a long breath. This was the job—the moving chess pieces, the sacrifices, the losses. "What does she want done about the girls?"

Eileen blinked a few times, her lips pressed together. "The Syndicate is the priority, then Aeron, then Katherine."

"Alright," Izz said, but shook her head.

• • •

Izz's fingers flew across the keyboard, pulling all the files they had on Hale as a phone line rang in her earpiece.

"Yo," Dash said.

"I need an update on the transport of each team," Izz said.

"Since when?"

Izz bit back the growl trying to escape, irritation settling into her bones. Moving hundreds of assets without the tracking system took more coordination than they had time for. "Since right this second, asshole."

"Tampa and Georgia will be at the vaults by 9pm. The Raleigh team should be in within the next hour. And your newly appointed Firebirds two hours after."

"And when are you getting in?"

"In you? As soon as I get back," Dash said, and Izz smirked. "By seven."

"Make it six." She hung up the phone and looked over at Keara. Her hair was in a frizzy bun atop her head, a stylus clenched between her teeth as she worked on the schematics of Legacy Inc Headquarters. "What's going on?" Izz asked her.

"The block is still shut down from the 'chemical leak'. Mason set it up beautifully."

"Of course he did," Izz said. "Any sign of him?"

"No."

"Good. Your teams will be there by nine." Her phone buzzed in her pocket, and she took it out, Small Dick Derek scrolling across the screen. He had taken the bait. She answered. "If it isn't my favorite booty call."

"Can you be here in two hours?" Derek asked, right to the point, voice full of lust.

"I can be there in three," Izz countered, already standing up. She signaled for Rebekah to come take over the computer for her.

"Bring those toys again," he said and hung up.

Izz smirked. He was kinky in all the right ways, and she felt almost guilty for what she was going to have to do to him—almost. "Rebekah, can you finish this? I'm pulling up any file that mentions Hale."

"From memory?" she asked, eyes widening.

"Do you have a better way?" Izz asked.

Rebekah licked her lips and smiled. "I've got it. Have fun tonight."

Izz dragged her gaze over Rebekah's body, and the techie's cheeks reddened. "Tonight is simply business. I can show you what I consider fun one day." Izz winked and headed out the door. She took the steps two at a time to Maureen's room and hesitated before entering. She stopped knocking on Maureen's door years ago—she'd also never flat-out challenged Maureen's authority the way she had today—so she took a deep breath and knocked.

"Come in."

Izz pushed it open. Maureen looked up from the desk. She had the schematics of Legacy Inc on the screen, working in tandem with Keara on the plans. "Since when do you knock?" she asked, all aggression from earlier gone.

"Since I don't fancy another hole in my body. I'm heading to meet with Derek Hale. I'll get what I can out of him. Are you still wanting to move in tonight?"

She shook her head. "I want everyone ready to go at my command. But you have some valid concerns."

Izz smiled, the weight on her shoulders lifting. "I'll call when I finish."

"He was my least favorite cousin," Maureen said, a wicked smile crossing her face. "Treat him accordingly."

Izz took the stairs to Derek's place two at a time, the bag of supplies bouncing against her back. The door was unlocked, as always, and she entered the dimly lit apartment. He sat at the kitchen table, his blue button-up shirt undone, the dark blue tie tossed next to the tablet he was working on. He smiled when he looked up.

"I don't have much time," he said. "I got called into work—but I didn't want to miss this."

"Moving up?" Izz asked.

He nodded. "Yeah, my cousin needs me for a big job."

A genuine smile spread across her face. Maybe he would have more information than she thought. She slid off her shoes and tossed the bag on the couch. "We should celebrate."

Derek pushed the chair back, eyes on her, tongue darting

across his bottom lip as his eyes locked on her body. She closed the distance between them, scanning the room for cameras or security that may have been installed since the last time she was here. She cupped the side of his face, dragging her fingers down his jaw to his neck, itching to squeeze the information out of him. But she needed patience. She straddled his lap, his erection already bulging for her, and moved her fingertips to his chest. His eyes fell closed, head dropping back as she wound her hips against him. Her eyes fell closed too, a moan leaving her.

Their hips moved in sync, Derek's hands moving to her ass, tracing invisible circles, the light touches sending jolts of pleasure between her thighs. Dammit. She should have found someone to fuck before she'd left. She took a deep breath and placed both hands on his chest, stilling. "I brought some new ones to try," she whispered.

He bit his lip in anticipation. She stood, the chill hitting her legs, begging her to strip them both and sit back down. She retrieved the bag, pulled out a pair of soft restraints, and held them up with a single finger and a quirked an eyebrow, waiting for his confirmation, which she knew he'd give.

She brought the bag with her and dropped to her knees in front of him. She wrapped an ankle in the familiar, soft fabric, securing him to the kitchen chair. Her hand ran up his thigh, over his dick, and back down, repeating the process on the other side, while his hand fisted in her hair. He pulled her up for a kiss, and she obliged, raking her teeth along his lower lip when she pulled away. Tracing across his chest, Izz moved behind him, hands sliding over his shoulders and down to his wrists. She pulled them together, wrapped each one, and attached them to the chair. This was nothing new for them, but the zip ties she pulled out next were. She laid them out on the floor and pulled out another rope. She draped it across his chest, leaning close to his ear.

"One more?" She ran her tongue up and down his ear.

"Ye-yeah. I only have an hour."

"Oh, I'll have us both off in less than that," she assured, a smile tugging her lips. He sucked in a breath as the ropes cinched tight across his chest. She grabbed the zip ties off the ground and wrapped the first one over the soft fabric on his wrists, tightening enough to be secure, but not enough for him to notice the differ-ence. She placed a kiss on his neck again. "We need some music." She slid the other two zip ties beneath the chair and moved back into his view. He looked like he would fucking burst already, a hungry look crossing his face. Who knows, maybe she would unlock a new kink, and he would enjoy the torture. She picked the remote up off the couch and turned on the surround sound. "Shit. Where's your phone?"

"Table," he said, voice low.

She sauntered over, scanning the documents he had scattered about. The tablet had timed out, his phone sitting beside it. She plucked it off the table, tapping the side button. Pin code required. "Babe." She turned the phone around and pouted. "This isn't going to be fun without music."

He didn't even hesitate. "7-7-4-5-2-5."

Izz typed it in, the screen opening for her. Text messages, calls, his whole digital world now available. She turned on their sex playlist and then scanned the most recent texts with Oliver, but nothing jumped out. She put the phone down and turned back, straddling his lap again.

"This usually works better without our clothes on." A smile tugged at his lips, and he tried to lean in for another kiss, but the ropes held him in place.

"Usually," she agreed, hips moving to the beat of hip-hop music. But if she took off his pants, she would want to take off hers, and she had a job to do. She slid back down to her knees, her tongue dancing across his chest, caressing one nipple and then the other. His breath hitched, and she smiled, hands sliding to his ankles. She made quick work of the zip ties, tightening them hard.

He gasped, eyes snapping toward her. "What was that?" Izz's eyes darkened, and she pulled a switchblade from her pocket. His eyes widened, his body tensing against the restraints. "What the fuck?"

This was her favorite moment, when people realized she was more than a great piece of ass and that they were fucked—and not in the good way. "Where is Oliver?"

He tried to move, but the restraints held tight. She flipped the blade over and jammed it into his thigh. He screamed, and Izz reached for the remote, turning the surround sound up. She used the blade as leverage to pull herself to her feet. "Where is Oliver?" she said into his ear.

He glared. She picked the phone back up, typing in the code. If Derek had been part of the Syndicate, he'd be a low tier three operative; disposable; collateral damage. But he was also family—so allowed information he probably shouldn't have. She pulled the blade back out and dropped herself onto his lap, wiping the blood on his cheek. She turned the volume back down. "I don't have a lot of time. See, your boss threatened my boss, which makes this arrangement no longer possible. If you tell me what Oliver is up to —I'll let you go."

"So he can fucking kill me?" Derek said, his voice several octaves higher.

"Is Oliver a mercy killer, or does he enjoy taking his time?" Izz pressed the tip of the blade against his cheek, ripping the skin apart as she moved it centimeter by centimeter down his face, wondering just what kind of boss Maureen's brother was. Did they share the same twisted taste for vengeance? Izz almost wanted to leave him alive just to see. "Because my boss—well, she likes to take her time. Make sure each piece of flesh has been touched—

every crevice of the mind has been probed. And everything I learned? I learned from her."

He whimpered, body trembling beneath her. She'd made him tremble the last time she was here, too, but that had a much more satisfying ending.

"What does he have planned?" He refused to respond, lips pressed together like they could keep his secrets in. "Fine." Tossing the phone on the table, she turned the volume back up and grabbed the ball gag from the bag. It would keep the screams muffled, and she just liked the way he looked with it stuffed in his mouth. The blade danced across his chest, superficial but painful. He tried to talk around the ball.

"What was that?" Izz asked, bringing the knife to his other cheek. His eyes widened again, noises trying to get out. "You have information for me?" His head gave the slightest nod so as not to cut himself. She dragged the weapon down, slicing his face again before she released the gag and turned down the music.

"They're making a trade tonight."

"With who?"

"I don't know his name," Derek said. "Big scary guy. Ran a place called the Playhouse."

Izz rolled her eyes. Fucking Rufus. "What are they trading?"

He opened and closed his mouth a few times. Izz paced the small space, patience in short supply, and then threw the switchblade. It embedded in his shoulder, and she closed the distance in an instant, pulling a smaller knife from her waistband and pressing it against his balls. A half cry left him, the answer following. "They are trading some half-dead guy and some girl for a woman and her son!"

Izz moved the blade to his inner thigh and pressed, ripping the fabric of his pants and piercing the muscle. "That doesn't tell me anything. Who, Derek?"

He screamed. "I—I—"

Izz split the muscle as she moved higher up his leg, riding just beneath the femoral artery. A single twitch and he'd bleed out.

"Some programmer who's been missing for like a decade. The Graveyard hired us to find her." His voice rose in panic as her hand didn't stop moving. "That's all I know. Please," he cried out.

Izz paused. A programmer, who had been missing for a decade, and connected to Kara. Maybe Maureen was on to something with Storm. She pulled the blade out slowly. The blood soaked through his pants and dripped onto the floor beneath the chair. If Rufus had Storm, who was the boy? And who would Rufus want in return? "You said a half-dead guy?"

Derek's pale face nodded.

"And a girl? What girl?" He shook his head, eyes rolling, and then his head dropped forward. "For fuck's sake." This was why Hale failed in comparison to the Legacies and the Syndicate— they didn't have proper torture training. Every Alliance and Syndicate member underwent a year of torture training and a basic round of Sin. The top-tier teams were subjected to advanced Sin protocol. Made them fucking ruthless and nearly unbreakable. She wiped the blood off her blade on his shoulder and turned to the table. She unlocked the phone again, scrolling through all the messages. Ollie, Barnes, Sugar Lips—she smirked—and a list of others. Oliver's messages held no information—check-ins, reminders about meetings, and orders to show up tonight at the warehouse with the package. She opened Barnes' messages, more of the same, but with a less friendly demeanor.

She put the phone down and turned to the tablet. It too had a passcode. Would he be dumb enough? She punched in the same code and the screen opened to a map. Fucking rookie. A quick zoom-in showcased an industrial park thirty minutes away. A laugh left her, and she placed a kiss on top of his head, putting the devices and papers into her bag. She still had a few minutes before she needed to leave.

She tapped his face hard, rousing him. "What can you tell me about Oliver's sister?"

"Olivia?" The words were slurred. His head started to fall forward, and Izz threaded her fingers into his hair, holding it upright.

"Does he have another one?" she snapped. But then she asked again, because she didn't actually know. "Does Oliver have another sister?"

"No. That bitch is dead."

Izz backhanded him, releasing his hair so his head got the full effect. "So disrespectful."

"Why do you care?"

Izz turned the music back up and straddled his lap again, a yell of pain escaping him as her ass pressed down on the stab wounds. She moved against him and licked her lips. Fuck, she needed to get laid. Her fingers grasped his chin, tilting it up, and she placed her blade beneath his ear, leaning in close. "Silly boy. Olivia sends her love." She pushed up, and warm blood poured over her hand as his ear fell behind the chair, his screams drowned out by the music.

21

———

AERON

arnes escorted Aeron from the garage to an office several floors up. The room was furnished with a large wooden desk and a black high-back chair. But the couch to the left called her name, and Aeron headed straight for it. She dropped down, sinking into the soft leather as sleep begged her to finally join him, but the cold fabric came as a shock to her flush face. She must really be burning up.

"What's wrong with you?" he asked.

Aeron lifted her head, looking over at him. He sat behind the desk and pulled out a laptop from one of the drawers. He set it up, typing away, not sparing her a glance. "I'm dying," she said. Mason had talked about getting her to someone who could help. She'd hoped to find a medic after Rita's, maybe track down Dr. Shea. But the reality was no one could help her except the doctor who created the cocktail.

Barnes sat up a little straighter and looked at her over the screen. "What do you mean?"

"Are you dumb?" Aeron asked, closing her eyes. "It means exactly what I said."

He scoffed. "God, you sound just like him." He didn't pursue the topic, though, and she let the sound of typing lull her to sleep. Visions of Luke, of the dead, chased her in and out of consciousness, a tangle of misery and happy memories threading together. Her father's look of pride watched her from the distance, and she clung to him. She wanted answers—why did he lie to them about their mother?

"How'd it go?" An unfamiliar voice pulled her closer to consciousness, and the pressure of a hand on her head pushed the vision of her father aside. She fought against her body to move, to pull her eyes open, but her body remained locked in its current sleep cycle.

"Honestly? Not what I expected. She didn't even put up a fight," Barnes said. "But she looks rough."

The pressure on her head released. "She's feverish."

"She was favoring that shoulder pretty hard," Barnes said. "I can't believe it, though. What a stroke of fucking luck."

"It's karma. Did we get confirmation? Besides the word of a serial killer and a dying girl?"

"I found nothing in StormLink, but the system is jammed up," Barnes said. "If anyone knew, it would be her. Any luck on Rufus giving up the location?"

"No. I still can't believe you let him get his filthy hands on her and broke the fucking tracking system."

"Hey," Barnes said, defensively. "Whoever burnt down Legacy Inc broke it."

"And what about the Institute?" the man asked.

"She got her people in. I compromised what I could on the system, but their techie—Storm trained him, Ollie."

"We'll take care of him as soon as I handle Maureen—if it's her."

Ivan. They were talking about Ivan. Her sweet, naïve Ivan. *I love you.* His final words to her before she left echoed in her head. She didn't deserve his love, and he didn't deserve to die for any of them. She pulled against the invisible weight holding her down, trying to shake her head until her body caught up. Hands grabbed her shoulders, and she groaned. Pain seared through her left arm, and Aeron shot her right hand across her body, latching onto the hand touching her. She rotated it toward her and folded the wrist down with a snap.

"Son of a bitch," the unknown voice whispered, and the hand ripped free. Her eyes shot open, and she rolled to the side, tumbling off the couch, swallowing the scream trying to escape as she landed on her side. Everything hurt. Her head pounded, and her lips were chapped. How long had she been out?

"And she rises from the grave," the man said.

Aeron looked up. The man staring at her was dressed similarly to Barnes, except his suit was gray. Beneath the jacket was a matching vest over a white shirt, and his purple tie loosed at the knot. His eyes, however, danced with mirth behind his black-rimmed round glasses. His brown curly hair was kept tidy and close to his head, like his neatly trimmed beard. She pulled herself unceremoniously back onto the couch, sighing at the effort to even exist at this point. "That joke is only amusing the first time. By the third time, I promise you, you will wish you stayed dead."

He chuckled. "Good to see you awake, Aeron. I was worried."

"Why?" Aeron asked. "You could have saved yourself a bullet and made a small fortune."

"I'm not looking to collect, yet," the man said. "Oliver Hale, known to my close associates as Ollie. I run a security firm, not quite as impressive as the Legacy, though."

"I don't know what you're talking about," she said, but they had been talking about the Institute—they'd been inside. And they were threatening Ivan.

"We don't have to pretend it doesn't exist here. I mean, we really don't—it's gone. You seem to be the last remaining heir—

well, blood heir. There are a few straggling members holding on for dear life. Mason hasn't kicked the bucket yet, has he?"

She licked her lips, her body screaming for hydration. She didn't want to think about Mason, or the Legacy, or anything. "Do you have any water? Antibiotics? A bullet to put me out of my misery?" she asked. Barnes and Oliver exchanged a look, and Barnes picked up his computer and left the room without a word. "Was it something I said?"

Oliver removed his gun from inside his jacket, and she tensed. He took a seat on the couch, resting his hand with the weapon along the back of it, pointing lazily at her, but his eyes moved over her, taking in the cuts and bruises the same way Mason would. She looked away, his betrayals still raw. "Is it true your mother's alive?" he asked.

She swallowed the secret. She wasn't ready to talk about it. Believe it. Relive it.

"I'm not here to hurt you. On the contrary—I want to get to know you."

She could almost believe him. "Don't bother. You'll end up dead in the end. Everyone always does."

"Did you ever think it's everyone your mom meets that's cursed? Everything she touches, everyone she claims to care for, winds up broken or dead."

She hadn't thought of that, and the idea it wasn't all her fault sent a small sliver of hope to her heart. But she was the one who made the choices, pulled the triggers. She was the one who lied. She couldn't pass the blame anywhere. "Why do you care so much about my mother, anyway?"

"Because until a few hours ago, I thought she was dead."

"Welcome to the club," Aeron said. "If you think using me to get to her will work, you're wrong. She doesn't care about me. Never has." She swallowed hard at the painful reminder.

Oliver's eyes widened. "She abandoned you?"

Aeron didn't answer. She didn't want to be talking about Maureen. Because talking about Maureen brought Luke's slack face to the forefront of her mind. Her chin trembled, and she wiped at her cheeks.

He asked another question. "What happened to you, kid?"

Her eyes found a knot in the wooden desk to focus on, indignation burning in her chest. "Don't call me that."

"What are you, twenty-one? You are a kid. I'm old enough to be your dad," he said with a harsh laugh.

"Yeah, well, I killed my dad. And the Senior Assassin," she said, the confessions slipping from her lips like a busted dam, and it felt good to say the words. "Does that sound like kid shit to you?" She slid her left arm into her hoodie pocket, taking the pressure off the bullet wound. She could feel his gaze on her but, refused to look at him.

"And how does that disqualify you?" he asked.

"I've never been one," she said. "Legacy heirs aren't kids. We're assassins." The words were out of her before she could stop them, and she pressed her lips together and looked at him.

"I'm sorry about that," he said, sincerity in his voice.

She melted her look into a glare, not wanting pity from a man who kidnapped her, who was using her as leverage to lure her sister here to let Rufus do whatever he wanted, who was then going to use her against her mother. "Why are you working with Rufus? He's a terrible human being."

"He has something I need."

"You mean someone."

Oliver nodded. "And her safety is more important than anything else."

"Is that why you're willing to give up Katherine?"

"That and the added bonus of where I eliminate the last remaining heir of Francis Wayward. The end of Legacy Inc and the Legacy reigning family? How could I pass it up?"

"Are you going to kill me too?" she whispered. She was okay with dying, had accepted her fate. She yearned for it, but she didn't want to wait for it.

"I thought about it. You know, you look like your mother," he said, eyes darkening. A chill ran through her body. Mr. Wayward had said the same thing to her. "And my immediate reaction was to take the sins of the mother out on you. To make her feel the pain she put me through. But if she abandoned you, too..."

Aeron's mouth fell open. Abandoned her too? "You have no idea what she's done!" Aeron ground out, anger pulsing through her. "She didn't just abandon me, she destroyed me. Convinced my father to lie to me—to hate me. She tortured my—she tortured the humanity out of Luke. I had to put a bullet in his head. She's the reason Decius is dead. She's—"

"A terrible excuse for a mother," Oliver finished, his shoulders slumping forward.

Aeron nodded, blinking tears away, letting out a dry laugh. "You know, everyone used to tell me stories about her. How amazing she was! Kind. The epitome of a moral compass. All I saw was a monster."

"A momster, if you would."

Aeron snapped her head to look at him, eyes wide, a barely contained smile on his face. She couldn't help it. She laughed.

"Dad jokes. The best kind. I used to tell them to my son when he was upset. The more ludicrous, the easier to snap him out of his funk."

"How old is he?" Aeron asked, still chuckling, unsure if it was the absurdity of the joke or the complete inability to regulate her emotions anymore. But Oliver put her at ease. She didn't feel like a hostage. She felt safe. Her guard began to climb back into place because she was a hostage, and he would gladly put her in the grave at the end of the day. She couldn't trust him.

Oliver sobered. "He would have been twenty-three last month."

Another soul gone too young. "I'm sorry."

"You know, it never gets easier. He and his mother died fifteen years ago. Some days it feels like a lifetime, and others? Like I'm still holding their bodies, begging someone to bring them back."

Aeron swallowed hard. The images of her dead seared into her mind, her guard dropping again. He held the same pain in his eyes she saw every time she looked in the mirror. "What happened to them?" In their line of work, it could be anything.

He tilted his head in thought, lips pursed. "Your mother," he finally said. "My sister, trading secrets for power, and people for glory."

"They worked together? I'm not surprised," Aeron said. "She's a real fucking piece of work. If you want her dead, I'm on board. Katherine is on board, she. . ." Aeron caught herself. No one knew about Katherine's relation to Maureen, and it wasn't her secret to tell. "She hates her as much as I do." Oliver gave a soft laugh. "If you want to get to Maureen, get in line. She's a liar, and a terrible person. And she won't come for me. You're wasting your time." Aeron let out a long breath. "Where is your sidekick?" Her head swam again, body fatigue kicking back in as her emotional outburst waned. "I really could use that water."

"Why would you assume I'm using you for leverage?" Oliver asked.

"You're pointing a gun at my head."

"You nearly broke my wrist out of a dead sleep," he said, but held up the gun and then slid it home beneath his jacket.

"You kidnapped me to be traded to Rufus—Rufus of all fucking people," she said. "Because it is what we do. What this is. A life for a life. A lie for a lie."

"Fair enough. But that was before I learned your mom was still topside."

"And what difference does that make?"

"It makes all the difference!" he said, raising his voice, and then he pulled his volume down, his voice still thick with emotion. "Your mother—I wanted her to feel my pain, watch her family die in her arms." He took a deep breath, and Aeron stiffened. "I'd let all thoughts of vengeance die with her. You and Decius were young and widely out of reach to me. The Legacy protected you." Aeron swallowed hard, and he continued. "When your name came up on the hit list, I thought it was karma for my son being murdered. But when Rufus asked for your head? I knew something bigger was at work—never did I think my traitorous sister was still alive."

His sister? The words didn't make sense. That would make him her uncle? No. Not possible. Her mother was an orphaned child. Aeron had no family left, except Katherine, and she sure as hell wasn't going to tell Oliver about that. "You're lying."

"I'm not," he said, gaze boring into her.

She swallowed the lump in her throat, the mental games too much for her to keep track of. "If you're going to kill me, please just fucking do it. Rufus is right. My dead body would be enough. You don't need to make shit up."

"I'm not going to kill you, Aeron. Your mother betrayed and abandoned you the same as me. She left us broken. My sweet justice isn't to kill you; it's doing the one thing she never could."

"What's that?" Aeron asked.

"Save you."

The door opened, interrupting the moment, and Aeron sent a silent thanks to the universe. Barnes entered with a bottle of water and a medical bag, handing them over to her. She put the bag on the floor and opened the water, chugging it. "Derek said he'll be here."

"About time he steps up."

"I moved the boy to the office down the hall and posted Sandra out front," Barnes said.

Oliver nodded, grabbing the medical bag and opening it up. "How is he?"

"Fine. Sleeping."

"He's not fine. The kid is traumatized. The sooner we can get his mother, the better. What are the reports on Katherine?"

"No sign of her yet. You should take Aeron and the boy out of here."

Oliver shook his head. "I need her location, and Katherine seeing Aeron here is part of that deal. Besides, if he dies—we're screwed."

Barnes sighed. "Well, she burned all her bridges in the Playhouse. The most she has is Mason and the techie."

"What about the Reaper?" Oliver asked. Aeron looked to Barnes, too, biting her lip.

"He was leading the hunt for their heads, confirming the kills. And he hated her. The number of times I heard him bitching about her? I don't see him as a threat."

Oliver nodded, and Aeron scoffed, the water bringing a bit of clarity to her mind. They had no idea what they were dealing with —who they were dealing with. "What?"

"You won't see them coming," Aeron said, her guard all the way back up. He wanted to save her? He's her uncle? Ugh, he almost had her—she almost fucking believed him.

"We saw you," Barnes said with a smirk.

"And what are you seeing now?" Aeron asked, nodding to the darkened window. "Nothing. My people are better than yours."

"You mean the ones you fled from?" Barnes said. "Are you sure they'll even come for you?"

"I'm sure you'll be the one I point to when they show up, just so I don't have to hear the sound of your voice anymore." Oliver laughed beside her, and she glared at him.

"What do you need?" he asked, holding up the bag.

Probably nothing they had in there. Legacy had some of the

most advanced medical supplies the field had to offer. Legacy Inc had some of the world's most experimental trials. But if he was going to pretend to care for her, she wasn't going to complain about the accommodations. "Have any antibiotics?"

He pulled out an orange pill bottle. "Metronidazole?"

She nodded, and he tossed it at her. She opened, counting at least fifteen doses. "Can I keep this?" she asked.

"Sure. There's more where that came from."

She popped the pill in her mouth. He passed her another bottle of water from the bag, and the room went dark. It only took a moment for the emergency lights to click on. Oliver was on his feet beside Barnes, weapons drawn. Barnes' laser focus was on her, eyes glancing to the door. Oliver pulled out his phone.

"No signal?" Aeron asked and took another sip of water. His eyes flicked to her, and she smirked. "Told you—you wouldn't see them coming."

22

KAT

"Please give me some good news," Kat said into the phone as she headed to the cold room. Their rescue mission was creeping into suicide mission territory. They were short on people and time, and she hoped Griffin and Mason had come up with a better plan than 'just show up'.

"You're beautiful and a badass," Star said on the other end.

Kat smiled. "News, not facts."

"Carl eliminated everyone at the European headquarters that he didn't take with him. Everyone—cleaning crew, security, assets. It fucking reeks here."

"Damn it. How are the vaults?"

"Secure. There are even some funds lying around. It looks like he planned on coming back."

Kat paused in the hallway outside the glass doors. Just beyond them, Mason and Griffin hovered over the back of Dom's chair, Ivan down below, pointing at the screens. Overseas needed to be handled and out of her mind so she could focus on getting Aeron and Shay home safely. She could shift the headquarters to another outpost, but logistically speaking, it would be a nightmare. "How do you feel about a promotion?" Kat asked.

"What?"

"I need someone I can trust leading the European side. I need someone capable. You check both boxes."

"Kat…"

She could hear the trepidation in her voice. This wasn't a small ask. "It doesn't have to be forever," Kat said. "Once we are established here, you can come home if you want to."

"Yeah, okay," Star said, and Kat let out a sigh of relief. "What's first?"

"Let me see where Ivan is on StormLink and I'll send you more info. For right now, get the bodies cleaned up. There should be a secondary cleaning crew in the area unless Carl killed them, too." She hung up and stepped forward, the glass doors sliding open. All four men looked back at her, a map and blueprints on the large screen behind them. "What are we looking at?"

"Layout of the building. Storage area on the bottom floor, office spaces on the next three. Helicopter pad on top. Pretty standard looking."

A green dot flashed on the screen. Kat took a step forward. "Was that Rufus?" she asked, blood pumping faster through her veins.

Ivan nodded. "It's been spotty, but he's there."

"Any idea why he chose that place?" Kat asked and joined them at the desk. Griffin moved to her side, placing a kiss on her temple and winding a protective arm around her.

"It belongs to a subsidiary of Hale Security," Griffin said.

"Why would he be working with Hale?"

"Or why would Hale be working with him, is a better question," Mason said. "I think we can safely rule out Maureen at this point."

Fuck. "How many people can we spare to bring with us?" she asked.

"The vaults will be ready for transport tonight—we can't spare any of the reapers," Griffin said.

"Division Three?" Kat asked, looking at Mason.

"Not unless you want to leave here unmanned."

"I guess that just leaves us," Kat said. Griffin's arms tightened around her, and she leaned into him, letting out a long sigh. "Have we gotten in touch with Alexis? I don't trust her, but she's proven useful to me before."

"Negative," Dom said.

Damn it. "Keep trying," Kat said and looked over to Mason. "Carl eliminated the entire European headquarters. I put Star in charge."

"Is she up for the job?" Mason asked.

"For now," Kat replied. "Ivan, I need you to create a secure communication for her to reach out to the other overseas divisions and then look into Carl's finances. He said he had a bug-out account. See if we can access that and send the money to Star to start paying Ireland and the others."

He groaned, dropping his head back. "What about Dom?" he practically whined.

Dom looked back at her and smiled. Kat couldn't return it. The bags beneath his eyes and three-day-old stubble reminded her of the early days of their justice plotting—when rage and grief burned in their veins, fueling an unstoppable mindset. He slid his headphones off. "What's up?"

"I know how you feel about the overall violence, but I was. . ." Why was this so hard to get out? "I think it would be a good idea if you came with us in case Shay's there." Griffin's arms stiffened, and she stepped away from him.

Dom's brow furrowed, teeth sinking into his bottom lip. "Kat—"

"Please," she said before he could tell her no. "I haven't seen him in—it's been—" She took a few breaths. She hadn't laid eyes on Shay in person since she left him, brokenhearted, on the beach. What if he didn't even recognize her anymore? What if he blamed her and hated her? "Please?"

Dom nodded. "Yeah, of course."

"Mase, can you get him geared up?"

Mason met her gaze, lips pressed together, and she wanted to know what he was thinking. But he just nodded and led Dom out of the room. Ivan returned to the desk and took a seat, leg bouncing. He looked back at her. "Do you need anything before we head out?" she asked.

"Can I, uh, talk to you for a minute?" he asked, hand now fidgeting with the hem of his shirt.

"Yeah, what's up?"

"Uh, alone?" he said, voice cracking.

Kat looked back at Griffin, his eyes narrowed in suspicion. "Of course," she said, giving Griffin a small push. Ivan waited until the doors slid closed to speak. He turned in his chair to look at her, mouth open and closing a few times. "Spit it out," she finally said.

"I have combed through StormLink a hundred and fifty-seven times."

"That's oddly specific," Kat said and leaned against the desk beside him.

"It's oddly accurate," he said. "There is no way this program—any of the programs—could be running for as long as they have, with the updates they have had, without a backend worker."

"Yeah, Mike Barnes, and all his predecessors."

"No," Ivan shook his head and then turned to the computer. He pulled up what looked like a log box. "These are all the instances of when StormLink personnel logged in and did anything. It's pretty standard until the timeframe when Mike Barnes took over. And then he did a whole bunch of shady stuff. But this. . ." He typed away again, and another log box popped up. "This was hidden so deep within the program that I only knew to look for it because I know Storm. I was looking for a clue as to what Mason thinks I should know in order to rewrite it."

Kat took the mouse, scrolling up. The list seemed to never end. "How long is this?"

Ivan gave a small laugh. "That's the thing, Kat. These are Storm's original logs. They should have stopped when she died."

"But they didn't?"

"I didn't want to say anything to Mason, because if I'm wrong —well, that would be the worst thing I could be. But if I'm right..."

"Right about what?" Kat said, trying to drag the words from him.

"I'm not sure." He shook his head and took the mouse back, scrolling down to the bottom. "But look." He pointed to the screen. "There's a log from just a few weeks ago. And then another one a month before that. It goes back all the way to the beginning." He kept staring at the screen, no longer moving it, but she could see the tension in his shoulders. "He said she was dead. But what if..."

Kat's mouth dropped open. "You think Storm's alive?"

"I—I don't know what I think. But I know her work, and maybe she trained someone else, and they're out there, but..."

"Okay," Kat said, mind reeling back to Mason sharing about Storm, the pure anguish in his voice—the fact they never found a body. If there was a possibility that what Ivan said was true, Kat didn't doubt for a second Mason would go after Storm, and she couldn't afford to lose him yet. "Let's not say anything to Mason. We don't even know what it means. Mike Barnes could have doctored those," she said, nodding her head for his agreement.

He nodded too. "Yeah. That's true," he said, and she could hear him wanting to believe it.

"We need to focus on bringing Aeron home, and then I'll go down the rabbit hole with you," Kat assured. "Are you any closer to being able to fix the program?"

He nodded, shoulders relaxing. "Yeah. I think I am."

"Good. Keep working." She patted him on the back and left, turning the possibilities over. If Storm was alive—how had she managed to stay off Mason's radar for so long? Her granddad's? Maureen's? And if Mike Barnes had found what Ivan had found...

The pin from Rufus led them to an industrial park. She expected it to be somewhere off the grid, but he'd put them in the middle of a busy area with CCTV and traffic cameras on every corner. Perfect. Their faces would pop off every alert for the Underworld if they weren't careful. "You can drop the block, right?" Kat asked, looking back at Dom from the passenger seat.

He sat beside Griffin, two tablets running on his lap. "Yeah. But not for long. Maybe sixty seconds to get you in. It looks like they have a backup generator-—so it could be less than that."

"And what's the body count inside?"

"Fifteen."

She looked at Griffin. He sat straight, eyes closed, and fingers running along a blade in his hand. He opened his eyes, pure focus meeting her. She swallowed hard and turned back around, leaving him to his ritual. Three against fifteen. Possibly thirteen if Shay and Aeron were counted among them. But Rufus was more like four people.

"This is a rescue mission," Mason said, as if reading her mind. "In and out."

"What about Rufus?" she asked.

His jaw did the usual tick. "If we have both Aeron and Shay, take the shot if you have it, otherwise we're in and out." He pulled to the side of the road and parked. They were three blocks from their destination, the rest of their trek would be on foot.

Dom shivered beside her, tucked in the tree line half a block away from the warehouse, the tablet in hand as Mason looked over his shoulder. Kat adjusted the earpiece, trying to ignore the dread creeping in. "The goal is to get Aeron out, and Shay if he's there," she said, trying to tame the dread creeping in. "If Rufus gets his hands on me, promise you'll put a bullet in me."

"If Rufus has his filthy hands on you and I'm able to put a bullet in you, I can damn sure put a blade in him," Griffin said, danger in his voice that sent warmth to all the right places.

"But if it comes down to it—"

"I already told you," Griffin said. "I'm not going to let that happen."

"You have three guards on the outside," Dom said, lowering the tablet so they could see the heat signatures. "There are five people on the third floor, three in this office. The other two—looks like one inside the room down the hall and one standing guard." He moved the image, the green dot pulsing on the screen. He touched it, the name DEVIL popping up."

"That's fucking accurate," Kat said under her breath.

"Senior wasn't blind—he knew how dangerous Rufus is," Mason said.

"Well, he's on the main floor with six others," Dom added.

Kat eyed the building. It was scalable, but not easily, and her tricep twinged at the thought. "Easy day," she said, not feeling the confidence of the words. "I don't know if my arm will cooperate on a climb. Griff, you go up. Mason and I will take the ground floor."

"Rescue mission," Mason reminded, screwing his suppressor into place. "Ready?"

Kat nodded and looked up at Griffin. "Ready," he said, a smile sliding into place.

23

———————

AERON

"Go check on Rufus," Oliver said, gun trained on Aeron in the semi-darkness. She took another sip of water. She wasn't in a hurry to leave—Kat and Mason were going to be pissed at her. Griffin was going to be infuriated.

"What about. . ." Barnes nodded in her direction.

"Go," Oliver said again. Barnes glared at her before heading to the hallway, his shouts muffled by the closing door.

"I don't think he likes me," Aeron said.

"Shut up," Oliver snapped. He reached forward, grabbing her right arm and yanking her to her feet. The room swam, and she stumbled forward, landing on her knees. A flash of being in her driveway just days ago raced through her mind and she squeezed her eyes shut, her body tipping forward. Oliver's grip tightened, and he pulled her back up.

He led her to the darkened hallway, the emergency lights not doing much. Sandra stood guard outside a room down the hall near their exit. Her tall frame towered over Aeron, even in the distance. "Grab the kid," Oliver said.

Sandra retreated into the room, appearing moments later with a boy who looked about eight. His brown hair was a tangled mess on top of his head, and his brown eyes were rimmed red from crying. The school uniform he wore was dirty with piss and blood, and Aeron watched his entire body shake as they closed the distance in the hall.

Aeron ripped her arm free and dropped to a knee in front of him, looking for signs of injury, but he didn't have a visible scratch on him. So where had all the blood come from? She glared over her shoulder at Oliver—he was no better than Mr. Wayward, using kids as leverage. Glass shattered in the room she'd just left, and Sandra shot past her to meet the threat. Aeron smirked and met the boy's terrified eyes. "Things are going to get scary," she whispered. "Stick close to me."

He gave a small nod, and she grasped onto his wrist, turning to put herself between him and Oliver, who was already retreating toward them. "Go," he said.

Aeron shook her head. They weren't coming to hurt her. Footsteps pounded up the stairs, and she pushed the boy against the wall, crouching, ready to protect him. Hale's guards burst through the door, fully armed, sights on her. The first one held his aim as another stepped past and cleared the hall.

"The office," Hale said, sending them past. He pointed his gun at her. "Move."

A snarky response sat on her tongue, but the trembling body behind her made her swallow it. She didn't mind dying, but this kid didn't deserve that. She kept the boy behind her and descended the stairs. Gunfire met their ears as they neared the first floor, and the lights came back on.

"Out the back," Hale demanded. Aeron paused at the door, listening for movement. She heard nothing and cracked it open, scanning the area. The cold air engulfed them as they stepped outside.

"Right," Oliver said. Aeron turned right, guiding the kid along the side of the building, staying in the shadows. She glanced over her shoulder, Oliver's gun still on her as he too scanned the area. "Black sedan around back."

She slowed at the corner, peering forward. The boy looked too, before she could stop him. A dead man with half his face missing from a bullet wound met them. The boy let out a screech and threw himself at her, burying his face in her shirt, his breath labored. She wound her good arm around him and closed her eyes. Fuck.

"Move it," Oliver said.

"Fuck off," Aeron replied, the boy's sobs reverberating right through her. She leaned forward again. The coast was clear, and she escorted the boy forward, keeping his face pressed against her as they passed the body to the car.

"Him in the back, you in the trunk," Oliver said.

She glared, but opened the back door, trying to urge the boy inside. He clung harder to her. "C'mon. What's your name?"

"C-cass."

"Cass, that's a cool name. Listen, Cass, I need you to get in the backseat for me. I won't let anything happen to you. Do you trust me?" Cass nodded. "Good." She helped him into the back seat and dropped her voice. "I need you to close your eyes, cover your ears, and lay on the floor. Can you do that, Cass?"

His brown eyes widened, and he nodded. Aeron felt Oliver grab the back of her hoodie. She gave Cass a smile and a wink. He slammed his eyes shut and dropped to the car floor. Aeron let Oliver tug her back. She pushed the car door shut and spun toward him. Her left arm screamed in protest, but she kept moving. Her fingers slid down his arm to secure his wrist, forcing his aim to the ground, and her right elbow retracted across her body and shot toward his face. He blocked it and shoved her hard. She hit the car with a hiss of pain and rebounded.

"Using a kid as bait? You're fucking disgusting," Aeron said.

She kicked at him, pushing him further away from the car. He kept his aim away from her and she smirked. He really wasn't going to kill her—that would be his biggest mistake. She charged, running straight at him. They collided, Oliver's hands coming up to catch her. This time she grabbed the gun as they tumbled to the ground. She landed on top, disarming and slamming the weapon beneath his chin. She glanced up at the car—still secured.

"Give me the keys," Aeron demanded. He reached down toward his pocket. Aeron moved her leg just enough for him to slide his hand in and pull out a ring of keys. She plucked them from his fingers and locked the car. "Where's his mother?"

"Rufus has her," Oliver said. "He's the only one who knows where she is."

"Who is she?"

Oliver's eyes widened. "Watch out!"

Fingers dug into her hair and pulled her back. She dropped the gun and the keys as she caught her balance, hands flying to her hair. She spun around, scalp screaming from the familiar pressure. Aeron couldn't even fake a sneer. Terror filled her as Rufus licked his lips. "I am going to enjoy you so much." He tossed her to the side, Aeron's knees skidding on the asphalt.

Oliver scrambled to his feet, and from behind him, a figure emerged from the shadow. The sickening sound of metal striking a skull hit her ears, and she flinched. Oliver dropped forward, Barnes stepping around him. Aeron's mouth dropped open. The fucking snake. She hadn't even had time to get back to her feet and Rufus was on her again, fingers twining through her hair once more, pulling her back up.

"Oliver!" Aeron screamed.

"Will you shut the fuck up?" Barnes said.

Rufus pulled her close, tipping her head back. She braced her hands against his body, but it did nothing to stop him. He leaned forward, taking a deep breath by her neck. A whimper left her. "Oliver!" she pleaded, because he was her only hope at the moment.

"Oh, he's not getting up anytime soon, sweetie," Rufus said. "Let's go find Red."

24

KAT

The guard outside the door dropped silently when Kat pulled the trigger. Mason's hand paused on her shoulder. "I'm heading south." She nodded and crept forward toward the entrance. The small window allowed her to see a sliver of the room. Three fully armed guards trailed in and out of view, but she didn't see Rufus. He wasn't going to touch her. If she repeated it, it would be true. Her breath fogged in front of her as they waited for Dom's signal.

"Three, two, one," Dom's voice said in her ear. The room went pitch black, and Kat pulled the door open, firing three shots in the vicinity of the guards before tucking herself against the wall. The emergency lights clicked on, and Kat fired two more times, the bullets finding homes in a protective vest and a forehead. But the room had no cover, save for two vehicles and the lines of support columns. She sprinted for one of the huge metal beams in the middle, bullets just missing her, and she slammed her back against it. She glanced around the cool metal spying Mason doing the same on the other side.

"You've got company," Dom said into her ear. "Another person just showed up."

"Does anyone have eyes on Aeron or Shay?" Kat asked.

"Negative," Griffin said. "I've got three dead upstairs. Heading down."

"I dropped one," Kat said.

"Dropped one," Mason added. "No eyes on Rufus either."

"Kat, every heat signature is moving fairly quickly. There are three moving toward your six. I don't think Shay's here," Dom said.

Her gut sank. "Then we can't kill Rufus," Kat said into the comms. "If Shay's not here—we may never find him without Rufus. We're moving to capture and detain." She glanced back into the room—by her count, there should be at least five more hostiles. Someone would have information. "Can I get an affirmative on that order?" Kat said, heart beating hard against her chest, and she glanced over her shoulder toward the door.

"Copy," Mason said.

"Yeah, okay," replied Griffin, the disappointment clear in his voice. She let out a sigh of relief.

The door she'd entered flew open, and her knees went weak as Rufus stepped inside. He had his fingers tangled in Aeron's hair, holding her like a shield. Aeron's hands hung on to the one in her hair, her arms shaking with the effort. Kat pivoted to face him, leaning against the metal beam for support.

"Hey, Red."

She kept her gun trained on him. Mike Barnes stepped in behind him, his aim finding her first with a smirk, and then he turned toward Mason. He fired. Kat's heart dropped. Metal on metal rang as the round hit the barrier, and she'd never been so happy to hear that sound. Mason didn't fire back.

"Barnes, it seems you left a few things off your résumé," Mason said.

Barnes fired another shot, the bullet ricocheting again.

"We have never had a mole make it that far inside either Legacy before. Impressive," Mason continued.

Barnes stepped forward, but Rufus shot his free arm out, his head shaking. "Nice try, Mason," Rufus said. "But I know your head games. I only want Red. You can take this one back to Maureen." He shook Aeron, and Kat stepped forward. She caught a glimpse of Mason in the corner of her eye. The missing guards had surrounded him. He looked at her and shook his head.

"You know nothing about me," Mason said. He tossed his gun to the middle of the floor and stepped out, hands raised. Kat looked back at Aeron. Her eyes stared daggers at Rufus. The set of her chin, the snarl on her face—this was the girl she'd met at Rockstars, one ready to fight.

"I've got the two guards in the middle," Griffin's voice whispered in her ear. "Mase, you take the one to your right. Kat—"

"I'll take that deal, Rufus," Kat said, stepping forward, grip tightening on her gun. "I'll come quietly."

"Kat, no," Aeron said, shaking her head, wincing in pain.

Kat gave her a small smile and lowered her gun to the floor. She spied a knife tucked into Rufus' belt and flicked her gaze from it to Aeron twice. Aeron licked her lips, the tension in her hands lessening. "It's okay, Aeron. I'm ready."

Kat prayed Aeron caught the signal. A shot fired from behind her, and she stood back up, firing at Barnes' leg. She needed both of these men alive. He dodged it, and Kat adjusted to aim at Rufus as Aeron snatched the knife at his waist and dropped her weight. With surprising speed, Aeron swiped the blade through her hair and across Rufus' fingers as she ripped herself free. She raised the weapon to attack again, but Rufus kicked her back, swearing as blood spilled from his hand.

Once Aeron was clear, Kat fired. The bullet just grazed his shoulder, and she fired again, aiming for his leg, but the gun jammed. He smiled.

"Damn it." Kat backpedaled as he advanced. Panic surged through her, and she reached for her backup piece. She bumped squarely into a body, an arm pushing her aside. Griffin stepped past her, blades in each hand. But she couldn't enjoy the show. She dove for Aeron.

"Are you good?" Kat asked. Aeron nodded, taking several gasping breaths beside her. "We can't kill them—Mike Barnes and Rufus. We need them alive." Kat scanned the room. Mason moved from one guard to the next, the tranquilizer gun in hand. Where had Barnes gone?

Aeron scrambled to her feet. "There's a kid out there," she said and sprinted toward the outside.

A kid? "Damn it," Kat spat, getting to her feet.

But Mason hurdled past her. "I've got her!"

Kat let him go. He needed to be the one to save her—to ease his guilt for pushing her away.

"Kat, left!" Griffin called. Kat took a step left and turned. His blade whizzed past her face, and she looked at him, eyes wide. He had never missed a throw that badly. But instead of Griffin, Kat met Izz's amused smile.

25

AERON

*A*eron tucked the knife into her belt and sprinted back outside, Barnes already at the rear of the building. Her side hitched, and she ran faster, stopping at the corner of the building to look for Barnes. He leaned over Oliver, trying to rouse him, the keys already in his hands. Fuck. She kept her feet quiet as she crossed the open space between the building and the car.

"Come on, Ollie. I didn't hit you that hard," Barnes said, and she let her feet move faster, ducking behind the black sedan. Peering into the rear window, Cass remained huddled on the floor. Smart kid. She pulled the door handle, but it was locked.

Aeron knocked softly on the window and pulled Cass' eyes up. She pointed to the door handle. He didn't move. *Please,* she mouthed, smiling and waving him closer. The fear in his eyes remained, but he moved, ever so slowly, to the door and pulled the handle. It didn't budge. He unlocked it, and Aeron tried to open the door again, but it remained stuck. Fucking Oliver. She held up a finger and pressed it to her lips.

A shot echoed through the air, and Aeron crouched down, heart lurching to her throat as she scanned for the threat. Movement by the building called her—Mason—pressed behind the wall, eyes bouncing between her and Barnes.

I'll cover you, he signed.

No, she signed back. *They have a kid in here.*

He dropped his head back, and she didn't need to see his face to know a look of anger passed over it. The wall beside him exploded, and he retreated a few steps. Aeron dared a glance over at the car. Barnes pulled Oliver to his feet, his gun aimed at Mason. "Leave him," Oliver said. "Is the boy still in the car?"

Barnes looked back. Aeron didn't drop fast enough, his gaze narrowing at her. He shifted his aim and fired. "Drop!" she yelled at Cass, and she followed her own command. The crunch of bulletproof glass reached her ears, and she spun on her knees, peering into the car. Cass hadn't dropped. He sat frozen, staring at the distorted window, mouth open in a silent scream.

"Stop firing!" Oliver ordered. "Get him out of there."

Aeron slunk lower as the car door opened, and Cass' scream hit the near-silent night air. "Shut the fuck up, kid," Barnes said. Aeron's face contorted in rage, and she pulled out Rufus' blade. She moved to the driver's door, looking through the window at them. Barnes held Cass tight to his body, the gun hovering above his head. Cass' breath rose in puffs of fog, his whimpers tearing at Aeron's heart.

"I hate it has to come to this, Aeron. Hands up and come around the front of the car," Oliver ordered. He straightened out his suit, rolling his head from left to right, and picked his weapon up from near his feet, waving her forward with it.

"Alright," she said. "I'm coming out—don't shoot me."

"Oh, now you *don't* want to be shot," Barnes said. She stood, his look of hatred burning into her from across the parking lot. "More of a reason to do so."

"Shut up," Aeron said. "I'll make you a deal, Oliver. I'll come willingly if I can kill him." She nodded her head at Barnes and rounded the car, not daring a glance at Mason. He wouldn't take a shot now. They had Cass in the line of fire—and Kat said they needed Barnes alive. She'd said nothing about Oliver, though.

"You are not the first person to make that offer," Oliver said with a chuckle.

"Maybe that should tell you something," Aeron said.

"Do you have any idea what you've done?" Oliver asked.

"Hey, you're the one who kidnapped me. If you can't take the heat, stay out of hell." She flicked her wrist. The blade snapped back and then sailed forward. She dove for Cass, not looking to see if the knife landed where she intended, wrapping her arms around the boy and barrel-rolling to the side. The world around her spun as she landed hard on her shoulder. She pushed through, landing on top of Cass, covering his body with hers. Fingers dug into her gunshot wound, and the world darkened around her. The ground disappeared from beneath her as Cass was ripped from her grip. "No!" she screamed. More shots went off. Aeron struggled against the person holding her. They let go, and Aeron landed on a semi-soft surface. She forced her eyes open in time to see Barnes smile before he slammed the trunk shut.

26

IZZ

"Sorry about that," Izz said, staring at Kat.

Kat's gaze dropped from her to the Reaper kneeling beneath the barrel of Izz's gun. Blood seeped down his thigh, staining the floor, his hands raised in surrender. If she had any idea Mason would be here, she would have called.

Rufus laughed, rolling his neck and shoulders. Blood streamed down his face from Griffin's work. He'd have scars to match Maureen's—almost. "Perfect timing, as always," he said.

"Shut up," Izz said to him, lip curling. "We're leaving." Izz gestured to Rufus and to herself.

Izz could feel the wrath rolling off of Katherine. "No. I need him."

"Unfortunately, so do I," Izz said. "Let's go."

Rufus shook his head. "Not without Red." He took a step toward Katherine, and Izz reached behind her, pulling out her secondary piece. "You either come with me, or I shoot you right now."

"You won't—you need me," Rufus said.

Izz made a vomiting sound. "It's a matter of convenience for me. If I drop you now, it wouldn't matter," Izz lied. "Or I'll leave you for Mason to play with. Your choice."

His face darkened. "Fuck Mason," he nearly growled. Kat stepped backward, pulling Rufus' attention.

Before Izz could say anything, Rufus latched on to her, his bloody hand wrapping around Katherine's neck, his tongue darting out and licking her face. Izz was really going to vomit now. Motherfucker. She needed Rufus out of here before Mason came back and saw her. Griffin moved too, but Izz struck the pistol hard to the nape of his neck. He dropped to all fours.

She leaned over him so he wouldn't miss a word, keeping pressure on his head. "This is the last time I save you, Reaper."

"I didn't need your fucking help."

She gave a small laugh. "Didn't you? Now, I know where your loyalty lies—but if you think Maureen won't use this to try to break her, you haven't been paying attention." He nodded, eyes downcast.

A scream pulled Izz's focus. Rufus had Kat pinned against the metal column, blood smearing her neck as he squeezed her throat. Her eyes bulged, face red from the restricted blood flow. Rufus' other hand held a knife, tracing its way around her body. "He won't hurt her," Izz said. "I promise. Be a good boy and stay down." She rubbed his head affectionately as she pushed herself up and stepped forward. She jammed the gun right between Rufus' ass cheeks, and he stilled.

"No, I'm not happy to see you," she said. Rufus' hand relented on Kat's throat, her color returning to normal. Izz plucked the blade from his fingers. "We have an appointment with the boss lady, and you know how I don't like to disappoint her." A growl left him, and Izz rolled her eyes.

"I'm not done with you, Red," Rufus said, stepping away from Kat. She dropped to her knees, and Izz looked back at Griffin. He glared, but didn't move. Good boy. Izz blew him a kiss. "Get that fucking thing out of my ass!" Rufus spat.

Izz laughed. "Is that what you said last time?" she joked, pulling the assaulting object back so he could move. "C'mon. I'm parked out front." They ran for the front door, Izz taking stock of the bodies across the floor: two dead and three restrained. Kat would have plenty to funnel her anger through, and she wondered, did Kat play with her prey the way Maureen did?

"Izz!"

Izz looked over her shoulder. Mason sprinted from the other door, a hunger in his eyes that sparked a healthy dose of fear in her. Shit. "Go," she said to Rufus, covering him as he crossed the threshold. Mason aimed, but she fired first. He spun off course, blood exploding from his arm. And she bit back her apology.

"Come on," Rufus called.

She backed toward the exit, eyes on Mason. He took his shot from his knees; the bullet grazed her cheek. Her hand flew to her face, and she stumbled back. Rufus caught her and dragged her from the building, but not before Izz saw a look of hatred cross Mason's face. She swallowed hard. "Let's go."

The side of the building was free of people, except for the guard laid out on the sidewalk beside his brains. Rufus slammed the door on the passenger side, and Izz peeled out of the parking lot. A scream left him, and he slammed his fist against the dashboard, blood from his injured hand splattering across the car. He opened and closed his fingers, the flesh across the backs of his digits split almost to the bone.

She let him rage and ran her fingers across her cheek again, the skin burning. Was that a warning shot? Or had he simply missed? She glared over at Rufus. She'd only ever seen that look cross Mason's face when they spoke of him.

"You done?" she asked. "There are napkins and tape in the glove compartment. Wrap those things up."

Rufus rummaged through the glove compartment, pulling out a stack of napkins and duct tape. "I had her," he said, wrapping his fingers in the brown napkins. He grabbed the duct tape with his teeth and pulled, the sound filling the car, and wound the tape around his hand. "Fuck. Izz, she tasted so good." He ran his no longer dripping hand over his crotch, head falling back. "Her screams are the sweetest you will ever hear."

Izz hid the chill seeping through her body. She hated this monster. He gave Izz the worst kind of ick. But he'd taken a liking to her in a way that she nor Mason could explain, and they ran with it. Her chest constricted. Mason had never looked at her like that before, and she had to fight the urge to pull out her phone and call him. Explain to him. But she needed to find the truth about Storm first. And quick, before Mason killed her.

"You are disgusting," Izz said.

"I know." He shoved the bloodied duct tape back into the glove compartment and closed it.

"What do you know about Storm's disappearance?" Izz said, cutting straight to the chase.

Rufus laughed beside her. "I'm hungry."

"And I'm fucking horny. I guess we're all a bit unsatisfied tonight."

"I can—"

"Finish that sentence and I'll crash this goddamn car."

He laughed. "Hale delivered Katherine to me for that information, and you just took my prize from under my fingers—literally."

"Who else were you all trading for funsies tonight?"

"Doesn't matter."

"Matters to me," Izz said. He didn't answer. "Why are you so fixated on her? I could deliver you a hundred Katherines."

"Because Rosemary had promised her to me—I've waited years."

Izz licked her lips. Once Rufus had a scent, nothing strayed him from it. If Rosemary had been dangling Katherine for that long—no wonder he'd been so wound up. But he'd gotten a taste, and seemed pretty positive there would be another, since this was the calmest she'd seen him in years. But a beast in heat was easy to trick.

"Is Storm alive?" Izz asked. Information could be anything from the last person to see her to her corpse in a ditch.

He shrugged.

"This isn't fuck around season," Izz said. "What do you want in exchange for the information?"

"Katherine is non-negotiable," he said. "And I want Hale and Mike's heads."

Izz nodded. She couldn't deliver Katherine, but thanks to Derek, she knew where Hale would be. "I can give you Hale and Barnes. And if your information on Storm checks out, I guarantee Mason will hand-deliver Katherine to you."

The smile she caught on his face in the passing streetlights would give her nightmares. She waited while he thought it over, counting all the ways Mason and Maureen would kill her for doing this. How she would throw herself off a building for doing this. But there was no other option. Torture didn't work on him and if she wanted Rufus to give up the information on Storm, he needed to feel in charge.

"Agreed," Rufus said. "Now I need to eat, or I need to kill. You left me completely unsatisfied and I'm not responsible for what happens if one of those urges isn't met."

"Ugh, fine." The bright lights of a shopping center glowed in the distance. She sped up and flicked on the blinker. "Chicken or burgers?"

27

KAT

$\mathcal{F}$uck.

Kat fell to her hands and knees, gasping for air. She dropped her head to the ground, trying to catch her breath.

"Kat?" Griffin scrambled toward her, his hand touching her shoulder. Her entire body cringed at his touch, and she shoved him off.

"Don't touch me," she said, and sat back, leaning against the metal support.

"Babe." He moved his gaze over her, face darkening as it landed on her throat. "Oh, no," he whispered and reached out, but Kat jerked back again. A flash of hurt crossed his face, but he didn't push. Every inch of skin crawled from Rufus' mouth on her. She brought a hand to her raw neck, the ghost of his hand still there.

"What happened?" she asked, her voice coming out hoarse, vocal cords protesting their use.

He raked his hand through his hair. "I didn't see her coming."

"Since when is that a problem for you?" she snapped. He opened his mouth to answer, but Mason's shout interrupted them.

"Izz!"

Griffin closed his mouth, tilting his head. A shot echoed in the near-silent room, followed by a yell of pain from Mason.

Griffin jolted to his feet, gun drawn, holding a finger out for her to wait. Her chest continued to heave. Another shot, this one muffled, and then Griffin shook his head. "They're gone. Can you stand?"

Kat pushed herself up, refusing his help, and rounded the barrier. Mason grasped his arm, blood pouring down his fingers. He slid off his jacket, the wound looking like a through and through, and then slid it back on.

"Still think Maureen isn't involved?" she asked, fighting against the tearing sensation in her throat. "Fuck! Where's Aeron?"

"Barnes and Hale grabbed her before I could get there," Mason said. "I told Dom to start tracking them if he can."

"Great. So we lost Aeron, Mike, and Rufus."

"Well, we've got these guys," Griffin said. He'd grabbed two of the unconscious Hale guards by the top of their vests. "I've always wanted to play in the Interrogation rooms below the Institute." He shot her a wicked smile, but she couldn't return it. "Are we taking a car or. . ."

"No," Kat said. "We don't need to worry about Hale tracking us." He nodded and dragged the two bodies to the bay door. She pressed her com. "Dom. Bring the car around. We gotta go."

Mason grabbed the other unconscious body and dragged them over, a wound in the man's leg leaving a trail of blood along the way. The sight reminded Kat of her mother, Rosemary. She would torture them until they told her how often Mike and Oliver liked to take a shit. The thought lowered her heart rate.

She surveyed the area, looking for any information. The room was mostly empty. On the floor near the card table, she saw a cell phone and picked it up. "Check the cars," Kat said, flipping it open. This was Aeron's cell phone. She pocketed it and joined Mason at the SUV. "Anything?"

"It's clean," Mason said. Kat cupped the nape of her neck and dropped her head back, the pain in her throat increasing by the second. When she looked back down, Mason's eyes narrowed and he reached for her. She pulled away, and he kept his hand out. "What happened?" He reached again, eyes full of concern, and she let his light fingers grab her chin, turning her head from side to side.

"Rufus."

"I broke my promise," he said, frowning. "I'm sorry."

"I think Griffin broke his first," she said. The sound of sirens reached the warehouse, and Mason released her chin. They readied their weapons and moved to the bay door, tucking behind the wall as the sound of wheels speeding on the asphalt met them. Damn it. Hale must have called it in. Didn't matter. She would kill every last responder if she had to. But it was Dom. He skidded to a stop and jumped out of the car. "I rerouted their alerts, but they'll be here any minute!"

They each grabbed a hostage and heaved them into the rear of the SUV, and then piled inside, Mason taking the wheel, Kat in the seat beside him. The flashing lights of the police cars approached, and Mason slowed as they raced past. Kat held her breath until the lights were out of their rearview mirror.

"Well, that was a shit show," she said, resting her back on the seat and closing her eyes. She propped her hand on the top of her head, the pain in her tricep not nearly as bad as she expected. Or maybe the pain from Rufus was just fresher. The ghost of his grip on her throat still held tight, the image of Griffin on his knees seared into her mind. She turned around, adjusting in the passenger seat. Griffin's arms were crossed, his head tipped back, eyes closed, but she could see the flex of his jaw as he ran the night over too. "How did Izz do it?" she asked.

He opened his eyes, giving her a hooded look. "Get Rufus to heel?" he asked.

"No," Kat said. "Get you to."

He sat up straighter. "I told you—I didn't see her coming."

She shook her head. "What did she say to you?"

"Nothing," he answered.

"Don't fucking lie to me. She said something to you," Kat countered. "Right before she shoved the gun up Rufus' ass."

Griffin's eyes flicked to Mason. Kat glanced over as a look passed between the two of them, the kind Perry and she had shared on many occasions when they spoke in code. "What am I missing?" she asked.

"Nothing," Griffin said. "She said it was the last time she was saving us."

Kat narrowed her eyes. "Bullshit."

"Kat—"

"You have to tell her," Mason cut in.

Tell her what? The energy in the car shifted, a vice grip wrapping itself around Kat's chest. She unholstered her Sig, checked the rounds, and pointed it at Griffin. "Tell me what?"

Dom squeaked beside Griffin and pushed himself against the door. Kat glared at him until he fell silent.

Griffin heaved a sigh, pain crossing his face when he met her gaze. "It's. . ."

"If you don't tell her, I will," Mason said. "With Izz doing god knows what with Rufus—it's time."

"Tell me fucking what?"

"Kat, it's not what you think," Griffin said.

"I'm not thinking anything, except somehow Izz got the drop on you, and you let that fucker get his hands on me." Her skin burned with the thought. She didn't think a hundred showers or even a vat of acid would remove the feeling of his tongue on her.

"I knew she would help us."

"She just stabbed you in the leg," Kat said. "She's working with Maureen."

"I know, but she promised she'd keep you safe."

Kat scoffed. What alternate timeline did she step into?

"Griffin," Mason said, warning in his voice.

"Fine. But you have to believe me," he said, eyes pleading with her. "I love you. My loyalty is to you."

Kat pressed her lips together, not lowering the gun. "Why would anyone think it wasn't?"

"Me being in your life isn't an accident," he said. "After my parents were killed, I was scooped up by a woman who promised to keep me safe if I made a promise, too. There was a girl who needed a friend—a protector."

Pressure formed between her eyes, and she frowned. Another lie. Everything in her life except Shay had been a lie. She shook her head. "No."

"I was seven and terrified. Once a year, she would find me and ask how it was going. There were no ultimatums or threats, Kat. Just a simple 'are you still friends? Is she safe?' I didn't even know who she was. And then she stopped showing up for a few years. And I forgot all about her until a dark-skinned woman showed up one day, asking the same questions. I never saw the first woman again—until she stepped into your office the other night. I didn't even know it was her until she asked how her Katherine was doing."

Kat looked at Mason. "You planted him in my life?"

He shook his head. "Maureen did. I had no clue until later. The intention was to make sure you were never alone, afraid Rosemary would isolate you. After her car accident, Izz took over, and I learned what she'd done. Izz and I did our best to stay out of your way. It was clear by then you didn't need protection."

Kat lowered the gun, gears turning in her head as she looked back at Griffin. "Maureen planted you in my life."

Griffin leaned forward, pleading in his voice. "It doesn't matter—"

"It does matter," Kat said. "Because she thinks she has a pawn to use." Which meant Kat had a pawn to use.

He shook his head and closed the distance, reaching around the headrest for her face. "Babe."

Kat leaned into his touch, bringing her hand to his. The feel of Rufus washed away, and she closed her eyes, letting Griffin's warmth run through her. She slid her fingertips under the pads of his, then grasped his middle finger and ripped it backward, peeling his hand from her face. He snatched it away.

"Goddman, Kat!"

"I thought we were done with the lying to each other," she said, a mixture of anger and understanding swirling inside her. Did it really matter how they ended up here? He brought a peace nothing in this shitty fucking world could touch. But if she couldn't trust him?

"The only thing she did," Griffin said, his hands safely in his lap, "is hand-pick the man who will deliver her head to you on a silver platter."

He leaned toward her again, their lips now inches apart, his eyes begging her to believe him. There was too much history to untangle right now—too many lies to categorize while they fought for their lives. But she knew he loved her, and that would need to be enough. "I know. But if you ever put my safety into the hands of someone else again," Kat whispered. "I will fucking castrate you."

She felt his lips twitch into a smile as he closed the distance to her lips, the kiss soft.

"I'm sorry," he said again and sat back.

Kat reholstered her gun and glanced at Dom. He had pushed himself against the car door, eyes glued on the tablets. "Anything good, Dom?" she asked.

"I lost track of the car that had Aeron in it," he said. "But I have a clear follow on Spike and the Devil at the moment." He turned the tablet around and held it out to her. She accepted it, the GPS showing the pair heading south.

"You've been holding back," Kat said to Mason. "Izz and Rufus?"

He sighed. "The only person Rufus feared more than your granddad is Maureen. When she faked her death and Izz stepped in, he took a strange liking to her. He listens to her. I don't know why—but if Izz asked him to strip naked and jerk off in the middle of winter, I'm pretty sure he would."

"Ew," Kat said.

"So, is Rufus working with Hale or Maureen?" Griffin asked.

"That is an excellent question," Mason said.

Dom's phone chimed in his pocket, and he pulled it out. "It's Ivan. Hello?" He pulled the phone away from his ear and held it out to Kat. She took it.

"Ivan?" A loud alarm sounded, and she pulled the phone back. "Ivan!" she said louder.

"The reapers!" He yelled into the phone. "They've been—the vault in transport!"

"What?" Kat said. "What is that alarm?"

"Hold on!" It took a few moments, but the alarm ceased. She put the phone back to her ear. "Sorry. I didn't know it would be that loud," he said. "The reapers—they were hit in transit. The vault's gone."

28

AERON

*A*eron pressed her eyes closed, bracing against the inside of the trunk. The car took several harsh turns, each one sending a fresh wave of nausea through her as she rolled onto her shoulder. The road finally evened out, the speed picking up as if they were on a highway. Aeron released a long breath. She felt around the pitch-black area, searching for anything she could use as a weapon, or for an emergency latch—although she knew there wouldn't be one. This was a customized car, bulletproofed, and hostage-proofed if she had to guess.

She let out a scream of frustration. Was Cass in the car? Was he okay? Was Mason following them? There was no telling how long she would be trapped in here. Could be minutes, could be days. She laced her fingers together and laid them across her stomach, trying to claw through the fog sinking into her mind, the image of Cass the only thing she could focus on. The blood wasn't his—so his mother's? Someone else's? The uniform he wore screamed expensive private school, maybe even boarding school. Aeron shook her head, another round of nausea coming over her, and she couldn't be sure if it was from the terrible driving, or the cocktail she was ninety percent sure was frying her brain.

Aeron estimated they drove for at least forty minutes before the car decelerated. She adjusted her position, rotating so her feet would be the first thing Mike Barnes saw. The car stopped, and her stomach fluttered with nerves. She strained to hear sounds from outside—but it was silent—soundproofed. She braced on the back of the trunk, her feet ready to strike, and bit her lip, ears ringing in the silence. After what felt like hours, a soft click echoed in the space. She coiled her leg, eyes squinting against the sudden light to see her target. She struck as soon as there was enough space and kicked the figure back. Launching herself out of the car, Aeron landed in a crouch, glaring at Barnes. A quick sweep around the three-car garage confirmed they were alone.

"You should have killed me," Aeron said.

He pulled out his gun. "What makes you think I won't?"

She smirked and lunged again, pure adrenaline fueling her past the pain. Her hands cupped his outstretched hand. She snapped it first left then right, the sound of his carpal bones crunching bringing her a rush of pleasure. The gun slid into her hands. She racked it back, the round in the chamber flying aside, and fired. His scream filled the air as the bullet pierced his leg. Kat had said they couldn't kill him, she said nothing about maiming.

"Stop!" Aeron's finger paused on the trigger before she could pull it again, eyes not straying from Barnes, but he hadn't been the one to yell. "That's enough, Aeron."

She looked over her shoulder. Oliver stood in the doorway to a house, one hand resting on the back of Cass' neck, a pistol in the other. Cass' wide eyes met her, and she tried to give him a smile. He stood frozen, his face clean and wearing a pair of red flannel pajamas with bare feet. "Are you okay, Cass?" she asked. He gave a small nod, and Aeron nodded too.

"You're probably hungry," Oliver said. "Why don't you come inside?"

She raised an eyebrow at him and then looked back at Barnes.

He sat on the floor, applying pressure to his leg. She had just shot, what she assumed to be, Oliver's second in command, and he was treating her like an honored house guest. She looked between the two men, Oliver waiting patiently, his gun too close to Cass for her liking, and back to Barnes, staring daggers at her.

Aeron ejected the magazine, expelling the cartridges across the floor, the silence filling with metal pings as they bounced on the concrete. She disassembled the gun, tossed the pieces around the room, and then glared at Barnes. "Was that a better fight for you?" she asked. He didn't say anything, his lips pressed together to keep his howl of pain in, but if looks could kill. . . She laughed and turned toward Oliver, sliding her left hand into her hoodie pocket, swallowing back the pain. "I could use some food."

He regarded her with curiosity and stepped aside for her to pass. He released Cass' neck, and Aeron reached for him with her right hand. Tentatively, Cass grabbed on. She gave his hand a small squeeze, and they stepped into a massive kitchen. An island with a gas stove on one side and seating on the other was the main focus. To the right, the room opened into a living area, with a wrap-around couch, a fireplace, and large windows overlooking a back patio. Frost and condensation obscured most of the view. To the left, a hallway with a guard on post at the end.

"Are you just going to let him bleed out?" Aeron asked.

Oliver shook his head and pulled out a walkie-talkie. "George?"

"Yes, sir?"

"Barnes is in need of some assistance in the garage."

"Uh—sure. What kind?"

"Non-lethal gunshot to the leg."

Aeron's lips twitched. "How do you know it's non-lethal?"

"You would have aimed for his head if you wanted him dead," Oliver said.

"You're not mad at me for shooting your friend?"

"We had a bet going on," Oliver said with a shrug. "I bet you would shoot him with his own weapon if he didn't stop antagonizing you, and he bet the only way that would happen was if you pried the gun from his cold-dead fingers and shot his corpse. I bet he's real glad I won this one."

"You're punishing him for knocking you out," Aeron said. She pulled out a chair for Cass at the counter and took a seat beside him.

"That," Oliver said, "and you're family. Grilled cheese and soup?"

His words caught her off guard. "What?"

"To eat? It's really all I know how to cook." Aeron gave a half laugh. This man was making her grilled cheese and soup? "What's so funny?"

"You're not going to lock me up?" she asked. "Hide the knives?" She gestured to the butcher's block on the counter beside the fridge.

"Would that stop you from trying to kill me?" He rolled up his sleeves, grabbed two mugs from the cabinet, and filled them with water from the fridge. He placed them down on the counter.

"No," she said. Footsteps reached her ears, and Aeron leaned sideways. A man in jeans, a blue-threaded sweater, and a medical bag hurried down the hall. He glanced at them, nodded at Oliver, and then exited into the garage. A muffled scream sounded a few moments later, and Cass jumped.

"It's okay," Aeron said, pushing the water toward Cass. "Take a drink." He took a sip and then downed the entire cup. Aeron followed suit, the warm water sending nourishment throughout her body. She regarded Oliver in the light—her family. It didn't sound right.

"I don't think you'll do anything to put our young friend at risk," he said. "Besides. I have eighteen guards on this property, and in your condition, you can't fight them all."

Her condition. What could he possibly know about her condition—she didn't even know much about it. But she was feeling better. More like herself. Sure, her shoulder throbbed, and the occasional brain fog crept in, and the nausea. But she hadn't really eaten since she died—hadn't had the will to do much of anything other than sit in the loneliness. In her grief. She took another sip of water and looked at Cass, nodding for him to answer.

"Can I have two grilled cheeses?" he asked.

Oliver smiled at him. "Two grilled cheeses coming up. Aeron?"

She opened her mouth to answer and then snapped it closed, heart thumping in her chest. How did he do that? Make her feel so at ease? Let her guard fall. He could be poisoning them. Or just luring them into a false sense of security.

"Aeron?" Cass said. She shifted her gaze to him and spied the fear still on the edges of his posture, his hand resting in hers again. Oliver was right. She wasn't going to fight her way out of here—and she wasn't leaving Cass behind. But she needed to be careful. Oliver could turn out to be more dangerous than any threat she'd faced before.

"I'll have the same, and chicken soup if you have it."

Aeron wrapped the blue fluffy towel around herself and wiped the fog from the mirror. She leaned in, examining the hair at the crown of her head, hand running over the now shorter section. Grabbing onto a smaller curl, Aeron stretched it out. It was inches shorter than the rest of her hair, reaching only to her cheeks instead of her shoulders. When she let go, it coiled back up, tighter than the rest. Fucking Rufus. She grabbed her hair with her good hand and wound it until it coiled on itself into a bun. She tucked the ends in and then did her best to secure it single-handed with an elastic. It was loose, but it would do.

Oliver had put her in one of the seven guest rooms on the third floor of his oversized home, across the hall from Cass. She could shower, eat, and watch tv at her leisure. She would just have round-the-clock guards who kept their fingers on the trigger of their semi-automatic rifles.

The wound in her shoulder smelled infected. The surrounding skin was red and swollen, and a yellow discharge oozed from the crusted scab around the staples. She tried lifting her left arm, but it wouldn't budge. Her adrenaline did its job to save her, and now she was left with a useless limb. She grabbed her arm, trying to move it, and a cry broke from her. She let go, gripping the counter. Fuck. How would she be able to get her and Cass out of here?

She moved into the bedroom, opening and closing the dresser drawers, looking for clothes. She found a pair of pajama pants that matched Cass', and a black tank top. Her arm wouldn't cooperate, so she slipped her limp limb into the hole first and then pulled the garment over her head. A thin layer of sweat already formed on her forehead from the effort. For fuck's sakes. She needed something for the pain. A quick search of the room turned up zero meds. The antibiotics he'd given her probably lay abandoned in the back of the warehouse, or inside the trunk.

The room was a decent size. A queen bed in the middle, a cafe-style table and chairs near the window, and a small writing desk by the door to the private bathroom. The bed called for her, but she sat on the hard desk chair instead, swirling from side to side. Oliver said he had eighteen guards strapped for war and patrolling the property. Surely this wasn't all for her. Hell, if someone so much as bumped into her, she might collapse from the pain. So, what did Oliver have here that was so important? Or plan to have here? She leaned back in the stiff chair, dropping her head back. She needed schematics of the house, their location, and a working freaking appendage. A knock pulled her gaze to the door.

"Come in," Aeron said, too tired to get up.

The door swung open. George, still in his sweater, waved. "Oliver said you may need some assistance."

Aeron straightened up and nodded. He was sending his medic in? Her guard instantly raised. "How's Barnes?" she asked.

George's face revealed nothing. "He'll live." He left the door open when he entered. "What seems to be the issue? Oliver wasn't specific."

She spun in the chair toward him, and his eyes widened. The small part of her that thought she would be okay disappeared when he said nothing as he came closer. He dropped the medical bag, pulled out a pair of gloves, and put them on. Aeron clenched her good fist, a hiss of pain passing through her lips as he prodded the area. The discharge seeped out of the wound, and she looked away. He grabbed her wrist, slowly testing her mobility. Her vision tunneled. "Please, stop," she said between clenched teeth.

He grimaced and lowered the arm back down. "When did you get this?"

"A week ago?" Aeron wasn't sure how long it had been. The days all seemed to melt into each other like an endless nightmare.

"And when did you stop having full mobility?"

"Today."

He sat back on his heels and stripped the gloves off. "Did they take the bullet out?" Aeron blinked at him. Did they take the bullet out? She hadn't a clue. "How did they treat it?"

"I'm not sure," she admitted, her cheeks heating.

"Well, we'll need to remove the staples, clean the wound and re-secure it. Then I can start you on a slew of medicine, but first I'll need to see if the bullet is still in there before we do anything else."

"Aeron?" Cass' small voice called from the hallway. Aeron leaned around George. Cass' head peeked in the doorway. "Can I sleep in here tonight?" He hovered at the threshold, large brown eyes wide as they moved from her to George.

"Yeah buddy," Aeron said. "C'mon in. Dr. George is just checking my arm."

"What happened?" he asked.

"I died," she said, "but it didn't take." Lying to him wouldn't protect him, and he'd been with Rufus—who knew what the boy had already experienced. The thought pulled the Legacy kids to her mind, followed by Luke's haunting expression. A shiver ran down her spine and she shook the thought away, swallowing back the lump of emotion building in her throat. "Come here."

Cass moved closer and leaned into her. George quirked an eyebrow. "You didn't mention that you died."

"It's happened a few times," Aeron said. "It's hard to keep track. Are we handling this tonight?"

"I'm afraid if we don't, the damage will be irreparable."

Aeron nodded. "Hey Cass, do you like to play cards?"

"Sure," he said, stepping back. "I play blackjack, poker, spades."

Aeron's lips quirked. "Have you ever played war?"

It took three hours, five rounds of war, and all the self-control Aeron could muster to not curse George to hell at the top of her lungs as he worked on her shoulder. She missed the Institute and their top-notch medical. There were no LidoPen or pain blockers here, and George apologized profusely as he retrieved what bullet fragments he could while she glared at him.

Cass now lay on the bed beside her, tucked under her good arm, the other in a sling. The bathroom light slipped in from the cracked door, brightening the room for him. Her pain was down to manageable, and the sickly smell of infection no longer seeped from the wound. "Do you think my mom can come back from the dead, too?" Cass asked.

Her stomach flipped, kicking herself for her phrasing. "What happened to her?"

He shrugged. "I don't know. There was screaming, and a lot of blood. And then that man, the big scary one, dragged me away."

"Did he hurt you?" Aeron asked, already formulating all the ways she would help Kat dismember him. But to her surprise, Cass shook his head. They fell into silence until Cass' soft snores filled the room. Her stomach growled and she pulled herself out from underneath him to sit up. The world didn't spin, and she released a long breath before standing. The guards jerked to attention when she opened the door, one of them raising his rifle. "I'm going to get a snack," she said and walked past them. She heard the exchange of who was going to stay with Cass and who was going to follow her, and she smirked.

She built the map of the house as she walked, counting her pacing and peering down halls. She intentionally took the wrong turn, walking halfway down the hallway, deaf to the guard calling her back. They weren't going to shoot her unless she became a threat. But a disoriented woman—they would just yell and threaten. The kitchen lights were on downstairs, and unsurprisingly, both Oliver and Barnes were sitting at the breakfast bar. She caught a few words from Barnes before they spotted her. "Alexis sent word—Derek's dead. Tortured."

"Shit," Oliver said, the disappointment laced through the word. "Send Rufus a message, and we'll see if he responds, then have George ready him for transport."

Barnes lifted his gun with his left hand when she fully entered the room, as his right one was in a splint. "What do you want?"

"Food," she said, and continued her trek to the pantry. "And answers." She tucked the information away. Was Alexis working for Oliver? Aeron knew she hated that girl. She opened the pantry door, scanning the shelves. "Where do you keep your peanut butter?"

"Fridge," Oliver said.

Aeron quirked her eyebrow. That was where she kept hers, too.

She retrieved the peanut butter and strawberry jam from the fridge, and the bread from the counter. She pulled out two slices and reached for a butter knife in the dish rack.

"Don't even think about it," Barnes said. Aeron's hand hovered over the utensils, and she looked up. His gun was still on her. "Use the spoon."

Aeron tried to hold back her smile but failed. She gingerly, with two fingers, picked up the spoon and waggled it in the air. "This is just as deadly in my hands," she said and laid it next to the bread.

"Would you like a hand with that?" Oliver asked. Before she could answer, he rounded the island. He opened the jars and used the spoon to spread the jam and peanut butter on the bread for her. He grabbed a plate from the cupboard and put it down in front of the space beside him. "Have a seat."

Her appetite waned, but she sat anyway. "How do I know you're telling the truth about my mother?" she asked. "About who she is? I'm not doubting she killed your family." She took a bite of the sandwich. "She's a wretched person."

"She wasn't always," Oliver said. "She was actually a really sweet child. Wanted to be on Broadway, and was the most beautiful ballerina." He pulled out his phone, scrolling until he found what he was looking for. "See."

Aeron took another bite of the sandwich and looked over. It was a picture of a young ballerina on stage and a slightly older boy, around Cass' age, giving a standing ovation, the pride clear on his young face.

"I was her biggest fan." Oliver pulled the phone back. "That all changed when she moved to New York. Francis Wayward sunk his claws into her and turned her against her family."

Francis Wayward? Aeron racked her brain, the name seemingly just out of her reach. Francis. . . Luke's great-granddad. She shook her head, a headache forming behind her eyes as it did now whenever she tried to concentrate too hard. "That's just a picture of some kids," Aeron countered. "It proves nothing."

He held up the phone and snapped a selfie with her in the background.

"Hey!" she said, the violation of her picture being taken washing over her.

"Let's see what she thinks about her big brother and her last remaining heir hanging out."

Aeron scoffed. "Again—proves nothing." She finished her sandwich in silence, feeling better than she had in days. She brought the plate to the sink and grabbed a bottle of water from the fridge. It felt so normal, like this was any other safe house. But it wasn't—she wasn't free to leave. "Thanks for the sandwich," she said.

Oliver nodded. "Why did Katherine Wayward come to your rescue? Mason, I expected. But when Rufus said Katherine would be on the way for you. . ."

"We both have a vested interest in stopping Maureen," Aeron said. "And shutting down the hit list." She shot a look at Barnes. "You wouldn't know anything about that, would you?"

Barnes looked up from the laptop. "What is it worth to you?"

"Barnes—"

"No, I'll play," Aeron said. If she could get Barnes to shut down the hit list—even if they never let her go, Katherine and Betty would be free. "What do you want?"

Barnes and Oliver exchanged a look, and Oliver answered. "It's more what we need. Rufus has the location of a very important asset."

"Cass' mom," Aeron said.

"Yes. And he will only give the information in exchange for Katherine," Barnes said.

"Who is she?" Aeron asked.

"Not your concern," Oliver said. "Now, we saw on traffic cams that Katherine and Mason made it out of the warehouse. But Rufus left with someone else."

A wave of relief washed through her. They'd made it out. "Who did Rufus leave with?"

Barnes turned the computer around. "Recognize her?"

Hatred pulsed through her body. "That's Izz. My mother's right hand. Which means if you want Rufus, you'll have to go through her now."

"Fuck," Barnes said, turning the screen back around.

Aeron leaned against the counter. "What's your end goal, Oliver? Because from where I'm standing, you're fumbling, and fumbling hard. You lost your leverage with Rufus and all chances of saving Cass' mom. You're on Katherine's radar now—I promise you, that is a shitty place to be. And Maureen—well, you already know how dangerous she is, and if you have been in contact with my mother, you put a big shiny target on your back by letting her know you know she's alive. I know you were banking on having Cass' mom in hand, but you counted your chickens too early and dropped the fucking basket."

"Thank you for putting that so eloquently," Oliver said as he removed his glasses to pinch the bridge of his nose.

"Look, you seem like a decent guy. I don't know many other people who cook for their hostages and give them mid-tier medical care. But you are out of your depth here. With me, with these people," Aeron said. She took another sip of water, and he slid his glasses back into place. "Shut down the hit list, and I'll call Katherine right now. I'll tell her everything, show her you are the good guys, and we go after Maureen together, before Maureen gets her hands on Cass' mom. I get the feeling that is a bad place for her to be."

They exchanged a look, and Aeron grasped the counter. Her head swam, and she took another sip of water. The dizzy spells were becoming more frequent.

"Sir?"

She glanced toward the hall, George stepping into the kitchen. He looked exhausted, dark bags beneath his eyes. His gaze landed on her. "Aeron—you really need to be resting." She nodded, his sincerity both nice and unsettling. She didn't know what Oliver's true end game was, but if she could get him to believe that she believed him, then she was one step closer to getting her and Cass out of there. George turned to Oliver. "Shay's awake."

Aeron's ears perked up. Were they talking about Dr. Shea? George did a good job on her arm, but it was the vial from Dr. Jones that worried her the most, and possibly right up Dr. Shea's alley. But the familiar feeling of something just out of her reach Shea. . . Shea. . . Ivan had said something about an asset—Kat's asset.

Oliver's entire demeanor shifted, face darkening as he slid his phone into his pocket, eyes on Aeron. "I'm afraid it may be too late to take you up on that offer," he said, standing. "You two try not to kill each other. And Aeron? Make yourself at home."

29

KAT

"What do you mean, the vault is gone?" Kat said. Mason shot a glance at her, and she put Ivan on speakerphone.

"They were hijacked on the way to the warehouse. I got footage from the tractor-trailer cam, but I have no idea who they were," Ivan said.

"Casualties?" Kat asked, biting her lip as she waited for his answer.

"Five."

"Who made it out?" Mason asked.

"April. A bystander stumbled upon the wreckage before Dr. Shea arrived," Ivan said. "She's en route to the hospital."

"Fuck," Kat said. With StormLink down, they wouldn't even be able to check on her without popping up on security. "Thanks, Ivan." She hung up, not even wanting to voice the question on the tip of her tongue—what else could go wrong? It felt like the universe was sitting with a sniper rifle, waiting for her to ask.

Mason's hands tightened on the wheel, and he sped up. "We have a good amount of the files digitized," he said. "It's not a total loss."

"The reapers, though," Kat said. She dropped her head back. They drove in silence the remainder of the way to the Institute. The night ran over and over in her mind. She needed more information on Hale, and she wanted leverage on Maureen. Something that would knock her off her game—turn those on her team against her.

Mason pulled into the parking garage beneath the building, backing up to an elevator tucked in the corner. "These lead straight down to interrogation," he said. Kat caught the flash of anger in his eyes. He hadn't said much about Izz in the car, but she got the feeling that her running off with Rufus was a bigger betrayal than he was letting on. "I'll get them started."

"I'll go check on Ivan," Kat said. "Save one of them for me—if you can." It wasn't that she didn't want to be in interrogation, but Hale's guards were in the perfectly capable hands of Mason and Griffin. But the thought of leverage made her think of the untouched office upstairs—and what secrets were sitting behind those doors.

She and Dom found Ivan in the cold room with a box of pizza on the floor and cans of his favorite energy drink tossed on top of it. He didn't hear them enter, the sound of techno music blaring from his headphones. She plucked them from his head, and he jumped, spinning around, fists raised as if to attack as a high-pitched scream left him.

She quirked an eyebrow, holding up the headphones. "I could hear this across the room."

Ivan's hand flew to his chest. "Oh, my—you scared me."

"What do you have for me?" Kat asked, tossing the headphones onto the desk.

"Where's Aeron?" Ivan looked around her at Dom.

Kat's lip twitched into a grimace. "The mission was a failure. Hale grabbed Aeron and Izz took Rufus. Shay was nowhere in sight," she said, which was the only saving grace. If she had him slip through her fingers too?

"But Aeron—"

"Don't worry, we didn't leave empty-handed. Mason has our unlucky friends in interrogation now."

Ivan scrunched his nose. He reached behind himself and grabbed a tablet, passing it to her. "The footage from tonight. Maybe you guys can see something I don't."

She accepted the tablet. "Any update on April?"

"Minor bumps and bruises. Dr. Shea met them at the hospital —he's handling the discharge."

Dom rounded them and took a seat at his station. He'd been unusually quiet on the ride home. "Everything okay, Dom?" Kat asked.

He began to nod and then shook his head instead. "Do you think Shay is alive?"

She bit her lip, her hand sliding into her pocket, fingers closing over Aeron's phone. "I do. It's been a long night for all of us. Dom, why don't you go shower and eat something?"

"But the—"

"Ivan's got it," she said, putting her hand on his shoulder as he opened his mouth to protest. Kat drove her middle finger into the pressure point just above his clavicle, and his mouth slammed closed. He nodded in agreement. "Go," she encouraged.

He didn't need to be told twice. "Thanks."

Kat waited until he was gone to release the grip on Ivan. "Ow!" he yelled, shrugging her hand off and reaching up to massage the spot. "What the heck?"

She pulled out the phone. Someone had put the video of Shay on here, and she hadn't a doubt Dom and Ivan could track where it came from, giving them their first solid lead. But the thought of Dom seeing this—knowing what actually happened to Shay. Seeing the aftermath was one thing—to experience it? "There is a video on here—and I need to know where it came from, but Dom cannot know—he cannot see it."

Ivan took the phone from her. "Sex tape?" he asked, his eyebrows waggling.

"Torture video—of Shay."

Ivan's face paled. "Oh—I—"

"I wouldn't watch it if I were you," she said. "But I need to know how it got on there, where it came from, and if we can track the point of origin."

"Of course." He turned back to his computer and opened the top drawer, rummaging through the cords.

"Will my granddad's office open for me?"

He pulled out a black wire and plugged it into the phone. "Yes. Everything will open for you."

Perfect. "I'll be there if anyone needs me," she said. "As soon as you have an answer—"

"You'll be the first to know."

Kat stepped off the elevator into the bleak hallway, the large wooden double doors towering over her from the end of the corridor. The last time she'd been here, Perry had been by her side. She pressed her lips together and took several deep breaths before approaching them. The scanner whirled to life at her touch, and the lock disengaged, echoing around her. The metal handle sent a chill through her body, and she pulled the door open.

The office lights came to life around her, and she did an automatic scan of the room. This was not like his office at headquarters. It had a cozier feel—the rich history of the Legacy sprinkled throughout the room. The wall beside the door and the one to her right were lined with bookcases, filled to the brim with mismatched tomes and items that looked like they should be in a museum. The wall to her left was bare save a large mirror. Even the furniture added to the historical elegance of the room. A dark blue velvet couch sat to the left, a small coffee table in front of it piled with books, and the handcrafted oak desk where every Senior Assassin had taken their seat sat directly in front of her framed by a large window overlooking the city.

She neared the desk and placed the tablet down, running her hand over the wood. Unlike the one in the headquarters office—this one was marred and stained with small chunks missing, worn down with age. It looked like it had gone to battle alongside its owners. She pulled out the leather office chair—the newest piece of furniture in the room—and took a seat. The room seemed to settle around her and she let out a small laugh in the silence. He was dead. The fucking bastard was dead. And so were too many others. She sobered and scanned the room again. No obvious secret hiding place stood out—no oversized vaults taunting her.

She explored the desk, the drawers neatly organized with old files, office supplies, and a bottle of whiskey. No, a room like this held its secrets in the open. She moved to the bookcases. The wood matched the desk, with the same craftsmanship and attention to detail in the borders, the Legacy logo etched into square embellishments between each section.

She scanned the spines. She didn't recognize the titles or authors so she moved to the next set of shelves, these books more familiar: Tolstoy, Hemingway, Dostoevsky, Poe. The items on the shelf she thought were important seemed more like knick-knacks when she picked them up. A glass ball; a decorative dagger with a dull blade. She shook her head. Something wasn't right. She pulled out her phone and dialed Griffin.

He picked up on the second ring, the sound of screaming in the distance. "What's up?"

"Let me talk to Mason."

"Sure."

The screams of pain got louder, words audible as Griffin neared. "I don't know her!"

Mason's voice responded, his tone menacing. "Look again—who is she?" Silence, and then another wail of pain. She heard a muffled exchange of words, the screams moving away from the phone, and then Mason's voice. "Go."

"I'm in the Senior Assassin's office," Kat said, "but something's not right. There are no video feeds, no safes, or files. It feels—"

"Too small," Mason supplied. "The wall of books to your right. On the third separator from the left, you'll see the Legacy logo on a square embellishment."

Kat moved to the bookcase and counted to the third separator. "Okay."

"Open it," Mason said.

She felt around the edge of the square, giving it a tug, and it swung open like a small door revealing a black button. "No biometrics? No codes? Push the button?" she asked.

"Push the button," Mason confirmed. A loud click sounded from within the bookcase, and the shelves to her left swung open.

"Well, damn. Thanks." She hung up the phone and pulled the bookcase open. This was more like what she was expecting. The wall on the left was dedicated to security, with an entire line of monitors, all darkened at the moment. Straight ahead was a solid wooden table and chairs, with a remote and a book left on it, as if her granddad was going to come back and finish what he was working on. Shelves behind the table displayed weapons—guns and knives for easy access—and on her right was another bookcase filled with more old-looking books. There still wasn't an obvious safe.

She picked up the remote and pressed power. The screens lit up, 'no display' in the center of each. She pressed a few buttons, but nothing happened—she'd have Ivan fix that tomorrow. She put the remote down and picked up the dusty red leather-bound book instead. It was softer and heavier than she expected with the title, An Assassin's Guide, stamped onto the front cover. On the back, the circular cityscape logo was embossed with a date in the bottom left corner:1774. Kat lowered herself into the chair and opened the book. The off-white pages were thick and stained, and as she flipped through them she realized it wasn't a book, per se, but a handwritten journal. She moved to the first page. The title sat in the middle of it, the initials B.G.P. beneath it. A scan of the first few pages revealed it wasn't just a journal, but a code of ethics, and a set of bylaws written by the founders of the Legacy.

She closed the book and looked at the wall of leather-bound journals. There were hundreds of them. She moved to the book-shelf, running her fingers along the blank spines. She pulled out an emerald-green journal, looking at the back cover first. The logo sat in the center, the date 1976 in the lower corner. She turned it around. There was no title, just the initials J.L.P. She flipped through the pages, skimming the dates and notes. She smiled. It was essentially a black book. She returned it to the shelf and picked out another one, an orange leather one from 1995, titled *The Ballerina* by F.H.W. Francis Howard Wayward. Based on the date, he was her great-grandfather. But this one was not a black book. It recounted the life of a girl named Olivia. Kat skimmed the pages, Francis' writing of how he courted her to the Legacy at the age of sixteen, right out from beneath her father's nose.

She kept skimming, but only Olivia's name was mentioned. Every other person in the Legacy whom she had contact with was redacted, and there were several pages ripped out. But Kat gathered she married a Legacy member and she ran missions. At the end of the book, the writing became almost impossible to read. Elijah had killed him shortly after this was written, having poisoned him until his mind no longer functioned. She tossed it on the desk to ask Mason about it later.

She pulled a few more books, checking the dates and scanning the contents. They didn't seem to be in any order, black books from the 1840s beside detailed mission accounts from the late 1980s. It wasn't what she was looking for—but there was a wealth of knowledge—of power right here. A knock on the office door called her attention. She stepped out of the secret room and pushed the door closed. "Come in."

Mason entered, blood spattered across his face and chest, a bloody rag in his hands as he wiped them clean. "I couldn't save you one. They cracked faster than an egg in a vise." He tucked the bloody rag into his back pocket and looked around the room. "Did you find it?"

Kat nodded. "Do you know what's in there?"

Mason took a seat in front of the desk. "The original documents for the Legacy. I've only read one: An Assassin's Guide. Every full-fledged Legacy member had to, but I'm assuming it has the logs before everything was digitized."

Kat sat back down at the desk. "And stories," she said. "Personal accounts of missions. I wonder if my granddad ever wrote anything." She'd have to have another look. "What did our guests have to say?"

"They had never seen Izz before, so that's good news and bad. Good news—Maureen isn't working with Hale. Bad news— Maureen *is* calling Rufus home."

"What about Aeron?"

"They said she was simply bait for you. Hale and Rufus were making some kind of trade. They couldn't give names or anything."

"Could they give us a location?"

He shook his head. She released a long sigh, eyes falling on the tablet. She slid it across to him. On to the next problem. "Footage from tonight." She unlocked it, and Mason leaned forward as she pressed play. There was no sound in the video, so they watched in silence. A cloud of smoke plumed in the air. The tractor-trailer swerved and pulled to the side of the road, the reapers escorting it pulling up for security. Another explosion, reapers dropping. New cars pulling into the frame.

"Hold on." Mason hit pause on the video and zoomed in on a white sports car. "Motherfucker."

"What is it?" Kat asked. They couldn't see a single person with the quality of the video.

"That's Dash's car," he said, pointing at the screen. "What a fucking idiot." He shook his head, amusement in his laugh. "Do you know how many times I told him not to take that car on missions?" Kat just stared at him until he continued. "Maureen took the vault."

That was the least surprising news of the night. She brushed her knuckles across her lips. Maureen had the vault and Rufus, but Hale had Aeron, and she had no clue where Shay could be in this tangled web. "Let's switch gears," Kat said. "The vault and Rufus can wait. I need to know about Hale."

*I*zz parked behind Dash's car, the snow crunching beneath her tires as she pulled up to the main building of the New York Syndicate Compound. It had the same general setup as every other safe house compound they owned, a central building that was the hub for food and meetings downstairs, with the main office and three bedrooms upstairs. Behind that building were smaller cabins, each housing up to a six-man team. From the looks of the cars, they probably had about thirty or so assets.

The bed of the tractor-trailer sat between the garage and the main building, a handful of people setting up spotlights and heaters around the massive object hidden beneath tarps. Mason's crew had done the bulk of the work for them, securing the block, clearing the rubble, and loading the hunk of steel onto the bed of a truck.

"Don't talk to anyone," Izz said, looking over at Rufus. "Don't look at anyone, and for the love of killing, don't fucking touch anyone."

He held up the duct-taped covered hand. "Assassin's honor."

She stepped outside, Derek's dried blood on the back of her pants stiff as she moved to the vault, Rufus by her side. Maureen directed the chaos on the bed, the Firebird crew shivering as they worked. Eileen stood beneath one of the outdoor heaters, taking in the scene. She looked over as Izz approached. A smile started, but vanished when she spotted Rufus at Izz's side. "We'll meet you inside," Eileen said, eyes flicking to Izz.

"Good. I'm fucking cold," Izz said. She turned, grabbed Rufus by the arm, and directed him toward the house.

The warmth of bodies and noise assaulted her when she opened the front door. Two dozen assets crowded the room. Most sat at the long dining table that divided the space, a few hung in the kitchen area to the left, and on the three oversized couches to the right, sat Dash, Keara, and Rebekah. Izz shot Rebekah a smile, sliding her tongue between her lips, her teeth catching her bottom lip. Rebekah blushed, pulling her hair over her shoulder, and giving a seductive smile in return. Damn. This was going to be a good night.

"Izz!" Keara jumped out of her seat, coming closer, her face glowing with pride. "You should have seen it. Flawless."

"I'm sorry I missed it," she said, stepping into the house. Keara's face fell as her eyes dropped to the bloodstained pants she wore. "None of it is mine," she assured.

"You sure?" Rufus said over Izz's shoulder. "You look like you got your fucking period." He stepped into the entryway, and the entire room fell silent, eyes on them.

Before Izz could tell him to fuck off, footsteps treaded up the porch stairs, and Izz looked past Rufus. Maureen smiled at her, approval dancing in her eyes, and Izz let the warmth of it fill her. She stepped past Rufus into the house, Eileen right behind her. "Quit gawking," Maureen said. "Everybody out."

There was a collective groan of discontent. "It's freezing out," Dash complained.

Maureen glared, and he snapped his mouth closed. It only took a few minutes for everyone to grab their food and some extra blankets, and then head outside. Rufus took a seat at the table, pulling a box of pizza toward himself.

Izz rolled her eyes. "You literally just fucking ate." She snatched the piece from his fingers and took a bite, sitting on the edge of the table beside him. Rufus snatched the slice back. Eileen lowered herself into the seat across from them, and Maureen stood at the head of the table, leaning on her knuckles and surveying Rufus. He took a bite of the pizza, a smug look on his face that he didn't normally wear around Maureen. But he had them by the balls this time and knew it.

"So, Rosemary was telling the truth," Maureen said. "What do you know about Storm?"

He took another bite and grinned. "You seem to be missing some bargaining chips."

Izz slid her hand to her waist, fingers brushing her pistol, but Maureen's face remained calm. "And you seem to think I care if she's alive or not." Rufus' grin faltered. "You want Hale and Mike Barnes? Katherine? Give me something useful."

"You fucked up my night, you know that?" He sat forward in the seat, and Izz tensed, ready to pounce. "I already had everything I wanted right under my fingertips." He held up his bandaged hand.

"Let's call it even for your fuck up at the garage. I should put a bullet in you for that stunt."

"But you won't," he said with a sadistic smile. "Because you need me." Maureen held his gaze until he sat back. "How do I know you'll hold up your end?"

"Have I ever not held up my end?" Maureen countered. "Even after I was dead, you got your payments." Izz could practically see the tension between them.

He put the pizza crust down and straightened in the chair. "Fine. I'll take Izz in the morning."

Izz exchanged a glance with Maureen and Eileen. That felt too easy. Or were they just used to navigating around Elijah's road-blocks? Eileen seemed to be thinking along the same lines. "Why wait?"

"Because," he said, cupping his hands behind his head and leaning back in the chair. "Izz needs to bust a nut before I get back in the fucking car with her, and I'm curious as to what you'll find in that vault."

"Deal," Maureen said.

"Sabrina should have the vault open within the hour," Eileen said, looking at Izz.

"An hour is all I need," Izz said, heat pooling between her thighs at the prospect of an uninterrupted hour in pure bliss. The thought of Rebekah laid out in her bed was a vision of pure ecstasy. But she only had an hour—and the things Izz wanted to do to that woman would take all night long. "I'm going to shower. Send Dash up to my room."

Izz bolted upright, hand flying to her face, heart pounding out of her chest as the echo of a gunshot chased her out of her nightmare. Her cheek burned at the touch, and she took a deep breath. It was dark. Not a sound reached her from the other rooms, just the soft snores of Dash in the bed beside her. How long had she slept for? She checked the time on her phone; it was nearly three in the morning.

She swung her feet out of bed, the cold floor sending a chill through her body, and peered outside her window to the vault. The lights and heaters still ran, and two people stood guard outside the now open door. Excitement raced through her, and she pulled on pants, a hoodie, and a pair of socks before stepping into the hall. The light beneath Maureen's door lit the hallway. Izz stopped by, knocking and pushing the door open.

"Hey," she said, stepping into the room. Maureen waved her in without looking up. The room was the largest of the three, with a queen bed pushed against the right wall so a ten-person conference table could take up the majority of the room. Izz recognized the boxes from the vault piled on the floor, their contents spewed across the workspace. "Where's Rufus?"

"Working in the vault with Eileen," she said. "Might as well put him to use while we can." Maureen looked up at her, eyes flicking to her cheek. "He told me what happened."

Izz scoffed, the reminder of Mason a blow to her gut. They had been the perfect family: her, Eileen, Maureen, and Mason. She never imagined a day he would walk away from them—a time when he would abandon her. Her heart thumped hard, and it felt like a piece of her was missing. "I'm pretty sure I'm at the top of his list at the moment."

"Higher than Rufus?"

"He shot at me—not him," Izz said, the hostility in Mason's gaze burning into her heart. She could fix this, though. She could find out what happened to Storm and—and what? Maureen wouldn't share the information willingly with Mason. No. It would be used to torment him for defying her. And if Storm was alive? Whatever hell hole Rufus had her stashed in would be a luxury compared to what Maureen would do to the techie. Izz couldn't blame her—Storm had stolen everything from them, but the pain it would cause Mason sat in her gut like a stone. "Need help in here?"

Maureen shook her head. "I am regretting my earlier urge to make this as difficult as possible for them to go through. I did a fucking phenomenal job with it, though. Oh," she looked over. "Did you hear the news about Kara?"

Izz shook her head. She hadn't realized Kara was still on their radar with everything else going on.

"We secured a meeting. She'll be here in the morning. Go help Eileen. I'm sure she's at her wit's end with Rufus by now."

Izz wanted to know what she meant by secured, but the dismissal was clear in Maureen's tone. She would have to wait until tomorrow to find out—or she could just ask Eileen. The downstairs was empty, save for Keara at the kitchen table. Her laptop was open, and a steaming mug sat in front of her. She looked up as Izz entered, a weariness in her eyes that Izz recognized all too well. "How's the perimeter?"

"Clear," Keara said. "We did get a report from Home Base about some damage from an earthquake."

"I'll take an earthquake over this frigid weather anytime. Where's Rebekah?"

"Sleeping. We're working in six-hour shifts. But, um, you should know—she seemed disappointed you asked for Dash." Keara raised her eyebrows and took a sip of her drink to hide her smile.

Izz grinned. "Good to know." Coats hung by the side door, a line of boots beneath them. Izz stuffed her feet into the warmest-looking pair and pulled on the thickest and largest coat she could find. The blast of cold air bit at her face, and she stuffed her hands inside her pockets. Fuck this weather. She slipped and slid her way down the path to the vault, walking as close to the kerosene heaters as she could.

The bundled guards looked her way, but didn't move from beneath the heaters at the entrance to the vault. She stepped past them without a word. The inside of the vault was surprisingly bright and warm, which was a good thing because they would be out there for a while. Every box that had sat on a shelf had been dumped. Papers were scattered across the floor along with equipment, books, and weapons. Eileen sat on a folding chair with several neat piles of papers around her and smiled when Izz entered. Izz looked over to the still form of Rufus propped against the rear wall, a thermos by his side. His eyes were closed, and it looked like someone had tended to the cuts on his face. Izz squinted toward him.

"He's alive," Eileen said, distaste in her tone.

Izz felt her guard lessen. "Well, that's a shame." Izz dragged the other folding chair near Eileen and unzipped her jacket, slipping it off. "What is this I hear about Kara coming to the compound?"

Eileen let out a long sigh. "Rebekah tracked Kara down. Maureen sent what was left of the Blue Bloods and Serpents to retrieve her."

"Cool," Izz said, an unease settling into her stomach. "Because we're kidnapping CIA officers now." She sighed. "What are we doing here?"

"Organizing. Right now, it's by date. Each year has its own pile, and if the paper mentions Hale, it goes over here." She pointed to the smallest pile of the bunch. "She wants every ounce of dirt on him."

Izz grabbed a stack of papers and started sorting. Each page had a date on the bottom left. Maureen wasn't kidding—she had a document from 1990 followed by one from 2002 followed by another from 2021. She looked around. There were thousands of pages.

"Find anything interesting yet?" Izz asked, sorting through the stack in her hands, scanning the page for the name Hale, and then dropping it into its respective pile.

"I stopped reading after the first hundred pages. Most of it is coded, and without the entire document, it's hard to know which cipher to use."

"I'm surprised she let him in here," Izz said, nodding toward Rufus.

Eileen smiled. "She knew the documents were coded. His ability to read the human psyche far surpasses his ability to read a cipher. He lost interest after the first half hour."

"He normally doesn't sleep around people."

Eileen pulled an empty vial from her pocket. "He had some help."

Izz laughed and grabbed another stack of papers. They sorted for another hour, lapsing into a comfortable silence. Izz's mind wandered from the torture session with Derek to Rebekah. The woman always smelled so fucking good. And she had the ass of a goddess—it looked good in her pants, but even better in a bikini. Another fucking reason to leave this freezing hellhole. There were too many layers of clothes.

Izz reached for another stack of paper, but looked up to Eileen. Her body was tense, eyes reading the page in her hand. "What's wrong?" Izz asked. Eileen didn't answer. The page trembled in her fingers, and her eyes narrowed. "Eileen?"

Eileen put the paper on her lap and grabbed a stacked pile from the floor. It wasn't a large one, maybe twenty-five pieces. She shuffled through them, a sinking feeling in Izz's gut as she realized it was the 1996 pile. "Eileen." Izz reached out to grab the papers, but Eileen reached behind her, drawing her gun. Izz sat back, hands raised. Moisture gathered in the woman's eyes when she looked up. The gun stayed on her as Eileen flipped through the pages, putting them in order.

"Eileen," Izz said again, but there was no distracting her. Izz's heart beat painfully in her throat. She lowered her hands, reaching for her phone to warn Maureen. Her fingers barely brushed it when Eileen's eyes shot up from the paper, betrayal fresh on her face. It was like a knife in Izz's heart.

"Did you know?" She shook the papers at Izz, lowering the gun to her lap.

Izz licked her lips, unsure of what she'd found. Izz knew a lot that would make people look at her like that. "Know what?"

"Katherine's father?"

Izz swallowed hard. Oh. She did know that. "Listen—"

"Fuck off." She stood and headed out of the vault. Izz jumped to her feet to follow and looked back at Rufus. Damn it. Eileen was already outside. Izz stopped at the guards, the sound of the side door already slamming shut. "If he wakes up, shoot him—but do not fucking kill him. Understand?"

The guards nodded, and Izz raced inside. Keara was half out of her seat, eyes wide. "Izz—"

"Stay here," Izz said. "No matter what, stay fucking here." She took the stairs two at a time, the yelling already reaching her at the top, Maureen's door wide open.

"How could you not tell me?" Eileen yelled.

"It was a mistake," Maureen said, loud, but under control. "It didn't matter. I wasn't keeping her."

"Didn't matter?" Eileen's voice dropped, and Izz halted in the doorway. Maureen stood at the table, hands resting on it, Eileen stood just inside the door, her gun pointed at Maureen. "He was my husband. Of all the fucked-up shit you've done—I've been there for you. I've always been there for you. If you had told me—"

"You would have been there for me?" Maureen said with a harsh laugh. "You would have wanted to raise her together like a big fucking family?"

"You gave his daughter to Elijah! This whole time, there's been another piece of him out there. How could you?"

"Andrew would have never—"

"He would have loved her," Eileen said, shaking her head. "But you could never handle Andrew loving anyone but you. You fucking narcissistic bitch. Why come back from the dead when you pretend the kids don't exist at all? You never loved them—the second Andrew died, they stopped being useful to you."

Maureen's hand shifted. She reached for the gun secured beneath the table, and Eileen fired. Maureen spun out of the way, and Izz lunged for Eileen, pinning her to the ground and putting herself between them. "Stop!" Izz yelled.

It was a fruitless effort. Maureen's foot connected with the side of Izz's face. The pain radiating from Mason's shot forced her to roll away. She got back to her feet. The sight of the best friends fighting was all too familiar, except the energy was wrong. There were no playful quips or annoyed looks. They were out for blood.

"Maureen, stop!" Izz called out, but the words didn't make an impact.

Eileen scrambled to her feet before Maureen could get on top, tears on her cheeks, her voice breaking as it came out. "How could you?"

"I did what was best," Maureen said. "Bringing her in would have ruined everything we were building."

"You gave an innocent child to the fucking enemy!"

"Do you want an apology?" Maureen said with a laugh. "For me to tell you how it tore me up? How I threw myself into the Alliance with everything to not think about what I'd done?"

"Did Seamus know?" Eileen asked, the words a whisper.

"Does it fucking matter? He's dead."

"It matters to me!" Eileen yelled, her chest heaving. "Please— did he know?"

Maureen lowered the gun and shook her head. Izz saw the switch of her humanity in the set of her mouth. Shit. "No," she said matter-of-factly. "Are we done?"

Eileen's face twisted into pure hatred, and she lunged again. The hairs on the back of Izz's neck tingled. She looked toward the door as Keara stepped into view. Fuck. Izz moved to block her, but Maureen spun, and Izz saw the flash of silver in Maureen's hand, the gun firing.

31

KAT

Kat leaned against the counter in Mason's residence, watching the microwave countdown as it heated the leftover takeout. "So, from all accounts, Hale was a power-house of a firm until Storm built her program, giving my granddad an all-access pass to the CIA."

"Yeah," Mason said from the table. "We cut theirs and Onyx's numbers down to a third of what they were, forcing the merger. It was a shame, really. They were good people. Good at their job. Elijah just didn't want the competition."

"So, Oliver has beef with Legacy Inc—which no longer exists. Maybe I could talk to him, make an arrangement. I need people, and he needs power." The microwave beeped, and she took out the steaming container of Chicken Pho. She poured it into a bowl and returned to the table, blowing on it to cool.

"Wow," Mason said with a laugh.

"What?"

"You just made a completely diplomatic and reasonable suggestion without an ounce of vengeance in your tone after he attempted to trade your life to Rufus, took Aeron, and it's still up in the air if he has Shay."

She glared at him. "I'm not marrying the man. I'm simply trying to get everyone home alive this time. But I don't get it. Why take Aeron? If they wanted money, they should have killed her, or called to negotiate by now. Same thing if they wanted me in exchange for her." She took a bite of the food and closed her eyes, enjoying what she could at the moment.

"I don't know." His tone sobered. "I wish I knew how Barnes managed to infiltrate Legacy Inc."

"Don't beat yourself up. Granddad fucked a lot of protocols up near the end. Maybe he knew he was a mole the whole time," Kat replied.

Her phone buzzed, and she took another bite of food before any more bad news could come her way. It was a text from Ivan: the StormLink icon, along with a message.

> Ivan: username: Queen

> Ivan: pw: Qu33nStr!k3sB@ck!

Her stomach flipped, and she clicked on the icon. The screen darkened around the logo, pink clouds appearing behind it, pulsing a few times before the entire image disappeared, replaced by a login screen. She input the details and the home screen for StormLink appeared on her phone, an unread message waiting for her. She opened it.

From: GameMaster

-located the device that sent the video.

A smile spread across her face, and a laugh left her. "He did it," Kat said, standing up, excitement buzzing through her entire system. Mason looked up from the computer and she turned the phone around. "Ivan fucking did it!"

• • •

"I could kiss you," Kat said, half running into the cold room, Mason on her heels. Ivan turned in his chair, his cheeks reddening. "Are we back in business?"

"We are back in business," he confirmed.

"We didn't turn on the facial recognition spoofer yet," Dom said from his desk. "We'll lose all traces of Shay and Aeron from the system if we do, so I'm running their pictures through all the databases we now have access to."

"Perfect," Mason said. "What about tracking?"

"Anyone who has ever been tagged by any version of Storm-Link is now trackable," Ivan said. He pulled up a map. "I reorganized them. Red are Alliance, blue are Legacy Inc, and orange are the Syndicate."

"I could kiss you too," Mason said, his eyes glowing with excitement. "Where the fuck is Izz?"

"Hold on," Kat said, shaking her hands. "First things first— where did the video come from?"

"It was downloaded from StormLink right before Senior was killed," Ivan said. "The only person with that kind of access was Mike Barnes." Ivan typed away, and the map cleared of colorful dots, a singular green dot appearing in the countryside of Connecticut. He zoomed into the satellite image. It was a decent-sized compound, surrounded by a tall brick wall and woods. "Storm's tracking malware infected the device he used when he stole it, bypassing his IDPS—the intrusion detection/prevention systems. That's where Mike Barnes is —or has logged in to his computer as recently as an hour ago."

"Can you get into his computer?" Kat asked.

"Can I get into his computer?" Ivan said with a laugh. "Does rain fall from the sky?"

The doors to the cold room opened, Griffin joining them. "I got the message." He held up his phone and jogged down the few steps to meet her at Ivan's desk. "Any luck on the hit list?"

Dom tilted his head. "No, but if Mike Barnes has it on his computer. . ." The room fell silent, Ivan and Dom typing away.

"Anything?" Kat asked after a few minutes, her patience on edge.

"He's no slouch," Ivan admitted. "It will take some time. But we have their locations now, tracking, and borrowed eyes in the sky. Dom has been working to reconnect with the Legacy satellite, but—"

"We need to bring in a specialist for that," Dom finished. "That's outside our expertise."

"I'll put some feelers out," Mason said, and touched the screen, pulling back up the large map. He picked up the keyboard sitting on the nearby desk and typed in Spike. The map widened, a pin drop marking Izz's location. He zoomed in—Izz's red marker sitting in the middle of at least thirty orange dots and a singular blue one. Mason hovered the cursor over the blue dot. *The Devil.*

"So, we've got Hale and Barnes in Connecticut, and Rufus and the Syndicate in New York. What do you want to do, Kat?" Mason asked.

"I want to bring Aeron and Shay home."

"And Maureen?" he asked.

Kara's warning about keeping Maureen alive sat in the back of Kat's mind. She pulled out her phone, clicking on the StormLink icon, a thrill shooting through her again. Opening the messages, she clicked on StormTracer, and sent one before she could over-think it: *Back in Business.* She didn't know how long it would take for Kara to get the message, so she pocketed the phone.

"Maureen can wait for now. Kara wants her alive. Ivan, pull up the schematics on Hale's compound. Let's pay him a visit."

32

———

IZZ

aureen's shot filled the room. Keara's body spun, crashing into the doorframe. Izz cried and she dove for the girl, catching her body before it could hit the ground. Blood saturated her pink sweater, the bullet finding a home in Keara's chest.

"Mom?" Keara's voice was barely a whisper. Eileen untangled herself from Maureen, turning to find Izz holding her daughter. She skidded to her knees, hands already pulling up Keara's sweater.

"No. Baby, what are you doing here?"

Izz looked to Eileen for directions. She was their medic. She could fix this—she had to fix this.

"Rufus gave this to me." She held out a piece of paper, blood spattered on it. "Said it was important."

Izz took the note and opened it. *Went to secure my prize. Meet me at Pop's—7 am.*

Damn it. She glanced at Maureen. Her face was a twisted map of anger, but Izz didn't have time for her right now. Keara was shot. Izz turned her attention back to Eileen. "What do we do?"

Tears stained Eileen's face, her hands shaking where she

pushed on the wound near the heart. It had only been a few seconds, but there was too much blood on the sweater—Maureen must have nicked an artery. Eileen shook her head at Izz and looked back down. "You did good, darling," Eileen said, somehow keeping her voice steady.

"I don't feel good," Keara said. She moved to look down at her chest, and Izz cupped her chin, guiding her eyes back up. "I'm cold."

"It's this fucking place. Wait until you come and see me in Costa Rica. The temps are hot, the men are hotter."

Keara gave a laugh, blood spraying across her chin and onto Izz's hand. She pulled it away as Keara's body convulsed for a moment, and then nothing. The silence was deafening. Eileen laid her daughter down and turned to look at Maureen, Izz following suit. The battle of emotion warred behind Maureen's eyes, and Izz watched for the moment it landed. Her gaze hardened, nostrils flaring in annoyance, and a small twitch developed in her wrist. Izz clambered to her feet, stepping between them. She wasn't fast enough. Maureen pulled the trigger again, and Eileen's body dropped from a single shot to her head.

"What the fuck?" Izz said, panic clawing its way up her chest. "Maureen—"

"She would have done worse to me. Accident or not—I killed her kid. And I slept with her husband. Fuck. I can't believe I didn't think about that being in the vaults. It's been so long. . ." She put the gun down on the table. "What did Keara say?"

Izz blinked a few times, the whiplash of events hardly settling. Eileen was dead. Her confidant; her mentor; her fucking friend.

"Izz!"

"Rufus," Izz said, gathering her bearings. "Rufus is gone."

"He couldn't have gotten far—" Maureen fell silent.

Footsteps sounded down the hall. Who the hell else was here? Izz grabbed the gun from the table, readying herself. Dash poked his head around the door frame, his gaze landing on Keara and Eileen, then bouncing back up. "I—I heard the shots. I thought we may be—"

Izz let out a long sigh. Without looking at Maureen, she pulled the trigger, a pang of regret as Dash dropped in the hall. "Well, that fucking sucks," she said, stuffing down the uncomfortable feeling in her chest. They had a corporation to run, they had a job to finish. She looked at Maureen. "We can blame it on Dash. Nice and neat."

Maureen gave her a rare, appreciative smile. "This is why you have always been my favorite. We just get it. You go after Rufus. I'll do damage control here."

Izz passed Maureen back her gun and nodded. She stepped over the bodies, a hole inside her that she'd stuffed full of everything and everyone imaginable, ripping wide open, dragging her back to the day she'd met Eileen.

'I can give them to you,' a woman said.

Izz looked up from her brother's body, tears and snot running down her face. She didn't recognize the woman, but she didn't recognize most of the mourners there for Jason. The line of unfamiliar faces wrapped around the room, colleagues from the university and friends she'd only ever heard of coming to pay their respects. The reception line was short, however, just her and Jason's girlfriend Krista.

'The person who did this,' the woman whispered, eyes so intent on her that Izz shivered. 'I can give them to you.' The woman nodded for her to follow.

Izz's chest tightened. They hadn't found who murdered him. The cops were useless in their investigation—worried more about who had vandalized the town hall than a murdered black man. She'd tried going to the news stations, anyone, but her pleas had fallen on uncaring ears. She glanced at Krista in conversation with the English Department Head. Everyone here knew her—they worked together at the university, but Izz was simply known as Jason's younger sister. She touched Krista's arm, whispering a quick, 'I'll be back,' and followed the woman outside.

They took a seat on the stone wall surrounding the funeral home, facing the busy street. People going on like nothing has happened. 'Who are you?' Izz asked.

'My name is Eileen.'

'If you know what happened—why didn't you come forward? Tell the police?'

Eileen laughed. 'They are useless. Minions for a bigger useless idiot, who is a minion for a bigger idiot, and so on up the chain. Even if I did—how long would it take to serve justice? Months? Years?'

Izz looked up at her. Her brown hair was pulled into a bun, her green eyes sharp. 'Why are you telling me, then?'

'Because you have something in you—a hunger. I've seen it when you train, when you work, when the men give you a hard time.'

'You've been watching me?' Izz said, the violation sending a shiver down her spine.

'I'm a headhunter, Izz.' The way the word headhunter fell off her tongue, Izz got the impression she did more than just find talent. 'And I'm offering you a spot, a very exclusive spot among an elite set of people.'

Izz scoffed. 'I'm a bartender. I'm nothing special.'

'You're a fighter,' Eileen countered. 'And very alone right now. You can go back in there, watch those people mourn over your brother for the next hour, and then forget about him in the next month while you sit alone in your apartment wondering who stole him from you. Even the girl will move on, get married, have kids, and occasionally bring up the interesting fact that one of her early boyfriends was murdered.' The words ripped at Izz. The hole in her heart her brother filled after their parents were killed now gaping, the tattered pieces flapping in the wind.

'Why are you saying these things?' Izz asked, anger boiling in her gut. She stood, towering over the woman. 'Tell me who did this.'

Eileen's lips quirked, her head barely tilting up to see her. 'And what are you going to do with that name? Give it to the cops? Pay them a visit?' Izz swallowed hard, and Eileen continued. 'My offer first. You come work for me. A year apprenticeship. At the end, you get the name.'

'A year doing what?' Izz asked.

'Caring for a colleague of mine. She needs a guard and a friend, and I need someone I can trust. Someone who will do whatever it takes to protect her.'

Izz shook her head. She took some martial arts classes, but that didn't qualify her for anything. The whole conversation felt wrong. She needed to get back inside. 'I think you have the wrong person,' Izz said, taking a few steps back. Jason wanted her to finish college. Get a job in something she loved. Whatever this woman was offering—it didn't sound like finishing school was part of it. 'I have a plan.'

'And who is going to pay for tuition without Jason's position at the university?'

Izz froze in her retreat. She hadn't thought about that. His job secured her a free ride. But she couldn't afford to pay for rent on her part-time bartender's income, let alone a semester at school.

'You'll be compensated,' Eileen said. 'Highly compensated for your services. Room and board will be taken care of. Medical—we have the most advanced medical team in the US on call. And if you still want to take classes—we can figure out how to make that work.'

It sounded too good to be true. 'I'm not doing anything illegal,'

Izz said, but she stepped closer to the woman. A roof over her head, food on her table, medical? All the things Izz needed now that Jason was dead. Dead. The word tore through her.

'It's only illegal if the rules apply to you,' Eileen said with a smile. 'Where we're going? They don't.'

"Izz." Maureen's voice pulled her back to the present. Eileen had saved her—given Izz the life she loved, a family, a purpose. And now she was gone.

"Yeah, boss," Izz said, yanking her gaze from Eileen's body.

"Don't come home without the information on Storm."

33

AERON

"Who do you have up there?" Aeron asked. She rounded the counter and took Oliver's seat. Her head swam again. She reached up, pressing her hand into the fresh wound, the pain bringing the room into focus. Barnes ignored her, typing away on his computer. "It wouldn't be Dr. Shea, would it?"

"No." His phone buzzed. Whatever the message, it must be a good one, as a glint of victory reached his eyes. He closed the computer and picked it up, then stood, favoring his left leg. "Go to bed, Aeron."

She resisted the urge to kick out at the leg and let him pass. Words were exchanged down the hall, and her guard moved to the kitchen entrance. She raised her eyebrows and nodded at him. He didn't move, dark eyes watching her. With a heavy sigh, she stood, making a big deal of yawning and stretching. She assumed Shea was located on the second floor, and in her tired and delusional state, she may not remember how to get back to her room.

Voices and movement carried down the stairwell. Aeron paused halfway up the first flight, ears alert. "Move!" the guard called after her. She glanced over at him, but before she could even figure out where he might want her to move, he rushed forward and pushed her against the wall. The world swam as he jostled her arm, Aeron's knees going weak. She dropped to the step, but the guard didn't notice—or care—his attention on the group of people appearing at the top of the steps.

Bracing her head against the wall, she took several deep breaths and peeked between his legs. Barnes, Oliver, and George appeared on the landing, along with two guards escorting a man between them. Oliver's eyes looked at the guard and then dropped to her. Anger flashed across his face, and he took the stairs two at a time down to her, shooing the guard away.

"I didn't know you were moving him already," the guard said, thick New York accent coating the words. "I wouldn't have let her—"

"Move," Oliver spat, and the guard's legs disappeared from view, replaced by Oliver's bright eyes, his brows raised in concern. "Are you okay?"

"Fabulous," Aeron ground out, accepting Oliver's offered hand. Barnes and George passed behind him. George's mouth was set in a stern line, but Barnes smirked at her. She flipped him off. The guards passed by next. The first thing Aeron noticed about the man between them was a smile that creased the dark skin around his bright brown eyes, almost childlike, unaware of the danger he was in. His braids were unkempt, though, and on closer inspection, what she thought were wrinkles were scars. Hundreds of them. Her chest tightened, and she looked back to his gaze, seeing the trauma in them now—a mind that had protected itself and survived.

He waved when he noticed her, his smile somehow becoming wider. "Kat! Kat!" he called as the guards escorted him slowly down the stairs.

"Yes, we hear you!" Barnes half yelled. "You like cats. Shut up."

"Barnes," Oliver's voice warned.

Aeron's heart seized in her chest at Kat's name—because it felt like a name he called out. "Who is that?" she asked, watching as they patiently walked him down the stairs.

"My payment," Oliver said.

"You're giving him to Rufus?" Aeron said, incredulously.

"It's late, Aeron. You should go check on Cass." Oliver followed the others to the first floor before she could think of a response.

"You heard him," the guard said, coming back up to her. Aeron kept her eyes on the group until they rounded the banister and disappeared from view. Aeron took the steps two at a time, her mind racing. The man had clearly said Kat. Who was he? What had happened to him? The guard outside her room opened the door, a yawn escaping him.

She locked the door from the inside. Cass was still asleep on the bed, and Aeron slid in beside him. He turned toward her and wrapped his arm around her, snuggling in closer. Aeron gave a small chuckle and ran her hands over his hair. "Don't worry, kid," she said, sinking herself deeper into the pillows, her eyes becoming heavy. "I'll make sure we get out of here. And then we'll go and save your mom. She sounds way better than mine."

Gunfire startled Aeron awake, Cass scrambling on top of her as the semi-automatic rounds echoed through the air. Her stomach turned as he landed on her arm, and she tried to pull him off. "Cass," she whispered. "My arm—please." Cass' frightened breathing and stilled movements answered her. More bursts of shots jump-started her. She swung her legs out of bed and grabbed him by the arm. "Follow me."

She led him into the bathroom, the oversized tub the perfect hiding place. She helped him crawl in and then ran back to the room, grabbing the pillows and blankets to cover him. They wouldn't protect against bullets, but they would help him feel hidden and safe.

"I need you to stay here, Cass." His terrified eyes answered her. "Do you trust me?" she asked.

"Yes," he breathed.

"Do not move from this spot until I come back."

"How will I know it's you? That it's safe? My mom said we always need a code phrase."

Aeron laid the pillows down, and covered him with the blankets, leaving a small space for him to breathe. "You're a smart kid, you know that? What's your mom's name?" A thump hit the door, and Cass jumped, a squeak leaving him.

"Hannah. Hannah Smith."

"Well, your mom is right. We need a phrase." Another bang into the bedroom doors, gunfire just outside. Shit. "Koala," Aeron said, the first word coming to her mind. "The code phrase will be: Koalas eat ice cream."

He giggled, and Aeron didn't know if it was because it was funny, or because hysterics were kicking in. "Don't come out," she reminded and tossed another blanket over him. She turned off the lights and closed the bathroom door. Something or someone rammed into the bedroom door, shaking it on the hinges before it burst open. Aeron crouched, ready to fight. She didn't wait for Hale's guard to catch his bearings. There was no telling if he was here to hurt her or help her. She attacked, diving for his legs. He stumbled back, her good hand already secured on his rifle strap.

She rolled behind him, blocking his legs, and pulled. He tripped over her, hitting the ground hard. With a quick loop of the strap around his throat, Aeron drove her knee into his chest and twisted the material like a tourniquet, his face changing color, his body convulsing. He lost consciousness, and Aeron held on for a few more seconds.

Untangling the strap, Aeron looped it over her shoulder, sliding the rifle behind her. She reached down to his belt, unhooked his tactical knife, and slid the blade across his exposed throat, his body jerking beneath her. There was nowhere in her pajama pants to store the knife, and she was down to one working arm, so she tossed it on the bed. The hallway was clear, and she closed the door behind her, pulling the rifle to the front. She pressed herself against the wall, peering over the banister. There was no movement, and she hurried to the landing to check the next set of stairs.

These, too, were empty, but a ruckus sounded on the second floor, and Aeron hurried toward it. A body flew from one of the rooms, hitting the wall and dropping to the ground. They got back to their feet, but they hit the wall again as three blades flew through the room, finding homes in the legs and shoulder. Griffin stepped into the hallway.

A cry of relief left her. He looked her way, blade already in his fingers, and paused. "It is really fucking good to see you," he said.

"Same." A scream escaped the room he'd just left. Aeron raised her eyebrows and nodded toward it, but Griffin had already returned to the poor fool, now bleeding out on the ground.

"Where is he?" Griffin demanded.

"Fuck off," the guard said.

More tormented screams escaped the room, and Aeron hurried past them, coming up short in the doorway. It was a medical ward. This must be where George operated from. Straight ahead was an office space with computers and monitors. Then it opened to the left, six beds running down the room on one side with vital sign monitors and IV kits, and medical supply cabinets on the other. At the end of the room was another door, the word 'Supply' stamped across it.

The scream came from one of Hale's guards tied to the frame of the closest bed, Kat calmly shearing the skin from one side of his face with a scalpel. "Where is he?" Kat asked, her voice light as she wiped the blade clean on her cargo pants. The guard just shook his head.

"Who are you looking for?" Aeron asked, pulling Kat's attention up. A wicked glint met Aeron, and she smiled.

"Shay. He's an asset, and judging by the paperwork and medical supplies around, he was here."

The man's scarred face flashed into Aeron's mind. "He was. They took him out of here a few hours ago." Aeron's stomach flipped. "They were bringing him to Rufus."

Kat's eyes fell closed, annoyance and disappointment distorting her features. She turned to the guard. "How fucking hard was that?" Kat asked, squatting down. The man tried to lean away, but there was nowhere to go. Kat snapped his neck and stepped over the body. "I'm really glad to see you."

"What's the body count?" Aeron asked, adjusting the rifle. "I dropped one."

"I dropped six," Griffin said, coming back in, blood sprayed across his face. He looked feral, and every ounce the Reaper she'd learned about growing up.

"I dropped four," Kat said. She pushed her comm. "Shay's gone. We have Aeron. What's your body count?" She waited for whoever else was with them to respond.

"Mason dropped three. Has Hale pinned down."

"That leaves roughly five," Aeron said. "But Barnes probably took two with him. So three?"

Kat relayed the message. "Hale is calling for parley," she said. "Mason has eyes on one guard. That leaves two unaccounted for. Let's get down there and find out what the fuck happened to Shay."

Aeron let out a long breath, and the world tipped a wave of

nausea crashing into her as the adrenaline died down. The floor came up faster than it should, and Griffin's strong arms slowed her descent, his face hardly coming into focus. "Aeron?"

"Aeron?" Kat said, stepping into her line of sight. "What do you need?"

It took a moment for the nausea to pass, and she sat up. "I'm okay," she lied. Each wave of dizziness felt heavier, like she was being pulled down into the ocean fully clothed. "Griff, there's a boy named Cass in the bathtub one floor up. The first door on the right," she said, the idea of moving at all exhausting her. "He's terrified. Use the phrase 'Koalas eat ice cream', and he should come out."

"Of course. Here," Griffin said. He pulled the rifle from around her and handed her three throwing knives. He stood and headed out of the room.

Kat helped her to her feet. "I want to punch you in the face for leaving the safe house," she said.

Aeron cracked a smile. "It would be warranted. What happened to your throat?"

"Rufus," Kat said as they moved toward the hall. The world threatened to tip again, and Aeron waved Kat over for support. She looped Aeron's right arm over her shoulder as they headed downstairs. "I expected to find you locked in a room, chained to a chair, torture being administered."

"Hale has taken really good care of me," Aeron said. She stopped when they reached the stairs and looked at Kat. "You should know that he claims to be Maureen's brother."

Kat gave her a blank look.

"Yeah. My opinion too. But I shot Barnes, and then Hale fed me grilled cheese and soup, sent the medic to fix up my shoulder, and gave me free rein of the house, with a guard, of course."

"Why?" Kat asked.

"Because Maureen hurt him too, so he wants to save me."

Aeron rolled her eyes. "He has no idea about you, though. So, whether he is telling the truth or not, I'm letting him think he has me."

Kat bit her lip and nodded. "Okay. Let's go squeeze him for every bit of information he's got."

34

KAT

"How do you want to play this?" Mason asked in her ear. She stopped, looking down at the last set of stairs, Aeron's breathing becoming heavier as they moved. She didn't look good, her color waning with each step, and Kat wondered what kind of medical care she'd actually gotten. "Kat?"

What she wanted to do was give Hale a taste of torture. Make him piss himself and cry for her to let him go. But their time was limited. If Barnes had taken Shay to Rufus, they needed a location. She pressed the comm. "Aeron said they took Shay to Rufus. I need to know where they are, and if he loves his life enough to call it off."

"So... Am I torturing him?"

Kat laughed. "Not yet." Footfalls sounded on the stairs above them. Kat pulled her gun, and Aeron leaned back against the wall, blade poised to throw.

"It's us," Griffin called, coming into view, a prepubescent boy by his side. Griffin's eyes landed on Aeron first, and Kat glanced over. Her shoulders sagged in relief, and she held out her good arm. The boy raced toward her, and she pulled him in for a hug, her face wincing in pain. It was an odd sight, and it took Kat a moment to realize why—they were wearing matching red flannel pajama pants.

"Who's this?" she asked, nodding toward the kid.

"Cass," Aeron said. "Rufus grabbed him and his mother. His mother is who Hale wants, but only Rufus knows her location."

Cass' wide gaze stared at them, his grip tightening on Aeron as it landed on the gun still held out in front of Kat. She lowered it. "Hence the trade," Kat said. "It's okay. I like a little game of cat and mouse."

"How did you find us?" Aeron asked.

"Ivan," Kat said, motioning for them to follow. Aeron averted her gaze at his name. Kat wanted to say something, curse Aeron up and down, but now was not the time to hash it out. They rounded the banister, walking down the hall to the kitchen. Hale had been secured to one of the stools, his guard bound on the floor. Mason sat on the kitchen counter, one leg propped up as he took a bite of an apple.

Aeron escorted Cass to the other side of the counter and took the seat beside Hale, Cass on the other side of her. Griffin's hand found her ass as he walked by, a smile finding her lips. He leaned against the wall by the garage door, crossing his feet and pulling out a knife to fiddle with.

Kat's lip curled as she looked at Hale. This man had taken Shay. It was clear in the documentation upstairs. She pulled a picture of Shay from her back pocket. It was taken a few years ago during his birthday party at the compound. He looked so full of life—so happy. She laid it on the surface in front of him. "Where is he?"

Hale looked down at the image and back up. "He is on his way to Rufus."

His casual tone sent Kat's hackles on guard. "Call them back."

"I can't," Hale said with a frown. "We need the information Rufus has."

"The information will be no use to your corpse," Kat replied.

"No. But Cass' mom's life depends on it, and this is bigger than just me." Hale looked over at Cass. "I promised him we would bring his mom home safely—that's all I'm trying to do."

"Bullshit," Mason said. He jumped off the counter, tossed his apple in the trash, and then leaned forward on his elbows next to Kat on the breakfast bar.

"Not bullshit. Do you even know who he is?" Hale asked, a glint of malice in his eyes. "Who his mother is?"

No one answered, and Cass scooted closer to Aeron. Kat kept her gaze on her—her eyes were out of focus, and she swayed ever so slightly in the chair.

"Let me set the story for you. Mike Barnes infiltrates the most secure assassin network on the East Coast. His end goal? To steal the program that is whispered about—that keeps them in the good graces of the Graveyard. What did he find? Someone got to it first. There was a programmer already inside the system." Kat looked back to Hale, his face bright with anticipation. Her heart thumped hard in her chest, the words similar to Ivan's. Hale only had eyes for Mason, though. "He informed Elijah—doing what needed to be done to keep his cover and build the trust. Do you know who Rufus found when he went looking?" He flicked his eyes to her.

Kat's mouth was dry, and although she had an inkling of what he was going to say, she shook her head.

Hale looked back at Mason. "Your darling Storm."

Mason lunged at Hale. Kat grabbed the waist of his pants as he vaulted over the breakfast bar. He half dragged her across it with him, and Griffin came to assist, with Aeron moving to pull Hale's stool back.

"Get her name out of your mouth!" Mason said with a fury in his face Kat had never seen.

Hale smirked. "Storm and her seven-year-old son, Cass." His gaze flicked to the boy.

Mason froze, Kat and Griffin pulling him back to their side of the counter. Mason looked toward Cass, too, his normally schooled features a mess of confusion and pain. The boy cowered under his gaze.

"I remember when you came looking for her—torn up and willing to sell your soul for a scrap of information. Looks like it was you who chased her away," Hale said.

Aeron reeled her elbow back and slammed it into the back of his head, snapping it forward. "Shut up," she warned.

Mason licked his lips, moving closer to the boy. "What's your mom's name?" he asked.

"Han-Hannah Smith," Cass said, visibly shaking as Mason studied his face.

"What does she do for a living?" Kat asked.

"She's a travel agent," he said. "We get to go on big trips every year. We went to Disney World last year."

Kat looked back to Hale. "If Rufus is the only one with confirmation of her location and identity, how do you know she is who you think she is?"

"The Graveyard sent us an assignment for the first time in over a decade," Hale said, "right after Rufus grabbed the programmer. Said Legacy Inc couldn't handle this one—too personal. They had a programmer named Hannah Smith and her son Cass go missing and needed us to retrieve them. It didn't take much to put two and two together. Plus, Rufus confirmed with a picture—that tattoo on her hip was hard to see under all that blood, but it was just as I remember it."

Kat moved to stop Mason again, but he didn't react. He didn't even move, just studied the little boy. It'd been seven years, and

Cass was seven. He must be wondering the same thing she was—if Storm was alive, was that his son? "Are you retrieving her for the Graveyard or personal use?" Kat asked, cocking her head.

"Doesn't matter now," Hale said. "You're going to kill me, right?"

"If we were going to kill you, we would have already," Aeron said, leaning against the wall. Her complexion was ghostly, sweat breaking out across her brow, and before Kat could take a step, she fainted. Mason reached her first, vaulting over the counter, Cass racing to his side.

Kat tamped down the urge to join them and kept her eyes on Hale. "Shay isn't enough to get Rufus to turn over Cass' mom," Kat said, not feeding into the possible lie that the woman was Storm. "So, what else are you offering?"

Hale kept his eyes on Aeron. "Nothing. He was willing to make the trade for Shay."

Kat didn't buy it. "Call Barnes off," Kat said, grabbing the phone from the counter and holding it out. She shot a glance at Griffin, nodding toward Hale to untie him. Griffin obliged, stepping past Aeron's unconscious form. Mason met her gaze, a frown on his face, and shook his head. Fuck.

"Is she okay?" Hale asked, looking at Aeron, his shoulders slumped forward as Griffin slit the zip ties.

"Doesn't matter," Kat answered. "Call him off."

"That's my niece, you obnoxious bitch," Hale responded, sending her a glare.

"That's my sister, you fucking prick," Kat spat.

Hale's mouth dropped open. "Maureen?" he asked.

"I guess that would make you Uncle Oliver," Kat said with sarcasm thick in her words, but she saw something shift in Hale's demeanor.

"You're not Andrew's," he said. "Who do you belong to?"

Her nostrils flared. What a fucking dick. "I belong to myself," she said. "Shay is an innocent bystander in all of this. You saw his condition—I'm sure you saw his torture." She swallowed back the guilt and continued, "If Rufus wants me, he can have me. But Shay has suffered enough."

"You love him," Oliver said.

"Call him," Kat repeated, "and tell him you have a better prize —me." Hale nodded, rubbed his wrists, and reached for the phone. "On speaker," she said.

Griffin watched as he pulled up the number for Mike and dialed. The phone rang and rang. No answer.

"Again," Kat said, her chest tightening. They were too close now to lose Shay. But the phone continued to ring. Hale ended the call and looked up, his eyes full of remorse. "I can't even tell you where they are meeting," Hale said. "I'm sorry."

And Kat believed he actually meant it. "Send him a message," she said and pressed her comm as Griffin read over Oliver's shoulder. "Home base?"

"Yes, my queen?" Ivan said over her comm, and she caught Griffin's lips quirk.

"I need the location on the Devil, please."

"He's left the compound, heading east."

"Kat," Mason said. She glared at him, but it melted instantly. He'd scooped Aeron up in his arms, her body cradled against his, blood flowing from her nose, staining his shirt. "We need to get her to Dr. Jones. Now!"

Hale stood, concern etching his face as he looked at Aeron. "Is she okay?"

"She's dying," Griffin said, pushing Hale back into his seat.

Kat pursed her lips. They needed to intercept Shay, and Aeron needed to get help. "Do we have a location on Dr. Jones?" Kat asked Mason.

He shook his head. "He managed to make himself invaluable

enough that they didn't track him, but he will come when Maureen calls—no doubt about it."

Good. "Griff? I need you to return home." His face darkened, but he nodded. "She thinks you can be manipulated? Let's use that," Kat said. "We'll retrieve Shay and be right on your heels to pull you out."

"Tell them Izz gave you the location," Mason said, passing Aeron over to him. He shrugged off his jacket and laid it over her, then pushed the hair from her brow with a grimace. "Alone, Izz would throw you to the wolves, but she will not let Aeron die."

"What about the kid?" Griffin asked, looking over at Cass. He sat on the floor, staring at the spot where Aeron had just been.

"We'll keep him safe until we can get to his mom," Kat promised.

Griffin nodded and headed to the garage, Kat meeting him by the entrance. She held the door open. "Be careful."

He pressed a kiss to her lips, lingering long enough for it to feel like a goodbye. "You too."

She let the door fall shut without a backward glance, her focus on Hale and all the ways she would love to ruin his life. "Kill him."

Mason nodded. "Turn around, kiddo," he said to Cass and stepped forward.

"Wait!" Hale exclaimed, but Mason didn't stop. He pulled out his Sig, grasped Hale by the shirt, and dug the gun beneath his chin.

"You are useless to me," Kat said.

"You need bodies to go after Olivia—Maureen," Hale said. "I have bodies."

Kat held up her hand for Mason to wait. "Olivia?" Kat repeated, the name familiar, but she couldn't place it.

"Who is Olivia?" Mason asked.

"Maureen," Hale answered. "My sister Olivia is Maureen. And

I want her dead. I'll keep trying Barnes and I'll help you retrieve Shay. We want the same things."

Mason cocked his head. "We do need bodies—and the Syndicate is short themselves since the Playhouse."

Kat liked nothing about this man. He'd stolen Shay and Aeron. He'd tried to steal her Legacy. But they did need bodies. "Tie him up," she said. "If he doesn't provide what we need, we'll dispose of him on the way to Rufus."

35

IZZ

The car slid across the ice, Izz doing her best to maintain control. The heat blasted into the silence of Dash's car. Rufus had snagged hers, and Dash wouldn't be needing his anymore. But he hadn't changed to the snow tires yet, and she sucked at driving.

Eileen was dead.

The thought chased itself around her mind, through her center, down to her toes, but it didn't want to stick. Maureen had killed Eileen. That fact seared into her mind, like a lie that she should know better than to believe. But she'd seen it. Felt it. And it had to be done. The second Eileen learned about Seamus, there was no other logical option.

It took two hours and several encounters with the guard rails to reach Pop's. Izz parked the no longer pristine Audi beside her blue car. She was early—but so was he. He waved his duct-taped hand at her and rolled down his window. She did too, the icy air invading the space and she swore, wishing she hadn't left her jacket back in the vault.

"You wouldn't happen to have a med kit in that car, would you?" he asked.

"You wouldn't happen to know about Storm, would you?" she countered. He glowered, but nodded. She rolled up the window and turned off the engine. Her teeth chattered, but she grabbed the medical kit and got into the passenger seat of her car, grateful for the full-blast heat Rufus turned on for her.

The blood had seeped out of the tape, and she half-hoped his fingers needed to be amputated. "Let me see that thing." She cut the duct tape off and carefully peeled it up from his palm, pushing the fingertips in the direction they belonged. Her nose twitched in disgust as they slightly flopped forward again once the pressure of the tape was gone, but enjoyed the growl of pain Rufus gave. She turned his hand over. Aeron had gouged all four fingers above the second knuckle. There would be no saving the fingertip of his first finger. How he'd managed to nearly kill Kat and have it not fall off was a physical-phenomenon—the skin barely held it on. The middle two fingers she'd sliced into the bone, the skin and tendons working overtime. His pinky took the least amount of damage, a nasty cut down to the bone—nothing a little super glue wouldn't fix.

She let out a low whistle. "You're lucky. Any deeper and I'd be chucking all of these in the snow." She took the scissors she'd cut off the tape with and made a quick snip through the first finger. Rufus ripped his hand back, a snarl leaving him as the tip dropped into her lap. She pulled the duct tape back out of the glove compartment, ignoring the slew of curses Rufus aimed at her, and wrapped the bloody nub in tape. As quick as possible, she cracked the door, tossed the duct tape outside, and slammed the door closed, fighting off a shiver. "Give it here," she said, holding out her hand.

Izz took her time, not out of care, but to ensure the process was as painful as possible before she applied the LidoPen. Years of studying under Eileen walked her through the steps: clean, align, secure, apply antiseptic, cauterize if needed. The steps were easy. The voice in her head, however, tore at her.

He turned the bandaged hand over, testing his ability to bend it. He winced but had mobility. "It will do," he said. "Let's eat."

Marigold looked up from the hostess counter as they entered the blissfully warm building, her light brown skin dusted with freckles that danced when she smiled. She reminded Izz of Eileen. "Long time," Marigold said.

"Is our booth open?" Izz asked, unable to return the smile. She felt heavy—empty all of a sudden.

"Always," Marigold said. "Your usual?"

"Please," Izz answered. "And keep the hot coffee coming."

Izz scanned the restaurant as they walked to the back corner. Rufus' massive stature pulled almost every eye in the room. The blood on his shirt didn't help either. Most regulars, she recognized, and the few new faces didn't give off the aura she'd learned to expect from dangerous people—even when they were playing sheep. Rufus slid into the booth first, Izz taking the seat beside him. Here, they were out of sight of the front door, but with a clear view of anyone approaching the building.

Lucy, Pop's oldest daughter, brought over a pot of coffee and two mugs. Her graying hair was knotted atop her head, and her smile touched her eyes. "Morning loves."

"Hey, Lucy. How are the grand babies?" Izz asked, accepting the mug of steaming gold.

"Growing," she said with a smile. "Your food will be out shortly."

Izz sipped the coffee, the burning sensation a perfect distraction from her frozen lower digits and the tattered hole in her chest. She waited until Lucy turned the corner to say, "I know you didn't call me here because I can glue your fingers back together and enjoy a meal."

"Why does Mason want my head on a spike?"

"Awe, you having a bro-fight?" she said with a smirk and took another sip.

"Cut the shit. He's saved my ass more times than I care to admit. He was low on my radar of enemies."

"That's because he's the best." Rufus glared, and Izz released a long sigh. "You really don't know?"

"I could have just left," he said in explanation.

"July, 1997. Washington DC. The first Legacy/Legacy Inc mission."

He closed his eyes and tipped his head back. "Yeah—I kinda recall it."

"You executed a little girl in a pink dress," Izz said, the words falling from her, the secrets Mason had shared with her after intimate nights and hard kills.

A smile spread across his face, and he picked his head up. "Oh yes. I remember that. Why does he care?"

"That was his sister, you soulless fuck." She took another sip of coffee, gripping the hot cup until the skin on her palms and fingers burned. "I answered your question and saved most of your fingers. My turn: What do you know about Storm?"

Lucy arrived again, dropping off Rufus' two double bacon cheeseburgers and Izz's chicken pot pie. Her mouth watered at the smell, and she dug in, the steam warming her face. "If you all need anything else, just holler," Lucy said and disappeared back into the kitchen.

"Oh my goodness, this is so good," Izz said, and looked at Rufus, waiting for him to answer her question. But he glared at his bandage before picking the burger up with his left.

He took a few bites before responding. "Why'd you shoot Mason?"

She'd shot Mason to secure Rufus—to get the information about Storm. But she couldn't tell him that. "Because Maureen declared him enemy number one. And I answer to her." She took another bite of food. "Storm."

"She's alive," Rufus said.

The spoon paused halfway to her mouth. She'd expected information on what happened to her or the location of her body. Alive? Maureen would flip when she found out. No. Izz needed eyes on her first, and then to get her away from Rufus. She wasn't turning up without proof or she would find herself in an unmarked grave next to Eileen. "Where?"

"In a stash house. She's been there a few days, though. I need to go check on her. Hale apparently needs her coherent." The disgust in his voice chilled her. Rufus' philosophy was people could be coherent without their limbs.

"You're trading her?"

"Her location, for a walking corpse that will draw Kat out. And if it doesn't—then I can enjoy torturing him and send her the video. It's a win-win."

Izz let out a small laugh. "You need help moving bodies, being a hand down and all."

"And backup, in case Mike goes back on the deal. I'm short of friendly support at the moment."

"I'm not friendly."

"No," he agreed. "But you nearly killed your favorite fuck boy to save me, so..."

They finished eating in silence; the sun peeked over the tree line by the time they stepped back outside. In the light of day, Izz could see the damage to Dash's beloved car. Dents and scrapes and mud. He would be rolling in his grave. She popped the trunk to remove all traces of the Syndicate. She grabbed an emergency bag with extra food, clothes, and cash and tossed it at Rufus. The travel arsenal was locked beneath the trunk flooring, and she pulled it up, revealing a safe. She pressed her middle finger on the scanner and the lock disengaged. Inside, nestled in foam, were several pistols and boxes of ammunition, along with smoke and flash bombs.

"Give me a hand with these," Izz said. "The good hand." She pulled the weapons from their secured spots and passed them over. She double-checked the car for any identifying information, then turned it on and dropped a Zippo lighter on the seat. It lit immediately, and she enjoyed the heat for only a moment, sending a final farewell to her second favorite fuck boy. Rufus pulled the car around, and she hopped into the passenger seat. "Off to retrieve your bait?"

He smirked and peeled out of the driveway.

One thing Izz could always count on was Rufus' need for discretion. Their meeting place with Barnes was an abandoned house in the middle-of-nowhere-Connecticut. Literally. She was going to need a GPS to get herself home. Four cars idled in the driveway, her hand sliding to her hip for her gun.

"Relax," Rufus said. "Underworlders here for backup."

"I fucking hate Underworlders. They're slow and sloppy."

"And great for body armor," Rufus said, parking on the street. "Mike should be here any minute." He went to step out of the car, and Izz grabbed his arm.

"Her location, in case things go sideways."

He regarded her with mild disinterest, and she waited. "Our stash house in Brooklyn."

She quirked an eyebrow. He'd used one of their old stash houses, one she would eventually look in, and he knew it. What was his end game?

Izz stepped out of the car, surveying the area. The cars in the driveway were fogged up, and Izz stopped her approach, eyes dropping to the snow-covered ground. A single set of footprints went to the car doors, and then to the house in a perfect line. She pulled her weapon and took another step, her breath a cloud in front of her. She held her hand up for Rufus to freeze, spotting drops of crimson in the snow. Her gaze shot to the house, searching the windows for a sniper.

"They're dead," Izz said, not even checking. If they hadn't come out at her approach, they weren't coming out at all. They turned toward the house instead, trekking through the ankle-high snow to the semi-cleared steps. She took the stairs slowly, trying to keep her balance as the boots slid in the slush. The front door opened wide, and Izz raised her gun. Barnes stood in the entryway with a steaming cup of takeout coffee and a smile that screamed victory.

"About fucking time," he said, looking past her to Rufus.

"You killed my people," Rufus said.

"I pre-punctured your shields," Barnes said with a laugh and stepped aside so they could pass. The room was cold, but not empty. An unconscious man sat strapped to the chair, his dark complexion highlighted by slices to his face and blood dribbling down his cheeks. A man in a blue sweater sat beside him, tending to the wounds, and looking more uncomfortable than Dash when she suggested using a strap-on. God, she was going to miss that boy.

But the two guards leaning against the wall left Izz feeling under-dressed. They wore full tactical gear, their semi-auto rifles draped across their chests. "Didn't realize we were coming to collect the fucking President of the United States," Izz said, eyeing them with caution.

"These are my peace offerings," Barnes said. "For a future together."

"Future?" Rufus said, walking past her, eyes only for the man strapped to the chair. She could see his arousal and averted her gaze back at Barnes.

"Ours," Barnes said. "Hale sent word Mason and Kat are on

their way here. The only thing missing is a big fucking bow. The Legacies have fallen, and the Syndicate is next."

"Excuse you?" Izz said, adjusting her grip on the gun.

"Hale, will be taking that bitch out in a few days."

Izz's hand twitched, and before she could fire, Rufus slammed into her, knocking her to the ground. The air left her body, head smacking the wooden floorboards. Her lungs refused to cooperate so she could move, and Rufus leaned down, his hot breath hitting the side of her face. "Sorry, Izzy. I'll take my chances with Barnes over Maureen."

"Brush your fucking teeth," Izz said, an irrational anger gripping her at the nickname. Her lungs were back in working order, and she shot her right hand out, gripped the tips of his fingers, and twisted. He swore, pulling his hand back and creating space for her to move. She grabbed her gun off the floor and aimed at the man strapped to the chair. She had to get back and warn Maureen. "I'm leaving here, or he's dead."

"It's four on one," Barnes said.

"Two on one, and in my favor," Izz corrected, reaching behind her and removing her secondary piece, pointing it in the same direction but toward the guards. "I have no faith in your left-handed shot, and Rufus will dive in front of this bullet before he lets it land in his leverage. That leaves Dimwit one and two, and one of them still has their safety on."

Everyone except Rufus looked at the guards. She threw Rufus a kiss, fired a few shots, and raced out of the house.

36

AERON

*A*eron woke in the passenger side of an SUV, the seat leaned back, and the music so loud she was sure there would be some hearing loss. She turned her head to look at the driver, her skull feeling as if it weighed a hundred pounds. Griffin's intense profile met her, his hair pulled up with a dart stuck through it.

"Griffin," she said, but she could barely hear herself over the music. If she could move her arm, get his attention—but her left arm was useless, and her right seemed just as heavy as her head. "Griffin," she said louder. It did the trick.

He glanced over at her, and then looked again, the SUV swerving. He turned down the music and stopped the car, placing his hand on her head, his touch freezing. "Can you hear me?" he asked.

"Yeah, dipshit," she said. "I'm just having a hard time moving."

"Good. Stay awake. We're almost at the compound." He pulled back onto the road, the jokester she'd gotten to know nowhere to be seen.

"Where?"

He ran his tongue across his teeth before answering. "We're

taking you to Maureen's compound—to see if she'll let Dr. Jones take a look."

"No—Griffin. . ." Aeron fought to sit up, her body refusing the request. Going to Maureen would be a suicide mission for him. And what about Hale? Hale—her most recent memories returned to her: Mike Barnes, Hale, Cass. Her heart pounded, head swimming with the sudden rush of blood through her veins. "Where's Cass?"

"Safe. Mason and Kat will take care of him. Maureen is the best shot at saving you. I half expected you to be dead before we arrived."

"I'm not that bad," she said, although they both knew that was a lie.

"We're only a few minutes out. Since you're up—I'm going in undercover."

Undercover? It was clear as day that Griffin's loyalty was to Kat. "How?"

He grimaced. "Short version: Maureen planted me in Kat's life."

"What?" She managed to sit up, bracing herself on the dashboard. A jacket that didn't belong to her fell off her shoulders, and she shivered hard. She scooped the garment back up and pulled it on over her good arm.

"It was almost two decades ago, and after her car accident—I never saw her again. It's a long shot, but that's what we need at this moment. If she asks, I took you from Hale. No one else was there."

Aeron pulled the seat into an upright position and settled back against it, unease creeping into her stomach. "Why didn't they just let me die?"

His head snapped over at her, brow furrowed. "You're joking, right?"

"I'm not worth it," Aeron said, the feeling of guilt consuming her. "So many people are dead because of me. People are still dying, and for what? A liar? A murderer?" Luke's pleading eyes swam into her mind, and she closed hers, seeing the pain in them. She'd pushed him there.

"You saved Cass' life," Griffin reminded her. She had. The rush of purpose she'd felt when she'd seen him—it trumped everything in that moment. "And you saved Kat's life on more than one occasion. For me, that alone makes you worth saving."

A lump rose to her throat, and she nodded. Silence fell between them. The road, loud under the tires and slush hitting the undercarriage, filled the space. He pulled off onto an unmarked road and sped up. They drove between the snow-covered evergreens for half a mile, coming upon a guarded gate, a man waving him down. Griffin's grip on the wheel tightened, and he slowed, lowering the window.

"Sorry, sir, this is a private road," he said. "You'll need to turn around."

Aeron could almost see Griffin turn the charm on. "Tell Amara that the Reaper has a delivery." The man whipped up his pistol, but Griffin did not move his hands, Aeron catching a smirk on his face.

The guard didn't lower the weapon as he touched the comm at his throat. "Patch me through to Amara." They waited in silence, the man's eyes never shifting away from Griffin, and it took Aeron a moment to remember she had felt that way the first time she'd seen him in the Playhouse. But after playing cards and hearing him chase the kids around the house, she saw the man beneath the Reaper. The guard cleared his throat. "You can go through."

The gate lifted, and Griffin started their drive again, his posture stiffer. Aeron sat up straighter too, eyes scanning for possible danger. It was another mile before the tree line opened. The road widened around a bend to a line of people blocking their path, rifles at their sides. Griffin slammed on the brakes, skidding to a halt. Her mother stood in the middle of them, hands on her hips, eyes narrowed.

The reality of what they were doing landed on Aeron like a ton of bricks. "Griffin—just hand me over and leave. No one else needs to die because of me."

"Who said I'm dying?" He unbuckled his seatbelt and put the car in park. The half smile he gave did not ease the fear growing inside her. "There are things here far worse than death." Before she could respond to that morbid statement, he stepped out of the car, hands up near his shoulders. Aeron popped her door open. The freezing air hit her but did not slow her hasty exit. She stumbled, legs refusing to hold her full weight, and leaned onto the hood of the vehicle for support.

"What do you want, Reaper?" Maureen asked, closing the distance between them. Her eyes darted to Aeron, and Aeron saw a small flicker of concern like she had in the Playhouse, right before Maureen had attacked Rufus.

"Izz told me if I wanted to come home, I needed an offering. Well," he looked over to her, and although Aeron knew it wasn't real, the disgust on his face stung. "Here she is."

"Come home?" Maureen frowned. "I offered that in the office, and you refused."

"After careful consideration—I want to be on the winning side."

Maureen's lips quirked. "We'll see about that. Strip. Then I'll get some real answers."

Aeron swallowed hard, but it was all she could do. The world began to fade at the edges again, and her head pounded.

Griffin removed his hair dart, and the entire line of rifles raised. He shook his hair out and lightly tossed the dart away, and the line of rifles lowered. He moved to his belt next, pulling two blades from their sheaths. As if they took a collective breath, the rifles raised again. He paused with a smile that reached his eyes. "I have fourteen blades on me. Their arms are going to get pretty tired if they keep that up."

Maureen smirked. "Susie and Petra, watch the man strip down. Everyone else, back to work. If he wanted to kill us, he wouldn't have come down the driveway."

The group dispersed and two women approached Griffin, rifles at the ready. Aeron shivered as he removed his shirt, revealing two tattoos and a compilation of scars. Aeron turned as Maureen approached, taking Aeron in with interest. "Not the way I was hoping to have a conversation with you, but I'll take it." She looked over to Griffin again, now down to his black boxers, removing the blades from the sheaths in his boots. "What's wrong with my daughter?"

Anger swirled in Aeron's chest—she could have just asked her—but Aeron let Griffin take the lead. "Mason dosed her with a cocktail from Dr. Jones' laboratory to bring her back from the dead. From what I gathered, she's not reacting well," he said with a shrug and kicked off his boots, his bright blue socks with orange fish on them not what Aeron expected.

Maureen's face darkened. "Take him to the garage."

One woman secured his wrists, the other collected his clothes and weapons, and they escorted him around the bend. Maureen stepped forward and Aeron looked at her. Even though they were outside, Aeron felt as if the space was closing in on her. What would she even say to this woman? What did she need to say? Nothing. Everything.

It seemed Maureen wasn't in the talking mood, anyway. She nodded toward the car, going to the driver's seat. "Get in."

But Aeron couldn't move. Her joints ached, and as she tried to turn, the world went sideways, and she landed in a pile on the ground. The cold snow bit into her cheek, and she left it there, letting the darkness seep in. She could just go to sleep and forget all the pain. She could—

Get up, Aeron.

Aeron snapped her eyes open. The voice sounded like Decius, so clear she could swear he knelt by her head. Her heart worked overtime, and she pushed herself to her hands and knees, looking for Maureen, but she was nowhere to be seen. With the fresh wave of adrenaline, she got to her feet, finding her mother glaring from the car. With shaking legs, Aeron got herself into the passenger seat and shut the door, the clearest thought in her head since before Mason had tried to save her: if she fell asleep now, she would never wake back up.

Maureen said nothing to her as she put the car in drive and rounded the bend. They had been feet from the main compound. Cars were parked in front of a large cabin, where people were going in and out. Beside that was a tractor-trailer with a massive vault on the bed. Aeron sat up straighter and looked at Maureen. "Is that the Legacy Inc vault?"

"That it is," she said, pulling around the cars and tractor-trailer to park beside a garage-looking building. She looked over, giving Aeron the chance to see her in the early morning light. Aeron couldn't find a trace of the woman they'd seen pictures of while growing up. Her favorite picture had been in Mrs. Gale's study. The two best friends were at an old-fashioned milkshake shop, faces glowing and full of excitement. But that woman no longer existed. The scars across her face were deep and twisted. And the more Aeron looked at them, the worse they seemed to get. "What did Mason give you?"

Aeron blinked a few times. He'd told her what he'd given her, but like so much since she woke up, the words hadn't stuck. "I don't remember," she admitted. "But it feels like my brain is melting."

Maureen nodded and turned off the engine. She pulled out her cell phone and sent a text message. Aeron surveyed the surroundings while she waited for whatever would happen next.

Each entrance to the garage she saw had a guard, and behind them the vault was closed, two guards standing in front of it. "Dr. Jones will be here in twenty minutes. Let's get you inside."

"Is Mrs. Gale here?" Aeron asked, the thought of a friendlier face comforting.

Maureen's scars twitched. "No."

Maureen led her into the main cabin. She had to pause several times for Aeron to catch up, and Aeron didn't miss the annoyed look on her face. It brought a small feeling of satisfaction that Aeron couldn't explain, but she made sure to walk slower than she needed to. The cabin felt packed with people. Some milled about the kitchen area, and others lounged on couches on the other side of the room. Several people sat at a long table that dominated the room, bowls of food in front of them. All eyes turned to them, except a blonde woman who sat at the head of that table, eyes glued to her computer like Aeron had seen Ivan so many times before. Her heart thumped harder for a moment. He must hate her now.

"Everyone out," Maureen said. Aeron had never seen a group of people exit a room so quickly. "You too, Rebekah."

Rebekah looked up from the computer, fingers not slowing down. "I'll lose the trace on the car," she said.

"She probably already ditched it," Maureen replied. "Let it run." Rebekah's hands hesitated over the keyboard, but she nodded and grabbed a jacket on her way outside. "Take a seat, Aeron."

Aeron picked the closest seat and lowered herself down, her muscles sagging in relief. A bowl of leftover lasagna sat in front of her, and her stomach turned. She pushed it away. "Do you have water? Or tea?"

Maureen's lip curled, the barely contained distaste on her face, and Aeron fought the urge to tell her to forget it. But Maureen boiled a kettle of water and then brought over a mug of steaming liquid, an unmarked box of tea bags, sugar, and a glass of water.

"Thanks," Aeron said, unsure if she should even say that. The air was thick with tension, years of unasked questions sitting in the back of Aeron's throat. She wanted to ask why she'd left. Why she didn't come to them after her father died? Why she'd taken Luke? Why she didn't love them? Just—why? But Aeron couldn't read her body language, and just asking for a drink seemed to be a big enough burden.

Maureen took a seat across the table with her mug, mouth set in a line, and stared at Aeron. Aeron stared back, ignoring the warning her brain gave to look away. Maureen smirked in response and plucked a tea bag from the container. "English Breakfast," she said and put it in her mug. She put two spoonfuls of sugar in the steaming liquid and stirred, the spoon dinging against the mug filling the thick silence that sat between them.

Aeron copied Maureen's motions, grabbing a tea bag and adding sugar. But instead of sipping it, she just wrapped her right hand around it, letting the warmth work up her arm. Her tongue felt swollen, the sealed-away boxes inside her trying to jam themselves up her throat, demanding to be heard. She was one-hundred percent positive if she opened her mouth, she'd have no control of what would come out, so she kept it slammed closed instead.

Maureen broke their silence first. "I'll find out from the Reaper, one way or another, but how did you really end up here?"

Aeron licked her lips, brow furrowing. "He took me from Hale." Maureen's lip twitched at the name, the mass of scars moving as one. A jolt shot through Aeron, and she sat straighter in her chair, ready to move if she needed to. But Maureen didn't say anything, so Aeron continued, her voice finding its footing now that she'd spoken. "He claims to be your brother."

"What kind of brother allows your children to be put in danger?" she countered.

Aeron's lip twitched into a smile. She took a sip of her tea to hide it—that was exactly what she'd said about Maureen when Barnes had asked about her mother. "I imagine one that was betrayed, and his family murdered."

Maureen glared, but her voice was soft when she answered. "I didn't realize at the time that his family would be compromised."

"Would you have done it, anyway?" Aeron asked. "Whatever it was that you did?"

Maureen sat back in the chair and regarded her with a curious gaze. "The me today or the me fifteen years ago? We are vastly different people."

Aeron felt a pang of sadness with that confession. Everyone talked about how much love her mother had, but all she saw was hate and pain. It reminded her of Luke, of the person he became to protect the people he loved. "What happened to you?" Aeron asked, her voice low.

Maureen gave a harsh laugh and looked down at her drink, disappointment threading into her next words. "I lived."

Aeron's breath caught in her chest, the underlying pain in those words as raw as the phantom pressure of a suppressor to her forehead and gravel digging into her knees. Was this her future? Angry she'd been pulled from the grave, surrounded by people but utterly alone?

Maureen's phone chirped in her back pocket, and the moment passed. She pulled out her phone, the mode already switched. "Jones' ETA is four minutes. We'll meet him in the garage."

Grunts and shouts met Aeron as they stepped into the dimly lit garage. The smell of bleach assaulted her nose, and she followed Maureen blindly until her eyes adjusted. The garage had been divided into three sections. On the right was a white-tiled, sterilized area, with gurneys and emergency medical equipment. The middle area looked like a lounge, with tables and couches and a bar. On the left—where the grunts were coming from—was a torture area. There looked to be several private rooms, but in the corner, chains hung from the walls, a table of instruments in front of several chairs—like the one Luke had been strapped to, with IVs and monitors. They all were empty, save one. Petra and Susie stood on either side of Griffin. He looked up from the one he'd been secured to and smiled at her, blood smearing his teeth, before he shifted his gaze to Maureen.

"Not the welcome home I was expecting," he said. "Do I get the honor of a Sin trip from you? Or are we waiting for Eileen?"

Maureen's body stiffened beside her, and Aeron looked up, her own body tensing in response. Sin? It had destroyed Luke. "I'm giving the honor to Izz," Maureen said coolly.

No. He'd be forced to give them up, but more importantly, he would lose his spark—he would—Aeron's heart began to race, her breath not cooperating, and a loud beating sounded in her ears.

"Aeron?" Maureen's voice said close to her, and Aeron swore it held a smidge of concern. Aeron hoped it would be enough for Maureen to catch her, as the edge of her vision darkened, the sound getting louder, her world tipping sideways. "Hold on, Dr. Jones is here."

A set of hands caught her and lowered her to the cool cement. The world blinked around her: the ceiling, her dad, a bright light, Decius, another bright light—Shannon. Aeron smiled at her best friend, her insides feeling like they were going to burst out of her chest. Another bright light, and then a man she did not know—he had beady eyes, and a pointed nose, his black hair slicked back. She blinked several times, trying to bring Shannon back—but the man's puzzled face didn't budge.

"Which vial did he give you, Aeron?" the man asked.

The word vial jumpstarted her memory. "Vial 879," she said. The man's somber expression didn't help the panic.

"That's the one I isolated the rouge strain of Sin in," he said, looking up at Maureen. "Jump starts the body, but—"

"You need 880 to follow it up," Maureen said. "I had Izz bring your stock from Legacy Inc Headquarters."

The man nodded and looked back down at Aeron. She looked away from him to Maureen. "Am I going to be okay?" A wave of vulnerability washed over her as the words left her. But she wanted to hear her say it—have her mom tell her it was all going to be okay.

"You'll live," Maureen replied and looked away, the same disappointment slipping in from the table.

Aeron bit back a sob, not fully sure why she was crying. She was going to live—and her mom was displeased? Aeron kept her eyes on Maureen, willing her to look back, but when she finally did, Aeron's heart launched into her throat, Maureen's displeasure piercing any composure Aeron had left. Another sob left her, and Aeron looked away, a new hole opening in her chest she didn't know if she'd have the strength to box up.

Dr. Jones grabbed her chin, turning her head toward him to check her eyes again. She tried to push him off, but her arms wouldn't listen. "Don't worry," he said, his beady eyes narrowing. "I'm going to get you right as rain in no time."

37

KAT

"Get in," Mason said, popping the trunk. Hale glared at him. "It was good enough for Aeron, it's good enough for you."

Kat pushed Hale forward. "I thought we had an understanding," he said.

"We do," Kat said. "Get in." Hale slid into the trunk, glaring at her until it clicked closed. Mason had secured Cass in the backseat, and Kat peered in at him on her way to the passenger seat. The kid looked shell-shocked. She released a long sigh—she was so tired of kids being used in this business. She picked the laptop they'd found off the seat and dropped into the car.

"We can store him in interrogation rooms beneath the Institute," Kat suggested. "Dom and Ivan can keep an eye on Cass."

Mason turned on the car and backed out of the garage. "Sounds like as good a plan as any."

They pulled into the Institute, Dom meeting them in the garage by the interrogation elevators. He nodded in greeting, and Kat held out a laptop.

Dom tucked the computer under his arm. "Who is this special guest?" he asked.

Kat looked at Mason. He hadn't said anything on the drive, and every time she caught him looking at Cass, it was with a mixture of fear and concern furrowed in his brow. He wasn't ready to confront the possibility of this being Storm's son, let alone this being his son. "This is Cass," Kat said, opening the rear door. "He's a friend of Aeron's."

Dom smiled at the boy, a hand outstretched, coaxing him out of the back seat. Cass didn't move. "I'm a friend of Aeron's too," Dom said. "And one of her best friends, Ivan, is downstairs. We have a ton of video games and pizza."

Cass' face relaxed a little. "Does it have pineapples?"

Dom didn't move his eyes from the boy. "Do you want pineapples?" Cass nodded. "Then we will order another. C'mon." Cass inched out of the car, giving Kat a wide berth. He took Dom's hand, and Kat let out a silent sigh of relief as Dom led him inside.

She exchanged a look with Mason and looked at the trunk. "Ready?"

"Ready." They stood on either side of the trunk, guns drawn, and clicked it open. She expected him to lash out, attack, do anything after being locked in the trunk. Instead, he just laid there, fingers interwoven behind his head, a scowl on his face. Kat lowered her gun.

"I didn't realize how fucking disorienting being in this trunk was. We soundproofed it, and let me tell you, the designers were not kidding. The anxiety-inducing silence waiting for you to open it is on the money." He sat up slowly, raising his hands, and looked at Mason. "Have you decided what we're doing with me?"

Kat scoffed. Fucking men.

"Don't ask me," Mason said with a half laugh. "I'm not in charge here."

Hale adjusted his gaze to Kat. "My apologies."

"Get out of the car," she said. He obliged, and she waved him to the elevator, Mason joining them, taking the lead on the journey.

Kat hadn't been down to the interrogation rooms in years. They stepped into the end of a dimly lit hallway with doors spaced evenly throughout it, the closest one labeled 'Observation Room'.

"I thought we had come to an understanding I would cooperate," Hale said, looking at Mason, sweat dripping down his face. "I gave you access to my assets."

Kat rolled her eyes. At this point, he was doing it on purpose. "We did, and you did," Kat said. "But until I have eyes on Shay, we need you locked up safely, and no one gets in or out of these interrogation rooms."

"Which one?" Mason asked.

There were several options, but Kat wasn't taking any chances. Room four was rumored to induce nightmares just by being in it, and Hale sounded like he could use a few more nightmares. "Four."

They escorted him to the last door on the left. Kat unlocked it with her retinal scan, a small jolt of excitement coursing through her each time it worked. The putrid stench washed over them, and Kat choked back a gag. Hale paled. "This is how you treat an ally?"

"You should see how I treat my enemies," Kat answered, a wicked smile crossing her face. She pushed Hale into the room and slammed the door. The stench lessened, and she turned to Mason. He leaned against the wall, arms crossed, eyes on the floor. "What's going on?" He was distracted, and they couldn't afford for anyone to be distracted.

"Last time I was down here, Eileen and I had set up Luke." Kat's mouth dropped at the confession. "We needed time for me to help her escape, and took advantage of Luke's state of mind, fabricating a story that he wanted her tortured so we could make a plan and get her back to Maureen." Mason looked up. "You see, Maureen is not the same woman who started the Alliance. I know that, and so does Eileen. But it's hard to let go of that kind of friendship and loyalty. The Alliance was started out of love, and a fierce protection of family and team. And then something changed after Maureen's accident. She became obsessed with Sin and digging into people for the truth. She became more vengeful—ruthless. But Eileen has always stuck by her—always. Keeps her in check, balances out the crazy, and Maureen lets her. And I swear it's only because Eileen doesn't know the truth."

His words stirred uncertainty in her. "Truth about what?"

"Your father. He never knew either. And I was set to take the secret to the grave unless you straight up asked me for it. But," he paused, licking his lips, the words seeming difficult for him to find. "He should have had the opportunity to know. What Maureen did was—it was selfish and wrong. And if I had been older and wiser with a few less fucks to give, I would have told the truth to everyone involved. So, if you want to know—just ask."

Kat swallowed back the lump rising in her throat. "Where is this coming from?"

"If she's alive," he took a second to compose himself, and Kat waited, realizing he was processing the information about Storm. "I searched for her, Kat, and when I couldn't find her—I wanted her to be dead so she couldn't be used against me, and because dead meant she hadn't willingly left me behind. But what if she's not?"

"We don't know Rufus has her. He could be lying," Kat said. But she was positive Ivan had uncovered the truth—Storm was still alive. Or had been.

"A techie who's gone missing with a personal connection to Legacy Inc? A son that is seven years old? If that is Storm's son, he could be mine," he whispered, and the pain in his eyes tore at Kat.

From what she'd learned about Mason, fatherhood would be right up his alley. He'd fostered all the Alliance's children, and loved them more than their parents at times, filling the void she now saw in him. She'd always wondered about her father. Who had been unlucky enough to fall in love with Rosemary? Or

Maureen, she should say. Did they know about her and choose to walk away, too? But they hadn't.

"Was he a good man?" Rosemary had led her to believe he was trash. A man she had to put down for the betterment of both of them. A man who didn't want her.

Mason gave a small smile, sadness creeping into the corners of his eyes. "He was one of the best."

A weight lifted off her. Her gene pool wasn't completely fucked. She hadn't cared—she hadn't needed them, but the question of who he was popped up in the back of her mind more often than she cared to admit, and it would be a lie to say it didn't hurt to find out Rosemary hadn't been lying about him being dead. Then a small fear bloomed in her chest—if anything happened to Mason—she may never learn the truth. "Who. . . Who was he?"

"Seamus Gale." He kept his gaze on her the way people do when they are waiting for someone to put the pieces together.

It didn't take Kat long. "Gale. As in Eileen, Shannon, and Keara Gale?"

He nodded.

She had more family—more sisters; no, a sister. Shannon was dead. A sadness so deep crashed into her. Motherfucker. "Eileen doesn't know?"

Mason shook his head. "You were the most guarded secret, Kat. For the Waywards and Maureen. Until the accident, Eileen didn't know you existed, but as far as I know, she hasn't learned you were Seamus'."

"Is this why you kept telling me I can trust her?"

Mason shook his head. "No. You can trust her, because I trust her, and she knows Maureen is just a few moves away from being dethroned."

Kat mulled the information over. She tucked away the identity of her father for another day. There would be plenty of time to deep dive into who he was, warm up to Eileen and Keara, and maybe—just maybe—breach into that topic with them. Eileen's loyalty and the certainty that Maureen was on a path to self-destruction was what interested her since they sent Griffin and Aeron in blind. "How dangerous is Maureen to Aeron? To Griffin?"

"With Eileen there, she's not. We have the same goal of ending this feud."

"I'm a Gale," she said, pushing off the wall. "Katherine Gale." She smiled as they headed down the hall, the name feeling right. "That sounds fucking good."

"I always thought so," he said.

Kat bit her lip and nodded. If they were telling the truth, she needed to come clean before they went upstairs. "You should know something," she said as they stepped onto the elevator. "Ivan found Storm's log in the program." He turned to look at her, and she gave a small frown. "She logged in three weeks ago." His face became a mask, and she continued. "I had no idea her being alive was possible and thought Mike Barnes may have done something to alter them. Don't be mad at Ivan. I told him not to say anything."

Mason just stared at her for a moment. "Don't tell him anything yet," he finally said. "I don't want to get his hopes up and then bring home a corpse."

Kat nodded. The symmetry between Ivan's and Mason's desire to protect each other was not lost on her. She watched as his mask secured his feelings in a box for him to look at later. They all did it, learned to compartmentalize, learned to peek inside the boxes to feel things and remember their purpose. But very few ever took all those boxes back out. She knew Mason did—it was the only way he could be as vicious and as calculating as he was loving and kind.

The smell of pizza overwhelmed her as she and Mason stepped into the hall for the cold room. Lights flashed from the unusually dark room, and Kat sped up, worry running through her gut until the laughter hit her ears just outside the door and she paused. The main screen flashed, two avatars moving to the music that reached her as the door slid open.

Mason chuckled beside her. "They've turned it into a freaking arcade."

That was exactly what they'd done. Cass and Ivan stood in the open space, controllers in hand, attempting to move in sync with the characters on the screen. Dom sat on the steps leading down, a pizza in his hand. He looked back when the door opened, a smile on his face that faltered when he met Kat's disapproving stare. They were in the middle of two deadly rescue missions, with the head of Hale Security locked downstairs, and they were playing fucking video games?

"Turn it off," she yelled. Dom scrambled to hit the buttons on the remote, the screen going black. Ivan and Cass looked back, disappointment leaving them in whines and complaints until they saw her. Ivan shut his mouth, Cass' eyes widened, and he scooted behind Ivan to hide from her. "We are in the middle of two goddamn missions!"

The lights brightened, and Mason came down the steps to stand next to her. He held out a piece of pizza for her and she glared at it. He took a bite instead. "I'm sure Ivan has everything on alert," he said around the piece in his mouth. He chewed a few more times and then swallowed. "Right, Ivan?"

Ivan nodded and fumbled for a remote in his pocket. The screens turned back on, and the video game minimized to the corner. Their working screens moved back in place: The Storm-Link logo in the middle, the map tracking everyone on the right, facial recognition running on the upper left corner, a set of codes running in a box on the lower left, and a blank box sitting between the two.

"We were just helping Cass here feel more comfortable," Dom said. "Do you think I don't know how important it is to find Shay?"

Kat clenched her jaw and took a deep breath. She was wound too tight, too many lives rested on her shoulders. How many times had she and Griffin done the same thing—the confidence in their skill allowing them to play and live while they worked? She didn't have that confidence as their leader yet, and it was showing. She relaxed her shoulders. Dom would never compromise Shay, and Ivan would never compromise Aeron.

"Apologies," she said. "Why is that box on the left blank?"

"Oh," Ivan said with a sheepish grin. "That's the hit list. It's down."

Kat's jaw went slack. "How?"

"Mike Barnes' computer."

A weight lifted from her shoulders. One less threat to worry about. "Good fucking work."

"I didn't do anything," Ivan admitted. "He just left the web browser open."

Mason laughed beside her. "Bring up the feed for interrogation room four, on a smaller screen," she said, eyeing Cass. Dom nodded and stood, moving to his desk. He pulled up the feed, logs, and control panel. The room was dark, the infrared camera giving them eyes inside. Hale sat against the wall, feet drawn up, with his arms wrapped around his knees. "What is the protocol?" she asked Mason.

He pointed to the control box. "You have preset timers for some psychological warfare. Now he's not chained up, so some of the more subconscious torture won't work, but you have your standard flashing lights, water from the ceiling, sounds, and temperature control all right there."

Kat nodded. "Unless he gets rowdy, just leave him in the darkness. We may still need him, and if anything is going to break him, I want it to be my hands. Pull up Rufus' and Izz's locations."

The map enlarged, filling the main screen. Rufus' and Izz's

dots were together, moving at a decent speed toward the middle of nowhere. "Do we think that's where he's keeping Shay?" she asked.

"Would be my best guess," Mason said.

Kat bit her lip, running the scenarios in her head before settling on the one that had the highest probability of success. "Hale already gifted us the twenty assets, and he can't call them back now, and we have the remainder of Division Three. We leave April here to protect Dom and Cass if needed. Ivan, you roll with the squad. We need the eyes and ears of StormLink inside that compound. You can do that, right?"

Ivan looked at Mason. "Was that property linked through their tracking system?"

Mason nodded.

"It's probably still decoding. I'll put it to the top of the list."

"Good," Kat said, ignoring the fear crawling up her spine. "We're going for Shay and Rufus first. Ivan, you'll prep everyone else on the schematics and plans for the compound. I'll send them to you. I'm thinking a game of hide and go snipe and then a full-scale rush."

Ivan paled, but nodded.

"What about Hale?" Mason asked.

"I don't trust him," Kat said. "We descend on the compound without him."

Mason parked down the road from Rufus' location. They needed to use the long stretch of ice and snow-covered trees to mask their approach. According to Ivan, Izz had been here briefly but was already gone, heading back in the direction of the compound.

The cold bit at her nose and fingers and she followed Mason's lead. He knew Rufus like no one else, and she trusted him to keep them safe from any booby traps he may have laid out. There were none, though, and Kat let out a nervous puff of air as they neared the back of the house. The rear screen door hung off its hinges, and the faded, peeling wooden door would be an easy breaking point. The blueprints had shown a living room in front, a wall, and then the kitchen. Three bedrooms sat off to the sides. Rufus had at least Barnes, two of Hale's men, a medic, and whoever else he had managed to scrounge up from the Underworld. They needed only two people to make it out alive: Rufus and Shay. Everyone else would be dropped without question. Kat would walk in the front door, get a headcount, and Mason would take the lead from the rear.

She let out a long breath, nodding at Mason and breaking off in the tree line to round the front of the house. She ran her thumbs across her fingertips, nerves settling in. He was here. She couldn't explain it, but she *knew*—Shay was here. Four cars idled in the driveway, windows fogged. No one moved as she approached, and when she peered into the passenger side window, she realized why. They were all dead.

Snow crunched beneath her shoes, so there was no way to mask her approach. She took the stairs to the front door two at a time, coming up short as the door swung open. Rufus looked down at her, his frame blocking her view of the room and knowing how many people were inside. She scanned him instead, seeing the damage Aeron had inflicted on his hand, the white bandage soaked in fresh blood. Good, about time he got a taste of his own brand of torture.

"You came," he said.

"Where's Shay?" she asked, not wanting to engage in small talk.

His eyes dropped to the bruise on her neck, and he bit into his lower lip. Her nervous system went haywire at the hooded look in his eyes, and she fought the urge to step away. "You want to see?"

No, she didn't. Everything in her screamed to turn around and run. But she'd abandoned Shay once already—she wouldn't do it again. She plastered a smirk on her face instead. "My life for his, right?"

"I won't kill him," Rufus said "Strip—"

"Excuse me?" Kat said, unable to stop the look of disgust crossing her face.

"—your weapons and comm," Rufus finished. "But I wouldn't say no to a full strip search." A chill that had nothing to do with the temperature rocked her core. Her lip curled as she turned over her comm and weapons: three pistols and four knives. "Hands up." Kat raised them, unable to resist the urge to flinch as he ran his hands over her body in his search. He smiled, eyes heavy on her, and then stepped aside.

Kat ignored the look and entered the room, eyes immediately drawn to Shay. A knot filled her throat, and she couldn't breathe. He was strapped to a chair, recent cuts on his face held closed with strips of medical tape. Her feet moved faster than her mind, and she stumbled to his side, dropping to her knees in front of him. Of all the times she imagined seeing him again—it was never like this. His face was swollen, his left eye bloodshot, and when he looked at her, an emotional dam broke inside of her chest and she fought off the tears begging to fall, because he smiled at her. His beautiful, soul-warming smile that she missed every day for the last seven years. "Kat." His face lit up like he'd finally figured out the answer to a question he'd asked for ages.

The sob broke free, and she nodded. "I've got you, Shay." She reached up for him, the scars she'd only seen in photos raised across his face, but a hand grabbed her wrist before she could touch him. She snapped back into the room.

Hale's guard held tight. "Don't touch him," he said.

Kat turned her head back to Rufus, catching sight of just the medic and one other guard. "This is all you have? Two borrowed guards and a medic?" She looked back at the man holding her.

"Let go of me before I'm the last thing you ever touch," she said, the venom dripping through her words. It did the trick. He released her, and Kat spun on her knees, grabbed the rifle that hung strapped around him, and tugged. He stumbled forward, and Kat got to her feet, moving behind him, using the rifle to pin him against her. The other guard raised his weapon at her and she smirked. "You can't kill me," she half sang. Rufus wanted a long time to torture her. No one was killing her unless he was dead.

"But I can kill him." Barnes stepped into the room with Mason bleeding from his temple at gunpoint. "Let the dumbfuck go." Mason raised an eyebrow at her, and she looked at Barnes. He held his gun awkwardly in his left hand, and as she did the scan of his body, Mason's hand tapped his own thigh. Kat nodded in understanding—Barnes was compromised.

"You heard him," Rufus said.

"Yeah, but you know how good I am at following directions," she said and kicked the back of the man's knees, pulling his shoulders toward her. He dropped to a kneeling position. Mason made his move with Barnes as Kat cupped the man's chin and the top of his skull and twisted. He fell forward, and the other guard tackled her from the side, skidding them toward the front door. Before Kat could even push herself up, two shots echoed in the room. The guard's body dropped heavily on her, and she pushed him off as Shay's scream echoed in her ears. It was a sound that haunted Kat, and she scrambled to her feet.

Rufus stood behind him, a hunting knife driven into Shay's leg. His cries continued as Rufus wiggled the blade from side to side. "Kat!" he cried out, and Rufus pushed it deeper.

"Stop!" Kat yelled, getting to her feet. She removed the pistol from the dead man as she did. Hale's other guard and the medic lay at Shay's feet, and Mason had landed himself face down on the ground, his head beneath Rufus' heavy sole, Barnes' own blade at Mason's throat. Even without the threat of Barnes, she'd been under Rufus' boot many times and there was no getting up until he wanted you to.

"Pick one, Red." Rufus drew the blade from Shay's leg at a slow, excruciating pace. Shay's screams were the only thing Kat could hear, tearing into her. His body dropped heavily as the metal left his leg, and she breathed with him. But Rufus pulled Shay's forehead back, the blade moving to his neck instead.

Kat took a step forward. "Don't," she pleaded. Shay's wide brown eyes met her. Gone was the innocent man who lived in a bubble. The fear in his eyes pulled her back to her granddad's office. Gone was the protection his mind afforded him. He was very much present in this moment. "Kat," he said softly, tears filling his eyes, and her heart broke into a million pieces.

"Mikey and I are going to start at the same time. You chose," he said, a vicious smile on his face. "Three, two—" Kat didn't let him finish. She pulled the trigger. Shay's body went limp, and she fired again—Rufus stumbled back as the bullet landed in his shoulder to give Mason the opportunity to defend against Barnes. She tucked the gun away and lunged for Rufus, slamming into him, her blows not doing a damned thing, but giving her anger a place to go. He grabbed her neck, the bandaged hand wrapping around it. She snarled and reached up, pulling on his fingertips, and he howled in pain.

Rufus stumbled forward this time, and Kat retreated as Mason hit him from behind. Between the two of them, Rufus dropped to the ground. Mason slammed the muzzle of his Sig into Rufus' neck, and he finally stopped moving. "Damn Red. You are full of surprises." He licked his lips. "I did not see that coming."

"Where is Storm?" she asked, burying the guilt already wanting to drown her. Shay was past saving, and they needed to find Storm—and Mason, Mason deserved his shot at vengeance.

"You'll have to ask Maureen," Rufus said and smiled that awful smile at Mason. "I'll say hello to your sister for you." His left hand shot to his mouth before either of them could stop it. Rufus slammed his lips closed and swallowed.

"No!" Mason screamed. He tried to pry Rufus' mouth open, but his body convulsed as he foamed at the lips.

Kat watched in horror as their only lead died in front of them. No. No fucking way. Mason screamed, and she jumped. He beat on Rufus' chest, and Kat left him to grieve, moving to Shay's side. His head had fallen forward, the front of his shirt covered with blood. She took a measured breath, praying her instincts had been right. She tilted Shay's head, exposing the gaping wound at his neck. Rufus had severed his carotid artery before she'd gotten her shot off.

Relief flooded her. She let the tears fall and cupped the side of his face, her thumb running over the miniature scars from her mother and granddad. He deserved a quick death after the torment his life had become because of her. "I'm so sorry," she said to him. "You were the best thing in my world, and I loved you more than anything else." Memories long buried flooded her mind. Late nights on the beach with his family. Dancing under the moonlight. Hearing someone tell her they loved her. She had never heard those words before—from anyone—and she had clung to them like a lifeline.

"Katherine," Mason said in a way that made her believe it wasn't the first time he'd said her name. She wiped her face and looked over. He knelt beside Rufus, removing his personal belongings. "Barnes got away, and we have to get to the compound. Aeron and Griffin."

She looked back at Shay, slamming each box closed in her mind until the only memory of him was the smile on his face when he'd seen her. The innocent smile that drove her to vengeance in the very beginning. She placed a kiss on his forehead and stood.

Then she asked the only question that ever seemed appropriate to ask even, when you already knew the answer. "Are you okay?"

"I don't know how he found out about Faith," Mason said, shaking his head. "But he knew I would break him, the fucking coward. Are you ready?"

"Yeah." She grabbed her comm from the floor and tucked it back around her ear, pressing the transmit switch. "GameMaster, are our people ready?"

"We are outside the rally zone."

"Good. Let's go kill a whole lot of people."

38

———

IZZ

*I*zz checked the rearview mirror for the fifth time, but no one was following her. She pulled onto the highway, heading for New York, racking her brain for anyone she trusted enough to go check the safe house for Storm first. But no. The only people she trusted were Eileen and Mason. One was dead, and one was trying to kill her. Fuck. She pulled out her phone to dial Maureen, and it rang first. Maureen's number scrolled across the screen. That couldn't be good. "Go."

"I need you home," Maureen said. "The Reaper showed up with Aeron and claims you sent him."

What the fuck. She told that boy she was done saving his ass, but she'd grown too fond of him for Maureen to put a bullet in him before they had a chance to talk. "What about tracking down Storm?" Surely that was still a priority.

"Did you find Rufus?"

"Yes, along with Barnes. I got a lead and a warning," Izz said. Until she confirmed with her own eyes whether Storm was alive or not, she couldn't give Maureen any ammunition. Storm might be safer in Barnes' hands at the moment, especially without Eileen around to help her. Her chest ached at the thought. She was really on her own now. "Hale is coming for us. Tonight, or tomorrow, I'm not sure. Do you want me there or following the lead on Storm?"

"Come home. I need answers."

And without Eileen, Izz added in her head, Maureen needed Izz to administer the Sin. When Maureen engaged in true torture —the kind that fueled her—nothing else existed. She lived there, and short of a bomb going off, nothing would distract her. It made her effective, and watching it was just shy of orgasmic. But Maureen couldn't run the compound and engage in the type of torture Izz realized she wanted to do to Griffin. That poor boy. Izz huffed a sigh, looking for the next turnaround. "I'm on my way."

Izz pulled right up to the garage, parking beside an SUV she didn't recognize. Cameron waved at her from his post on the vault, and she jogged over to him. "How goes it?" she asked.

"Dash killed Eileen and Keara last night," he said.

Izz didn't need to fake the shock on her face. Hearing the news so bluntly rocked her. "Shut the fuck up," Izz said.

"And," he lowered his voice, "the Reaper showed up with some girl—Dr. Jones is working on her now."

"Is Amara in the garage?" Izz asked. He nodded, and Izz reached into her pocket, pulling out her wallet and passing him a hundred-dollar bill. "Keep it up."

Izz's feet slipped and slid underneath her on the way to the building. Mark opened the door for her with a smile and a friendly hello. She cocked her head and stepped inside, realizing as the door closed, word of her needing a new fuck boy would be the hot topic of the compound. Fucking idiots. The spot was already filled by Rebekah—if she'd have her.

The lights over one of the medical tables were on with the curtains drawn, and Maureen sat at the bar, eyes on her drink. But

Griffin's low groans greeted her, and she put on a smile. "Looky, looky," she said, redirecting her path to him. He'd been stripped down to his boxers and adorable fish socks. The wound she'd gifted to him on his thigh had been reopened—probably by Petra, by the look of the work: sloppy and unnecessary. He had several cuts on his face—nothing to take away from his handsome features, thankfully, and he still had all his teeth when he smiled.

"Move him to room one," Izz said.

"We already have someone in room one," Petra said.

Izz looked over her shoulder at Maureen. Room one was Maureen's personal torture chamber—who did they have in there already? "Then move him to three." She joined Maureen at the bar, accepting the glass of whiskey offered. "I heard Dash went off the rails," Izz said and took a sip of the warm liquid. She dropped her head back, the burn of the alcohol a welcome as Eileen's dead eyes came to the surface.

"A real shame," Maureen agreed.

"Who's in room one?" Izz asked, cutting straight to the chase.

Maureen's devilish smile, which normally excited Izz, sent a shiver through her instead. "A surprise. Come look."

Maureen sauntered around the bar. Izz left her drink on the counter and followed her to room one—the sound of whimpering reaching her ears as the door pushed open. Maureen had taken inspiration from the Playhouse when they designed these rooms. The walls were dark, the lighting terrible, and a drain for easy clean up sat in the middle of the floor, behind which a metal chair with restraints was secured to the ground. In this chair sat a slim woman, her head covered in a black sack.

Izz entered the room, circling the unfortunate soul to have captured Maureen's wrath. She reached up for the bag, curiosity eating at her. "May I?" Izz asked.

Maureen's expression glowed in anticipation. "Please."

Izz ripped the bag off, the woman's straggly, graying, brown hair frizzing around her face. She tried to duck her head, but Izz pushed her chin up, gently moving the hair from her face. Kara Lourde looked up with terror in her eyes. She was in her late fifties, and although she may have at one time been a beast in the field, she was now a paper pusher, and her lack of physical fitness for an agent disgusted Izz.

"Isn't she perfect?" Maureen asked.

"She'd be perfect in her own office, signing over the fucking contracts to us," Izz said before her brain caught up with her mouth. This would be when Eileen would step in. Agree with Maureen, but then convince her Izz was right. But there was no Eileen to convince anyone of anything—because she was gone. "I thought you said we were setting up a meeting. What the fuck is this?"

Maureen ignored her outburst. "Meet the woman who has been hiding Storm—and her son—for the past seven years."

Izz's mouth dropped open. So Rufus was telling the truth—and Barnes might know it. Storm was alive—or had been recently—and she had a kid. She regarded the woman again, pity seeping in. This was no longer about contracts and money. Maureen was back on her vengeance shit, and in front of them sat the woman who unknowingly assisted Storm in the biggest fuck-you campaign against Maureen.

"A son?" Izz said, the word soft in her mouth.

"I can't wait to get my hands on him," Maureen whispered, mirth in her voice.

"He's a kid," Izz countered, positive Maureen wasn't suggesting what it sounded like.

"I—I—don't know where they are," Kara said, her voice shaking. "I told you."

"And I believe you," Maureen said. "But I am curious about what our girl has been up to these last seven years, and who the father of that boy is."

Izz didn't like the sound of that. Storm deserved every ounce of torture that Maureen wanted to bestow on her. She had known who she was crossing—but her son? Izz would stake her life on it that he was Mason's, and Izz shuddered to think of the ways Maureen would use the boy to torture them both.

Izz covered Kara's head again and stepped outside, waiting until the door clicked closed to speak. "The lead on Storm—"

"I'm not worried about it," Maureen said, returning to the bar, and Izz followed. "Find out what Mason's plans are from the Reaper, so I can put my full attention on our honored guest."

Izz opened and closed her mouth a few times, trying to figure out how to best tell Maureen she was insane. Barnes and Rufus could be on their way to Storm right now. "But Storm. . ."

"Will be handled," Maureen snapped. "If Rufus gave her up to Barnes, then I go after Barnes next. He's talented, but he follows the money. And he owes me."

"You know him?" Izz said, incredulously.

"He went by Mike Salone, back in the day. Oliver's best friend. He hated me, well, hated the fact that Oliver and I were so close. There certainly were parts of me he loved. But should Ollie find out just what his best friend had been up to all those years ago, well, I'm not worried about them. I've got the threat from Hale under control. You concentrate on the Reaper."

The reminder that Maureen had been hiding her entire past slapped Izz in the face. She let out a rough laugh and grabbed her unfinished drink off the bar. She tossed the liquid back and wiped her mouth, trying to drown out the fact she was halfway outside the inner circle now—which was no longer a circle. It was just Maureen. "How is Aeron?" Izz asked. She was genuinely curious, but wanted to see how far removed her best friend had become. "I heard you called in Dr. Jones."

"Mason had snagged Vial 879," Maureen said, pursing her lips.

"The one from the vault."

Maureen nodded. "It's laced with Sin. Mason didn't know you needed vial 880 to counteract the negative side effects."

"Fucking hell," Izz said, shaking her head. Sin after an emotional tragedy was when it was most effective—she couldn't imagine the hell Aeron had just gone through.

"The Reaper got her here just in time. Said he stole her from Hale." Maureen took another sip. The relief Izz thought she would see learning Aeron would be okay wasn't there. There was nothing there—just indifference. A chill ran down Izz's spine.

"She was in the warehouse. I didn't see where she went. Could be telling the truth." Izz straightened up. "But I didn't give him this location. Probably Mason making sure Aeron doesn't die." Maureen granted her a smile, and the look warmed Izz, releasing the tension in her chest. "I'll find out exactly what they're doing here, and what their end game is."

Izz put her glass down and headed to the medical ward. She peeked in on Aeron. She lay sleeping peacefully with the monitors beeping steadily. "All good, Doc?"

Dr. Jones' beady eyes looked up from his clipboard. She hated this man, but had to respect his work. He could work miracles if he wanted. "She's good. Got a strong heart. I foresee a full recovery."

"How long?"

"Physically? Whenever she's ready to wake up. I added a few extra compounds in order to speed up the healing."

"How about mentally?" Aeron had endured so much trauma in a short period—Izz couldn't imagine she was doing well upstairs.

"I did an adjustment for the Sin, so she should be feeling more herself when she wakes up. But ultimately, it will be up to her to decide."

Izz gave one last look to Aeron. She sent a silent hope she would be just fine and moved to the locked cabinet, her retinal scan unlocking the case. She grabbed two vials of Sin and two of the antidote before heading over to relieve the girls of their charge. Room three was smaller than room one but had a similar layout: a single chair secured in the middle of the room with a table to put her drink and torture tools. They'd strapped him to the new chair, an IV already hooked up. "I've got it from here."

They excused themselves. Izz put the vials on the table and leaned against it, drumming her fingers beneath the ledge. Griffin's stare bore into her. "I heard you can't keep my name out of your mouth," she said. "Perhaps I can put something else in there?"

"Is she okay?" he asked.

Izz huffed a laugh. "She will be. This can be super simple, Reaper. I won't even give you the Sin—why are you here?"

He kept his mouth closed.

"Griffin—I watched you grow up. I don't want to do this, but if I don't get answers…"

His resolve didn't waiver. She picked up the yellow vial first— the antidote. The problem with using Sin against someone who held your secrets too—you were both in a sinking ship. But if you gave a small dose of the antidote first, you could guide the Sin more effectively. A secret she'd learned from Eileen. She drew the liquid into a syringe.

"What are you doing?" he asked.

"A little guide to help keep our little secrets tucked away, in case the boss lady wants to come in for a check," she said. She pushed the serum into his IV, then filled a new syringe with the bright blue liquid and sat on the table watching the clock on the back wall. She needed a five-minute buffer, at least. The time moved faster than she thought it would—the loop of Eileen and Keara on the floor occupying her mind. At last, she slid off the table and inserted the syringe. "Ready?"

Griffin looked up, his mouth set into a scowl, but there was no hiding the pain in his eyes.

"If you just tell me," Izz said.

"I can't," he whispered and swallowed hard, looking back down at the blue liquid. "You'll have to drag it out of me."

Izz hesitated, her teeth sinking into her lower lip. She'd taken the lead on Sin dozens of times, but this didn't feel right. She huffed out a long breath and removed the syringe. Maybe she was just tired—or maybe she knew that Sin wasn't the only way to get the answers they needed. Griffin's surprised gaze met her.

"Why did you bring Aeron here?"

"Dr. Jones is the only one who can help her," Griffin said.

"And why did you stay?"

"I told Maureen—I want to be on the winning side."

Izz shook her head. "I've had a pretty shitty few days," Izz confessed. "Normally torture would get me right in the mood to do my favorite thing—fuck someone until we both forget where we are, sweating and screaming in pleasure. But you know what?" She stuck the syringe back in the bottle and deposited the sin inside, tearing the label to indicate it was a tainted vial. She put it on the table and looked back at him. "I don't even want to do that. What are you doing here?"

Griffin gave her a measured look before answering. "Mason said you and Eileen would save Aeron. Kat just got her back from the grave. I would do anything to keep her from experiencing that kind of pain again," he said. "My goal was to deliver Aeron. What you do with me after that, I don't care." He nodded toward the table. "Go ahead and dose me and get your gears turning. Rub one out while I scream in torment. It will take days for my ghosts to work through me, and there will be nothing left when they're done to spill your secrets. I guarantee it."

Fucking hell. What were they doing? Torturing the kids they swore to protect—hunting them down. No. Fucking no. She shook her head and began to pace, rubbing the back of her neck. Eileen would know what to do. Mason would know what to do.

"Having a crisis of conscience?" Griffin asked with humor in his voice, although she could hear the relief as well.

She ignored him. If she wanted answers, there was an easier way. And now that she knew Storm was alive. . . She pulled out her phone and dialed Mason. It only took two rings for him to answer. "Go."

"I can pump your boy full of Sin just to get myself a little wet, or you can tell me what the fuck is going on."

"You tell me. You shot me first," Mason said. Izz pursed her lips, but he continued before she could answer. "Doesn't matter. You have the most impeccable timing. Listen, do you hear that?"

Izz strained her ears. "I don't hear anything."

"Listen again."

The sound of a suppressed sniper rifle firing reached her through the phone. Izz's stomach dropped, and the phone went dead. She raced out of the room and closed the door. Maureen looked up from her phone. "I don't hear any screaming," she said, disappointment in her tone.

"Fuck Griffin. Mason's breached the property," Izz said. "We're under attack."

39

KAT

The snow soaked through Kat's pants, her ass cheeks freezing. She and Mason sat in one of the two raised guardian angel positions in the back of the compound, its previous host some forty feet down on the ground. They were waiting for Division Three assets, Gigi and Linda, to take their post. Kat glanced longingly at the twisted body on the ground. She wished they hadn't shoved her off the platform. She could have sat on her.

"How's his vitals?" Mason asked as he hung up the phone.

"Heart rate dropping," Kat said, pulling Griffin's stats up on the screen. His blue dot now sat alone in the room, Izz's red dot in the main area. Ivan hadn't been able to access the camera in the compound because they had all been disconnected, but he had manipulated the biometric security protocols, granting her and Mason unrestricted access to the entire compound. "No indication of Sin in his system."

Mason let out a long breath. "That was fucking dumb luck."

"But did you have to tell her we were here?"

"The Syndicate runs on protocols." He reached for the tablet in her hands, moving the screen and zooming into the garage. "If Izz wanted to hurt him, she wouldn't have called. She was looking for help, but I don't know why. What I do know is wherever Maureen goes—Izz goes. She's her shadow, so if we keep eyes on her, we will have Maureen. Look, they're leaving the garage. They'll leave him locked up there, and the garage will go on lockdown—no one in, no one out. Aeron should be there too—that's Dr. Jones' lab to the right." He readjusted the dead woman's comm in his ear and returned to his prone position, looking back through his scope. "They're safe for the moment. Let's drop a few more while we can."

Kat sighed and lifted her spotter's scope, finding their next target. It'd been years since she'd been in this role, and it wasn't like riding a bike. They were close enough that she let Mason work his killer magic while she located and confirmed his targets. A tall-looking man in a blue puffy jacket stepped into view behind the furthest cabins from the garage. He moved toward the three other bodies they had dropped—just like the others had. "Target in range," she said.

"Roger," Mason replied. "Target in sight."

"Send it."

Mason took a breath and pulled the trigger. The man dropped.

"Got 'em." she confirmed.

"There's movement in the compound," Ivan said in her ear. "G and L almost to you." Kat scanned the tree line behind them, spying the sniper team on their way.

"Maureen's called for a rodeo," Mason supplied, hand on his ear. Kat looked at the screen, the little orange dots converging in the main building. Mason glanced over and smiled. "Like I said. . . protocol. Send in the first wave."

The gunfire echoed in the vast compound as she and Mason sprinted across the open area between the tree line and cabins, Gigi and Linda covering their approach to the garage. "Talk to me, GameMaster," Kat said.

"The cabins you're coming up on are clear from trackables. Syndicate is down ten, Hale down six, Div Three holding strong."

Mason smirked as he looked in the window of the closest outlying cabin. "Sounds like he's giving game stats. This one is empty."

Even though they could track the Syndicate, it was only for those in the system. There was no telling how many new people she'd brought in since the Playhouse, but so far it didn't look like any. "That's great, GameMaster, but where's the bitch?"

"Izz just left the main cabin, heading back to the garage."

"Heading that way," Kat responded. They cleared three more cabins, finding not a soul in sight. She leaned against the outside of the last building, peering forward to see the garage. She pressed her comm. "Guardian Angel One, are we clear to fly?"

"Negative," Linda responded. "Four hostiles coming up from the left. Stay grounded."

"Roger," Kat said.

"Queen," Ivan said in her ear. "I've got eyes in the buildings. Repeat eyes in the buildings."

Mason let out a laugh. "Maureen turned back on the feeds—she's looking for us."

"Let's help her out," Kat said, and then into the comm, "What are you seeing, GameMaster?"

"She's in the garage with Izz—she's. . ."

"She's what?" Mason growled.

"She's staring at the camera, holding Aeron at knifepoint."

Kat dropped her head back against the cabin and side-eyed Mason. "Not a threat?"

Mason jumped on the comm. "Can you locate Eileen?" Silence met them. "GameMaster?"

"Queen, Ghost, you two are clear to fly," Gigi said.

"Fuck this," Kat said and sprinted around the corner, Mason

on her heels. She skidded to a stop, grabbing onto the door frame for support. She lowered her face in front of the scanner. The door clicked open, and she stepped inside, raising her Sig, with Mason on her six.

Maureen sat on top of the bar in the middle of the room with Aeron pinned in front of her. One hand wrapped over Aeron's shoulder, pulling her chin to expose her neck, and the other pressed the tip of a dagger into her throat, the skin already split, blood trickling down the blade.

Izz stood behind them. She poured a glass of whiskey and held it up in greeting. "Would you like one?" she asked. "You look like you could use one."

Kat glared, her face twisting in disgust. "Fuck off. You good, Aeron?"

"Yeah, just some family bonding," she said, voice strained.

Kat gave a small laugh and took a step forward. "I don't think that's how it's supposed to work," Kat said.

Maureen pulled the blade back, waving it toward them, the blood creeping down Aeron's throat like a small red river. "I'm genuinely curious," she said. "What did you think you would accomplish here?"

"Feed's down!" Ivan's voice rang in her ear as he shouted. "There's movement from Hale's guys." Kat tried to listen, but Maureen was still talking.

"—to know you. Explain a few things."

"What?" Kat said, losing the context of the conversation. She pulled the comm from her ear and glanced over at Mason. His comm was still in, brow furrowed. She looked back at Maureen. "I missed like ninety percent of that."

Maureen's face darkened, and she returned the dagger to Aeron's throat. Aeron pressed her eyes shut, straining against their mother to get away from the blade. "*Have kids,* they say. *It's the greatest joy of life.*" Maureen scoffed. "You were the biggest mistake of my life."

"I'm not a fucking mistake," Kat said, blood boiling in her veins. "I'm your goddamn Legacy—people may hear of you, but they'll remember me."

Maureen stared for a moment and then laughed, the blade cutting deeper into Aeron's neck. If they weren't careful, she'd slice Aeron's throat by accident. "You're going to die here, and no one will remember your name. Katherine Nobody."

"You're right," Kat said, a sudden warmth filling her chest. "I'm not your Legacy. I'm my father's."

Maureen's smile dropped as if a switch had flipped inside her. Kat could see the mirth turn into coldness, and she swallowed hard. "It's a shame, then, that you'll never get to know the rest of your family. They're dead."

Mason's gasped breath was like a shot in Kat's heart. "What?" he asked.

Izz looked up from her glass, eyes red, a frown on her face that looked so out of place that it caught Kat off guard. "Remove your vest and comms," she said, rounding the bar. "Drop your weapons on that table to your right."

"Where's Eileen?" Mason whispered. "Keara?"

Izz's sad eyes hardly looked at Kat, landing heavily on Mason as she shook her head. A knot lodged itself in Kat's throat. They were dead? The knot dropped into her chest, the familiar rage building, and she turned her gaze on Maureen.

"Did you kill them?" Kat demanded. "Your best friend and her daughter?"

"An unfortunate turn of events," Maureen admitted. "But necessary. And the only reason I haven't finished you two yet is I need information. Now be a good girl and follow the directions."

Blood pounded in her ears. She was going to rip Maureen limb from limb if it was the last thing she did on this earth. But

Maureen had not relented on Aeron's throat, so Kat swallowed her words and tossed her comm and gun to the table, reaching over to remove her vest.

"C'mon, Mase," Izz said. "Don't make this harder than it needs to be. Gear off."

40

IZZ

"Harder than it needs to be?" he whispered. "You can't be serious."

"I have never been more serious," Izz said. Mason's hatred burned into her as he removed his vest, weapons, and comm. Every sly comment that would normally fall from her lips stayed jammed in her throat as she ran her hands first over Kat, and then Mason as she searched for more weapons. She wanted to tell him the truth about Storm and Eileen. But how could he believe her now?

Her hands slid down his torso, feeling the familiar map of muscle and scars. His body twitched as her fingers passed over the stretch of skin just above his hip that made his eyes roll to the back of his head as she worked him in bed. She moved to his legs and then finally to his waist. Her fingers lingered on his belt buckle. He'd killed with that belt. He'd tied her with that belt and fucked her for hours. She gave the buckle a small tug, and Mason's eyes shot to hers, a burning in them that was mostly hate, but she saw the underlying desire and curiosity as her tongue caressed her lips. She left it in place and turned back to Maureen. "All clear."

It took two trips to move the stockpile of weapons behind the bar. She poured another glass of whiskey before returning to stand between Maureen and their invaders. "Sit down," Izz said, motioning to the closest table and chairs.

Mason and Kat exchanged a wary glance and took a seat. Katherine leaned back in hers, looking around Izz toward Maureen. "If you're going to kill us, just fucking do it already."

"Don't say things you don't mean," Maureen replied and hopped off the countertop, dragging Aeron over to join them at the table. "I'm in a particularly murderous mood." She pushed Aeron down, forcing her to sit. The slice at her neck bled freely, and Maureen kept the hand with the blade resting at her shoulder. "Sending the Reaper to his death to save Aeron—bold move." Izz glanced at Kat, but the words rolled right off her as if she knew it was a lie. "What were you expecting to achieve here?"

Rapid gunfire echoed outside. There was no telling who was winning—but it didn't matter. The most important players were right here. The three in front of them remained silent. Aeron pressed her fingers to her neck, eyes downcast; Katherine glared at Maureen, lips pressed together; and Mason—Mason sat back in the chair, legs spread, one arm over the back of Katherine's chair with a smirk on his face. "Spit it out, Mason," Izz said.

"I have to give it to you. . .what is it you prefer to be called these days?" He cocked his head at Maureen. "Should I go with Olivia? The traitorous daughter and sister? Perhaps Maureen, the head of the Alliance, set on freeing the Legacy children from centuries of bondage, but who sold her own child for freedom? Or Amara? The woman too scared of her own life to come back from the dead."

Fuck. Mason always knew how to get underneath Maureen's skin. From the corner of her eye, Izz caught the twitch of Maureen's hand. Izz shot her hand out, knocking the blade off course. It flew between Kat and Mason. Kat jumped back, but Mason did not move, and his smile grew wider. "Why don't we just go with Bitch?"

"Mase," Izz warned, silently begging him to be quiet. He didn't look at her, though.

"Do you still use the same locks on the interrogation chairs? The custom ones?" he asked. "I've only been gone a short time. I'll take a bet you didn't have the chance to change them yet."

Izz's gaze shot to the room she'd left Griffin in. The door was open, and she'd definitely closed it. A quick scan showed no signs of the Reaper.

"Find him," Maureen ground out.

Izz headed toward the room. She'd only gotten a few steps when Mason pounced. His arm snaked around her body and her feet left the ground. She landed hard on her back, and they became a tangle of limbs and curses. A commotion ensued at the table, but Izz couldn't look to see what was happening. Mason landed on top, straddling her. His fist rained down on her face. She covered and bucked her hips, but it did little to lessen the blows.

"Mase, stop!" Izz begged. The barrage of blows halted, his hand moving to her throat, his weight too high to move, and he pressed in on her arteries.

"Give me one good fucking reason." The intensity of his words vibrated down to her throat, his face contorted in rage.

"Because you know me." The grip on her throat loosened, the rage slipping from his face.

A shot echoed around the room. They both froze, heads whipping over to the table. Panic surged through her: which sister was dead? Izz shoved Mason off, and he stood, backing up several paces from her, frozen as if he'd seen a ghost.

"Oh hello, Mason!" Hale said with a smile. He yanked Aeron to her feet like a rag doll, brushed off her clothes, and tilted her chin to look at the cut on her neck. Aeron shoved him off and backpedaled. Maureen stood beside him, straightening out her shirt with one hand, the other one aiming her gun down at Katherine, where she lay on her back, Maureen's foot planted solidly on her throat.

41

KAT

Kat's throat screamed in protest as Maureen's shoe pinned her to the ground. She glared at Hale. How the hell had he gotten out of the interrogation room?

"Tie Mason to the chair this time, and then go look for the Reaper," Maureen said, glancing away from Kat toward Izz. Kat couldn't move her head to see, but from the sounds of it, Mason didn't put up a fight. Maureen smiled down at her, and Kat shivered. There was no mirth or any emotion in her eyes at all. They were cold—like her granddad's. "I have zero fucking use for you. Mason has sins he needs to answer for, and Aeron—well, I didn't pull her from the grave for shits and giggles. Until I get my hands on Storm and her son—I won't need Sin for him to relive the worst day of his life when I can just replay it for him, live and in color. It worked so well for Elijah. Look at how broken you are."

Kat kept her face a mask, but inside her entire soul shook with fear. This was it. Kat could see it in her eyes. She was going to die at her mother's hand. She would never get to say goodbye to Griffin or Aeron. But she would see Perry again, and Shay. Her sweet, sweet Shay. It was a fitting end.

"No!" Aeron screamed.

Kat twisted her face in defiance. "Go ahead and put me out of my fucking misery because I'm telling you the same thing I told Rosemary. One of us is leaving here in a body bag."

From her limited vision, Kat saw Aeron lunge. Hale grabbed her around the waist as Maureen pulled the trigger. Kat squeezed her eyes shut. The shot fired, and the chair beside her exploded, the pressure leaving her throat. She rolled away from Maureen, heart slamming hard enough to crack her ribs. Shaking, she looked up to see a blade protruding from Maureen's shoulder. She got to her hands and knees, her body shaking as if she'd been left out naked in a snowstorm. Someone vaulted over her, and she ducked in response, catching sight of Griffin's untamed hair as he tackled Maureen to the ground.

Kat pushed herself to her feet and grabbed Maureen's fallen gun, taking in the full sight in front of her. Griffin, in just his boxers and bright blue fish socks, had Maureen pinned face down on the ground. The knife she'd thrown was in his hand pressed against her throat, blood already making a small pool on the floor. Mason held Izz on her knees, standing behind her with his belt wrapped around her neck, Izz's face a strange mixture of pleasure and fear. And Hale was the odd man out, Aeron held securely against him. His gun, however, was pointed at Katherine.

"Let my sister go," Kat said.

Hale frowned and shook his head. "No. I'm going to need you to let *my* sister go."

Kat laughed. "That is never going to happen, and you know it. How the hell did you get out?" Kat tried to keep her mind on basic solutions like they hadn't locked the door. Not the other scenarios, like everyone in the building was dead.

"You've been underestimating us from the beginning," he said.

"Are they dead?" Kat asked. "My people." She didn't want to be responsible for that—for the death of Dom, too? April? Cass?

"We're entering a new era—less violent, but twice as deadly. I didn't need to touch them to prove my point. I'm here."

She didn't believe a word that came out of his twisted mouth. She kept the gun trained on him and retrieved her comm from the bar top, placing it in and immediately pulling it back out. Ivan's voice screamed into the earpiece. "Mobile to Queen! Mobile to Ghost!"

"This is Queen. I need an immediate update on Home Base."

She kept her eyes locked on Hale, waiting for the worst news. "Everything looks fine, are you—"

"Good to go. Standby," she said and disconnected the comm. She asked Hale again, "How?"

"Storm," he said with a shrug. "It's amazing what people do to protect their children." Kat glanced at Mason, but his face remained a mask. His grip on the belt, however, tightened, and Izz struggled to breathe, her eyes beginning to bulge.

"Where is she?" Kat demanded.

"We had a deal, Ollie. Don't tell her a damned thing," Maureen said from the ground. Oliver's gaze wandered to Maureen, and Kat looked too. Griffin secured her head to the cement with his free hand and a knee on her back. His hair hung over his bare shoulders, and his mischievous grin sent a spark through her.

"She killed our family, Oliver," Aeron said. Kat looked over as Aeron adjusted in his grasp. "You can't trust her. Doesn't matter what she promised you."

"She promised you in exchange for what she stole from me."

Aeron's jaw dropped open, and Kat gagged, unable to even form the disgust into words.

"Just fucking shoot him," Mason yelled.

"You'll never find Storm without me," Hale said. Kat grit her teeth at the fucking smile on his face. Maybe she would pull each tooth from his mouth before she killed him.

"Let me up," Izz tried to yell, and Mason released the pressure.

"Don't you say a fucking word either," Maureen ground out.

"You're not in a position to make demands," Griffin's low voice warned.

"What are you going to do, torture me?" Maureen asked, sneering up at Kat.

"Oh, no," Kat said. "I know you would enjoy that. I think I'm going to lock you in a dark room until you've gone completely mad, and once I'm tired of listening to your cries, then I'll put a bullet in your head." Maureen glared at her. Kat's gaze returned to Mason. "Your call," she said, nodding at Izz. She saw the flicker of regret in his eyes, and he tightened the belt.

"Wait!" Izz called out, tears sliding down her cheeks from the lack of oxygen. "I know where Storm was."

"You bitch!" Maureen yelled, straining against Griffin's hold on her, the knife slicing deeper into her throat, and she stilled again.

"Mase, please," Izz begged. "I'm a dick, but even I wouldn't lie about this. We have Kara, too." Kat shot a glance back at Maureen, but her face remained stoic, eyes cold on Izz.

"Where?" Mason loosened the belt, and Izz dropped forward, taking deep, gulping breaths.

"Room one."

Kat nodded for him to check, although he would've gone anyway, and looked back at Hale. Izz moved to her feet.

"Don't even think about it," Kat warned. "I will blow Maureen's brains out and make you clean them."

Izz shot an angered look toward Maureen, removing the belt and running a hand over her neck. She dropped into a chair. "I would love nothing more than for you to kill her," Izz said, leaning against the table for support. She looked up at Mason when he returned. "She fucking killed Keara and Eileen. I couldn't stop it— I'm sorry."

Mason nodded. "Storm," he said to Izz. "Is she dead or alive?" Kat could feel the fear in his words as they passed his lips.

"Alive as far as I know," Izz said and then looked back at Kat, gesturing at Maureen. "We were supposed to be protecting you all. Instead, I let her rip our family apart."

"Family?" Maureen laughed. "You've been fucking the man who turned my children against me and who ripped the Alliance apart bit by bit." She moved her hateful gaze to Mason. "You've been loving the man who said he would do anything for me, and then destroyed my world."

"You destroyed your own world when you slept with Seamus," Mason said. He moved to the bar and collected his gun before squatting down beside Maureen's head. "And you sealed your fate when you handed the love child to Elijah in return for his silence. You've always been so worried about making sure other people's sins caught up with them. Now it's your turn."

Kat swallowed the heavy stone that seemed to lodge in her throat. She turned to Izz. "Do we need her?"

"What?" Izz asked, taken aback.

"Do we need her to find Storm?" Kat clarified.

Izz shook her head. Good. She nodded at Griffin, and he hesitated for a moment, then picked up his hands. Maureen's glare didn't leave her as Kat said, "All yours, Mase."

There was a moment of silence, then his shot echoed around them, Maureen's body jumping once and then going limp, the red halo forming around her head. It was the most perfect sight Kat had ever seen, but she didn't admire it for long. She shifted her focus and aim back to Hale, who released Aeron and put his arms up. "And do we need him to find Storm?" Kat asked.

"I know where she was," Izz said. "But if Barnes got a hold of her already, he may prove useful."

Kat curled her lip in disgust. "Fine. Secure him."

Hale's bravado faltered as Griffin, covered in blood—both his and Maureen's—sauntered toward him, looking completely unhinged in just his boxers and socks. He was, without a doubt, the sexiest human she had ever laid eyes on. Before Griffin reached them, Aeron spun around and punched Hale across the face, the sound of flesh-to-flesh filling the room. Hale grabbed his jaw and looked at Aeron in shock. She decked him again, and Griffin smiled like a lunatic as he secured Hale's arms, encouraging Aeron to take another swing. A genuine smile filled Kat's face. This was her family.

"If you ever want to share. . ." Izz said as they watched Griffin force Hale to his knees and Mason bring over zip ties.

"I'll leave that to you and Mason," Kat said with a laugh and moved to stand next to Aeron—her eyes on Hale. "You okay?"

"I thought he might be a good guy," Aeron said and turned to face her, a frown forming. "Thank you for not giving up on me."

"We can call it even for the two times you saved me from Rufus," Kat said.

"Are you okay?" Aeron asked.

"Me? I'm not the one who was pulled from death."

"Seamus Gale is your father?"

Kat opened and closed her mouth a few times, and then settled on nodding, the words unable to leave her. For a moment, she'd imagined meeting Eileen and Keara in a new light—learning about Shannon. They'd worked briefly together—she had worked with her sister and had no clue. She changed the subject. "How are you feeling?"

"Whatever Dr. Jones did, I feel. . .alive. Not like I'm on the brink of death or wishing for it. But I'm not ready to come back yet. I need space. Time to process."

Kat nodded. "The seat's yours when you are ready."

Silence dropped between them, and Kat realized she hadn't heard a single gunshot from outside. She turned the comm back on. "Queen to Mobile Unit. I need an update. It's quiet out there."

"That's what I was trying to tell you," Ivan said, exasperated. "Hale's people pulled out—not sure where they went. But the remainder of Syndicate has been rounded up to the main cabin and locked in. Div Three is on patrol outside of it. No casualties on our end."

Kat furrowed her brow. "How did you manage that?"

"It's like a video game," he said. "And when you can hack into the enemy comms and give them orders, they follow them."

Kat chuckled. If he stuck around after this, the two of them could do some amazing things. "Outside is contained," she said, loud enough for everyone to hear.

"Am I allowed to ask for a status update?" he asked.

"Pumpkin and Whiskey Killer are good to go," she supplied.

"She's okay?" Ivan's voice cracked.

Kat met Aeron's confused look, and she smirked. "Yeah, Whiskey Killer is just fine."

"No, she's not," Griffin said, joining Aeron. "She owes me a bottle of Macallan. An expensive bottle of Macallan," he said loud enough for Ivan to hear. Ivan stuttered and then disconnected the comm on his end. Kat laughed, catching the color rising in Aeron's cheeks. "It's good to see you among the living still," Griffin added.

"It's good to be here," Aeron said and bumped her good shoulder into him. She gave Kat a smile and retreated to one of the chairs near Izz, leaving Kat and Griffin alone.

"Did you find Shay?" Griffin asked, looking down at her.

The question sent a buzzing through Kat's veins, and she furrowed her brow. "He didn't make it," she said, not wanting to elaborate in front of everyone. Griffin's face fell, and he reached out, pulling her into her chest. She let his warmth engulf her, the tears falling onto his bare chest as he rubbed her back. She'd failed Shay. What would Dom and Gunnar say when they found out? Would they hate her as much as she hated herself? Or would they feel that moment of relief she had, knowing he was no longer suffering and trapped in his own mind?

She took a deep breath and buried the box one more time.

They weren't finished yet. Yes, they saved Aeron. Yes, they rid the earth of their godforsaken mother. But Barnes had his grimy hands on Storm, and Kat owed it to Mason and Ivan to find her.

Griffin placed a kiss on her head. "Should we grab Kara?" he asked.

She nodded, taking the moment to compose herself before stepping back. "Yeah. And remind her she should have taken my offer to begin with."

She looked at Mason as Griffin disappeared from view. He squatted over Maureen's body, staring at it the same way Izz did from her seat—anger, regret, sadness. She must have been a great woman at one time. A friend. A lover. A leader. Decades of choices together boiled down to your closest friends gunning for your head. Kat hoped she would never end up like that—but the track record for leaders in their field didn't look pretty.

"Hey, Mase, you ready?"

He pulled his eyes away and looked at her, wiping the tears from his cheeks. He nodded, the pain and regret slipping away, a cold focus shifting into place as he flexed his jaw. "We need to find Storm," he said.

Kat nodded. "Since Hale didn't seem to appreciate our ally treatment, I think it's only fair he experiences the true enemy treatment of Interrogation Room Four. Care to show me how it's done?"

A sadistic smile spread across Mason's face as he stood. And if he wasn't on her team, Kat would have been terrified. But he was on her team—and always had been. The thought warmed her, and she returned his smile as he said, "It would be my honor. Lead the way, boss."

THANK YOU

I hope you enjoyed The Assassin's Storm. Sign up to find out when the next installment, The Assassin's Alliance, will be released!

If you would like access to exclusive content and updates on the next books in the series, join my newsletter. If you enjoyed this book please consider leaving a review to help other people fall in love with this world too!

ACKNOWLEDGMENTS

The biggest thank you goes to my husband and kids. Their constant patience and encouragement as I move from part-time writer to full-time author has been the cornerstone of my success and sanity.

To my Beta Team and critique partners, the real MVPs in a writer's arsenal. Without your genuine interest in this series, words of excitement, and the more than occasional curses flown for justice of my characters, this book wouldn't be done. Kristina, Dietrich, Kadee, April, Shannon—thank you for believing in this story.

Elle and Courtney—finding you in Okinawa has been the biggest blessing. Thank you for being the best writing group. I'm going to miss you both!

To my developmental editor, Cora, who not only kept me on track but pushed me to finish the book bible, spent hours pouring over all three manuscripts to keep the timeline accurate, and brought the graphics in my head to life—I appreciate you so much!

A huge thank you to Colby, your constant support and excitement keep me coming back to the keyboard on rough days. And to Malia, who has helped me create merch to bring the Assassin's world to life. You both are amazing!

To the BookTok community has been welcoming with open arms. I cannot express enough the joy and motivation getting to know so many of you has brought me.

To the applause gallery—Jenna, Anya, and James. Celebrating

as each chapter's edits were completed was genuine motivation. *Cheers & Applause!*

And a very special thank you to Shannon W. Your unbelievable support in my dream and potential of this series is humbling, and without your vision, The Assassin's Sin audiobook would not be a thing. I am forever grateful to call you my friend.

ABOUT THE AUTHOR

After a childhood filled with James Bond marathons with her father, Libby brings to life a world of assassins and badass heroines.

When not writing, Libby spends her time enjoying the art of jiu-jitsu or napping. She loves English Breakfast tea, campfires, and loud music.